BEAU IDEAL

BEAU IDEAL

BY

PERCIVAL CHRISTOPHER WREN

"Judge not the Play, before the Play is done
Her plot hath many changes: every day
Speaks a new scene; the last act crowns the Play."

Hank: "All a matter of what's your own private
'*Bo Ideal*', as they call it. . . ."
Beau Sabreur.

LONDON
JOHN MURRAY, ALBEMARLE STREET, W.

First Edition . . . *July* 1928

DEDICATED TO
WILLIAM FARQUHARSON
THE
GOD-FATHER
OF
BEAU GESTE

CONTENTS

NOTE

This book, while a complete and self-contained novel, is the last of the trilogy—*Beau Geste*; *Beau Sabreur*; *Beau Ideal*.

PROLOGUE

THE heat in the *silo* was terrific, and the atmosphere terrible.

A whimsical remark from the man they called Jacob the Jew, to the effect that he wondered whether this were heat made black, or blackness made hot, remained unanswered for some minutes, until a quiet voice observed in good French, but with an English accent:

"It is the new heat, Jacob. Red hot and white hot, we know. We are now black hot. . . . And when I have to leave this quiet retreat I shall take a chunk of the atmosphere . . . a souvenir . . . keep it in my haversack."

The man spoke as one who talks against time—the time when sanity or strength shall have departed.

"Good idea," mused another voice with a similar accent. "Send a bit to one's National Museum, too. . . . You an Englishman?"

"Yes," replied the other. "Are you?"

"No . . . American," was the reply.

Silence.

The clank of irons and a deep groan.

"Oh, God," moaned the wounded Spaniard, "do not let me die in the grave. . . . Oh, Mother of God, intercede for me. Let me die above ground."

"You are not going to die, Ramon," said the Englishman.

"No indeed," observed Jacob the Jew. "Certainly not, good Ramon. No gentleman would die here and now. . . .

9

You would incommode us enormously, Ramon. . . . I go the length of stating that I absolutely do prefer you alive—and that's the first time you've heard *that*, Ramon. . . . Worth being put in a *silo* for."

"That's enough, Jacob," said the Englishman; "hold your tongue."

The irons clanked again, as though the sick man turned in the direction of the last speaker.

"You'll keep your promise, Señor Caballero?" moaned the dying man. "You *have* forgiven me? . . . Truly? . . . You'll keep your promise? . . . And the Mother of God will come Herself and tend your death-bed. . . . If you don't, my dying curse shall blast . . ."

"I'll see to it, Ramon," said the Englishman quietly. "Don't bother about cursing and blasting. . . ."

"You'll see that I die kneeling! . . . You won't let me die until I kneel up? . . . You'll hold my hands together in prayer . . . my head low bowed upon my breast? . . . And then you'll lay me flat and cross my hands and make the Sign of the Cross upon my forehead. . . ."

"As I promised, Ramon."

"You'll let God *see* that I fear Him. . . . *He wouldn't mistake me for my brother?* . . . He wouldn't visit my brother's sins on *me*?"

"God is just," said the Englishman.

"Yes, my poor Ramon," observed Jacob the Jew, "I greatly fear that you'll find God just. . . . But don't say that you have a brother, Ramon?"

"*Nombre de Dios*, but I have, *hombre*! . . ." gabbled the Spaniard. "And he is in Hell . . . *Seguramente*. . . . He was an enemy of God. . . . He hated God. . . . He defied God. . . . And God took him and broke him. . . . *Caramba!* It is not fair the way God . . . *Yes*. . . . *Yes*. . . . *Yes*. . . . It *is* fair, and God is good, kind, loving and—er—just."

"Yes. *Just*—Ramon," said Jacob.

"If I could find your nose, my friend," said the American,

turning in the direction of the last speaker, "I would certainly pull it."

"I will strike a match for you later," replied Jacob, a man famous among the brave for his courage ; brilliantly clever, bitterly cynical, and endowed with a twofold portion of the mental, moral and physical endurance of his enduring race.

"God will not punish me for my brother's sins, will He, Señor Smith ? " continued the Spaniard.

"No," replied the Englishman, "nor him for his own."

"Meaning him, or Him ? " inquired Jacob softly.

"We punish ourselves, I think," continued the Englishman, "*quite* sufficiently."

"*Mon Dieu !* " said a cultured French voice, "but you are only partly right, *mon ami*. Woman punishes Man, or we punish ourselves—through Woman."

"Bless ourselves, you mean," said the Englishman and the American immediately and simultaneously.

"The same thing," replied the Frenchman. And the utter stillness that followed was broken by a little gasping sigh that seemed to shape a name—"*Véronique*."

"*Basta !* . . . *My brother !* . . . *My brother !* . . ." babbled the Spaniard and sobbed, "God will distinguish between us. . . . *Gracias a nuestra Madre en el cielo ! Gracias a la Virgen Inmaculada.* . . . *Un millón de gracias.* . . ."

"And what of this accursed brother ? Surely no brother of *yours* committed an interesting sin ? " inquired Jacob.

"*Cá !* It was the priest's fault," continued the Spaniard, unheeding. "We were good enough boys. . . . Only mischievous. . . . Fonder perhaps of the girls and the sunshine and the wine-skin and the bull-ring than of religion and work. . . . My brother *was* a good boy, none better from Pampeluna to Malaga—if a little quick with his knife and over-well acquainted with the smuggler track —until that accursed and hell-doomed priest . . . No ! No ! No ! . . . I mean that good and holy man of God —cast his eye upon Dolores. . . .

" Oh, Mother of God ! *He killed a priest. . . .* And he defied and challenged God. . . . And I am his twin brother ! . . . God may mistake me for him."

" God makes no mistakes, Ramon," said the Englishman. " Excuse my playing the oracle and Heavy Father, but—er—you can be quite sure of that, my lad."

" Yes, yes, yes—you're right. Of course you are right ! How should God make mistakes ? . . . Besides, God knows my brother, *well.* He followed him. . . . He warned him. . . . When he swore he would never enter a church again, God flung him into one. . . . When he swore he would never kneel again, God struck him to his knees and held him there. . . . Because he swore that he would never make the Sign of the Cross, God made a Sign of the Cross, *of* him."

" Quite noticed the little man, in fact," observed Jacob the Jew. " Tell us."

" My brother caught the priest and Dolores. . . . In the priest's own church. . . . My brother married them before the altar . . . and their married life was brief ! . . . But of course, God knew he was mad. . . . As he left that desecrated church, he cried, ' *Never will I enter the House of God again ! . . .*'

" And that very night the big earthquake came and shattered our village with a dozen others. As we dashed through the door—the old mother in my brother's arms, my crippled sister on my back—the roof caved in and the very road fell from before our little *posada*, down the hillside. My brother was in front and fell, my mother still in his arms. . . . And where did he recover consciousness ? Tell me that ! . . . *Before the altar,* upon the dead body of his victim, the murdered priest—who thus saved my brother's life, for he had fallen thirty feet from the half-destroyed church-roof, through which he had crashed. . . . Yes, he had entered the House of God once more ! . . .

" It was to South America that he fled from the police —to that El Dorado where so many of us go in search of what we never find. And there he went from worse to worse than worst, defying God and slaying man . . . and woman! For he shot his own woman merely because she knelt—just went on her knees to God. . . . And one terrible night of awful storm, when fleeing alone by mountain paths from the soldiers or *guardias civiles*, a flash of lightning showed him a ruined building, and into it he dashed and hid.

" It may have been the rolling thunder, the streaming rain, or an avalanche of stones dislodged by the horses of the police who passed along the path above—I do not know —but there was a terrible crash, a heavy blow, a blinding, suffocating dust—and he was pinned, trapped, held as in a giant fist, unable to move hand or foot, or head. . . .

" And, when daylight came, he saw that he was in a ruined chapel of the old *conquistadores*, kneeling before the altar—a beam across his bowed shoulders and neck ; a beam across his legs behind his knees ; a mass of stone and rubble as high as his waist. . . . And there my brother *knelt*—before the altar of God—in that attitude of prayer which he had sworn never to assume—and thought his thoughts. . . . For a night and a day and a night, he knelt, his stiff neck bent, but his brave heart unsoftened. . . . And thus the soldiers found him and took him to the *calabozo*. . . .

" The annual revolution occurred on the eve of his garroting, and he was saved. Having to flee the country, he returned to Spain, and sought me out. . . . Owing to a little smuggling trouble, in which a *guardia civil* lost his life, we crossed into France, and, in order to get to Africa and start afresh, we joined the Legion. . . .

" *Válgame Dios !* In the Legion we made quite a little name for ourselves—not so easy a thing to do in the Legion, as some of you may know. There they fear nothing. They fear no thing, but God is not a thing, my friends. *Diantre !* They fear neither man nor devil, neither death nor danger—but they fear God. . . . Most of them. . . . When they come to die, anyhow.

" But my brother did not fear God. . . . And his

escouade of devils realized that he was braver than they
. . . braver by that much. . . . And always he blas-
phemed. Always he defied, insulted, challenged God. He
had a terrible fight with Luniowski the Atheist, and
Luniowski lost an eye in the defence of his No-God. My
brother fought with awful ferocity in defence of his God—
the God he *must* have, that he might hate and revile Him
—the God Who had sat calmly in His Heaven and watched
Dolores and the priest. . . .

" In Africa there was little fear of his finding himself
flung into a church, or pinned on his knees before a chapel
altar ! We aren't much troubled with chaplains and
church-parades in the Legion !

" But one day my brother saw a lad, a boy from Provence,
a chubby-faced child, make the Sign of the Cross upon
his breast, as we were preparing to die of thirst, lost in a
desert sand-storm. . . . My brother, with all his remaining strength, struck him upon the mouth.

" ' *Sangre de Cristo !* If I see you make that Sign
again,' he croaked, ' I'll do it on you with a bayonet.' . . .

" ' If we come through this, I *will* make the Sign of the
Cross on you with a bayonet,' gasped the boy hoarsely,
and my brother laughed.

" ' Try,' said he. ' Try when I'm asleep. Try when
I'm dying. . . . Try when I'm dead. . . . Do you not
know that I am a *devil* ? Why, your bayonet would melt.
. . . *Me !* The Sign of the Cross ! . . . *God Himself
could not do it !* '

" And next day my brother was lost in that sand-storm,
and the Touareg band who found him, took him to the
Sultan of Zeggat. . . . And the Sultan of Zeggat *crucified*
him in the market-place, ' as the appropriate death for a
good Christian ! ' . . . Wasn't that humorous ! . . . "

Silence.

" Yes, God made a Sign *of* my brother," said Ramon
the Spaniard, and added, " Help me to my knees, Señor

Smith, and keep each word of your promise, for I think I am dying."

Silence. . . .

And then a cry of "*Dios aparece*" from the dying man. Jacob the Jew, great adept at concealment, produced matches and struck one.

The flare of the match illumined a deep-dug pit, its floor hard-beaten, its walls sloping to a small aperture, through which a star was visible. It had been dug and shaped, for the storing of grain, by Arabs following a custom and a pattern which were old in the days when Carthage was young.

It was now stored, not with grain, but with men [1] sentenced to punishment beyond punishment, men of the Disciplinary Battalions, the *Compagnies de Discipline*, the "*Joyeux*," the "*Zephyrs*," the *Bataillon d'Infanterie Légère d'Afrique*—convicted criminals.

The light from the burning match revealed a picture worthy of the pencil of the illustrator of Dante's *Inferno* —a small group of filthy, unshorn, emaciated men, clad in ragged brown canvas uniforms which, with the grime upon their flesh, gave them the appearance of being already part of the earth to which they were about to return, portions of the living grave in which they were entombed.

Some lay motionless as though already dead. One or two sat huddled, their heads upon their clasped knees, the inward-sloping sides of the *silo* denying them even the poor comfort of a wall against which to lean.

Beside a large jug which held a little water, a man lay upon his face, his tongue thrust into the still-damp earth where a few drops of water had been spilt. He had drunk his allowance on the previous day.

Another looked up from his blind search, with sensitive finger-tips, for grains of corn among the dirt.

[1] A prohibited and illegal form of punishment.

As Jacob held the match aloft, the Englishman and the American gently raised the body of Ramon the Spaniard from the ground. It was but a body, for the soul had fled.

"Too late," said Jacob softly. "But perhaps *le bon Dieu* will let him off with eight days' *salle de police* in Hell, as it wasn't his fault that he did not assume the correct drill-position for dying respectfully. . . .

"No use heaving him up now," he added, as the head rolled loosely forward.

Without reply, the Englishman and American lifted the dead man to his knees, and reverently did all that had been promised.

And when the body was disposed as Ramon had desired, Jacob spoke again.

"There are but five matches," he said, "but Ramon shall have two, as candles at his head and feet. It would please the poor Ramon."

"You're a good fellow, Jacob," said the Englishman, ". . . if you'll excuse the insult."

Jacob struck two matches, and the Englishman and the American each taking one, held it, the one at the head, the other at the feet, of the dead man.

All eyes were turned to behold this strange and brief lying-in-state of the Spanish smuggler, court-martialled from the Legion to the Zephyrs.

"Pray for the soul of Ramon Gonzales, who died in the fear of God—or, at any rate, in the fear of what God might do to him," said Jacob the Jew.

The Frenchman who had observed that Man's punishment was Woman, painfully dragged himself into a sitting posture and crawled toward the body.

"I have conducted military funerals," said he, "and remember something of the drill and book-of-the-words."

But what he remembered was not available, for, after the recital of a few lines of the burial-service, he fainted and collapsed.

"This is a very nice funeral," said Jacob the Jew, "but what about the burial?"

§ 2

Suddenly a man leapt to his feet and, screaming insanely, beat the wall with his manacled hands.

"Come! Come! Smolensky" soothed the huge grey-haired Russian who had been Prince Berchinsky. "We mustn't lose our heads, comrade. . . . I nearly lost mine once. . . . Sit down. . . . I'll tell you about it. . . . Hush now! . . . Hush! And listen. . . . Yes . . . I nearly lost my head once. It was offered as a prize! Think of that! There's an honour for you!

"It was like this. . . . I was with Dodds' lot at Dahomey, you know. He was almost a nigger himself, but he was a soldier all-right, believe me. Faraux was our Battalion-Commander and General Dodds thought a lot of him—and of us. It quite upset Dodds when Faraux was killed at the battle of G'bede, but he kept the Legion in front all the same. . . . So much in front that he lost me, *le Légionnaire* Badineff. . . .

"I was with a small advance-guard and we were literally pushing our way through that awful jungle when the Amazons ambushed us. . . . Wonderful women those Amazons—far better fighters than the men—braver, stronger, cleverer, more soldierly. . . . Armed with short American carbines and *coupe-coupes*, they're no joke!

"I don't want to fight any better troops. . . . Not what you'd call good shots, but as they never make the range more than about twenty yards, they don't miss much! . . .

"Well, it wasn't many minutes before I was the only man of the advance-guard who was on his feet, and I wasn't on those long. . . . For these she-devils were absolutely all round us, and as three or four rushed me with their *machetes*, one of them smashed me on the head, from behind, with the butt of her carbine. . . . Quite a useful bump too, *mes amis* . . . for it put me to sleep for quite a while. . . ."

"Lost your head, in fact," put in Jacob the Jew.

B

" No, no," continued the old Russian, " not yet . . . but I nearly lost my wits when I recovered my senses . . . if you understand me. . . . For the ladies had divided my property among them to the last rag of my shirt, and were now evidently turning to pleasure after business.

" Dahomeyan is not one of the languages which I speak. . . . I only know fourteen really well . . . so I could not follow the discussion closely. . . . But it was quite clear that some were for fire and some for steel. . . . I think a small minority-party were for cord. . . . And I was under the impression that one merry lass capped the others' laughing suggestions with the proposal for all three ! . . .

" Do you know, it was for all the world like a lot of nice little girls sitting on the lawn under the trees with their kitten, joyously discussing how they should dress him up, and which ribbons they should put round his neck. . . .

" You know how they laugh and chatter and pull the kitten about, and each one shouts a fresh idea about the dressing-up and the ribbons, and the fun generally. . . . Well, those nice little girls discussed dressing me—for the table—though it wasn't a ribbon they proposed putting round my neck. . . . And undeniably they pulled me about ! . . .

" I could not but admire the way they had tied me up. . . . I was more like a chrysalis in a cocoon than a bound man. . . . They *were* playful. . . . Good actresses too—as I realized afterwards. . . . When they saw that I had come round, one of them, eyeing me archly, drew her finger across her throat, and the others all nodded their approval.

" The young thing got up, took a bright sharp knife from her waist-belt, and came over to where I lay against the bole of a tree.

" Grabbing my throat with her left hand, she pulled up the loose skin and began to cut, just as the Leading Lady called out some fresh stage-directions—whereupon she grabbed my beard, pulled my head over to one side, and put the point of the knife in, just below my ear. . . . I closed my eyes and tried to think of a prayer. . . .

" When it comes to it, having your throat cut is the nastiest death there is. . . .

" And just as I was either going to pray or yell, there was a loud burst of laughter, and the girl went back to her place in the jolly group. . . . The Leading Lady then, as far as I could make out, said :

" ' Now we must really get to business or the shops will be shut ' . . . and told another lassie, who possessed a good useful iron-hafted spear, to put the butt-end of it in the fire, explaining why, with appropriate gesture. . . .

" It was evidently quite a good idea, for the girls all laughed and clapped their hands, and said what a nice party it was. . . .

" While the spear was getting hot, they propounded all sorts of other lovely ideas, and, over the specially choice ones, they simply rocked with merriment. . . . It *did* seem a pity that one couldn't follow all the jokes. . . . When the pointed haft of the spear was glowing nicely, its owner picked it up, and stepping daintily across to me, held the point a few inches from my eyes. . . .

"Not unnaturally, I turned my head away, but, saying that that wasn't fair, the Leading Lady and the Soubrette made one jump for me and grabbed my head. . . .

" Fine strong hands and arms those ladies had. . . . I couldn't move my face a fraction of an inch. . . .

" And slowly . . . slowly . . . slowly . . . that red-hot point came nearer and nearer to my right eye. . . . It seemed to approach for hours, and it seemed to be in the centre of my brain in a second. . . .

" When it comes to it, *mes amis*, having your eyes burnt out with a red-hot spear-haft is the nastiest death there is. . . .

" But when my right eye seemed to sizzle and boil behind its closed lid, and to be about to burst, my young friend changed her mind, and began upon the left . . .

and when the iron was just about to touch it she remarked, in choice Dahomeyan, I believe :

" ' Dammit ! The blooming iron's cold ! ' and, with a joyous whoop, bounded back to the fire, and thrust it in again. . . .

" Shrieks of laughter followed, and loud applause from the cheap seats.

" Meanwhile the ladies hanged me. . . ."

" *Hanged* you ? " inquired Jacob the Jew. " Don't you mean they cut your head off ? . . . You said you lost your head, you remember."

" No, my friend," replied Badineff, " I said I *nearly* lost it. . . . Not completely—as you have lost your manners. . . . What I am telling you is true. . . . And if you don't like it, pray go elsewhere. . . ."

" There's nowhere to go but Heaven, I'm afraid," was the reply . . . " being in Hell—and Earth being denied to us. . . . But pray finish your story, as it is unlikely we shall meet in Heaven. . . ."

" Yes. . . . They hanged me as neatly and as expeditiously as if they had had the advantage of an education in Christian customs. . . . They simply jerked me to my feet, made a noose in a palm-fibre cord, threw the end over the limb of a vast tree, hauled upon it and danced around me as I hung and twisted. . . .

" They say a coward dies many times. . . . That was undoubtedly one of the occasions upon which I have died. . . .

" When it comes to it, *mes amis*, being hanged by strangulation—and not by mere neck-break—is one of the nastiest deaths there is. . . .

" But evidently they let me down in time and loosened the rope from about my neck, for bye-and-bye I was staring up at the stars and in full enjoyment of all my faculties. . . . Particularly the sense of smell. . . .

" The intimate smell of Negro, in bulk, is like no other smell in the world. . . . There is nothing else like it, and there is nothing to which one can compare it—and here is a curious fact which should interest the psycho-physiologist. . . . Whenever I wake, as we of the Zephyrs do, dumbly sweating or wildly shrieking, from a ghastly nightmare, I can always *smell* Negro, most distinctly. . . . Very disgusting. . . .

" Curiously enough, these fearless savage fiends, who will charge a machine-gun with the utmost bravery and with a spear, are arrant cowards at night . . . in mortal fear and trembling horror of ten thousand different devils, ghosts, djinns, ghouls, goblins and evil spirits. . . . And when I came to, they were huddled around me for pro-tection. I was almost crushed and buried beneath the mass of them as they lay pressed round and across me. . . .

" As I was still most painfully bound, I can only suppose that I was, in myself, a talisman, a *juju*, a mascot, or shall I say, an *ikon*.

" And they had gathered around me in the spirit in which simple peasants might gather round a Calvary, and were using me as some might use a Cross, a holy relic or a charm. . . .

" Yes, to this day I smell that dreadful odour—dreadful because of its associations, rather than of itself—in my worst nightmares and delirium of fever or of wounds. . . .

" I can smell it at this moment. . . .

" I have passed some bad nights—one, impaled on bamboo stakes at Nha-Nam in Tonkin—but this was the worst night of my life . . . almost. . . .

" And in the morning the ladies awoke, made no toilette, and gave me no food. . . .

" But they had given me a faint hope, for I could not but realize that, so far, they had only tortured me by not torturing me at all—and it seemed that they might be keeping me, not only alive and whole, but without spot or blemish, for some excellent purpose. . . .

" They were ! . . .

" And when I discovered it, I was inclined to wish that they had killed me with fire or steel or cord—as they did all of our men whom they took prisoner. . . .

"For some reason, possibly on account of my unusual size—I was a fine specimen in those days, six foot six, and with golden hair and beard—they were taking me to good King Behanzin at Kana, as an acceptable gift for a burnt-offering and a bloody sacrifice unto his gods and idols. . . .

"There was a story afterwards, that Behanzin had been told by his sooth-sayers and medicine-men, that he would undoubtedly beat the French if a strong *juju* were made with the blood of a white cock that had a golden comb. . . . One of our officers, Captain Battreau, said I probably owed my life to my golden comb. . . . I have a very white skin where I am not sunburnt. . . .

"Anyhow, the ladies took me along—by the inducement of *machete*-points and rhinoceros-hide whips chiefly—to Kana. . . .

"I don't know whether we marched for a day or for a week. . . . Yes. . . . I was strong in those days . . . for I believe I ate nothing but raw carrion, and my arms were bound to my body the whole time, as though with wire. . . .

"Kana stands on a hill and is built of earth, clay, and sun-baked bricks, inside a great high wall, yards in thickness. . . .

"We entered through a gate like a tunnel, and, by way of filthy narrow red-earth streets, came to a second, inner wall, which surrounded the royal palaces, *hareems*, temples, and the House of Sacrifice. . . .

"The yelling mob that had accompanied us from the outer gate, crowding and jeering and throwing muck at me—though they kept well out of reach of the weapons of the Amazons—evidently feared to enter this inner city, for that is what it amounted to. . . .

"And I was handed over to a guard of long-speared ruffians and filthy priests who slung me into a big building and slammed the huge double gates. . . . As I staggered forward in the darkness, I slipped on the slimy, rounded cobble-stones, sprawled full-length and collapsed. . . .

"There was a loud roaring in my ears—not the conventional roaring in the ears of a fainting man, but the buzzing of millions of billions of trillions of huge flies, that soon so completely covered me that you could not have stuck a pin into my body without killing one. Their blue-grey metallic bodies made me look as though I were clad in a complete suit of chain-mail. . . . And I could not move a finger even to clear my eyes. . . . I could only blink them.

"And as my eyes grew accustomed to the gloom, I saw that the whitish gleaming cobble-stones were the skulls of men, sunk in the red earth. . . . And I realized why I was being nauseated by a terrible slaughter-house stench. . . .

"It *was* a slaughter-house. . . . The House of Sacrifice, of Kana, the Sacred City of King Behanzin of Dahomey. . . .

"That was another unpleasant night, *mes amis*. . . . Oh, quite unpleasant. . . . We are in clover here—pigs in clover. . . . But, mercifully, I was at the end of my tether, and I had now so little capacity for suffering, that I was not clear in my mind as to whether certain things that happened that night were real or imaginary, fact or nightmare. . . .

"They were real enough. . . . And in the morning I found I was, even as I had either dreamed or realized—actually inside a great wicker bottle or basket, from the top of which my head protruded. . . .

"I could not move a single muscle of my body save those of my face. . . .

"The priests and executioners had been busy during the night, and I was now like a mummy in its bandages, neatly encased in the Sacrificial Basket, all ready to play my helpless part in the bloody ritual of their unspeakable religion. . . .

"Half-dead as I already was, my one hope was that the Service would be short and early—the sacrifice soon and quick. . . . It is most uncomfortable to lie in a bottle with nothing to support your head. . . .

" I could see nothing, and hear little, by reason of the huge flies . . . but I was aware of tom-toming and shouting without, and hoped that it concerned me. . . . It did. . . . The gates of the House of Sacrifice were thrown open and a number of guards, priests, and executioners heaved me up from that terrible floor and carried me outside.

" Oh, the sweetness of that morning air—even in an African town. . . . It almost made me want to live. . . . And oh, the relief to have one's head freed from an inch-thick covering of flies. . . .

" The great Square of the inner town—a Square of which the sides were formed by, shall we say, the Palaces, Cathedrals, Convents, Monasteries and Municipal Buildings of King Behanzin—was thronged by hundreds and hundreds of warriors, both men and women. As my guards carried me across to the biggest of the buildings, all these people fell back to the sides of the Square, leaving the centre empty, save for me and my guards.

" In front of the palace, an ugly clumsy building of red earth and baked clay bricks, sat Behanzin, King of Dahomey, on the Royal Stool. Around him were grouped his courtiers. . . . I think that His Majesty and they formed one of the least pleasing groups of human beings I have ever encountered—and I have known quite a lot of kings and their ministers. . . .

" As I have already observed, I do not speak Dahomeyan, and at that moment I deeply regretted the fact, and equally so, that none of them understood Russian or even French. . . . However, French I spoke, in the vain hope that a word or two, here and there, might be understood.

" A few were, as I will tell you. . . .

" My speech was brief and blunt. . . . I told Behanzin that he was the nastiest king I knew . . . the ugliest . . . the foulest . . . the filthiest . . . the most abandoned and degraded. . . . And I should be much obliged if someone would remove me from a world which he contaminated. . . .

" I had not finished even these few and well-chosen

words before I was again seized by my porters and carried to the very centre of the Square, and there abandoned.

"Immediately the Public, obviously well accustomed to these out-door sports and pastimes, fell into perfectly straight lines on each of the sides of the Square, and assumed the position of sprinters at the starting-point of a race—but each with a *coupe-coupe*, knife, axe or spear in his right hand—and looked to His Majesty for the signal.

"The King rose from his royal stool, raised his spear aloft and gazed around. . . .

"I also gazed around, having just grasped the under-lying idea of the National Sport, a game in which I had never hitherto taken part, nor even seen. . . .

"Of course—how stupid of me—it was a race-game, a go-as-you-please, run-walk-hop-or-jump. . . . And my head was the prize!

"I wondered whether His Majesty had gathered that my brief address was not couched in diplomatic language. . . . He certainly now prolonged what was, to me, a painful moment. . . . He stood like an ebon statue, his white ostrich feathers nodding in the breeze, his handsome cloak hanging gracefully from his great shoulders, his spear uplifted, motionless. . . .

"When that spear fell, I knew that every competitor of those hundreds surrounding me, would bound forward like a greyhound unleashed. For a few seconds I should see them race toward me, their bloodthirsty faces alight with the lust of slaughter, their gleaming weapons raised aloft. . . . And I should go down, the centre of a mael-strom of clutching hands and hacking blades. . . .

"I wondered what would be the reward of the proud winner of the King's Trophy—the head of the white cock with a golden comb . . . the essential ingredient for the making of the strong *juju* that was to defeat the French. . . .

"That black devil, Behanzin, stood steady as a rock, and there was absolute silence in that great Square, as all awaited the fall of the flag, or rather the shining spear-head. . . .

" A woman, standing in a doorway, giggled nervously, and a crouching sprinter, presumably her lord, looked back over his shoulder—only to receive her sharp rebuke for taking his eye off the ball. . . .

" Another woman dashed forward and handed her husband a *machete*, taking his spear back into the hut. . . . I imagined his saying to her, just before he left the house, ' Tatiana, my dear, run upstairs and find that new *machete* I ordered last week. . . . I think it's on the top of the wardrobe in my dressing-room, unless that wretched girl has put it somewhere.' . . .

" And then I glanced again at the King. . . . Even as I did so, the raised spear-head, which probably had only been uplifted for five seconds after all, began to travel slowly backward. . . . And there was an audible intaking of breath. . . . Evidently the giving of the signal had begun, and in the fraction of a second, the broad, bright spear-head would come flashing downward. . . .

" I closed my eyes. . . .

" *Boom . . . BANG!*

" I nearly jumped out of my bottle. . . .

" *Boom . . . BANG!*

" Two shells had burst in Kana, one just above the inner wall, the other in the corner of the Square itself. . . .

" Our guns ! . . . Our guns ! . . .

" The runners were running indeed—for their *own* heads. . . . King Behanzin ' also ran ' . . . if indeed he did not get a win or a place. . . .

" I was forgotten . . . before ever the third and fourth shells arrived. . . . Oh, God ! I was *not* forgotten ! . . . There was *one* competitor left ! . . . I supposed he felt attracted by the walk-over. . . . As he dashed toward me, straight as an arrow, yelling madly, a great spear in his hand, I saw that he was one of the group of courtiers . . . the man indeed who had stood nearest to the King. . . .

" I admit, *mes amis*, that it seemed to me a little hard, more than a little hard, that with the flight of all those hundreds and hundreds of murderous slayers, this solitary one should prefer my life to his own . . . should not realize that the match was abandoned . . . the race scratched . . . the proceedings postponed. . . .

" A fellow of one idea. . . . A case of the *idée fixe*. . . . No sportsman, anyhow. . . . The sort of man that steals the Gold Cup. . . .

" I had been through so much, *mes amis*, from the time that that Amazon had hit me on the head, that I really rebelled a little at this last cruelty of a mocking Fate.

" Saved by the bursting of the shells at the fifty-ninth second of the fifty-ninth minute of the eleventh hour, and then this one solitary, implacable madman to fail to realize that I had been saved ! . . .

" Nearer . . . nearer . . . he came—and by the time that he was a few yards from me, he and I were alone in that great Square. . . .

" Would he drive that huge spear through my body, and then clumsily hack my head off with the edge of its broad blade ?

" How I hoped that the next shell would blow his limbs from his body, though it killed me too. . . . Another bound and he would be on me. . . . I closed my eyes— and the Nightmare Slayer flung his arm round me, and, in execrable French, panted :

" ' You tell Frenchies I be verra good man, massa. . . . I belong Coast . . . belong French shippy. . . . I good friend loving Frenchies. . . . I interpreter. . . . I show Frenchies where old Behanzin bury gin, rum, brandy, ivory. . . .'

" Another shell burst. . . . And the Nightmare Slayer tipped my basket over, and, flat upon the ground, the lion and the lamb lay down together. . . .

" That, *mes amis*, was how I nearly lost my head. . . .

" We must not lose ours here, for, as you perceive, there are far worse places than this one. . . . I rather like it. . . ."

§ 3

A long heavy silence was broken by Jacob the Jew.

" The lad we want here is the bold bright Rastignac . . . Rastignac, the Mutineer. . . ."

" Oh, did you know him ? " said the Englishman.

" What about him ? " asked the Frenchman.

" What *about* him ?　Ho, ho ! . . . He gave the Government some trouble, one way and another. . . . They stuck him in the Zephyrs, but they didn't keep him long.　What do you think he did ? . . .

" He used to carry a flexible saw-file round his upper gums from one cheek to the other, and they *say* he carried some little tool that he used to swallow—on the end of a string, with the other end tied round a back tooth—on search days.

" Well, he filed his manacles and got out. . . . And he killed two sentries, absolutely silently, by stabbing them in the back of the neck with a long darning-needle, to which he had fitted a tiny wooden handle. . . . There is a spot, you know, at the base of the brain, just where the skull rests on the backbone. . . . The point of a needle in *there* . . . just in the right spot . . . and *pouff !* . . .

" Rastignac knew the spot, all-right.　And when he was clear, and dressed in a dead sentry's uniform, did he run off like any other escaping prisoner ? . . . Not he. . . . He broke into a Public Works Department shed . . . took a pot of black paint, and a pot of white, and some brushes, and marched off at daybreak, as bold as brass. . . ."

" Where to ? " inquired the American.

" To the nearest milestone," chuckled Jacob the Jew, " . . . and neatly touched up the black *kilometre* figures and their white border. . . . And then to the next. . . . And the next. . . .

" When patrols passed, he gave them good-day and exchanged jokes and the latest news, for cigarettes and a drink. . . . They say he visited several camps and made himself useful, with his paint, to one or two officers, and reported some rascal who had smeared one of his nice black figures because he wouldn't give him tobacco ! . . .

" And so he painted his way, milestone by milestone, to Oran, where he reported himself, produced the dead sentry's *livret* and leave-papers, and was wafted comfortably, by *Messageries Maritimes*, to France. . . ."

" Well, and what would he do if he were here ? " asked a querulous voice. " We may suppose that your Rastignac had neither the wings nor feet of a fly. . . . And if he were here and got us out, where could we go ? . . . More likely to have caused the death of us all. . . . Like those two devils Dubitsch and Barre nearly did to their gang. . . ."

" What was that ? " asked Badineff.

" Why, these two unutterable swine were with a working-party in the *zone dissidente*, and at night were in a little perimeter-camp made with dry cactus and thick heavy thorn. . . . Their beautiful scheme—and they nearly brought it off—was to creep out on a windy night and to set fire to these great thorn-walls of the zareba ! This stuff burns like paper, and they'd got hold of some matches. . . . It mattered nothing to them that the remaining ninety-eight of their fellow-convicts would inevitably be roasted to death in the process. . . . Those two would easily escape in the confusion, while the men of the escort were vainly doing their best to save the rest of the wretched prisoners. . . . *Their* position, as you may imagine, would be just that of a bundle of mice tied together by their tails and packed round with cotton-wool soaked in kerosene. . . .

" As luck would have it—the luck of the other ninety-eight, anyhow—the first match was blown out, and a sentry had seen the glare of it. . . . He fired and challenged after, wounding Dubitsch and so flustering Barre, who had the matches, that he dropped the lot and was unable to strike another before the sentry was upon him. . . ."

" What happened then ? " asked the Englishman.

" The Sergeant-Major in charge of the escort simply returned them to their place in the gang—but took care that the gang should know exactly what had happened. . . ."

" And then ? . . . " prompted the Englishman, when the man stopped, as one who had said enough. . . .

" Oh—they died . . . they died. . . . They died that same night, of something or other. . . . Judging from their faces, they had not died happily. . . ."

" Sounds as though you saw them," observed Jacob the Jew.

" Quite," observed the narrator laconically.

" Not like poor dear little Tou-tou Boil-the-Cat," observed Jacob.

" What happened to him ? " asked the Querulous Voice.

" Oh, he died . . . he died. . . . He died suddenly, one night, of something or other. . . . But no-one was able to judge from his face whether he died happily or not. . . ."

" Tell us about him," suggested the American.

" About Tou-tou Boil-the-Cat ? . . . He wasn't a nice man. . . . Made quite a name for himself, Montmartre way, before he went to the Legion. . . . There was some talk about a Lovely Lady, the Queen of his Band. . . . Wonderful golden hair. . . . Known to all kind friends as *Casque d'Or*. . . . They say he cut it off. . . . Her head, I mean. . . . Got into bad trouble in the Legion too. . . . Life sentence in the Zephyrs. . . .

" A brave little man, but he hadn't the other virtue that one rather demands. . . . No. . . . Something of a stool-pigeon. . . . There were thirteen convicts in a tent . . . a most unlucky number . . . but it was soon reduced to twelve, through M'sieu Tou-tou Boil-the-Cat giving information that affected the career—indeed, abbreviated it—of one of his comrades. . . .

" Yes . . . thirteen went forth from that tent to labour in the interests of France's colonial expansion that sunny morning, and only twelve returned to it, to sleep the sleep of the unjust, that dewy eve. . . . A round dozen. . . .

"But they did not sleep through the stilly night, though the night remained quite stilly. . . . And behold, when another bright day broke, those twelve were now eleven. . . .

"The guard, who was but a simple peasant man, could *not* make the count come to more than eleven. . . . The corporal—possibly a shade more intelligent, could not by any means make the count a dozen. . . . The Sergeant, a man who could count quite well, swore there were but ten and one. . . . Not the Commandant himself could make us twelve ! . . .

"With the help of a bottle of absinthe he might make us twenty-two—but even then he realized that he should have seen twenty-four. . . .

"No. . . . Tou-tou Boil-the-Cat was gone. . . . Gone like a beautiful dream . . . or like the foul brutish night-mare that he was. . . .

"And that, you know, puzzled our kind superiors. . . .

"For, as it happened, it was quite impossible for anyone to have escaped from the camp that night—full moon, double sentries, constant patrols, and all-night wakefulness and uneasiness on account of expected Arab attack. . . .

"But gone he had. . . .

"We were interrogated severally, and collectively, and painfully . . . until they must have admired our staunch-ness and the wonderful cleverness of the missing man. . . .

"We eleven slept in the tent for a month . . . and the country round was scoured until not one grain of sand was left upon another, and there was not a locust, a scorpion, a serpent nor a vulture, whose *dossier* was not known. . . .

"And at the end of a month the whole camp moved on. . . ."

"Did they ever find him ? " asked Badineff.

"No . . . *they* didn't," was the reply. " The jackals found him. . . ."

"Where ? " asked the Englishman.

"Under the sand that had formed the floor of the tent of the eleven . . ." was the answer.

"Sounds as though you were there . . ." said the Querulous Voice.

"Quite . . ." replied Jacob the Jew, and yawned.

§ 4

The sun had risen and set once more, causing a spot of light to travel slowly across a portion of the interior of the *silo*, with the search-light effect of illuminating brilliantly the tiny area upon which it rested, while leaving the rest of the place in darkness darker than that of night.

There was curiously little movement, and less sound, in the *silo*—the uneasy stirring of a nightmare-ridden sleeper, a heavy sigh, a faint groan, the clank of a chain. Talk had ceased, and scarcely a sentence had been uttered for hours.

The last subject of general conversation had been that of the cause of their abandonment to a lingering and terrible death in that dreadful tomb. Speculation had wandered from sudden Arab attack and the annihilation of the Company, to the familiar theory of wanton malice and deliberate devilish punishment. Men, condemned from the Legion for military "crimes," had advanced the former theory; civilian prison criminals, the latter.

The Frenchman who had attempted to recite the Burial Service had accepted neither of these views.

"We are *forgotten*," he had said. . . . "We are the Forgotten of Man, as distinguished from our friends the Touareg, the Forgotten of God. It is perfectly simple, and I can tell you exactly how it happened.

"As you may be aware, *mes amis*, a list of *les hommes punis* is made out, by the clerk of the *Adjudant*, every morning, before the guard is changed. The form on which he writes the names is divided into columns showing the class of punishment and the number of days each man has still to do. . . . And the clerk of the *Adjudant*, God forgive him, has written the number of our days under the heading *salle de police,* or *cellules,* or *consigne,* and has left the column ' prison,' blank. So, each day, our sentences are being reduced by one day, in those places where we are not, and the Sergeant of the Guard for each day, observes that there are no men in ' *prison,*' for the column so headed is blank. . . . We are *not* in ' prison ' because we are not recorded as being in ' prison '—and therefore we cannot be released from ' prison.' . . ."

And Jacob the Jew had observed :

" Convincing and very cheering. . . . Monsieur must have been a lawyer before he left the world."

And the man had replied :

" No. . . . An officer. . . . Captain of Spahis and in the Secret Service—about to die, and unashamed. . . . *No !*—I should say *Légionnaire* Rien of the Seventh Company of the Third Battalion of the First Regiment of the Foreign Legion. . . . I was wandering in my mind. . . ."

§ 5

" Tell me," said Jacob the Jew (or Jacopi Judescu, the Roumanian gypsy). " What was really your reason for that sloppy feeble ' kindness ' to Ramon Gonzales. . . . I am a philosopher and a student of that lowest of the animals, called Man. . . . Was it to please your Christian God and to acquire merit ? . . . Or to uphold your insolent British assumption of an inevitable and natural superiority ? . . . You and your God—the Great Forgivers ! . . . ' Injure me—and I'll forgive you *and* make you feel so damned uncomfortable that you'll be more injured than I am.' . . . Aren't you *capable* of a good decent hate or . . ."

" Yes. I hate your filthy voice, dear Jacob," replied the Englishman.

" No. Tell me," persisted Jacob. " I loathe being puzzled. . . . Besides, don't you see I'm going mad. . . .

c

Talk, man. . . . These corpses. . . . Why did you
behave like that to Ramon Gonzales ? . . . He betrayed
you, didn't he ? . . . I would have strangled him. . . .
I would have had his eyes. . . . Didn't he betray and
denounce you after you had found him in the desert and
saved his life ? . . . To Sergeant Lebaudy ? "

" Yes. He recognized me—and did his, ah—duty,"
was the reply.

" For twenty-five pieces of silver ! . . . Recognized
you as one of the Zinderneuf men he knew at Sidi, and
promptly sold you ? . . .

" Consigned you to sudden death—or a lingering death—
for twenty-five francs and a Sergeant's favour ! . . . And
here the Judas was—wondrously delivered into your hand
—and you 'forgave' him and comforted him ! . . . Now
why ? . . . What was the game, the motive, the reason,
the object ? Why should a sane man act like that ? . . .
What *was* the game ? "

" No game, no motive, no reason," answered the Englishman. " He acted according to his lights—I to mine."

" And where do you get your ' lights ' ? What flame
lit them ? "

" Oh—I don't know. . . . Home. . . . Family. . . .
One's women-folk. . . . School. . . . Upbringing. . . .
Traditions. . . . One unconsciously imbibes ideas of
doing the decent thing. . . . I've been extraordinarily
lucky in life. . . . Poor old Ramon wasn't. . . . One
does the decent thing if one is—decent."

" You don't go about, then, consciously and definitely
forgiving your enemies and heaping coals of fire on them
because you're a Christian."

" No, of course not. . . . Don't talk rot. . . ."

" Nor with a view to securing a firm option on a highly
eligible and desirable mansion in the sky—suitable for
English gentleman of position—one of the most favourable
residential sites on the Golden Street. . . ."

" Not in the least. . . . Don't be an ass. . . ."

" You disappoint me. I was hoping to find, before I

died, one of those rare animals, a Christian gentleman—who does all these funny things *because* he is a Christian—and this was positively my last chance. . . . I shall die in here."

"I expect Christianity *was* the flame that lit those little 'lights,' Jacob. . . . Our home and school and social customs, institutions and ideas are based on the Christian ideal, anyhow. . . . And we owe what's good in them to that, I believe. . . . We get our *beau idéal* quite unconsciously, I think, and we follow it quite unconsciously—if we follow it at all. . . ."

"Well, and what *is* it, my noble Christian martyr?"

"Oh, just to be—decent, and to do the decent thing, y'know."

"So, indirectly, at any rate, you returned good for evil to Judas Ramon Gonzales because you were a Christian, you think?"

"Yes. . . . Indirectly . . . I suppose. . . . We aren't good at hating and vengeance and all that. . . . It's not done. . . . It isn't—decent. . . ."

"But you puzzle me. What of Ramon the Judas . . . Ramon who sold you? He was a *great* Christian, you know. . . . A staunch patron of your Christian God. . . . Always praying and invoking your Holy Family."

"There are good and bad in all religions, Jacob. . . . I have the highest admiration for your great people—but I have met rotten specimens. . . . Bad as some of my own. . . ."

Silence.

"Look here, Christian," began Jacob the Jew again. "If I summoned up enough strength, and swung this chain with all my might against your right cheek, would you turn the other also?"

"No. I should punch you on the nose," said the Englishman simply.

Silence.

" Tell me. Do you kneel down night and morning and pray to your kind Christian God, Englishman ? The forgiving God of Love, Who has landed you *here* ? " asked Jacob the Jew.

" I landed myself here," was the reply. " And—er—no. . . . I don't pray—in words—much. . . . You won't mind asking questions for fear of being thought inquisitive, will you, gentle Jacob ? "

" Oh, no. . . . Let's see now. . . . You forgive the very worst of injuries because you are a Christian, but not *because* you're a Christian. . . . You do as you would be done by, and not as you've been ' done ' by. . . . You don't pray in words, and hold daily communion with your kind Christian God—you regard Him as a gentleman—an English gentleman of course—who quite understands, and merely desires that you be—decent, which of course, you naturally would be, whether He wished it or not. . . . And you'll punch me on the nose if I smite you on the cheek—but you don't even do that much to anyone who betrays you to a dreadful death. . . . And really, in your nice little mind, you loathe talking about your religion, and you are terrified lest you give the impression that you think it is better than other people's, for fear of hurting their feelings. . . ."

" Oh, shut up, Jacob. You'd talk the hind leg off a dog."

" What else is there to do but talk ? . . . And so you are perfectly certain that you are a most superior person, but you strive your very utmost to conceal the awful fact. . . . You're a puzzling creature. . . . What is your motivating force ? What is your philosophy ? What are you *up* to ? . . ."

" Well, at the moment, I'm going to issue the waterration. . . . Last but one. . . . " said the Englishman.

" I can't understand you English. . . ." grumbled Jacob.

" A common complaint, I believe," said the Englishman. The quiet American laughed.

§ 6

" Should any gentleman here survive, I wonder if he would be so extremely obliging as to write to my Mother," said the French ex-officer later. " She is an old lady—quite alone—and she foolishly cherishes a fondness for a most unworthy son. . . . Darling Mother ! . . ."

The Englishman and the American memorized an address in Paris, and each declared that he would not only write to Madame de Lannec, but would visit her, give her her son's last message, and assure her of his gentle happy death from honourable wounds received in the service of France, and describe his grand military funeral.

Neither of these two men would admit that he also was already in his grave.

" Been in lots of tighter places than this," said the Englishman.

" I've been nearer death too," observed the American. " Been dead really. . . . In this same Zaguig. . . ."

" Ah—an unpleasant place, Zaguig," said the Frenchman, " I know it well," and added, " I, too, have occasionally been in danger. . . . But I finish here. . . ."

" Never say die," urged the American. " Personally, I refuse to die. . . . I've got a job to do, and I intend to live until it's done. . . ."

" Same here," agreed the Englishman. " I must be getting home to tea shortly. . . . My wife. . . ." He coughed.

" Ah, *mes amis*, you wish to live. . . . I, on the contrary, wish to die," whispered the Frenchman, and shortly after became delirious and raved—of " Véronique," of a terrible painter and his devilish picture, of a Colonel of Chasseurs d'Afrique, of a Moor of the Zarhoun whom the speaker had apparently killed with his bare hands, and of his mother. . . . But chiefly of " Véronique "—until he sank into a state of coma.

In the morning, the spot of light fell on his face and he

awoke and, from time to time, spoke rationally, though he did not appear to realize where he was.

He desired the services of a priest, that he might " make his soul." On either side of him, the Englishman and the American did what they could to soothe his passing, and Jacob the Jew produced his last scrap of biscuit for the nourishment of the sick man. . . . He offered to chew it for him if he were unable to masticate. . . .

" It's a privilege to die in your society, *mes amis*," said the Frenchman suddenly, in a stronger voice. " To die with men of one's own sort. . . . Officers once, doubtless, and gentlemen still. . . . I am going to add to the burden of debt I owe you. . . . But I am going to give you something in return. . . . My dying assurance that you are going to live. . . . I most clearly see you walking in the sunshine, free and happy. . . . Walking towards a woman—a truly beautiful woman. . . . She loves you both—but one far more than the other. . . . You fight on her account . . . your weapons are generosity, unselfishness, sacrifice, self-abnegation, the love of a man for his friend. . . ."

Silence.

" Poor chap," murmured the Englishman, staring across at the almost indistinguishable form of the American. " Wandering again. . . . He seemed better. . . ."

No reply came from the darkness where the other crouched beside the dying man.

" And this is the further request I have to make of you. . . . Will one of you go to the little cemetery and stand by her grave and say :

" ' *As he died he spoke of you. . . . He spoke only words of kindness and love. . . . He did not breathe one word of reproach. . . . Only kindness, love and gratitude.*'

" She will be able to understand—now. . . .

" And will you take violets—a few violets, from me. . . .

Always they were her flower. . . . A few of the beautiful
big violets that welcome one home from Africa. . . . Once
I kissed an old grandmother who was selling them on the
quai at Marseilles, and gave her a gold piece. . . . They
were not violets she sold to me. . . . They were *France*
. . . they were *Home* . . . they were *Véronique*. . . .
Their odour was the distilled soul of the sweetness of all
that is in those three wonderful words. . . . France,
Home and Beauty. . . .

"Oh, God . . . I can smell violets. . . .

"Véronique, did ever you see violets again without
thinking of me ? Did I ever see them again without
trembling from head to foot, without wondering how my
frozen brain could function . . . how my burning heart
could beat. . . .

"Forgive me, gentlemen. . . . But you never saw her.
. . . She was God's triumph. . . . Yes, often I called her,
'You Evidence of God'—for such beauty and wonder and
untellable glory of womanhood was final proof to me of the
existence of a great good God of Beauty.

"And Beauty *is* Truth—and Goodness."

Silence.

Jacob the Jew crawled painfully toward the spot of
light.

"You can give him my water-ration," he croaked.

"*Stout fella!*" said the Englishman, in his mother-
tongue.

The American started, as a slight jingle of iron indicated.

"*Say that again, will you?*" he said in English.

"I said, '*Stout fella*,'" replied the Englishman.

"*Merciful God!*" whispered the American ; and the
dying Frenchman raised himself on his right elbow, and
endeavoured to point with his left hand.

"*Véronique!*" he cried. "I did my best. . . . I *did*
save you from Dummarcq—the great César Dummarcq
—the world-famous painter, the idol of Paris, the huge

vile pig, the half-mad cruel devil. . . . *No—he is there!*
. . . Do not move! . . . Do not stir hand or foot . . .
a hair's-breadth—or he will shoot. . . . He will shoot
you, not me, the fiend!"

He sank back upon the ground.

"Dearest Mother! . . . I nearly broke your heart
when I told you I would marry her. . . . And you nearly
broke mine when you said that I should not. . . . An
artists' model. . . . True. . . . César Dummarcq's
model. . . . But a model of beauty and grace. . . .
Lovely in all her ways and thoughts and movements. . . .
César Dummarcq's model. . . . But a model for all
women to copy. . . . Every fascination and charm of
mind as well—witty and clever and of the sweetest
disposition. . . . With her, one laughed. . . . One
laughed the whole day through. . . .

"Oh, but she was *dear*—dear and sweet and a living
charm. . . . Was it her fault that she had no heart?
No fairy, mermaid, elf, sprite, no magic princess from the
golden castle on the crystal hill, ever *has* a heart! . . .
So I gave her mine—to break. . . .

"Oh, that terrible picture! . . . Véronique, how was I
to know that he had painted us, all save the last few
touches? . . . The jealous devil! . . . He did not even
love you. . . . You were merely his model, his chattel,
his property. . . . No one must take you from him—
not even to marry you. . . .

"Behind that sinister black curtain. . . . A pistol in
his hand. . . . My arms about you as I implored you to
be my wife. . . . Your terrible shriek as you saw him
appear . . . smiling . . . smiling . . ."

Silence.

The Frenchman's voice changed completely. It was as
though an entirely different personality possessed his body.

"No—don't move, my young cub! . . . Move hand
or foot, and our fair and frail young friend will have her

beauty marred! . . . Oh, a *great* picture! . . . '*FEAR!*'
by *César Dummarcq* . . . the greatest portrayer of human
emotions, of all time. . . . Yes . . . '*FEAR!*' . . .
Do you *fear*, little cockerel? . . . Do you fear you have
brought death to your mistress? . . . I *am* Death! . . .
Death the great Artist! . . . Oh, ho! his macabre com-
positions! . . . His lovely colours of corruption and
decay! . . . The great César Dummarcq's greatest
picture—'*FEAR!*' . . . Now keep still. . . . See, I
lay the pistol on this table beside the easel. . . . Ah!
would you! . . . You'd rise from that rug, would you?
. . . *Down*, dog! . . . Would you murder this woman
whom you love so much? . . . That's better. . . .

"No, my dear Véronique, do not faint. . . . Just
a minute. . . . Your glazing eyes staring from the
white mask of your face. . . . '*FEAR!*' Aha! . . .
Wonderful models! . . . One has to go to some trouble
to find them, of course. . . . That's right, popinjay—
excellent! . . . Moisten your lips with your tongue
again. . . . See, little pimp, I think I will shoot her,
after all—as I have finished her face. . . . Yes—you a
little later. . . . Another marvellous picture! . . . She
lies on the divan—same attitude—blood on her breast,
a thin stream trickling down her white arm, a stain on
the white bear-skin—lovely colours! . . . And you?
. . . One arm and your head and shoulders across her
body. . . . The rest of you on the rug—much the same
position as now. . . . A bullet-hole beneath your ear.
. . . I am not too near, here, I think. . . . No. . . .
What shall we call the second picture? . . . '*REVENGE!*'
. . . No, a little banal. . . . What about '*FINIS!*'
. . . No. . . . No name at all, I think—a '*problem*'
picture. . . .

"Oh? . . . You think *I*'ll make a fine picture on the
guillotine, do you? . . . That's where you're wrong,
puppy. . . . This is going to be a *crime passionel*. . . .
Glorious advertisement for the great César Dummarcq. . . .
Anyhow, the present picture is going marvellously. . . .

"'*FEAR!*' . . . Never was *FEAR* so portrayed before. . . . Hi! *Down*, dog! There . . . That bullet stirred her hair. . . . Stirred your heart too by the look of you, you little hound. . . ."

Silence.

" *Ce bon Monsieur César Dummarcq* would seem to have been a gentleman with a sense of humour," murmured Jacob. " I would we had him here."

" To jest with us ? " inquired the Englishman.

" No, for us to jest with *him*, I think," replied Jacob.

Silence.

" Water ! " gasped the Frenchman.

" Mine," said Jacob.

" We'll all contribute," said the American.

The Englishman took the jug to the ray of light and carefully measured water into an iron mug.

" A good spoonful each, left," he said, stepping gingerly between two corpses.

The Frenchman drank avidly. Upon this little stream of life-giving water his conscious mind seemed to be borne to the surface.

" Thank you ! . . . Thank you, gentlemen ! " he said. " I do hope I have not drunk more than my share. . . . I was not noticing. . . . One of you will see to that for me, will you not ? . . . Get them on the *quai* at Marseilles, and put them on her grave in the little cemetery. . . ."

" Why certainly, of course," said the American. " Where is it ? "

" . . . And tell her that my last thoughts were of her. . . . She will understand now. . . . She understood nothing when she died. . . . She was like that when I saved her from the Beni Zarkesh. . . . God is very good and He had taken away her understanding. . . ."

Silence.

" . : : That roof. . . . In the starlight. : : : He was twice as big and strong as I, that Moor. . . . But I killed him with my bare hands, as I had killed the watchman dozing at the foot of the stair. . . . Oh, that lovely silent struggle, with my hands at his throat. . . .

"And she thought I was de Chaumont, her Colonel of Chasseurs d'Afrique. . . . His name was Charles. . . . She called me ' *Charles* ' as I carried her to the horses. . . . She called me ' *Charles* ' through the brief remainder of her life. . . . She died calling me ' *Charles.* ' . . . A little hard for me to bear. . . . Yes, I suffered a little. . . . I had thought bitterly of Charles de Chaumont and I had written him a rather terrible letter when, on the strength of his rank and seniority, he declined my challenge to a duel. . . . But I am grateful to him for his kindness to her, and for making her so happy all those years. . . . He must have loved her truly. . . . Who could help it ? . . . And how she loved him ! . . . She must have been happy as the day is long, for she had changed but little. . . . A girl when I lost her. . . . A woman when I found her. . . . Even more beautiful, if that were possible. . . . The mad are often very lovely. . . . An unearthly beauty. . . . Very terrible. . . . But I firmly believe her last days were happy. . . . She had forgotten that *hareem*. . . . And I was her adored *Charles de Chaumont !* . . . Yes. . . . Unconscious fingers can play a fearful threnody upon our heart-strings. . . . Can break them one by one. . . . " *Véronique* . . . *Véronique* . . ."

Silence.

"Is he dead ? " asked Jacob, later.

"Yes," said the Englishman, and coughed slightly.

"Well, do you know," said Jacob, " I think I shall join him. I have always been deeply interested in the Hereafter, and I confess to being a little weary of the Here. . . . Yes, I think it's time to go."

" Are you talking about committing suicide ? " asked the American.

" Not at all," replied Jacob. " I am talking about being murdered and taking it upon me to shorten the process. I have no strong views on the subject of man murdering his fellow-man on the scaffold, or against the wall at dawn. But this slow murder is quite indefensible, and I feel justified in expediting my end."

" You'll look a most awful ass if they remember us and a release-party comes, after all," said the Englishman.

" I shall look very nasty, anyhow, by the time a release-party comes," was the reply. " So will you, my friends. And you will have suffered a few hours or a few days longer than I. . . . Either the Company has moved on, and there are a few more miles of the Zaguig-Great Oasis Road, marked, or else there was a sudden raid and the Company is obliterated. . . . Anyhow—I've had enough."

" Don't give up, Jacob. Don't be a coward," said the Englishman.

" No, I will not give up—my right to dispose of myself ; the only right left to me," was the answer. " No, I will not be a coward who dare not step uninvited into the next world. . . . What do you do, my friend if you sit on a tin-tack ? You promptly remove yourself. I am going to remove myself. I have already sat too long upon this particular—ah—tin-tack."

" Rot," said the Englishman.

" You're beat," said the American.

" You can't commit suicide," said the Englishman.

" It isn't—' decent,' I suppose," smiled Jacob.

" That's it," said the Englishman. " It's a rotten thing to do. One doesn't commit suicide ! It's not done. It isn't—er—decent."

" A matter of opinion," said the Jew. " Is it better and wiser to suffer indescribable agonies of the mind, and ghastly tortures of the body, for days, hours, or seconds ? It seems to me to be more logical to let it be a matter of seconds."

" Well, logic isn't everything," said the Englishman.

"Most of our best impulses and ideas are illogical. . . . Damn logic. . . . Love is illogical."

"Surely," said the American.

"Yes. Life is illogical and death is illogical, and God is illogical," said Jacob. "And it is also perfectly illogical to lie here and die of thirst, starvation, heat, suffocation and insects for another twenty-four hours when you can do it in twenty-four seconds. . . . Good-bye, my friends! May we meet again and discuss our discoveries concerning God, Jehovah, Allah, Christ, Mahomet, Buddha and the other manifestations of man's incurable anthropomorphism. . . . *Adieu!* Or *au revoir*—whichever it may prove to be."

"Hi! Here! Hold on!" cried the Englishman.

"You! Jacob!" called the American.

"Well?" chuckled the Jew.

"Look here," said the Englishman, "be decent, Jacob. You objected to Ramon dying at all."

"Ah—he was the first," replied Jacob, "and there was some hope then. . . . There are only we three now, and one more corpse will not further discommode you. I beg you to believe me that I would not have done this were all the others still alive—not even though I knew there would be no release. . . .

"To have done that would not have been—' decent,' " he added with a chuckle.

"Look here, Jacob, will you do me a favour?" asked the Englishman.

"I shall be most delighted," was the reply. "It will be my last opportunity. And it will have to be soon," he added, his weak voice growing perceptibly weaker.

"Well, I want you to promise to wait another day," said the Englishman. "Only another twenty-four hours. Just till the spot of light falls on the Frenchman's body again. . . ."

"Come on, Jacob," urged the American. "Stick it till then. Please yourself after that. But I believe we'll be saved to-morrow."

" Too late," was the whispered reply. " I have opened a vein. . . . When you want it, you'll find the piece of steel in my right hand . . . razor-edge one side, saw-edge the other . . . Pluck up your courage and come along with me, both of you. . . ."

Silence.

A deep sigh.

The Englishman and the American found it was indeed too late.

§ 7

" *Now*, my friend," said the American, " we can attend to our own little affairs ! . . . Do you know that our meeting in here is one of the most astounding things that have *ever* happened ? . . . Do you know you are *the one man in all the world I have been looking for* ! . . . And *this* is where I find you ! . . . I did my damnedest—and then Providence took a hand. . . . Heaven helps those, etc. . . ."

" I am afraid I don't quite understand," began the Englishman.

" You certainly don't. . . . I don't myself. . . . We're dreaming, of course. It's delirium. We aren't in any *silo*. . . . *You aren't John Geste*."

" But I *am* John Geste ! " gasped the Englishman.

" You aren't John Geste and I didn't spot you directly you said ' *Stout fella*,' in English. And I didn't hear you call your wife ' Stout fella ' at Brandon Abbas when you were kids and . . . Oh, my God !

" Where's your hand, man. . . . Oh, *John Geste ! John Geste !* . . . We'll be out of here to-morrow, boy. . . . We *can't* die here. God doesn't mean us to die and rot in this hole that was ordained to be our meeting-place. . . . Ordained from the beginning of Time as the place where I should find you, after all. . . . And Isobel's well and only waiting to be happy as soon as she hears you're coming home to—er—tea, John Geste! . . . And I was to tell you Michael didn't take the ' Blue Water ' from under the cover. It wasn't he who stole it. . . . And I'm going mad, John Geste—mad with joy—and starvation, and weakness, and happiness. . . ."

" Hadn't noticed the happiness much," said the Englishman. " What are you gibbering about, my dear chap ? Who *are* you ? How do you know my name—and about Isobel ? "

He coughed slightly. " I'm delirious, I suppose. . . . Both delirious. . . . Both dreaming. . . ."

" We're both dreaming the same dream then, John Geste. . . . I want to tell you. . . ."

An ominous clink of metal and a sigh were audible above the feeble croaking of his voice.

" Here, what's up ? . . . You listening ? . . . Here, *wake up.*"

The Englishman had collapsed and lay inert, unresponsive, either in a faint or the last sleep of all.

§ 8

The arrival of the spot of sunlight found the American moistening the lips of the dying Englishman with the remaining drops of water.

" Worn out," he murmured later. " God ! I feel as strong as a horse now ! . . . He had given up hope before I recognized him. . . . Oh, Isobel . . . I've found him and he's dying. . . . No, God can't mean that. . . . I'm talking out loud. I must catch hold of myself. . . . Help me, God, for I am going to help myself—to help them."

The American crawled across to where lay the body of the strange man known to his fellows as Jacob the Jew.

Feeling over the corpse he found the right hand and in it a piece of wonderfully-tempered steel, which, together with a few matches, the man had somehow hidden from those whose duty it had been to search him. Securing it, he returned to the side of the Englishman, and once again endeavoured to revive him.

Panic seized him as he realized his efforts were unavailing. Putting his lips to the ear of the unconscious man, he whispered urgently, and his whisper quickly grew to a hoarse shout.

"*John Geste! John Geste! Come back, John Geste!* Come *back*, man! You *can't* die! You can't die, *now*, John Geste! I've *found* you. . . . *Hi! John Geste!* Think of Isobel. . . . Isobel! . . . Isobel!! *Isobel!!!* Do you hear me? . . . Do you hear me, John? Fight, man! Fight for your life! . . . Think how Beau would have fought! . . . Beau Geste. . . . Think how Digby would have fought. . . . Digby Geste. . . . Fight, John! . . . Fight for Isobel. . . . Come back. . . . Isobel! . . . Isobel!! *Isobel!!!*"

As though the name had reached his semi-conscious mind, the dying man stirred. The other crowed inarticulately, and suddenly fell quiet.

"Wish I knew something more about that blood-transfusion stunt," he murmured in his normal voice, as he deeply incised the side of his wrist, forced open his companion's mouth, and pressed the bleeding wrist firmly against it.

"Excuse me, son," he said, and laughed hysterically.

THE STORY OF OTIS VANBRUGH

" A lean man, silent, behind triple bars
  Of pride, fastidiousness and secret life.
  His thought an austere commune with the stars,
  His speech a probing with a surgeon's knife.

  His style a chastity whose acid burns
  All slack, false, formlessness in man or thing;
  His face a record of the truth man learns
  Fighting bare-knuckled Nature in the ring."
                                    —*John Masefield.*

  *A man's place in the scale of civilization is shown
  by his attitude to women. There are men who regard
  a woman as something to live with. There are others
  who regard her as someone to live for.*

CHAPTER I

I SHALL never forget my first sight of Isobel Rivers—a somewhat foolish remark, in view of the fact that I have never forgotten any glimpse I have ever had of her. I don't think I have even forgotten any word that she has ever said to me. Nay, more, I do not believe I have forgotten any word that I have ever said to her.

It was, as was most fitting, one of those truly glorious English spring mornings when one is consciously glad to be alive, and unconsciously aware that God's in His Heaven and all's well with the world.

I was on a visit to the home of my maternal grandmother at Brandon Regis and had that morning walked out from the big old house which was half farm and half manor, where my yeoman ancestors had lived since Domesday Book, or before.

I suppose it was the utter glory of that lovely morning, and not a premonition that this was to be an epochal day in my life, that made me feel so joyously exalted.

I had walked a mile or so, in the direction of Brandon Abbas, and was seated on a gate that opened into one of those neat and tidy English fields that always look to me as though they were tended rather by parlour-maids than by agricultural labourers. I was whistling merrily, and probably quite tunelessly, when a dog-cart, its small body perched high on big spidery wheels, came smartly round a bend in the high-hedged narrow lane to which my face was turned.

On the front seat were two boys, extraordinarily alike, as I saw when the horse was brought to an extremely sudden stand-still at my gate. Back to back with these obvious twins, sat a boy and a girl, the boy an unmistakable younger brother of the twins, and the girl younger still.

They were an astoundingly handsome quartette, and the girl's face was the loveliest I had ever seen.

It is still the loveliest I have ever seen.

I will not attempt to describe her, as it is foolish to attempt the impossible. I can only say that the face was typically Anglo-Saxon in its fair loveliness of pale golden hair, large, long-lashed eyes of corn-flower blue, perfect complexion and tender mouth, faultless and sweet.

The boy who was driving the restless and spirited horse, addressed me in a form of words, archaic and unusual.

" Prythee, gentle stranger, seated pensive on thy gate, and making day hideous with shrill cacophony. . . ."

" Doesn't look coffiny to me," interrupted his twin.

" Nor too blooming gentle," said the boy behind him.

" And I am *sure* he was making day delightful and wasn't a bit s'rill, and he isn't a stranger now we've talked to him," said the girl.

" Good-morning Madam, and gentlemen," said I, stepping down and raising my cap to the lovely little maiden who had spoken in my defence.

" Have it your own way, pups," cried the first speaker, as the three boys gravely and gracefully returned my salute. " He's not a stranger within our gate, nor on it, now ; he is making day beautiful with uninstrumental and unearthly music. . . ."

" Do you mean an unearthly row ? " asked his twin.

" No, vulgarian ; I meant heavenly music. Music such as ne'er was heard on earth before—let's hope ! . . . But what's all this got to do with the dog ? The dog may be dying while we trifle thus—dying of a broken heart."

" Oh, don't say such dreadful things, Beau," begged the little girl.

" Nothing dreadful about that," replied the boy called Beau, manfully checking the horse's obvious desire to bolt. " Compliment to the dog. D'you mean to suggest that the callous brute is *not* by now dying of a broken heart ? "

" Spare a father's feelings," requested his twin, and wiped away a tear. " It's *my* dog. . . . And what we want to know, Sir, if you could be quiet for one second, is—er—have you seen a dog ? "

" Often," I replied, trying to enter into the light inconsequent spirit of this joyous charming band.

" Where ? " they inquired simultaneously.

" Oh, Wyoming, Texas, Oregon, Nevada. . . ."

" Nirvana ? " inquired the owner of the dog. " Then dogs do go there. Good."

" California," I continued. " Boston, New York, Paris, London, Brandon Regis. . . ."

" He's getting ' warm,' " said Beau.

" Brandon Abbas ? " prompted his twin.

" I'm not certain," I replied. " I rather think I did, though. . . ." And here the little girl broke in.

" Oh, do stop talking nonsense, Beau and Digby and John. . . ."

" Not talking at all," said John, through whose arm the girl's hand was tucked.

" Well *do*, then, and say something sensible," was the feminine reply, and she turned to me.

" We've lost our dog, and he can't have been in *all* those funny places you said. Have you seen her here ? Will you help me find her—for I do love him so ? "

" Why, *of course* I will," I said, and added impulsively, " I'd do anything you asked me. *I'll* find him if he or she is alive."

And the twins on the front seat, promptly assisted by John, thereupon simultaneously chanted what appeared to be a family *cliché*.

" *Oh—isn't—he—a—nice—boy.* . . . *He—must—come—and—play—with—us.* . . . *Won't—Auntie—be—pleased.* . . ."

" What's the dog like ? " I inquired of the one whom they called Digby. " What breed, if any ? And what sex ? " as there seemed to be a variety of opinions on this point.

" Sex ? Oh—er—she's a bitchelor—feminine of bachelor, you know," replied Digby. . . . " As to what she's *like*," he continued, " that's a difficult question to answer. She's rather like. . . . No, she isn't. . . . She isn't a bit like a giraffe, really. . . . No. . . . She's rather like—a dog. Yes. . . . She is. . . . And she is one of these new Andorran Oyster-Hounds. . . ."

" Oh, good ! That's helpful," I said appreciatively, while four pairs of bright young eyes summed me up. I was being weighed, and most earnestly I hoped I should not be found wanting.

" An idea," I exclaimed. " What name does she answer to ? "

" She never answered *me*," replied Digby, and turning to his twin inquired, " Did she ever back-answer you, Beau ? "

" Never a cheep out of her," was the reply. " Not a word. Sulky beggar."

" Not at all," contradicted John, "merely respectful. . . . Reserved, taciturn chap. . . . Strong silent dog."

" Well, she always answers *me*, anyhow," asserted the little girl warmly. " She always *smiles*. . . . He has a most lovely smile," she added, turning to me.

" Now we're getting on," I declared. " I'm to search for a dog that is very like a dog and answers with a smile. . . . Now what is the likeliest way to win her smile ? What shall I call her when I see her ? "

" Call her home," said Digby.

" I don't know *what* you'll call her when you see her," said Beau. " Have you a kind nature and a gentle tongue ? . . . You must tell us later what you *did* call her when you saw her. . . . Especially if you called her it in American."

" Darned gosh-dinged gol-durned dod-gasted smell-hound ? " suggested Digby.

" I've never heard the expressions," I replied, " but I'll

try to remember them if you think them appropriate. . . . But to get back to the dog."

" It's what we want to do," replied Digby, " or to get her back to us. You don't know the state I'm in. . . . Am I out in a rash ? "

" No. In a dog-cart," said Beau, " and you won't be in that long, when we start playing chariots. . . . Well, good-bye, old chap. Thanks awfully. I hope you haven't bored us—I mean we haven't. . . ."

" Stop, stop, Beau," cried the little girl, turning round and thumping the boy's broad back. " He's going to be a search-party and we haven't told him what he wants to know, yet. . . . I think he's most awfully kind and nice. . . . And we ought to help him to . . ."

" Oh, *yes*, Beau," said Digby in a tone of deep reproach, " when he's in such trouble about a dog. . . . Of course we must help him. Now let's see," he continued. " It's got four canine teeth."

" I should think all a dog's teeth are canine," observed John judicially.

" And five toes on his fore-feet."

" That makes twenty," remarked Beau.

" And four on each hind one. . . . He wags his tail from left to right ; not right to left. . . . You get the idea, don't you ? Like a pendulum. Or an Aberdonian his head, when asked to subscribe."

" But hasn't she a *name* ? " I interrupted.

" A *name* ? " replied Digby. " Now that's an idea. That's really helpful. Oh, yes, I know she's got a name because I was at the christening—but I've clean forgotten most of it. . . . What's her name, Beau ? "

" Well—I always call him Jasper Jocelyn Jelkes, but I think of her as Mrs. Denbigh-Hobbes of The Acacias, Lower Puffleworth."

" Oh, do stop rotting," begged John, and turning to me assured me that the dog's name was Simply-Jones, though generally addressed as Mr. Featherstonehaugh—whereat the little girl was moved to climb down on to the step at the back of the cart, and jump to the ground. Coming round to where I stood, she seized my arm and proceeded to lead me down the lane.

"Come away from those sillies, American Boy," she said, "and I'll just tell you all about it, and you *will* find her for me, won't you? She is Digby's dog, but it's me she loves, and I know she's grieving and sorrowing like anything, for she has such a nice loving nature and a good heart. Her name is Joss and she's middle-sized and middle-aged and sort of middleish altogether—not exactly a spaniel nor a terrier nor a hound, but just a dog, and if you call 'Joss, Joss, Joss, Joss, Jossie!' in a kind sweet voice, rather high, she'll run to you and smile like anything. You'll know her by her smile. You *will* find her, won't you? Our home's at Brandon Abbas—Auntie is Lady Brandon."

"If she's alive on this earth, I'll find her," I said.

"Isobel! *Hi!* Isobel!! *Isobel!!!* Come on, if you want to be Boadicea," came borne on the breezes, and with a "*Thank* you, nice American Boy," and a smile that went straight to my heart—and also to my head—Isobel turned and scampered back.

Later, while searching the world for Joss, I had another glimpse of this party.

The dog-cart driven at a reckless gallop across a great lawn-like field, contained a boy and a girl, both wearing fencing-masks, the girl, armed with a bow and arrow, returning the fire of two presumed Roman soldiers who, with javelin and arrow, assailed the chariot, skilfully driven and controlled by a charioteer.

I was relieved to observe that the horse was apparently accustomed to these martial exercises, and that the chariot came round in a graceful curve before reaching the ditch-and-hedge at the end of the field.

§ 2

Being a strictly truthful person, I cannot say that I found Jasper Jocelyn Jelkes, *alias* Joss, for it was really she who found me. What her business may have been, I do not know, but she was visiting at High Gables, my grandmother's house, when I returned for lunch.

As I emerged from the shadows of the avenue, I beheld a very nondescript dog sunning herself on the lowest of the white steps of the porch, and smiling, most positively smiling, with extreme fatuity and foolishness, at my Grandmother's tiny Pekinese, a microscopic by-product of the dog-industry, which found no favour in my sight. Lifting up my voice to the level of the hope that rose in my heart, I invoked the smiling caller, in the very tones and accent in which I had been instructed, and in the most mellifluous and wooing way at my command. The excellent Joss, for such, beyond peradventure of a doubt, her conduct proved her to be, lolloped straightway to my feet and sitting on end, smiled and smiled and was not a villain, I felt sure.

" Joss ! " I cried, patting that smiling head. " *Dulce ridentem Lalagem amabo* ; grinning idiot ; Minnehaha, Laughing Water ; I'm *very* pleased to meet you. . . . You shall lead me, gentle Jossie, like a blind man's dog, straight to Brandon Abbas, to the house of Aunty, to those delightful boys and to—Isobel. Are you a bit of a card, Jossie ? For my visiting-card you shall be. . . ."

Oh, to be seventeen again ! Seventeen, on a most glorious English spring day, the day on which you have first encountered the very loveliest thing in all the world— that is to remain, for ever, the very loveliest thing in all your world.

CHAPTER II

AFTER lunch, on that day of days, with Hail Smiling Joss as my sponsor, excuse, and loud note of introduction, I " proceeded," as they say in the British Navy, to the great house of Brandon Abbas, after so feasting the excellent dog that it seemed highly probable she would again lose herself in the direction of High Gables.

Up a few miles of avenue of Norman oaks I tramped, from the Lodge at the gates guarded by heraldic beasts well known to students of Unnatural History—the Returning Wanderer straining at the leash and obviously striving to compose her features to a mask of becoming gravity, tempered by gladness while chastened by shame.

Arrived at a large square of mossy gravel surrounded by a dense shrubbery, I beheld a great porch and an open door through which I had, in passing, a glimpse of a panelled hall, gleaming floor, and suits of armour. A passing glimpse, because it was clearly obvious that Joss intended me to pass, and my will was not brought into conflict with hers, as I heard shouts and peals of laughter from the band of whom I was in search.

Guided by the now excited dog, I crossed a rose-garden and, by a path through some great old elms and beeches, reached an open space of turf which was a view-point overlooking half the county.

As we burst from the gloom of the wood into the sunshine, a hubbub arose ; the four, now augmented by several others, converged upon me, and, with a shriek of joy, as she sped forward ahead of the rest, the little girl literally flung herself upon me, threw her arms about my

58

neck, and kissed me warmly. Truth compels me to add that she promptly did precisely the same to the errant Joss, who instantly abandoning her expression, pose, and air of a Misunderstood-but-Hopeful-Dog, stood upon her hind legs, her paws against her mistress, wagged her tail and her tongue, and smiled and smiled to the point of laughter.

"Oh, Stout Fella!" cried Beau. "Splendid! Good scout!"

"Put it right there, Mr. Daniel Boone—or are you Kit Carson? Or Buffalo Bill? Or the Pathfinder? . . . Anyhow, you're the Dogfinder," said Digby, extending his hand, and wringing mine powerfully. . . . "A father's thanks . . . The Prodigal Dog . . . Good mind to *kill* the fat-headed calf!" and seizing the dog in his arms, he rolled upon the ground in apparently terrific combat with the savage beast, who, with horrid growls and furious barks, worried the throat of her fiercely-stabbing antagonist, and bloodlessly bit him with all her canine teeth.

"In the end, I die, having saved all your lives from a mad dog, and so find a hero's grave," announced Digby. . . . "The dog was born mad," he added, and lay motionless, while the Andorran Oyster-Hound surveyed her toothwork, wagged her tail joyously, and seated herself upon the chest of her victim.

The youngest brother, meanwhile, having slipped his hand inside my arm, while he critically watched the progress of the fight, stood by my side as I waited— holding the grubby little paw which Isobel had thrust into my hand—and feeling unreasoningly and unreasonably happy.

"I say," said the boy, "you ought to join the Band. Will you? Would you like to?"

"Oh *yes*," chimed in Isobel. "*Do*, American Boy. . . . Have you ever been tortured by Indians, or been the Victim of a Cruel Fate, like Mazeppa? Do you think we might roast you at the stake? . . . We've all got mustangs, and Joss is quite a good wolf or coyote. She's being a wolf now, and she's not mad at all—not even half-witted."

"Not nearly half," agreed Digby, arising. "Er—this is—er—the Captain—Michael Geste, Captain of the Band. I am Digby Geste, Lieutenant of the Band. The object on your right hand is John Geste, or Very Small Geste, or Not-Much- of the Band. The female prisoner is Isobel Rivers, the Music of the Band. The beautiful woman enthroned yonder is Claudia, Queen of the Band ; and the gentleman at present struck dumb by toffee-on-the-jaw, is Augustus Brandon, and can't be helped. I may add that, as you doubtless suppose, he is not such a fool as he looks. How could he be ? . . . The small fat boy and girl on the pony are twins, Marmaduke and—er—Marmaduchess. Marmaduke's step-mother, who eats vinegar with a fish-hook three times a day, says he is Wholly Bad. We call him the Wholly of Whollies. Marmaduchess is of course the Roly of Polies. . . . These camp followers—scamp-followers—er—no, that won't do, as they follow the Captain, are Honorary Members of the Band. In view of your great services, I have the pleasure . . ."

"You'll have the pleasure of bread-and-water and six of the best, if you don't take a holiday," interrupted the Captain of the Band, and proceeded most warmly to invite me to become an Honorary Member of "Beau Geste's Band," and to take part in all its doings, for so long as the country was enriched by my presence, and whenever my inclinations prompted me so to do.

Gratefully accepting the Band's hospitality, I was initiated and enrolled, and quickly appointed stage-manager of its activities in its Western American manifestations, and became its authority upon the dark ways of Red Indians, Bad Men, Buffalo Bills, Cow-boys, Deadwood Dicks, and other desperadoes.

I won my spurs (but did not wear them) by finding myself able to catch, mount, and ride a horse that was loose in the paddock. A horse that had never been ridden before and apparently intended never to be ridden again. . . .

After a most delightful tea with these extraordinarily charming young people, I walked back to High Gables feeling happier, I think, than I had ever felt in my life. It was a rather wonderful thing to me, a lonely stranger in a strange land—for there was nobody but my Grandmother and her servants at High Gables—suddenly to find myself a member of so attractive a society, a family so friendly, so welcoming, so uncritically hospitable that, almost on sight, they had admitted me to membership of their Band, with all the privileges attaching thereto. . . .

But as I lay awake in bed that night, the picture most vividly before me was the beautiful face of the darling child who had given me that sweet spontaneous kiss of gratitude and innocence.

It surely was the nicest thing that had ever happened to me.

§ 2

I shall be believed when I state that I missed few opportunities of accepting the warm invitation to " come again soon " which invariably accompanied the farewells at the end of each of my visits to Brandon Abbas. The more I saw of the three Gestes, the better I liked them, and I knew that I could never see too much, nor indeed enough, of Isobel Rivers—that lovely little fairy ; charming and delightful child ; ineffably sweet, and absorbingly interesting, little friend. . . .

Of the boys, I liked John best ; for, in addition to all the attributes which he possessed in common with his brilliant brothers, he was, to me, slightly pathetic in his dog-like devotion to the twins, who ruled him with a rod of iron, chastened and chastised him for the good of his soul, kept him in subjection, and loved him utterly. In return for their unwavering and undemonstrated love, he gave them worship. They would have died for him, and he would have died under torture for them.

Yet, at the same time, I like Beau enormously ; for his

splendour—and it was nothing less—of mind, body and soul; his unselfish sweetness and gentleness, and his extraordinary "niceness" to everybody, including myself. Even when he had occasion to punish a member of his Band, it appeared to me that the victim of his arbitrary justice rather enjoyed the honour of being singled out, even for admonition and the laying on of hands. . . .

But then, again, I liked Digby as much ; for his unfailing mirth and happiness. He was a walking chuckle, and those who walked through life with him chuckled too. He was merriment personified ; his day was a smile ; and if he fell on his head from the top of a tree, the first use he made of his recovered breath was to laugh at the extraordinarily amusing funniness of Digby Geste's falling thirty feet and nearly breaking his neck. . . . He was the most genuinely and spontaneously cheerful person I ever met, and somehow one always laughed when Digby began to laugh, without waiting for the joke.

Isobel was their pet, their fairy, their mascot, their dear perfect play-mate ; and Claudia was their Queen—" Queen Claudia, of Beau Geste's Band "—held in the highest honour and esteem. They loved and obeyed Claudia ; but they petted and adored Isobel.

I suppose Claudia was of an immaculately flawless beauty, charm, and grace of form and face, even as a young girl— but personally I never liked her. There was a slight hardness, a self-consciousness and an element of selfishness in her character, that were evident—to me at any rate, though not, I think, to the others. Certainly not to Michael Geste, for she was obviously his *beau idéal* of girlhood, and he, her self-constituted paladin and knight-errant. When they played "tournaments" she was always the Queen of Beauty, and he her Champion, ready, willing and able, to dispose of all who disputed his (or her) claim that she was the loveliest damsel in all the world. . . .

Nor could I like Lady Brandon, fascinating as she was to most. She was kind, gracious and hospitable to me, and I was grateful—but *like* her I could not. She was an

absolute re-incarnation of " Good " Queen Bess, and I do
not think any living woman could have better impersonated
Queen Elizabeth than she, whether on the stage or off.
Although beautiful in her way, she was astoundingly like
the portraits of that great unscrupulous Queen, and, in my
belief, she resembled her in character. She was imperious,
clever, hard, " managing " and capable. She was very
queenly in appearance and style, given to the cherish-
ing of favourites—Michael and Claudia especially—and
extremely jealous. She was a woman of strong character
and could be both ruthless and unscrupulous. At least,
that is the impression I formed of Lady Brandon—and I
am very intuitive, as well as being a student of physiog-
nomy, and possessed of a distinct gift for reading character.

No, I disliked Lady Brandon and I distrusted her—and
I thought that she and Claudia were not unlike in character.
. . . I was very intrigued when my Grandmother dryly
remarked, " Henry VIII is, I believe the ' *Rex* ' of Brandon
' *Regis*,' " when, in reply to a question of hers anent Lady
Brandon, I had observed, " She reminds me of Queen
Elizabeth. . . ."

She resembled the Queen, too, in her power of inspiring
great love in men, a noble love, worthy of a nobler
object. . . .

On one of my visits to the Band, I was scolded for my
absence of several days—I had been to London, on business
of my Father's—and told that I had missed the chance of a
lifetime, a chance of seeing and hearing a veritable Hero
of Romance, a French officer of Spahis, son of a senior school
friend of Lady Brandon's, who had been week-ending at
Brandon Abbas, and who had for ever endeared himself
to the children, by his realistic and true tales of Desert
warfare, and of adventures in mysterious and romantic
Morocco.

Promptly we ceased to be Red Indians, Knights of the
Round Table, Crusaders, Ancient Britons, Big Game
Hunters, or anything else but Spahis and Arabs, and the
three Gestes and I spent a portion of our lives in charging—

mounted on two ponies, a donkey and a carriage-horse—a *douar* of gorse-bushes stoutly defended by a garrison of Arabs clad in towels, sheets and night-shirts and armed with pea-shooters, bows and arrows, lances, swords and spears, toy rifles and pistols which made more sound than sorrow. . . .

The Band certainly "lived dangerously," but accidents were few and slight, and the absolute freedom permitted to the children, as soon as morning lessons with the Chaplain were finished, was really not abused. Being trusted, they were trustworthy, and the Captain led the Band not into temptation irresistible, nor into more than right and reasonable danger.

This chaplain was a puzzle to me. I felt certain he was essentially good, honourable and well-meaning; but he struck me, in my youthful intolerance, as being too weak and feeble in character to be worthy of the name of man. Certainly he was well-placed in the skirted cassock that he wore; and that, together with his sweet and gentle face and manner, seemed to put him in a class apart—neither man nor woman, just sexless priest. He loved the children devotedly—and was more like a mother than a father to them. Lady Brandon, he obviously adored. He too, was one of this queenly and imperious woman's favourites, and her handsome face would soften to a great gentleness when she walked and talked with him upon the terrace.

It was an extraordinarily interesting household, and when the time came for me to return home and prepare to go to Harvard, I was extremely sorry.

It was with a slight lump in my throat that I spent my last afternoon with the Band, and with a miserable turmoil in my heart that I said good-bye to them. They, too, seemed genuinely sorry that I was going, and seriously considered John's proposal that they should accompany me *en masse*, at least as far as Wyoming, where they might remain and adopt the profession of cow-puncher.

I think I walked back to High Gables that afternoon as quickly as I had ever walked in my life, for I was trying to walk away from myself, from my misery, from the sense of utter loss and desolation.

I was astounded at myself. . . . Why was I feeling this way ? What had happened to me ? I had not felt so wretched, so bereaved, so filled with a sense of loss and loneliness, since my Mother died. . . . I was like a man who, stricken with some sudden mortal pain, strives to account for it, and cannot do so. . . .

Isobel had put her arms round my neck and kissed me good-bye.

" You *will* come back soon, nice American Boy ? " she had said. And I had positively been unable to answer anything at all. I could only laugh and nod my head in assent.

That night, being absolutely unable to sleep, I rose from my bed, dressed, and, creeping quietly from the house, walked to Brandon Abbas to see, as I told myself, how that ancient pile looked by the light of the full moon. . . .

Next day I began my journey, suffering horribly from home-sickness—sickness for the home of my heart— Brandon Abbas. Each mile that I was carried, by train and ship and train again, from that lovely place, increased my misery, and when at length I reached my Father's ranch, I had hard work to hide it from my sister Mary, that dear determined and forceful young woman. My Father—my hard, overbearing, autocratic Father—was not given to noticing whether others were wretched or not, and my kid sister, Janey, was too young. Noel, the eldest of our family, was still " missing," and my Father professed neither to know nor to care where he was. . . .

However, I soon began to enjoy my sweet unhappiness, and I lived on horseback until the day came when I must go East to college, and leave this free and glorious open-air life behind me.

As a matter of fact, I went willingly enough, for I loved books, and desired above all things to become a fine scholar. . . . I considered " My mind to me a kingdom is,"

E

to be a grand saying if one could say it (to oneself only, of course) with real truth. . . . I could never understand Noel's flat refusal to study anything but horses, Nature, and the lore of the Indian and the Plainsman ; nor his oft-expressed view that education is not of books but of life. Nothing, according to Noel, could educate one for life except life itself ; and books and schooling could but educate one for more schooling and books, the examination-hall, and the realms of false values. And yet he read the books that he liked, my wonderful brother Noel—but to school and college he would not go, and thither not even my dynamic and violent Father could drive him.

" Honour thy father and thy mother " . . . We could not do otherwise than honour Mother, as well as love her almost to the point of adoration.

What shall I say of my terrible Father ? We did honour him. We respected him and most certainly we obeyed him—all of us but Noel, that is. Noel ceased to obey him as soon as he was big and old enough to stand up for Mother.

His refusal to go to school and college was, I believe, due to his wish, that he might be near her and take her part. Nor did he leave home until the day when he found that in his wrath he had pulled his gun on Dad, and realized that he had to choose between that sort of thing—and departure.

He departed, and returned after a quarter of a century in such wise as I shall relate.

My Father was not a bad man. He was a very " good " one. He was not cruel, vicious, nor vindictive ; but he was a terror and a tyrant. He crushed his wife and broke her spirit, and he turned his children into rebels, or terrified " suggestibles."

Noel and Mary were rebels. Janey and I were cowed and terrified.

Of all the marvellous deeds for which, as a child, I worshipped Noel, his defiance of my Father, was to me by far the most wonderful.

At different times, my Father in his austerity and tenacity reminded me of Abraham Lincoln ; in his rugged and ferocious " piety," of the prophet Elijah, John Wesley, Brigham Young, and John Knox. There was something in him, too, of Mr. Gladstone, of Theodore Roosevelt, and a good deal of William Jennings Bryan at his most oratorical, most narrow, and most dogmatic.

And there was undoubtedly something in him of King David of Jerusalem. Yes, most undoubtedly there were many points of strong resemblance between my Father and that brave, strong, wily man, that pious and passionate king.

And a king, in his own wide realm, my father was, brooking scarcely a suggestion, much less a contradiction, from any man—a king terribly and unhappily aware of the state of sin in which lived all his subjects, especially those of his own household.

He believed that the Bible had been dictated—in English of course—by God, and that to take it other than literally was damnation and death. He almost flogged Noel *to* death when, at the age of sixteen or so, the latter impiously dared to wonder how Noah gathered in both the polar bears *and* the kangaroos, for his menagerie, and how he built the fifty-thousand-ton liner necessary for the accommodation of all the animals and their food.

This was after Father's return from a trip to Europe to buy a twenty-thousand-dollar pedigree prize Hereford bull, and the finest pure-bred Arab stallion that money could purchase.

During his absence, Noel had caught out the overseer, a pious-seeming hypocritical rascal, in whom Father firmly believed ; had thrashed him, and run him off the Ranch.

Undoubtedly Noel had saved Father a great deal of money and unmasked an unmitigated rascal, and for this, I verily believe, Father hated him the more, and never forgave him.

Yes, Father certainly spoilt Noel's life and made him the wanderer that he became.

To this day, when I have a nightmare, and I have a good many, it is generally of a terrible conflict with my Father, and I awake sweating and trembling with indignation, rage and horror.

For, in the dream, he always rushes at me, bawling invective, his face inflamed with rage, and, seizing me by the throat he raises his cutting-whip to thrash the wickedness out of me, as he so often did in reality. And, to my horror, I find myself clenching my fist to smash that mask of mad ferocity, and then I realize that I am about to strike my own Father, in my indignation that I, a grown man, should be treated thus.

It sounds nothing, but it is a *dreadful* dream.

" Honour thy father " . . . I believe that Mother worshipped him and feared him, and I believe that I, subconsciously, hated him most bitterly, while I consciously respected and feared him.

To the world, our little western world, he was a great man—a man of his word, a strong man, a dangerous man to cross, a good friend and a bad enemy.

One of Mary's *obiter dicta* on the subject of Father sheds a great light on his strong and complex character.

" Father has never done wrong in his life," said she, " for whatever Father does is right—in the sight of Father."

Mary inherited much of Father's strength and force of will, as well as much of Mother's attractiveness.

She was a girl of character, and what she set her heart on, she got. If Father's strength were that of granite, iron and adamant, hers was the strength of tempered steel, for she was pliant and knew when to bend that she might not break. She managed Father and refused to be crushed. Where Noel openly defied and fought him, she secretly defied and out-manœuvred him.

Father certainly loved her—as men do their daughters—and I think Mary loved him, up to a point.

§ 3

Much as I enjoyed everything, from books to base-ball, at glorious Harvard, I found myself obsessed with the desire to visit England again. Nor was it wholly due to a yearning to see the fine face of my kindly-caustic Grandmother Hankinson once more. Greatly I yearned to revisit Brandon Regis at the earliest opportunity—for Brandon Regis is but a pleasant walk from Brandon Abbas.

I wanted to see the Geste boys again—and I wanted to see Isobel. . . . That's the plain fact of the matter—I wanted to see Isobel. Every single separate day of my life I wanted to see her.

I do not say that, during my Harvard years, I mooned about in a hopeless state of calf-love, a ridiculous young sentimentalist, nor that her lovely little face came ever and ever between me and the printed page, and was always in my mind, sleeping and waking, playing and working— but I certainly admit that I thought of her regularly. . . .

It was my practice nightly, on laying my head on the pillow, to project my mind to the Park of Brandon Abbas, and to enter into a lovely secret kingdom of my own, and there to dwell, happy, remote, and in lovely peace, until I fell asleep.

This kingdom was shared by Isobel, and we two—devoted friends—did delightful things together; had wonderful talks ; explored a world of utter beauty ; and walked hand-in-hand in a fairyland of joy and fun and laughter. . . .

I am not sure but that this was my real life, at that time ; this and the dreams that followed almost invariably, when I fell asleep. Certainly, it was so real that I looked forward to it each day, and if not consciously doing so, was always half-aware and semi-conscious of something delightful that was in store for me, something good and sweet and precious, something " nice " that was coming to me. And when I analysed this feeling of joyous promise I found that it was my soul's anticipation of its visit to the Kingdom of Enchantment where Isobel would meet me and we would walk and talk and laugh together in our Paradise Unlost.

When a sleep-dream followed the consciously induced day-dream, I always awoke from it to minutes of ineffable happiness, a happiness experienced at no other time and in no other way. . . . I felt *good*. . . . And I realized how singularly blessed was Otis H. Vanbrugh, above other men. Nor did the corollary escape me—how incumbent it was upon me to keep myself fit to enter our lovely secret kingdom, and worthy to meet Isobel there.

I do not think that what are supposed to be the inevitable and terrible temptations of wealthy young men at College, existed for me at all. Late hours would have been hours that made me late for the Secret Garden ; the odour of wine was not one that would mingle favourably with that of the dewy roses there ; nor could one who was daily privileged to commune with Isobel, find the faintest possible charm or attraction in the halls of the Paphian dames. . . . So I filled my days with work, read hard and played hard, lived dangerously when living in the West, pursued with ardour there the study of International Law and of the ways of the mountain lion and of the grizzly bear, and earned the warm approval of my brave and hardy sister, Mary. . . .

And imagine if you can, the frame of mind in which, at the end of my College days, I sailed for Europe—on a visit to a life-long friend of my Father's, who was then our Ambassador to France—and incidentally to visit my Grandmother at Brandon Regis. . . .

As I stepped from the Southampton-London boat-train at Waterloo Terminus, another train was in the act of departure from the opposite side of the same platform, and gliding forward with slowly increasing speed. At a window, waving a handkerchief to three young men, was a girl, and, with a queer constriction of the heart, a rush of blood to the head, and a slight trembling of the whole body, I realized that the girl was Isobel Rivers—the child Isobel, grown up to most lovely girlhood . . . wonderfully the same and yet different. . . . She had put her hair up. . . .

In the baggage-car of my own train were my cabin-trunks and portmanteaux. In the hands of a porter were already my suit-case and grip. Without ceremony, I rushed across that broad platform, threading my way through the crowd like a football-forward in a hurry. As I reached the now quickly-moving train, seized a door-handle and ran swiftly while I turned it, an official of some sort made a grab at me and shouted, " Stand back ! You can't get in there, sir," in fiercely indignant remonstrance, not so much at my daring to break my neck as at my daring to break a railway bye-law.

" Hi ! You can't get in there," he roared again.

" Watch me," I replied, eluding him, and swung myself on to the foot-board as the door came open. . . . " I won't hurt your train," I shouted back, as he was left gesticulating in sorrow and in anger, at the end of the platform.

In the compartment that I then entered, were three Englishmen and an Englishwoman. Not one of them looked up as I took my seat, nor spoke to me nor to each other during the long hours of non-stop run that ensued. . . .

Wonderful people, the English ! . . .

And there I sat in that antediluvian non-corridor car through those long hours, my baggage abandoned, my hotel reservation unclaimed, my destination unknown ; but with the knowledge that Isobel Rivers and I were in the same train and that I should speak to her just as soon as that prehistoric Flying Dutchman, or Roaring Rocket, reached its destination or first stopping-place.

In spite of cold, hunger, disorientation, and a certain slight anxiety as to the ultimate fate of my baggage, those were, I verily believe, among the happiest hours of my life ; and when the train slowed down—it must have slowed down, I suppose, though no change of speed was to me perceptible—to decant its phlegmatic inhabitants at Exeter, I, the last man into that train, was certainly the first man out.

§ 4

Isobel, I am most perfectly sure, was really unfeignedly
glad to see me, and Lady Brandon very kindly pretended
to be.   I knew that Isobel was glad because, as she recognized me, that wonderful sparkle—a kind of dancing light,
that indescribable lighting-up, as though with an internal
illumination, that always signalized and beautified her
joy—came into her eyes.   One reads of people dancing
with pleasure and jumping for joy.   Isobel did not do
these things, but her eyes did, and one could always tell
when a gift or a jest or any happening had given her real
pleasure, by watching her eyes.

I had often heard John Geste say " *That'll* make Isobel's
eyes shine " when there was something amusing to tell
her, or some piece of good news ; and I thought to myself
that surely no-one could conceive a more glorious and
wonderful way of spending his life than in bringing this
beautiful light to Isobel's eyes.

Imagine, if you can, the joy that it gave me to realize
that I had been able to do it now.

" Why," she said as I approached and raised my hat,
" the nice American boy ! . . .   Oh, how lovely ! . . .
The boys *will* be sorry," and she gave me both her hands
in the most delightful and friendly manner.

Lady Brandon gave me both fingers in a less spontaneous
and friendly manner that was nevertheless quite pleasant,
and—God bless her—invited me to share their compartment
in the train to Brandon Abbas and their carriage which
would meet them there.   She displayed none of the surprise
that she must certainly have felt on learning that there was
no luggage problem, as I had no luggage.   Beneath her
half-kindly, half-satirical gaze, I did my best to conceal the
fact that, on catching sight of Isobel, I had abandoned
everything but hope, and dashed from one train to the
other.

I do not know whether selected prophets, such as Elijah,
ever found ecstatic joy in their rides in fiery chariots and

similar celestial vehicles, but I do know that my short ride by train and carriage with Isobel, was to me the highest summit of ecstatic joy—a pure happiness utterly indescribable and incommunicable—the higher, the greater, and the lovelier for its purity.   And it was not until I was deposited at High Gables after leaving Isobel and Lady Brandon at Brandon Abbas, that my soaring spirit came down to earth, and, it having come to earth, I was faced with the problem of explaining my unheralded arrival and the absence of further provision than a walking-stick and one glove.   Also, alas, with the realization that I should not see Isobel again, as she and Lady Brandon were going to Wales on the morrow, and, later on, to Scotland on a round of visits.   They had been staying in London with the boys, who were now setting off for a walking-tour in Normandy.

However, *I had seen Isobel* and received confirmation—if confirmation were needed—of the fact that not only was she the most marvellous thing in all the world, but that everything else in the world would be as nothing in the balance against her.

I have mentioned this trivial and foolish little incident—which ended next day with my return to London and the pursuit of my baggage—because it was on this night, as I lay awake, that there came to me the great, the very greatest, idea of my life—the idea that I might conceivably, with the help of God and every nerve and fibre of my being, some day, somehow, contrive to make myself worthy to love Isobel and then—incredibly—to be loved by Isobel, and actually to devote my life to doing that of which I had thought when her eyes sparkled and shone at seeing me.

It is curious and true that the idea had never occurred to me before, and I had never envisaged the possibility of such a thing as not only loving her, but being loved by her in return, and of actually walking hand in hand along the path of life in the spirit of sweet and lovely companionship, as we did nightly in our Dream Garden. . . . And there,

I remember, a little chill fell upon my heart and checked my fond imaginings, as it occurred to me for the first time that the Dream Garden was a creation of my dreams alone, and not of Isobel's as well. There we met and talked and walked and were dear friends, with a reality as great as that of anything in my real and waking life—but of course, it was only *my* dream, and the real Isobel knew nothing of the Dream Garden.

But did she know nothing ? Why should I assume that ? Suppose—only suppose—that she dreamed it, too ! Suppose Isobel had this curious and wonderful double life, as I had, and met me in her dreams precisely as I met her, night by night ! Absurd, of course, but much too lovely an idea to discard with even pretended contempt. I would ask her the very next time I saw her. How unutterably wonderful if she could tell me that it was so ! . . . More-over, if it *were* so, it would mean *that she loved me*—and, at this, even I laughed at my own folly. Still I would ask her the very next time we met. . . .

But the next time we met, I asked her something else.

CHAPTER III

I SUPPOSE that among the very happiest days of my whole life were those I spent on my next journey from New York to Southampton and Brandon Regis. I must have seemed insufferably joyous and pleased with myself. When not actually whistling or singing with my mouth, I was doing it in my heart. I loved everybody. What is less certain is whether everybody loved me. I loved the glorious sunshine, the perfect sea, the splendid ship, the jolly food, the passengers, every one of them, the young, the old, the merry, the grumpy, the active, the lazy, the selfish, the unselfish. . . . If all the world loves a lover, surely a lover loves all the world . . . the great grand glorious world that lies at his exalted feet. . . . The world that contains, and exists to contain, the one and only woman in the world. . . .

I loved the stars, the moon, the marvellous night-sky, the floor of Heaven pierced with millions of little holes through which shone rays of the celestial light—and I sat late and alone, gazing, thinking, dreaming, longing.

I loved the dawn, and late as I may have sat upon the boat-deck at night, I was there again to see the East grow grey and pink and golden, there to welcome and to greet the sun that ushered in one more milestone day upon the brief and lovely road that led to Brandon Abbas and to Isobel.

Brandon Abbas and Isobel! . . . One day, when a poor rich youth whom I comprehended in my universal love—in spite of his pimples, poor jokes, unpleasing ways and unacceptable views—asked me if I were going to

75

Paris, and I replied, "No—to Brandon Abbas," and he, astonished, inquired where that might be, and I answered :

"Next door to Paradise," he rightly concluded that I was out of my mind or else drunk. Doubly right was he, for I was beside myself with joy and drunk with happiness.

Yes ; I loved all things ; I loved all men ; and greatly I loved God.

At Southampton I let the boat-train go upon its foolish way to London, and at the terminus hotel of the South Western Railway I awaited the far far better one that meanders across the green and pleasant land of England to the little junction where one may get one better still, one that proceeds thence to Exeter where waits the best of all—the final and finest train in the wide world—that carries its blest occupants to Brandon Abbas.

I was not sitting in a train made with mortal hands, but in a chariot of fire that was carrying me, ecstatic and uplifted, to the heaven of my dreams, my night-and-day dreams of many years.

From the station I drove, in what to the dull eye of the ordinary beholder was a musty, mouldy carriage, drawn by a moth-eaten and dilapidated parody of a horse, to High Gables, and was welcomed with the apparently caustic kindness and grim friendliness with which my wonderful old Grandmother Hankinson hid her really tender and loving nature.

And next day I walked over to Brandon Abbas.

I remember trying, on the way, to recollect some lines I fancied I had read. Were they written by the Marquis of Montrose or had Queen Elizabeth scratched them with a diamond on a window-pane for the encouragement of some young adorer ? Was it, "*He either fears his fate too much, Or his deserts are small, Who dares not put it to the touch, To win or lose it all.*" . . . ? Something like that anyhow, and probably written by Montrose.

Well, my deserts were small enough, and at times I feared my fate, but I was certainly going to put it to the touch before I went away, if I stayed for a year or a life-time.

I was going to tell Isobel that I loved her—had loved her unceasingly and increasingly, from the moment that I had seen her, a lovely child sitting in a dog-cart, and much concerned about a dog.

True—I was utterly and wholly unworthy of her, but so was everybody else. I had nothing to recommend me but an absolutely perfect and unquenchable love— but I was not ineligible from the point of view of such a person as Lady Brandon, for example. I was a foreigner, an American, but I had roots in this very soil, through my Mother. I was obscure and unknown, but that could very quickly be put right if I became Isobel's husband. That alone would be a great distinction, but I would undertake to add to it, and to promise that Isobel's husband should one day be the American Ambassador to St. James's, to Paris, to St. Petersburg—any old where she liked. . . . President of the United States of America, if she set her heart on his being that. . . . I was very far from being poor, and should not be far from being very rich, someday.

Thirty-cent things of that sort would be quite germane and material in the eyes of Queen Elizabethan Lady Brandon. To my mind, the only really relevant thing was that I loved Isobel to the point of worship and adoration, and that this love of mine had not only stood the test of time, but had gained from Time himself—for the wine of love had mellowed and matured, grown better, richer, sweeter, nobler, year by year. . . .

Poor boy ! . . .

I turned in at the Lodge gates, and walked up the long drive of which I knew every Norman tree.

Good old Burdon, the perfect butler, fine flower of English retainerhood, was in the hall as I appeared in the porch, and greeted me in the perfect manner of the perfect servant, friendly, welcoming, respectful.

But Her Ladyship was Not at Home. . . .

Miss Claudia was Not at Home. . . .

Miss Isobel was Not at Home. . . .

Mr. Michael, Mr. Digby, and Mr. John were Away from Home. . . .

Nothing for it but to leave my cards and depart, more than a little dashed and damped.

I walked down the drive less buoyantly than I had walked up it. It actually had not entered my silly head that one could go to Brandon Abbas and not find Isobel there. . . . The sunshine was not so bright nor the sky so blue, and what had been the sweet singing of the birds, was just a noise. . . .

And as I rounded a turn in the drive, my heart rounded and turned and drove, for a girl was riding toward me, a little girl on a big horse. The loveliest, dearest, kindest girl in all the wide world. . . .

My heart turned right-side-up, pulled itself together, and let me get my breath again. . . . *Isobel*. . . .

The sun shone gloriously bright and warm, the sky was a deep Italian blue, the English song-birds were birds from Paradise—and Isobel held out a gloved hand which I took and pressed to my lips as she smiled sweetly and kindly and said :

" Why ! It's our nice American Boy come back ! I *am* so glad . . . Otis . . ." and then I knew that something was wrong. Her voice was different ; older. Her face was different ; older. She was unhappy. . . .

" What is the matter, Isobel ? " I asked, still holding her little hand as she bent toward me from her big horse.

" Oh . . . Otis. . . . How did you know ? . . . *John has gone*. . . . The boys have gone away. . . ."

Her lip trembled and there was a suspicion of moisture in her eyes.

" Can I help ? . . . *Let* me help you, Isobel," I begged.

" There's nothing you can do—thank you so much," she said. " It's nice of you. . . . I am so glad to see you again, Otis. . . . I have been so wretched. There is no-one I can talk to, about it. . . ."

" There is," I said. " There's me," and I think that
moment marked the absolute top-most pinnacle of happiness that I have ever known, for Isobel pressed my hand
hard.

" I'll tell you a great secret," she said, and smiled so
sweetly through the unshed tears that I could scarcely
forbear to reach up and lift her from her horse, lift her into
my arms, my heart, and my life.

" I'll tell *you*, Otis. . . . Keep it a secret though," she
added. And then Isobel said the words that in that second
cut my life into two distinct halves. . . .

" *John and I are engaged to be married. . . .*"

No—she couldn't have said that. I assured myself
that she had not said *that*. These queer hallucinations
and strange waking dreams ! . . . She had not said that.
. . . I was not standing staring and open-mouthed, and
watching, watching, watching for years and life-times and
ages and æons, while two great tears slowly formed and
gathered and grew and rolled from her eyes. . . . One
did not splash upon my hand as she said :

" And he has had to go away. . . . And I am so
miserable, Otis. . . . We were engaged one evening and
he was gone the next morning ! . . . And I have no-
one to talk to, about him. . . . I am so *glad* you have
come. . . ."

But a tear *did* splash on my hand. She *did* say it.

" You and John Geste are engaged to be married,
Isobel ? " I asked, gently and carefully, very very gently
and very very carefully, to keep my voice level and steady,
to keep myself well under control. . . .

I heard myself say the words, and I watched her face
to see whether I had said them normally. . . . Or had
I not said them at all ? . . . I had uttered some words
certainly. . . .

Her face did not change. . . .

" Yes, Otis," she said. " And I had to tell somebody !

. . . I am glad it was *you*. You are the only person, now, who knows. You'll be the first to congratulate me. . . ."

Yes. *I* should be *the* first person to congratulate her !

" I congratulate John—and you—Isobel," I said, " and from the bottom of my heart I hope that every hour of your life will be a happy one."

"Thank you, Otis," she said. " That is nice and dear of you. . . . Oh, I shall be almost too happy to breathe . . . when John comes back. . . .

"You'll come and see us again, won't you ? Aunt Patricia will be delighted to see you. . . . And we'll go for some rides, you and I. . . . I do so want to talk to you—*about John*."

Words of excuse rose to my lips. I must go to London to-morrow. I must hurry over to Paris. Some business for my Father. After that I must go quickly back to America, and so forth. . . . But before I had spoken, I had a swift vision of a face I knew well, though I had only seen it in dreams. A hard clean-cut cruel face, grim, stern and stoical, the face of that Indian Chief who was the father of my father's grandmother—the face of a man from whom no sign of anguish was ever wrung, a man to whom pain was as a friend, proven and proving.

"Thank you very much indeed, Isobel," I said. " I shall love to ride with you—and—talk about John." . . .

(Thank *you*, also, great-great-grandfather.)

Yes, it would give her pleasure. I would ride with her —and *talk about John !*

During the next month I saw Isobel almost daily, Lady Brandon occasionally, the Chaplain once or twice, and the girl, Claudia, from time to time.

Isobel and I talked unceasingly of John. I thought of things that would please her—dug up what had been fragrant joyous memories.

She did not tell me where he was, being, I supposed, pledged to secrecy, and I asked her no questions as I realized that there was some secret which she was hiding.

It occurred to me though, that it must be a mighty strong inducement, an irresistible compulsion, that took John Geste from Brandon Abbas on the day after the declaration of his love for Isobel!

And then, thank God, she went away to stay with friends, and I fled to Paris, plunged into the wildest dreariest round of dissipation (Good God! is there *anything* so devastatingly dreary as pleasure pursued?) and quickly collapsed as reaction set in, reaction from the dreadful strain of those days with Isobel—Isobel and the ever-present absent John.

I was very ill indeed for some weeks, and, when able to do so, crawled home—dropped back again, the burnt charred stick of that joyous rocket that had rushed with such brilliant soaring gaiety into the bright sky of happiness. . . .

Finished and down—like a dead rocket. . . .

§ 2

Things were, on the whole, rather worse than usual at home. My Father was becoming more and more tyrannical and unreasonable, and my sisters were reacting accordingly. Strong Mary, the rebel, home from College, was fast approaching both the snapping-point of her temper and the frame of mind in which Noel had cast off the dust of the ranch from his feet and the shackles of his Father from his soul, mind, and body.

Weak Janey, the "suggestible," was fast approaching the end of her existence as an individual, a separate identity, and was rapidly becoming a reed, bending in the blast of her Father's every opinion, idea and wish; a straw upon the mighty rushing waters of his life; thistle-down floating upon the windy current of his mental and physical commotions.

While firmly believing that she loved him, she dreaded the very sound of his footsteps, and conducted the domestic side of his affairs in that fear and trembling of a Roman

F

slave for the master whose smile was sole reward and whose frown portended death.

Filial love is a beautiful thing, but the slow destruction of a character, a soul, a personality, an individuality, is not.

Poor Janey did not think. She quoted Father's thoughts. She did not need or desire anything ; she lived to forestall and satisfy Father's needs and wishes. She did not live any life of her own, she lived Father's life and existed to that end.

Janey was abject to Father, and propitiatory to Mary. Mary was defiant and rebellious to Father; and sympathetic but slightly contemptuous, to Janey.

Father was protective, overbearing, loving, violently autocratic and unbearably irritating toward both of them. Apparently he simply could *not* forbear to interfere, even in things in which he had not the faintest right to interfere, and in which a different type of man would have been ashamed to do so.

Of me, he was frankly contemptuous, and what made me boil with anger was not that, nor the way in which he treated me, but the fact that *I was afraid of him.* Time after time, I screwed up my courage to face him and out-face him, and time after time I failed. I could not do it. His fierce eye, his Jovian front, quelled me, and being quelled, I quailed.

It was reserved for my Father to make me a coward, so poor a creature that I could not even stand up for my sisters against him.

But the enemy was, of course, as always, within. Deep down in my unconscious mind were the seeds sown in babyhood, in childhood, in boyhood—the seeds of Fear— and they had taken such root, and grown so strong a weed-crop that I could not pluck them out. When I conceived the idea of refusing to obey some unreasonable order, of asserting my right to an opinion, of remonstrating on behalf of one of the girls, I was physically as well as mentally affected.

I stammered and stuttered—a thing I never did at any

other time. I flushed and paled, I perceptibly shook and trembled, and I burst into a cold perspiration. My mind became a blank; I looked and felt and was, a fool; I was not sufficiently effective even to irritate my Father, and with one frowning piercing stare of his hard eyes, one contemptuous curl of his expressive lips, I was defeated, silenced, quelled, brought to heel.

Do not think that our Father was deliberately and intentionally cruel to any of his children. Cruelty is a Vice, and Vice was the abhorrent thing, the very seal and mark of the Devil—footprint of the cloven hoof. Did he not spend his life in the denunciation of Vice in every form and manifestation—though with particular abhorrence and detestation of, peculiar rage and fulminations against, *Sex*—its, to him, most especially shocking and loathsome form ?

He was not cruel, but his effect upon us was, and it drove Mary and me to the decision that home was no place for us. . . . We had decided independently—I, that I could not work for, nor with, my Father on the ranch, nor live with him in the house : she, that any place in the wide world would be preferable to the house in which her Father intended that she should live and move and have her being, wholly and solely and exactly as he in his wisdom directed.

We discovered our decisions to each other and agreed to act together when the time came ; and, as soon as possible thereafter, to rescue Janey from the loving thraldom and oppression that would turn her into a weak, willless and witless old maid, an ageing servant in her father's house, before she had been a girl.

It was the " old maid " aspect of affairs that particularly enraged Mary on behalf of both Janey and herself. For on the subject of " young whelps loafing round the place," our Father grew more and more unreasonable and absurd. A presentable man was a suspect, a potential " scoundrel," a thinker of evil who would become a doer of evil if given the slightest opportunity. To such we always alluded as

" Means "—by reason of Father's constant quotation of the Shakespearian platitude :

"The sight of *means* to do ill deeds, makes ill deeds done."

Any sort or kind of non-business communication between a man and a woman was, unless they were married according to the (Protestant) Christian Dispensation, undesirable, wrong, improper ; and avowed friendship between them was little better than Sin, Vice—nay, was almost certainly but a cloak for Sin.

Strong Mary, the rebel, suffered most perhaps ; weak Janey and I suffered much, certainly. But we stuck on somehow, for some reason—" the inertia of matter," apathy, custom, loyalty to Father, and the feeling that our defection would hurt him more even than his interfering, regulating tyranny hurt us. Most of all perhaps, because we knew that Janey would never have the courage nor the " unkindness " to leave him.

It was a very wretched time indeed for me, apart from the fact that I was so spiritually bruised and sore and smashed. My dreams of Isobel came no more, and my day-dreams of her were poignant suffering. I tried to fight the lethargy, the hopelessness, the selfish sorrow of my soul, and to throw myself into the work of the ranch, to live on horseback a life of constant activity, and to find an anodyne in labour.

But I was selfish. . . . I nursed my sorrow. . . . I thought, young fool that I was, that my life was permanently darkened and that none had plumbed such depths of suffering as I.

And I worked on, hopelessly, sunk in a deep and dark Byronic gloom. . . .

§ 3

It was a dead hand that released Mary and me from the irksome dependence of our captivity. I do not know whether the hand provided " the means to do ill deeds "

in providing us with the opportunity to leave our Father
and our home, but it certainly gave us the power to choose
our paths in life, and we promptly chose the one that led
straightest out into the world of men.

The said hand was that of a Bad Old Man, a meretricious
ornament of the city of San Francisco, a gay dog, a buck,
a lover of Life, who was, alas, my Father's cousin, once his
partner, and known to us from our earliest days as Uncle
Joe. He had all our Father's strength of will and character ;
his ability, grit and forcefulness ; his uncanny business
skill and his marked individuality. But he had none of
his fervid piety ; none of his Old Testamental patriarchal
self-importance ; none of his self-righteous domineering
violence ; and, I fear, but little of his moral integrity,
virtue, and highly-conscious rectitude.

In spite of this latter lamentable truth, we children
loved him, as our Mother had loved him—and as Father
hated him. He corrupted us with treats, gifts, sympathy,
and support ; he took our part when, as so frequently
happened, we were in disgrace ; and he endeavoured to
sow in our young breasts the seeds of revolt and rebellion against what he considered harshness and oppression.

For some reason I was his favourite. I amused him
intensely, and he apparently saw in me merits and virtues
which were hidden from other eyes. And the misspelling
of a word in a letter that I wrote to him, changed my life
and Mary's life, the lives of my Father and of Janey, and
indeed of very many other people—for it was the cause
of his leaving me a very large sum of money indeed, the
money that was my ransom from bondage—and Mary's
ransom too.

It had been my innocent and disinterested custom to
write a letter to Uncle Joe, upon the occasion of his birth-
day. On one of these anniversaries, I, being some seven
or eight years of age—and having just discovered the
expression " hoary old age "—wrote my annual letter and
concluded by wishing him eventual safe arrival at such

penultimate years. But having acquired the phrase by ear and not by eye, I misspelt a word.

The hoary sinner was delighted beyond measure, roared with laughter, shouted with joyous amusement, and swore then and there that he would make me his heir and leave me every last red cent of which he died possessed! He then rushed forth brandishing the letter, in search of all to whom he might impart the jest, and for days and weeks the bars of San Francisco's clubs, restaurants, saloons and hostelries echoed with laughter and my Uncle's shame.

Such conduct gives the measure of the wickedness of the man who had been a thorn in the side of my Father— until the day on which the latter felt that he could prosper without him, that Mammon of Unrighteousness, and cast him forth; the man who had been our dear, dear friend; the man to whom Mary and I owed our salvation.

And at this critical moment he died—and he left me all his money.

Of course, what was mine was Mary's, and at the earliest moment we fared forth together, " to seek our fortunes "—though not in the material sense, and to see the World.

A drop of regret in the cup of our joy was the fact that we found it utterly and completely impossible to induce Janey to come with us. She would not " leave Father "— the simple truth being that she lacked the courage to tell him that she was going with us, the courage to let us tell him that she was going with us, the courage even to slip away with us, or to run away and join us after our departure.

There was nothing for it but to leave her at home, though with the most urgent entreaties to join us at any time that she could induce Father to permit her to come, or pluck up sufficient courage to come unpermitted. . . .

Our idea was, of course, to make straight for Paris— the name of which place, Mary declared, was but an abbreviation of the word "Paradise"—and after sating ourselves with its wonders, make the grand tour of Europe. After that we were going to settle down in Paris, and I was going to obtain employment at our Embassy, for I had no liking for the profession of rich-man's-son and idler. Mary was going to keep house for me—but I doubted that it would be my house that she would keep for very long, and so I think did she. . . . Anyhow, that was roughly our programme, and, after what seemed an age of delay, we set forth, without the paternal blessing, to see how far we should carry out the scheme.

CHAPTER IV

LIFE in Paris was, to Mary, wholly delightful, and to me was at least as good and as bad as life in Wyoming. In point of fact it was wholly lacking in savour wheresoever I might endure it—but in Paris the heavy cloud, that was our Father, was on the far western horizon and no longer obscured the sun—a further exemplification of the ancient truth that they who flee across the sea change nothing but their sky.

Our friends at the Embassy were more than kind to us, and before we departed for London, Rome, Venice, Naples, Athens and finally Algiers, we had a large and delightful circle of acquaintance, French, American and English.

Mary is one of those girls who are " very easy to look at," and the young men of our circle looked. They also danced, dined, drove and flirted with her to her heart's content, if not to theirs.

As I spent my money very freely, she was soon reputed to be the usual fabulously wealthy American heiress, and the report did not lessen her popularity.

Prominent among her admirers was a much-decorated and be-medalled Colonel of Zouaves, a man who might have sat for a portrait of a typical Sergeant of the Old Guard of Napoleon Buonaparte. He was a middle-aged self-made fighting soldier—a man of the kind that one rather admires for excellences of character than likes for graces of mind and person—and I fear he amused Mary almost as much as he loved her. For he was obviously and hopelessly in love, and I do not think that the dollars in any way gilded the refined gold of *La belle Americaine* in the eyes of the

tough and grizzled Colonel Levasseur. . . . Poor fellow !
. . . Bravely playing his part in the ballroom, or at the
garden-party, he reminded me, when dancing attendance
on my sister, of a large bear heavily cavorting around a
young deer—though I realized that the Colonel would
remind me still more of a large bear if I saw him engaged
upon his real business, which was fighting.

Here again was coincidence or the hand of Fate—or as
some, including myself, would prefer to say—the hand of
God. For when, after our European travels, we reached
Algeria to bask in winter sunshine, Colonel Levasseur was
preparing to set forth, as the point of a lancet of " peaceful
penetration," to the fanatical city of Zaguig, a distant hot-
bed of sedition and centre of disaffection, a desert Cave of
Adullam wherein the leaders of every anti-French faction,
from eastern Senussi to western Riffian, plotted together
and tried to stem the flow of the tide of civilization.

They stood for savagery ; for blind adherence to the
dead letter of a creed outworn ; for ferocious hatred of
all that was not sealed of Islam ; and for the adminis-
tration of rapine, fire, and slaughter impartially to those
who brought, and those who accepted, northern civilization
and its roads, railways, telegraphs, peace, order and cultivation of the soil. . . .

While Zaguig remained secret, veiled, inviolate and aloof,
there could be no safety, and, as Colonel Levasseur put it,
Zaguig was a boil that the French must lance—that there
might be health in the body-politic of a great and growing
colony, a future granary and garden and farm for the
sons of civilization.

Colonel Levasseur showed better in Algiers than in Paris,
and he showed best of all in Zaguig at the head of his men,
in his element and on his native heath—or his adopted
heath.

For, later on, as I shall tell, I yielded to Mary's impulsive
yearnings to go and see a " really unspoilt " desert town,
and I accepted Colonel Levasseur's invitation to visit him

there, an invitation that coincided with her disillusionment
at Bouzen, a spoilt and vulgarized place at the end of the
railway, a plague-spot where alleged " desert " Arabs
spoke broken French and English to the trippers, and
richly earned broken necks every day of their ignoble
touting lives.

And to Bouzen from Zaguig came Colonel Levasseur—
ostensibly to confer with the Commandant of the big
garrison there—fairly quickly after learning that Mary was
shedding the light of her countenance on that already
well-lighted spot.

He took Mary riding on horse and camel, turning a
withering Colonel-glare upon the gay and gorgeous subal-
terns who had hitherto danced attendance upon her. . . .
He amused her and he had the inevitable appeal of the
strong man who has done things, who has a fine and big
job and holds it down.

And he played up to her growing love of the desert,
for she had succumbed to its lure and its loveliness of sunrise, sunset, space, colour, cleanness and enduring mystery.
Also he told her that *this* was not the desert—that she had
not yet seen the real desert, nor set eyes on a genuine
inhabitant thereof, Bedouin, Senussi, Touareg, nor any
other. . . . Also, that now was her chance, her chance
to cross a tract of the genuine desert-Sahara and see a
genuine desert-city, a lion's den whereof he had effectually
cowed and tamed the lions. . . .

I asked Mary if the acceptance of his very kind and
attractive invitation might not be construed as portending
her acceptance of the inevitable proposal of marriage which
would most surely ensue, if we entered the said lions'
den—whereof Colonel Levasseur was now the lion-tamer—
but only to receive the enigmatical reply that sufficient
unto the day is the proposal thereof, and that if I did
not take her to Zaguig, Colonel Levasseur would.

The which there was no gainsaying—and Mary is a
witch whom there is no gainsaying.

The delighted Colonel Levasseur, for some reason, inferred that I had had a helpful hand in Mary's decision to accept his invitation. And he expressed his gratitude to me in various ways, in spite of my denial of deserts.

One took the curious form of insisting upon showing me " life " in Bouzen, by night—*recherché* " life " not seen of the tripper, but solely of the elect—such as highly placed executive officials, for example, only by whose grace and favour, or ignorance and blindness, such " life " could exist.

Most men accept an invitation of this sort, and offer a variety of reasons for so doing. Some allege that " life " is, and must be, interesting to any intelligent person, and murmur " *nihil humanum . . . a me alienum puto,*" adding that none but the fool misses any rare, genuine " local colour " that may be seen ; and that, in any case, one would not like to hurt the feelings of the good fellow who had gone to the trouble of providing the opportunity.

As these were precisely my authentic reasons for accepting the invitation, I went with the worthy Colonel—and mine eyes beheld strange things.

We set forth after Mary had said her good-nights, she imagining that we were also about to seek our respective chaste couches.

Nothing was said to her on the subject of our expedition lest she insist upon joining us, and we be put to the shame of telling the truth or of abandoning the tour of the select improprieties. Incidentally I noted, in my mental *dossier* of the Colonel, that he was unselfish enough to devote to me time that might have been spent with Mary had he chosen to announce some different form of nocturnal entertainment, and also that he was of the type that could go straight, from looking upon the face of the beloved lady, to where every prospect pleases only a man who is vile. . . .

Let us, however, concede that it takes all sorts to make a universe, and humbly thank Allah for the diversity of his creatures.

As I had anticipated, I found, once more, that the deadliest, dreariest and dullest pursuit upon which the mind and body of man can embark is the deliberate pursuit of pleasure—that butterfly that flies indeed if chased, but will often settle if ignored—settle and delight the soul of the beholder.

I suppressed all yawns, endeavoured to simulate a polite if not keen interest, and failed to give the worthy Colonel the impression that I was enjoying myself.

So when he asked me if I were doing so, I said:

"Yes, indeed, Colonel" . . . and added, "It is the only thing I *am* enjoying" . . . whereat he laughed, commended my bluntness which matched his own, and promised that I should find the next place stimulating, for I should there encounter the Angel of Death.

I assured him that I was unready, unfit, unworthy; that I did not desire to encounter the Death Angel with all my imperfections on my head; unshriven, unassoiled and unannealed. . . . So young. . . . So promising. . . .

"Wait till you have seen her," replied the Colonel, and I withdrew my objections and listened, as we drove through the silent streets, to his account of the lady whose disturbing and deterrent title was "the Angel of Death," a title well-earned, I gathered, and well-given in return for disservices rendered. . . .

Well, it would be something to make the acquaintance of an incarnate Death Angel, especially if one might then plead fear of anti-climax as an excuse for abandoning the pursuit of pleasure, going straight home, and prosaically to bed.

As the car stopped at a gate in the high wall surrounding a native house and garden, on the outskirts of the town, I, in Hunnish vandal mood, murmured certain lines learned in childhood from Uncle Joe:

> "The Death Angel smote Alexander McCloo
> And gave him protracted repose;
> He had a check shirt and a number nine shoe
> And a very pink wart on his nose."

Well, the Death Angel smote me also, that night, but did not give me protracted repose (nor any protracted lack of repose—at the time).

The brightly-lit scene of our entertainment was the typical compound of the typical house of the wealthy town-Arab, the soft-living degenerate *hadri*, for whom the son of the desert has so great a contempt.

Our host, one Abu Sheikh Ahmed, a rotund well-nourished person with a bad squint, a bad pock-pitted face, and an oily ingratiating manner, received us with every evidence of joy, pride and respectful affection. He seemed grateful to us for existing; declared that all in his house was ours; that we were, each of us, his father and his mother both; and that Allah had this night been merciful and gracious unto him in that He had caused the light of our countenances to shine upon him and illuminate and glorify his humble gathering of guests.

Colonel Levasseur received these transports with dignity and restraint—particularly restraint—and informed me in English that Abu Sheikh Ahmed was a carpet-dealer and had the distinction of being the wickedest, most untrustworthy and most plausible old scoundrel that he had ever met.

" He'd be the first to fly to the Commandant with completest revelations of any plot that could not succeed; and the first to shoot him in the back, or cut his throat, in the event of one that did succeed," said he. " So we take him at his true value and use him for what he is worth. . . . He'll give us an amusing show anyhow. . . ."

He did; a show of which there were two items that, as far as I am concerned, proved quite unforgettable; the one for its hideousness, the other for its beauty—and its sequel.

The former was a " turn " by a troupe of Aissa dervishes, and consisted of maddeningly monotonous music and dancing—the twirling and spinning dancers quickly and obviously falling into a state of hypnosis; of a disgusting exhibition of self-mutilation by means of knives and skewers, driven into the arms, chest and legs and in some cases through the cheeks and even the tongue; of the eating of burning tow; and of the genuine chewing and actual swallowing of quantities of broken glass.

It is not given to the Sons of the Prophet to know the joys of a " next morning " head, as teetotalism is a primary essential of Muhammedanism, but I was moved to ponder the sensations of a " next morning " stomach, after an indiscreetly copious feast of broken glass.

Colonel Levasseur had seen this sort of thing before, and regarded it with the cold eye of familiarity, if not boredom.

" Enjoying yourself ? " he asked me, when the din and devilry were at their climax.

" Not even myself, this time," I replied, and was very glad when these holy men completed their exhibition of piety, and departed. The odour of sanctity was as unpleasing as the saints from whom it emanated.

I do not know whether Mr. Abu Sheikh Ahmed was an amateur of entertainment sufficiently skilful to appreciate the value of contrast, and deliberately to preface the beauty of the next item by the bestial ugliness of this one. Probably not—but certainly the vision of loveliness, that now enthralled the gathering, lost nothing by the juxtaposition.

In the centre of one side of a square, three sides of which were rows of Arab notables, and the fourth, the high white house, the Colonel and I occupied plush-upholstered European arm-chairs of astounding ugliness, while our host and his young son sat cross-legged upon the sofa of the same afflicted and afflicting family, the six pertaining small chairs being allotted to his chief friends, or enemies, who awkwardly sat upon them in dignity and discomfort.

In the guest-surrounded square, servants spread a large thick carpet, a carpet whereof the sheer beauty made me blush—for the European furniture that affronted it and the perfect night and the austere grace of the snowy draperies of the assembly. . . .

A current of awakened interest now ran through the latter, a movement that announced the arrival of an awaited moment. There was an atmosphere of pleased anticipation that indicated both the *pièce de résistance* and the certainty of high entertainment therefrom.

Brilliant teeth flashed white, as bearded lips parted in joyous smiles. Almost I fancied that pink tongues licked, beast-like, anticipatory, appreciative.

Our host beamed upon us, a pleased and pleasing smile of promise and of pride.

" Behold the Angel of Death," murmured Colonel Levasseur, and a woman appeared at the entrance to the house, walked disdainfully to the carpet, threw off a gauze veil and gazed calmly around.

There was a murmur of admiration, wonder, praise—and appraisal ; and I heard Colonel Levasseur sigh and gasp with a little catch of the breath. There was something very simple and elemental about poor Levasseur.

And there was something indescribably arresting, fascinating, wonderful about the real and remarkable beauty of the girl. . . . She was at once pretty, lovely, beautiful and handsome . . . quite indescribable. . . . Yes. . . . She was astounding. . . .

To begin with, she was so fair that you thought her European until you realized her blue-black hair, unbelievable black eyelashes and eyebrows and the Oriental moulding of the cheek-bones and lips—so brunette and Oriental that you thought her the true Arab Princess of a dream of an Arabian Nights' tale, until you realized her white skin, her rose-pink cheeks, her obviously northern complexion and European blood.

Of her figure I can but say it was worthy of her face. It was perfect, and what was to be seen of her neck and limbs was as white as flesh can be. . . .

She was a human flower. . . . An orchid—a white orchid marked with scarlet and with black. And as these flowers always do, she looked wicked—an incarnate, though very lovely, potentiality for evil.

Catching sight, I suppose, of Colonel Levasseur's gay uniform, she came straight to us, or rather floated toward us on her toes, her graceful arms and hands also appearing to float upon the air, quietly waving around her head and body like thistle-down and like gracefulness personified. One forgot the crudeness of the music, for she subordinated it to her purposes, and, becoming part of her and her movement, it was beautiful.

Straight to us she came, and at me she looked, giving no glance of recognition to the chagrined Levasseur. With a deep, deep curtsy of mocking homage and genuine challenge, that broke her slow revolving dance at my very feet, she sank to the ground, and, rising like a swift-growing flower from the earth—like Aphrodite herself from the wine-dark sea—she gazed straight into my eyes, smiled with the allure of all the sirens, Delilahs, Sapphos, Aspasias, Jezebels and Cleopatras that ever lived, and whispered—to me—as if she and I were alone in all Africa . . . alone in the gracious night, beneath the serene moon and throbbing stars . . . alone together, she and I, at the door of our silken tent under the graceful palms of our secret oasis . . . she and I, alone together upon the silken cushions and the silken carpet spread upon the warm honey-coloured sands. . . .

Good God in Heaven—what was this ? I struggled like a drowning man . . . I *was* a drowning man, sinking down . . . down . . . hypnotized . . .

" *No! No!* " I shouted. " *No! . . .*" The only flower for me was an English rose. . . . What had I to do with orchids of Africa ? Had I really shouted ? . . . What was she whispering ? . . . French ? . . .

" *Beaux yeux bleus !* . . . *J'aime les yeux bleus !* . . . *Baisez-moi !* . . . *Aimez-moi !* . . . *Venez avec moi* . . . *après !* . . . I lov' you so. . . . *Je t'aime !* . . . *Je t'adore !* . . . Kees me, sweetheart. . . . Crrrush me in your arms, darling. . . . *J'ai attendu. . . . Et tu es arrivé* . . . *J'ai attendu* . . . *depuis longtemps* . . . *il y a longtemps* . . . *J'ai attendu. . . . Et tu es arrivé.*

. . . Maintenant. . . . Baisez-moi ! . . . Embrassez-moi, mon amant Anglais . . . ah . . ."

She was talking French. . . . Was she speaking at all ? . . . Was she talking faulty French and broken English, with the accent of the educated French-and English-speaking Arab ? . . . No. Her lips were not moving—but her eyes were holding mine ; burning into mine. . . . Her eyes were great irresistible magnets drawing my soul through my eyes into hers and through them, down into her soul where it would be lost for ever, engulfed, held, drowned, destroyed.

"*No !* " I shouted, and burst into a profuse perspiration as I clung with the strength of despair to—to—sanity, to self-respect, to honour . . . to Isobel. . . .

And then I shook off the shackles of this absurd folly— or this devilish, hellish danger—and was an ordinary tourist from the north smiling at this ordinary dancing-girl of the south. . . .

But . . . and I shivered slightly . . . she was not ordinary . . . Neither in her evil loveliness, nor in her evil, conscious, or unconscious, hypnotic power, was she ordinary.

Had she actually spoken ?

Had I actually cried aloud ?

With a real effort, I wrenched my eyes from hers, and glanced around. The Arabs were watching her as a circle of dogs a luscious piece of meat—which is what she was to them.

Levasseur was smiling cynically and without amusement.

" You are favoured, my friend," he growled, as she floated away on her toes—her hands and her arms floating about her as she did so.

" Did she speak to me ? " I asked.

" Not that I heard," he answered in surprise. " She certainly intends to do so, though. . . . Beware, St. Anthony. . . . They don't call her the Angel of Death for nothing. . . ."

G

I decided that neither she nor I had uttered a sound, that she had paused before me for but a moment—and yet I *knew* that, if ever she spoke to me, she would speak in faulty French and broken English, with the accent of those Arabs who have learnt a little French and English—as many of the town-dwelling Arabs do, for purposes of business.

This was interesting, a little too interesting perhaps. It was also absurd, utterly ridiculous, perfectly impossible. I could have sworn that I had shouted " *No !* " at the top of my voice, and had recoiled violently.

Obviously I had uttered no sound and had not moved in my arm-chair. . . . But why was I trembling from head to foot, and wet with a cold perspiration that had no relation to the pleasant temperature of the night ? Why did I recover my normal serenity and self-control in inverse proportion to her proximity ?

While she swayed mockingly before an Arab who sat in the most distant corner of the square, her back toward me, I took my eyes from her and turned again to Levasseur, as the Arab, his face transfigured, his burning eyes riveted on her face, his clutching hands extended, rose slowly to his feet.

" Who *is* she ? " I said, controlling my voice as best I might.

" Who *is* she, M'sieu' St. Anthony ? " mocked the Colonel, evidently still a little piqued. " She is the Angel of Death, as I think I have already told you."

" Well ; tell me a little more about her," I said, shortly.

" Well ; she is what you see she is—and a good deal more. . . . Among other things she is the daughter of a very famous Ouled-Naïl dancing-girl. . . . Eh, *mon ami*, but a dancing-girl of a beauty. . . . Of a beauty . . . of a fascination . . . of an allure . . . *ravissante !* " and the Colonel kissed his stubby fingers and waved them at the stars, his somewhat heavy, bovine gaze momentarily aflame.

" Ah ! the marvellous . . . the incredible . . . the un-

tellable 'Zaza Blanchfleur,' as we called her. . . . But
that was a woman . . . a houri from Paradise. . . ."

"And the father?" I broke in upon the rhapsody.
"A Frenchman I suppose?"

"Said to be an Englishman," replied the Colonel.

"Certainly European," I observed.

"Oh, but yes, it leaps to the eye, that; does it not,
mon ami? That white skin, those unpainted cheeks. . . .
Yes, they say he was an Englishman. . . . The Death
Angel believes so, anyhow . . . and her great desire in
life is to meet him."

"Filial affection is a wonderful thing," I observed.

"It'll prove so, in this case," said the Colonel. "For
if the little angel gets near enough, she'll cut his throat till
his head falls backward—*boump!*—so. . . . Yes; she
loves all Europeans—especially the English—for her
father's sake!"

"What! Ill-treated her, I suppose?" I said, my eyes
again turning to where the girl beguiled the Arab, and was
now bending over backward towards him, that he might
place a coin of gold on her forehead among the gold coins
of the *sokhab* tiara that adorned it.

"No, no," murmured the Colonel lazily, as he gazed
at the smoke that was curling from his cigarette. "She
never knew him, I believe. It's her mother she wishes
to avenge."

"Ill-treated the mother?" I asked.

"Well; I wouldn't say *that*. . . . He merely did—er
—what one does. . . . One tires, of course . . . of the
loveliest of them. . . . One gathers that *ce bon Monsieur
Anglais* took her from the Street of a Thousand Delights
away out into the—er—Desert of One Delight. . . .
An individualist, one perceives. . . . Installed his *chère
amie* in the desert-equivalent of a flat or a *maisonnette*—
probably a green canvas tent from London. . . . A desert
idyll. . . .

"A great lover, one would say, this Englishman . . ."
mused the Colonel. "Of a certainty he captured the heart

of our Zaza—and broke it. . . . No . . . nothing cruel.
. . . He just dropped it—and it just broke . . . like
any other fragile thing that one drops. . . . He left
her. . . .

"She was never the same again, our little one. . . .
She became positively nun-like. . . . And then, a little
strange . . . *distraite*. . . . Other-world and other-where,
one would say . . . even in moments of love. . . . And,
in time, a little mad. . . . And then more than a little
mad. . . . And then quite mad. . . . Oh, mad as
Ophelia. . . . And through these years, the years of
hoping . . . the heart-sick years of hope deferred . . .
the heart-broken years of realization . . . the years of
growing insanity . . . the years of madness, she talked
of him. . . . Always she talked of him and his return. . . .

"Yes, of a truth, he broke her heart."

"One does not somehow imagine the heart of a Zaza
Blanchfleur to be very fragile," I observed.

"That is why I say this Englishman was a great lover,"
said Levasseur. "For certainly the little one's heart had
been taken up—and dropped—before. . . . By General
and by Subaltern . . . by civilian and by sheikh . . . by
aristocrat and by plutocrat . . . by the richest and by
the handsomest. . . . Had been dropped—and had
gracefully rebounded to be caught by the next. . . .

"But when the Englishman dropped it, it was shattered
—and Zaza Blanchfleur lived with a broken heart until
she died of a broken heart. . . .

"And the Angel of Death desires earnestly . . . oh,
but *earnestly*—to meet her papa. . . . And, meanwhile,
any white man serves her purpose—her purpose of revenge
. . . serves to glut her hate, to fill her coffers and to slake
her passion to avenge her mother."

"She must have adored her mother," I observed.

"Everybody adored her mother," said the Colonel
sententiously, and heaved a deep sigh, a sigh that, one felt,
claimed one's sympathy and the tribute of a tear. . . .

The Angel of Death—and certainly she moved with the lightness and grace of a being endowed with wings—came circling, gliding, floating toward me again.

Row upon row of enigmatic dark faces. . . . Hundreds of hard watching eyes. . . .

The fierce-looking hawk-faced young Arab, with whom she had coquetted, arose from his place, and came round the outside of the square of intently-staring onlookers, until he was behind the chairs occupied by the Colonel and myself.

"Have you a gold coin?" asked Levasseur. "She is going to favour you again. The correct thing is to lay a twenty-franc piece, or a sovereign, on her forehead, when she bends over backward with her face turned up to you."

Should I avoid her gaze this time—refuse to look her in the face? Absurd—a half-caste dancing-girl of the bazaars of Bouzen. . . .

She was before me again, and I was a captive fly about which a lovely and bejewelled spider was weaving the bonds from which there is no escape but death. . . . Her arms were weaving . . . weaving . . . weaving . . . mesmeric . . . hypnotic . . . compelling. . . .

She approached yet closer.

With a great mental and moral effort I wrenched my mind or soul violently from hers, and thrust my hand into my pocket for a coin. I would simply follow the "custom of the country"—signify my approval of her skill in the usual manner, tip this perfectly ordinary dancing-girl—and then tell Levasseur I was more than ready to return to the hotel. . . .

The Angel of Death saw my movement in search of money, but instead of turning her back to me and bending over until her face looked up into mine, she threw herself at my feet, knelt with arms out-stretched, and bringing her wonderful face closer and closer to mine, whispered:

"_Chèri!_ . . . _Beaux yeux bleus!_ . . . Lov' me! . . . I lov' you! . . . Kiss me, Beau'ful blue-eyes. . . . Kiss me! . . . Quick! . . ."

Now, Heaven knows, I am no saint, and I know I am
no priggish pompous fool. . . . There could be no earthly
harm in my kissing this girl. No more harm than there
is in any snatched under-the-mistletoe kiss. But the last
kiss that I had ever exchanged, had been with a dear little
child at Brandon Abbas—ah, how dear!—a sweet and
lovely little angel; an Angel of Life, if this was the
Angel of Death. . . .

I did not want to hurt this dancing-girl's feelings, but
neither did I want to kiss her. In fact, I wasn't going to
kiss her, whatever happened.

"*Kiss* her, man," snapped Colonel Levasseur, disgusted,
I suppose, at the stupid, graceless and cold-blooded Anglo-
Saxon.

"Thanks—but I never kiss," I said, both to the girl
and to him.

The Colonel snorted; the girl's eyes blazed; and I felt
an uncomfortable fool.

Simultaneously the young Arab made some movement
behind my chair, Colonel Levasseur shouted something at
him in Arabic, and the girl thrust her angry face almost
against mine.

"*Kiss me!*" she whispered tensely, and the eyes, that
had seemed to blaze, narrowed, and looked as deadly cold
as those of a snake.

I shook my head.

"I never kiss people," I said, and before my lips had
well closed, her right hand went to her sash, flashed upward
and fell with a sharp and heavy blow on my shirt-front,
exactly over my heart. . . .

I felt no pain. . . . That would come. . . .
Numbed. . . .

Levasseur sprang to his feet, hurled the young Arab
back, and seized the girl's wrist as though to snap her
arm.

"You she-devil!" he growled and, as she laughed
mockingly, glanced from the knife that gleamed in her
hand, to my breast.

I laughed also—a somewhat nervous laugh of relief.
She had not stabbed me as I had supposed. She had
struck with all her strength, but in the moment of impact
she had turned the point of the knife inward, and had
merely struck me with the clenched fist that held the knife.

It was over in a second, and she was whirling away
again upon the tips of her toes. But few had seen what
actually happened—and they had merely seen a girl offer
a kiss, receive a refusal, and give a blow.

Turning swiftly from the girl to the jealous Arab, Colonel
Levasseur showed something of the tiger that undoubtedly
lurked beneath the heavy and somewhat dull exterior of
the man.

What he said, I did not catch ; but the Arab recoiled
from the ferocious glare of the French officer's baleful
eye, the gleam of his bared teeth. I thought the big
clenched fist was about to crash into the Arab's face, but
it shot out with pointed finger, as the Colonel concluded
with an order, shouted as at a dog.

" *Imshi !* " he roared. " Get out of it, you black hound !
. . ." and the Arab slunk off toward the compound gate.

Impassive faces seemed to harden . . . hundreds of
watching eyes to narrow. . . .

Our host, apparently petrified with terror and amazement, now pulled himself together, rolled off his sofa, and
prostrated himself before his guest.

When he had finished his protestations of grief, horror,
outrage and alarm—perfervid declarations that he was
shamed for life, his face blackened for ever, his salt betrayed,
his roof dishonoured, his fame besmirched, his self-respect
destroyed, his life laid in ruins—by the action of the vile
criminal whom the Colonel had so rightly driven forth
into outer darkness—Levasseur quietly remarked :

" *Bien !* I hold you responsible then, that every
movement of that seditious, insolent dog, Selim ben Yussuf,
is reported to the *Bureau*. . . . And look you, Abu
Sheikh Ahmed, if he sets foot in Zaguig without my knowing
it, on your head be it. . . ."

" On my head and my life, Excellency," replied Abu Sheikh Ahmed, touching his forehead and breast, as he bowed humbly before the angry Colonel.

Levasseur then thanked him for the entertainment, bade him continue the music and the dance until we were well away ; and then, with a brief, " Come along, Monsieur Vanbrugh," marched off to the door, our host trotting beside us, voluble to the last.

" What was wrong with the good What's-his-name—Selim ? " I asked as we seated ourselves in the waiting car.

" A cursed great knife, my friend," replied the Colonel, " broad and sharp and curly. . . . That's what was wrong. . . . His hand was on it as I happened to glance over my shoulder. . . . I believe that both he and the girl each thought the other was going to stab you, and so neither did. . . ."

" Oh, nonsense, Colonel," I laughed, " she was only giving me a little fright because I refused her kiss, and he was just being dramatic—to please her. . . ."

" Ah, well, my friend," replied Levasseur, " doubtless *you* know the Arab best—and particularly Mademoiselle the Angel of Death and Monsieur Selim ben Yussuf, who is literally mad for her."

" Who is he ? " I asked.

" The son of the Sheikh of an extremely powerful and important tribe," was the reply. " An old man whose friendship is worth a very great deal to us. . . . Make all the difference at Zaguig. . . . Worth a whole brigade. . . . He's very loyal, friendly and peaceable, but things will be different when his mantle descends to Master Selim—if our fool politicians let it. . . . I'd shoot the dog on sight, if I had *my* way. . . . Let's stop the car and walk a bit, shall we ? I've been sitting down all day."

I was quite agreeable. We got out, and the Colonel bade the soldier-chauffeur return to his quarters.

" Are these streets at all dangerous at night ? " I asked my companion, as we strolled along through the silent moonlit dream-city of whitest light and blackest shadow.

" *That* is, very—in more ways than one," he replied, pointing up a somewhat narrower lane, the entrance to which we were just passing. " There are a good few murders, up there, in the course of the year. . . . We can go that way. . . . It's rather interesting."

" Murders ? " I observed, as we turned into the street. " Robbery ? "

"Yes. Robbery . . . Jealousy . . . Hate. . . . Sometimes the spider kills the fly. Sometimes the fly is a wasp and kills the spider."

It was a strange street. Silent as Death ; wide awake and watchful as Life : furtive and secret as Night : open and obvious as Day.

There was no movement, no sound, no invitation ; but there were eyes, there were open doors that looked like the mouths of tombs, there were mystery and evil and danger in the black shadows, in the very moonlight, the air. . . .

As we passed the first open door, I saw that it framed a curious picture. Back in the darkness, with which a small native lamp struggled feebly, sat a perfectly motionless figure, bedizened, bejewelled, posed, suggesting an idol dressed up for a barbarous religious ceremony, or the priest of such an idol, watching through the night before its shrine. No movement of the body of this priest or idol caused the slightest change in the reflections from bright jewels, shining gold, or gleaming cloth of silver, the slightest sound from heavy armlets, chains, anklets, girdle or bracelets—but, as we passed, the eyes followed us, gleaming. . . .

And so in the next house . . . and the next . . . and the next ; so in every house in the silent listening street, the waiting, watchful, motionless street, which the bold and hardy man beside me had declared to be very dangerous. in more ways than one.

"Interesting people, those Ouled-Naïl dancing-girls," observed Levasseur. "They've danced, and they've sat in this street, for a couple of thousand years or so. They danced for Julius Cæsar and Scipio Africanus—and for Jugurtha too—as they danced for you and me, and for old Abu Sheikh Ahmed. . . . Roman generals took them to Rome and French generals take them to Paris. . . . There isn't much they don't know about the art of charming. . . . A hundred generations of hereditary lore. . . . Most intriguing and attractive. . . ."

"A matter of taste," I observed. "Personally I'd pay handsomely—to be excused. I don't see how a bedizened, painted, probably unwashed, half-savage Jezebel is going to 'interest, intrigue, and attract,' a person of any taste and refinement."

I spoke a little warmly and wondered whether I did protest too much, as I thought of the Angel of Death.

The Colonel was faintly annoyed, methought. Perhaps he, a person of taste and refinement, had been interested, intrigued and attracted.

"One of them attracted the Englishman to some purpose," he growled. "He took her from this very street. . . . I could show you the house. . . . Zaza Blanchfleur. . . . He treated her like a bride. . . . Regular honeymoon. . . . Fitted out a splendid caravan, and went off a long way into the desert. . . . Oh, yes, she interested *him* all right, and for quite a while too. . . . And what about her daughter, the Angel of Death? She has interested a few people of taste and refinement, I can tell you! . . . Some names that would surprise you. . . ."

"And did she sit in this street too?" I asked.

"Of course she did, at first. . . . But she has walked in a few other streets since . . . Bond Street: Rue de la Paix: Unter den Linden: Nevsky Prospect: the Ringstrasse: Corso: Prado: Avenido: visited nearly all the capitals of Europe, she says."

"What's to become of a girl like that?" I asked.

"Oh—marry a big Sheikh and go out into the desert

for good—or a rich Moor and go into a *hareem* in Fez—
stay here and amass wealth—go to Paris, Marseilles or
Algiers—she may die a princess on a silken bed in a Sultan's
palace, or on the floor of a foul den in Port Said. . . ."

The Colonel sighed, and the subject dropped.

CHAPTER V

AT Zaguig, Colonel Levasseur was in his element, monarch of all he surveyed, and greatly he loved playing the monarch before the amused eyes of Mary, who enormously enjoyed the opportunity of " getting nearer to life " as she called it, and " seeing the Oriental on his native heath," unoccidentalized and undefiled—or unpurified and unregenerate.

Zaguig contained nothing European, and it intended to contain nothing European if it could help it. Unfortunately, its representatives had not even that moderate degree of straight speech and fair dealing which prevails in European diplomacy, and hid the bitterest hate and most evil intentions behind the most loving protestations, honeyed words and outward signs of friendship.

I am not a politician nor a world-reformer, neither a publicist nor a sociologist, and I have no views to offer on the subject of the ethics of the " peaceful penetration " of an uncivilized country by a civilized one. But nobody could travel southward from Bouzen, contrasting the Desert with the Sown, without perceiving that the penetration was for the greatest good of the greatest number, and ultimately for the whole world's good, inasmuch as cultivation and production succeeded fallow waste ; order and peace succeeded lawlessness and war ; and the blessings of civilization succeeded the curses of savagery.

Not always are the " blessings " immediately recognized for what they are, by their unconsulted recipients.

Certainly, in this case, there could be no two opinions on the subject of whether the penetrated approved the process. They were not altruists and they were fanatical Mussulmans with an unfathomable contempt for all Christians and all other God-forgotten Infidels. . . . Particularly was this true of the Zaguigan dervishes, marabouts, mullahs, priests, preachers, and teachers, for Zaguig was what is known as a "Holy" City, and it was wont to make a most unholy mess of any unauthorized intruder. . . .

Probably Mecca and Medina themselves were not more hopelessly reactionary and murderously fanatical than Zaguig, and certainly they could not have approximated more closely to the state of Sodom and Gomorrah than did this Holy Spot. . . .

However, the tide of civilization was encroaching upon the hitherto undefiled sands that surrounded it ; waves of progress were lapping against its very walls ; and the first wavelets of that irresistible ocean were the men of Colonel Levasseur's Military Mission.

It was in this peculiarly unholy Holy City that Mary met the man who instantly awoke her keenest interest, admiration and approval ; who later won her devoted love ; and ultimately became her husband.

Mary was—wholly unconsciously, I believe—becoming very interested in the subject of love and matrimony, and had, I feel sure, been wondering whether her twin soul might not be right there, when she sojourned in New York, London, Paris, Monte Carlo, Algiers, Biskra, and Bouzen respectively, where charming eligibles abounded.

To think that he should be in Zaguig where nothing abounded but unwashed Zaguigans, heat, dirt, smells and an almost unadulterated orientalism . . . !

I liked the handsome, hard, clean-cut Major Henri de Beaujolais from the first ; and he attracted me enormously. To the simplicity and directness of the soldier he added the cleverness and knowledge of the trained specialist ; the charm, urbanity and grace of the experienced man of the world ; and the inevitable attractiveness of a lovable and modest character.

He combined the best of two nations, with his English public-school upbringing, and his English home-life of gentle breeding, on the one hand, and his aristocratic French birth, breeding and traditions on the other. . . . I heard that he was as brave as a lion, extremely able, and likely to go very far in his profession—quite apart from the fact that he was the nephew of a most distinguished general and related by marriage (through his uncle's wife) to an extremely powerful and prominent politician.

We first met him at dinner at Colonel Levasseur's table, and I was surprised to note that Mary's attitude to him was anything but encouraging and kind. In fact she rather annoyed me by apparently endeavouring to annoy him. I taxed her with this after he had gone, and asked if she disliked him.

" *Dear* old Otis ! " she smiled, and added later . . . " Why—no—why should I ? . . . I altogether like him . . . and *then* some . . ."

" You certainly hid it," I observed, and,

" Did I ? . . . Did I ? " she asked.

Whereupon I also waxed wily, and remarked :

" He reminded me of d'Artagnan. . . . Just that swaggering self-confidence and assurance . . . a faint touch of the somewhat gasconading swash-buckler . . ." and got no further.

" What ! " interrupted Mary, " *Are* you as blind as a mole with a monocle *and* as stupid as a fish with a headache ? . . . Why I never met a more modest unassuming man in my life ! . . . You couldn't prise a word out of him—about what he has done. . . . Not with a crow-bar. . . ."

" Ah ! " I observed profoundly, and chuckled, whereupon Mary marched off to bed.

I love Mary, and I love to watch her at work. What she wants, she goes for ; and what she goes for, she gets. Our Red Indian streak is, at times, fairly strong in her, and shows particularly when she is in danger. . . . Then she is the coolest thing invented, and apparently at her happiest. . . . It shows also in a certain relentless tenacity, a determination to achieve her purpose—and, I may add, a certain recklessness—not to say unscrupulousness—with which she handles obstacles and opposition.

The idea that entered my mind that memorable evening remained, and it turned to a certainty. As the days went by, and Mary saw more and more of Henri de Beaujolais, she grew more and more interested in him, and he in her. . . . All his spare time was devoted to "making her visit agreeable," and to satisfying her insatiable thirst for knowledge of North Africa and the Africans.

Poor Colonel Levasseur could but acquiesce, and show a delight that he did not feel, when she assured him of how enormously she was enjoying her stay in Zaguig—thanks to Major de Beaujolais' wonderful knowledge of the place and people, and his extraordinarily interesting way of imparting it.

"Yes," thought I to myself in the vernacular, "Mary has fallen for Major Henri de Beaujolais, and Major Henri de Beaujolais has fallen for Mary—though possibly he doesn't yet know it. . . . But he is certainly going to know it—if the first part of my surmise is correct."

I was filled with hope and joy, for he was just the man I would have chosen for my sister to marry, and I longed to see her married and with a home of her own. . . . A woman needs a home more than a man does—almost more than she needs anything—and our own home in Wyoming was no "home" at all. . . .

It did not greatly surprise me, when, entering the spacious tiled breakfast-room, with its great pillared verandah, one morning, to hear de Beaujolais remark, as he turned to go :

"Well, I have warned you, sir, and done all I can. . . . We're sitting on a powder-magazine and there are quite a lot of lads inside it—*striking matches*. . . . And one of them is our friend Selim ben Yussuf too ! . . . There's going to be a big explosion—and a conflagration as well—and pretty soon. . . ."

" Won't you stop and have some coffee . . . before it happens ! . . ." smiled Colonel Levasseur in a particularly irritating manner ; and, with a haughty salute, de Beaujolais strode from the room, his face set and scowling.

" Wonderful noses for a mare's-nest, these Intelligence people," smiled the Colonel. " Have you seen Mademoiselle this morning ? . . . Been out riding ? . . . Wish I could find all the spare time these Intelligence fellers can. . . . *I* can't go riding with her every morning. . . . Yes, nothing but mare's-nest after mare's-nest, full of addled eggs—like the Intelligence feller's brains. . . . Yes, addled. . . . Another mare's-nest now—revolt, rebellion, mutiny, murder, massacre and I don't know what all ! . . . I suppose the Secret Service must justify its existence and earn its pay somehow. . . . *Intelligence*, eh ? . . . Pity some of them haven't *got* a little. . . . Ah ! Here's Mademoiselle. . . . Bring the coffee at once, Alphonse. . . . *Bon jour, ma chère Mademoiselle Vanbrugh*, you look like the morning itself—only cool . . . cool . . . always cool. . . ."

One afternoon within a week of the delivery of these *obiter dicta* by the wise Colonel Levasseur, I received a message, at the Residency, from de Beaujolais, bidding me hurry to his quarters. The messenger, a fine Spahi, named Achmet, de Beaujolais' orderly, calmly informed me that my sister, the Sitt Miriam Vanbrugh, was in great danger and that I was to go instantly, on the horse that he had ridden. It appeared that de Beaujolais himself had come to the Residency to find me, and had taken my sister's maid away with him. . . .

. . . At least this was what I gathered from Achmet's curious mixture of French, *sabir* and Arabic.

I rushed down to the street, guided by Achmet, who ran swiftly before me ; rode to the house near the Bab-el-Sûq where de Beaujolais lived, fearing I knew not what, and noting the strange emptiness of the bazaars, lanes, squares and streets, due, I supposed, to the fact that there was a big parade and review in the great Square of the Minaret. . . .

Arrived at de Beaujolais' quarters, I dismounted in the courtyard at the back of the house, gave the horse a smack that sent him trotting to the stable, and dashed up the wooden stairs. I either kicked down or opened the first door to which I came, and found two Arabs in the room. One of them announced himself to be Major de Beaujolais —I recognized the voice after I had heard the name— and said that Mary was in his bedroom with her maid, dressing up as an Arab female. . . . The massacre was to be for that evening, and not a foreigner would survive it, save those who successfully hid themselves. . . . He had sent for me to look after the girls and to share their chance of escape by hiding, in disguise, until a punitive expedition arrived. . . .

So it had come ! . . . De Beaujolais had been right and Levasseur wrong, criminally wrong. . . . And Mary was in the heart of one of the most dangerously fanatical towns in the world, at the moment of a *jehad*, a Holy War upon infidels, their slaughter and complete massacre. . . . Mary and her excellent English maid, Maud Atkinson. . . . And I was to disguise myself as an Arab and hide in a bedroom with them—hide cowering, trembling, sickening, starving, until the arrival of a relief-force from Ain-Zuggout or somewhere ! . . .

One thing was fairly certain, Mary wouldn't consent to do anything of this sort—and I said so. . . .

" What about the troops ? " I asked.

" Not a chance," replied de Beaujolais. " They are hopelessly inadequate in number, and they couldn't be worse placed than they are. . . . Scattered about the city. . . . If you hide here, you'll be the only white people alive by midnight. . . . It's absolutely your one and only chance. . . ."

" Mary won't stay hidden here for days," I said. " And I don't like the idea much for myself, either. . . . Let's hear what she's got to say about it," and we went into the next room, followed by the other " Arab "—a Captain in the French Secret Service, named Redon.

Mary, calm and cool as ever, appeared more interested in the Arab clothes than in the prospect of death and destruction.

" Look here, Mary," I said. " What about it ? Will you lie low here and keep the place all silent and shut up, and wear those clothes in case anybody gets a glimpse of you—and wait until the relief-force comes ? "

" Answer's in the negative," she replied, observing the effect of her head-dress in a shaving-mirror. " These what-is-its over the face don't give a girl much chance, do they ? . . . The just and the unjust. . . . the fair and the unfair . . . all start from scratch, so to speak. . . . Er—no—Otis, I am not paying a long visit. . . . What's Major de Beaujolais going to do in the massacre ? Show great Intelligence and offer us sure, but Secret, Service— or which ? "

And then de Beaujolais made the devastating announcement that he was going to clear out, cut and run—before the show started, if he could. . . . He had at that moment got his orders from the dirty, ruffianly-looking " Arab " who was Captain de Redon. . . .

And I, at that moment, got something too—the idea of a lifetime ! *He should take Mary with him*, wherever he was going ! . . . It would save her from the massacre, and it would, moreover, throw her and de Beaujolais together in the protracted intimacy of a desert journey.

And that would surely lead to the lasting happiness of both of them ! . . . In the imminence of battle, murder and sudden death, I thought of orange-blossoms, bridal veils, and the Voice that breathed o'er Eden. . . . I suppose it was because I knew that it was hopeless and useless for me to think of such things in connection with myself, that I so often thought of them for other people. . . .

And it promptly appeared that my bright idea had not occurred to me alone, for Mary observed that since Major

de Beaujolais was escaping, she and her maid might as
well escape with him. She said it as one might say : " If
you're going to Town too, we might as well catch the same
train."

But de Beaujolais apparently had other views.

He declared that it was utterly impossible. He was
going on a secret mission of the greatest delicacy, danger
and importance. . . . He simply could not take women
with him. He repeated his suggestion that I and the two
girls should lie hidden in that house, and take our chance
of surviving till a French column arrived.

I was glad that Mary did not for one moment suppose
that I should do anything of the sort—do anything, in
fact, but join my host and his men and throw in my lot
with theirs.

For herself, she merely brushed de Beaujolais' refusals
and explanations aside, and made it clear that no masculine
trivialities and puerilities of politics, Secret Service, or
Special Missions, were of sufficient importance to be talked
about—much less considered as obstacles in the path of
Miss Mary Vanbrugh.

When he waxed urgently explanatory and emphatically
discouraging, finishing by an absolute and uncompromising
refusal, she merely did not listen, but bade the departing
Achmet to take along the portmanteau that Maudie had
brought—to wherever he was going. . . .

And so extremely vehement and final was de Beaujolais'
negative, so absolutely convincing his reasons for refusing
to take her, that I was certain he longed to do it, and
was but fighting what he believed to be his own weakness.
I conceived him to be in the horrible position of having to
leave a girl, with whom he had fallen in love, to the mercies
of the men of Zaguig—or else take her with him, to the
greater danger to herself and the greatest danger to the
success of his mission. . . .

To my mind, the second alternative was wholly preferable, and I set about doing what I could to bring it to
pass—for it gave Mary not only a chance of life, but a

chance of happiness. . . . Also, I am bound to confess, because it transferred to the broader shoulders of de Beaujolais the terrible responsibility of saving her. . . .

"Take her, for God's sake," I said, "it is her only chance. . . . She will never hide here. . . . She'll come back to the Residency with me, and use a rifle. . . . She is as good as a man. . . . You say there is no shadow of hope. . . . Think of the end then. . . . I can't shoot her. . . . There is at least a chance for her with you. . . ."

"Against my instructions and orders," he said, his face a study of conflicting feelings. . . . "I have to travel as light as possible ; as swiftly as possible—and with the irreducible minimum of followers. . . . More people means more kit and camels . . . more delay . . . less speed. . . . And she'd never stand the journey. . . . Wholly against my instructions and almost certain death for her. . . ."

"And this is absolutely certain death for her," I said.

I wished I could see Mary's face, but it was hidden beneath the out-door garment that covers the *purdah* Mussulman woman from the crown of her head to the soles of her feet. Not even her eyes were visible through the strip of muslin that covered the aperture left in the thick material, to permit the wearer to see.

Captain de Redon added his voice to mine—evidently sympathizing to the depths of his gallant Gallic soul with his unfortunately-situated friend ; with a girl in terrible danger ; and with the girl's brother, pleading for her life. Probably he saw, as clearly as I did, that the one thing de Beaujolais longed to do, was to give way. . . .

And give way he did, with every appearance of reluctance and ill grace.

"Very well," he said. "On Miss Vanbrugh's head be it. She and her maid can leave with me—provided she understands that my business is not to save her, but to serve my country. . . . I shan't let her safety or life stand in the way of duty, for a second. . . ."

I wrung his hand and I knew that Mary was safe. . . .

He'd do his duty, all-right, but he'd make it square with the safety of the woman he loved. . . . Yes, he certainly loved her, whether he knew it or not—and a terrific load was lifted from my mind.

A few minutes later, they were all in the street—still empty and silent, I was glad to see—and on their way to the house of the wealthy and friendly Arab, Sidi Ibrahim Maghruf—a party of entirely ordinary and convincing natives ; de Beaujolais, a Sergeant-Major Dufour, Captain de Redon, Mary, and Maud Atkinson—the last-named, in her invincible ignorance and cheerful cockney courage, thoroughly enjoying the whole business.

De Beaujolais refused to let me come with them to the house of his friend Ibrahim Maghruf, where the caravan was waiting, as I was not in Arab dress, and begged me (since I refused to quit the town with him, and then take my chance in the desert), to hurry back to the Residency. I was to tell Colonel Levasseur of the arrival of Captain de Redon with orders for de Beaujolais' instant departure, and to try to get the fact into the good Colonel's thick skull that the revolt would break out that very night. . . .

I gave Mary a warm and loving embrace, kissed the place where I imagined her mouth to be, and murmured in the neighbourhood of her ear :

" God bless you, darling girl . . . " and added a *cliché* of our childhood anent " a buggy-ride with a nice young man."

That Mary heard and understood my allusion was indicated by the fact that I received an entirely perceptible jab in the sub-central region of my waistcoat, as I took my arms from about her neck.

Crushing down my feelings of loneliness, apprehension and anxiety, I told myself that Mary was in splendid hands, and, hurrying out from that boding and oppressive house, I quickly lost myself, completely and hopelessly, in the maze-like tangle of alleys, bazaars, winding lanes, and crooked streets, that lay between it and the Residency.

The atmosphere of the place was inexpressibly sinister —sly, minatory and enigmatic. There was no-one to be seen, but I felt that I was seen by a thousand watching eyes. . . . What lurked behind those iron-barred window-spaces, those lattices, gratings, slightly opened doors ; behind those high blind walls, and upon those screened balconies ? . . . Frequently the lane through which I hurried was roofed completely over, and was a mere tunnel beneath the upper rooms of the houses that formed its sides.

As I emerged from one of these and turned a corner into a narrow bazaar of tiny shops, each but a shuttered hole in the wall, I heard a heavy murmur such as one may suddenly hear when approaching the sea-shore and emerging into the open. . . .

It was indescribably menacing and disturbing, this growing noise as of a hive of infuriated bees, and it quickly grew into the most terrible sound there is—the blended roar and howl and shout and scream of a vast infuriated mob of maddened men, yelling and blood-lusting for rapine, fire and slaughter. . . . The man who can hear it unmoved is a man of iron nerve, a superman indeed—for a mob is infinitely worse and wickeder, more destructive and dangerous, than any single member of it. It is the most wild and savage of all wild and savage beasts ; and is infinitely powerful, with its innumerable hands to rend and slay and burn, its innumerable brains to think of evil things for those hands to do.

I was certainly frightened.

The appalling noise increased in volume and came nearer.

I was lost—and knew not which way to turn to avoid the mob nor to rejoin my friends, those splendid soldiers —many of them Africans—who would die to a man, without thought of parley or surrender.

To die fighting with them would be nothing—an ex-hilaration, a fierce joy—but to be torn to pieces in these stinking gutters, handled and struck by these foul bestial brutes, trampled to a jelly of blood and mud and mess . . . there could be no more dreadful death. . . . The loath-

some indignity of it—a white man struggling impotent
in the hands of blacks—his clothes torn from his body . . . !

That was what frightened me, not Death—for he was
a fellow I was quite willing to meet whenever he came
along. . . .

§ 2

As the noise made by the mob—the noise varying from
the roaring of ten thousand lions to that of a mighty sea
breaking on an iron-bound coast in a terrific storm—rose
and fell, advanced and withdrew, when I turned corners,
entered narrow gullies or crossed open squares, I prayed
that Mary was out of the city and safely on her way.

I fervently blessed de Beaujolais and his thought for
her; his fetching her maid and me; his final decision to
take her with him. I could not refrain from contrasting
him with Levasseur—who had invited her to Zaguig that
he might impress her and that she might see him in the
most favourable conditions.

Well—he had invited her to Zaguig for his own ends
and had so been instrumental in bringing de Beaujolais into
her life. Long might de Beaujolais remain there!

And suddenly I turned another corner and found, with
utter dismay, that I had walked round in a circle; for in
the open space where several lanes met, lay a dead horse
that I had seen an hour or two earlier, and, not very far
from it, lay the corpse of an Arab.

The sight—an unpleasant one—of the man's body,
gave me an idea. My object was to rejoin Levasseur
and to be of use; but it was absolutely certain that I
should never reach him in European clothes. I should be
torn to pieces by the mob, killed by the first gang I ran into.
Dressed as I was, my one chance of life was to creep into
some hole and hide. Dressed as an Arab, I might make
my way to the Residency, and get into it—if I were not
shot by its defenders.

Disguised as an Arab, I might be able to approach and

shout, in French, that I was one of them. Dressed as a European, I couldn't shout to the mob that I was really an Arab in disguise—and get away with it. There wouldn't be time to shout, for one thing.

The dead man's clothes were filthy, and they were soaked in blood. He had certainly been in bad trouble. . . . Could he be another Secret Service man, like de Redon ? One who had fallen by the way ? I should somehow feel less compunction about putting on his foul *burnous*, if he were. . . . Should I put his things on over my own, or discard European clothing entirely ? . . . I should have to look " right " about the head and feet, anyway. There wouldn't be much point in going about with European boots and trousers sticking out at one end of a *burnous* and a European sun-helmet at the other.

But what should I look like, if a gang came round the corner, and saw me sitting in the gutter, swapping clothes with a corpse ?

These thoughts flashed through my mind in the moment that I reached the body. Apparently the man had been stabbed, or run through, with a sword.

He had bled very copiously, and I glanced at the trail which connected him with the gate of a compound. . . . No, I couldn't squat down in the open street, pull off my boots and trousers—fancy being caught without one's boots and trousers—and change clothes with a corpse ! . . . Or could I ? . . .

And right here the corpse fetched a deep groan and settled the question. I could not pull the clothes off a dying man. . . . If I could do nothing to help him, I could at least leave him to die in peace.

I turned and hurried away, wondering which of the five streets that entered the square was the one by which I had followed Achmet from the Residency to de Beaujolais' quarters. They all looked alike to me, and I had been too anxious about Mary to take any note of the winding route by which we had come. . . . I found that I was following the trail left by the wounded Arab, and

saw that it led into the compound of an apparently un-
occupied building, and to the foot of an outside stair-case
that went up to the flat roof.

As I halted, there was a sudden burst of nearer noise,
the sound of men running as well as shouting; and,
glancing over my shoulder, I saw that, two or three hundred
yards from where I stood, a mob was streaming across the
end of the alley down which I was looking. Any one of
the running men might at any moment glance in my direction—and in a very few minutes it would be, " Good-
evening, St. Peter," for mine.

I dashed into the compound, up the stairs to the roof,
and found myself in the presence of some half-dozen
Arabs—all dead. . . .

" Dirty work at the cross-roads ! "

The place was like a butcher's yard, a slaughter-house—
also a perfectly private dressing-room provided with an
assortment of that kind of fancy-dress of which I was in
such desperate need. The garments were all filthy, more
or less torn, and plentifully bloodstained ; but I realized
that this was all to the good, since my object was to make
my way through streets swarming with the scum of the
city, similarly apparelled, and many of them similarly gore-
bespattered. In point of fact it was amazing good luck that
I had happened upon this sinister and revolting shambles.

Promptly I divested myself of my outer clothing and
boots, and got to work.

It was the nastiest job I have ever undertaken, and there
were moments when I was tempted to resume my own
clothes, take one of the Arab swords that lay about, and
run amok. Still more was I tempted to scurry back to
de Beaujolais' quarters and hide. . . . I could find the
place by returning to where the dead horse lay. . . .

I suppose that if I were a strong silent man with a big
chin (and a thick ear or two), I should have proceeded
coolly and swiftly with my task, and should have swaggered
forth from that house " every inch an Arab," correct to
the last detail.

In point of fact I felt ill and shaken ; I was very frightened
and nervous ; and I could scarcely control my trembling
sweating fingers.

Possibly most other ordinary people would have felt
nearly as bad as I did ?

It was growing dark. . . . The sky was lurid with the
glare of great conflagrations. . . . There was a ceaseless
nerve-shattering mob-roar, a roar punctuated by hideous
howls, rifle shots, and the crashes of volley-firing. . . .
I was in the midst of a select assembly of corpses, and their
hideous faces seemed to grimace in the waning and flickering light. . . . I had to pull them about, to get their
clothes from them—their beastly blood-sodden clothes . . .
and they resented this, and clung to their rags with devilish
ingenuity. . . . And there was viscous slimy blood upon
my hands. . . . There were knotted strings—and the
knots would not come undone—and this made the owner
of the garment grin and grin and grin at me, and shake his
horrible head as I tugged and tugged, the perspiration
streaming from me. . . . And once stepping back, I
slipped and stumbled and, in saving myself from falling,
I trod upon the chest of a man lying behind me, and my
weight drove the air from his lungs through his throat,
and the dead uttered what seemed a loud cry—the ghastliest, the most loathsome, the most terrifying sound that
I have ever heard : the dead voice of a dead man raised
in loud protest against the indignity, the defilement of
my treading foot. . . .

I hear that sound in nightmares to this day. . . .

From that man I took nothing, though I coveted his
burnous and great curved dagger. . . . I dared not touch
him, lest his dreadful glazed eyes turn to mine, his horrible
snarling mouth shout at me again, his dead hands seize
me by the throat. . . .

Yes, I was certainly frightened by the time I had
wrested a complete Arab outfit from those reluctant
corpses, and I was certainly sick by the time I had rubbed
a mud of blood and dust and dirt upon my hands and

arms, my feet and legs and—it makes me shudder to think of it even now—upon my face. . . .

Having dressed, I wound a filthy cotton thing about my neck, chin, mouth, nose and ears, almost to my eyes, beneath the head-cloth I had transferred complete from its late owner's head and shoulders to my own ; picked up a knife and a sword ; and fled from the horrible scene of my unspeakable labours.

As I emerged from the compound, a man dashed from a side-turning into the alley in front of me, and came running swiftly in my direction.

I raised my sword and waited, realizing that my ghastly work up above must, at any rate, have made a terrible spectacle of me, and that standing there, bloody, grim, silent, well-armed, I was scarcely likely to be attacked by one man—nor by any number, until I had to speak, or my disguise was penetrated. . . .

The running man drew near, and I saw that he was a filthy ragged creature, gaunt and wild, carrying a great staff in one hand and a rosary in the other. Flecks of foam lay in white spots on his mangy beard. . . . One of those bestial " holy " beggars, so full of divinity that there is no room for humanity. . . .

As he rushed by, a few yards from me, he glanced in my direction, took me for a fellow tough, and yelled something or other, in Arabic—a profession of faith or an incitement to slay and spare not—and I got a clear glimpse of his face.

It was Captain de Redon.

Dashing after him, I laid my hand on his arm, raised my sword and emitted a meaningless howl. He swung about, cursing me vehemently, and up went his long staff. He looked as pleasant and easy to tackle as a hungry grizzly bear. . . . And he did not know me—nor dream that I was anything but the Arab thing I was trying to appear.

" This one's on you, Captain," I remarked.

His staff and his jaw both dropped as he stared.

"*Mon Dieu!*" he said. "Who are you? . . . I thought I was the only . . ."

"Otis H. Vanbrugh," I told him. "Major de Beaujolais introduced us an hour ago."

"*Mon Dieu!*" he said again. . . . "But you have made good use of your time, Monsieur! You took me in completely. . . . What happened? . . . I am going back to de Beaujolais' quarters to see that everything is all-right. . . . No papers undestroyed. . . . He had to leave rather hurriedly. . . . And I want another bite of Christian food, for I'm starving. . . . Also a scrap of soap if I can find some. . . . Very useful for pious foaming at the mouth. . . ."

As we hurried along, I told him how I had lost my way in trying to get from de Beaujolais' quarters to the Residency, and of my finding the dead men on the roof.

"A queer business," he said. "But corpses will be sufficiently common before to-morrow. . . . And your idea is to rejoin Levasseur and take a hand? . . . You'll have to be careful. It would be bad luck to get through the mob safely and be shot by the Zouaves. . . .

"Your sister is safely away," he continued, and went on to tell me how he had accompanied de Beaujolais' party to one of the gates, and had been able to divert a mob from that quarter, lead them running to imaginary loot, and, by dashing round a corner and over a wall and through a house and garden that he knew, to get into one of the tunnel-like bazaars and shake them off.

"Perhaps you'd better stick to me for a while," he concluded, as we entered de Beaujolais' place. "If anybody speaks to you, howl and hit him. . . . Sure sign that your heart's in the right place and that you're feeling good to-day—nice and fanatical and anti-French. . . . We'll get as near to the Residency as we can without being shot, and I may be able to get you in. . . . If not, you'll have to manage it, somehow, to-night. . . . Call out in French and say that you want to speak to Levasseur. . . . It'll be a risky business for you, though, between the Arabs and the Zouaves. . . ."

"But aren't you going to join your comrades too ? " I asked. "The one of us that got in first could warn them to look out for the other—if we failed to get in together."

"No," replied de Redon. "My job is outside. I'm going to play around with the lads-of-the-village, and speak that which is not true. . . . Just when they are going to start something, I yell that a French army is round the corner. . . . Or I accidentally drop this club on top of the head of the most prominent citizen, at the moment of his maximum usefulness to the community he adorns. . . . Dupe and mislead the poor fellows as effectually as if I were a professional labour-agitator, in fact. . . ."

I liked this Captain de Redon, a cool, competent and most courageous person. As he ate the leg of a fowl, and swiftly searched the two rooms that de Beaujolais had occupied—presumably for papers or other traces of its late occupant—he chatted as though we were not both in imminent danger of a beastly death, and about to go out and look for it.

It was a most interesting and amusing thing to hear a cultured and very delightful voice, speaking excellent English, issue from that dirty ragged scarecrow, skinny, mean and repulsive-looking.

Gazing at him in some amazement, I had an idea, and went to a small framed mirror, a cheap bazaar article, that hung on the wall of the back room.

I was positively startled. Sick and sorry as I had been at the time, I had done my work well—and had so smeared the handful of blood, mud, dust and dirt into my face and eyes that there was not a vestige of my white (or red) skin exposed. The said face was a most revolting, bestial, and disgusting spectacle—barely human in its foul filthiness. . . . No wonder that de Redon had not recognized me nor dreamed that I was a Christian. . . . As I stared at myself, I was glad that Isobel could not see me.

"Ready ? " said de Redon, in the doorway. . . . "Excuse my rushing you. . . . We'll get as near the Residency as we can. . . . When we're among the simple villagers, you just follow me and do more or less what I do. . . . If anybody seems offensive or gets inquisitive, hit him—or else spin round and round, and howl. . . . And, look here—if we get in front of the troops, throw yourself on the ground and be a wounded man. . . . If you go running towards them dressed like that, you'll be shot or bayoneted. . . . Wait for a chance to crawl near enough to shout, in French, to Levasseur or an officer, as I said. . . ."

I thanked him and forbore to remark that I had played Red Indians before—and with tame Indians who had themselves trodden the war-path in their time.

We went down into the street and hurried in the direction of the big square, not far from which was the Residency.

De Redon evidently knew every inch of the route, each twist and turn, and he went so fast that I could only just keep him in sight as he kept vanishing round corners and into dark tunnels.

Every moment the horrible noise grew louder and louder as we came nearer to the scene of the fighting.

As we turned from a foul gully into a broader street, a gang of looters came running round a corner a few yards from us.

Waving his staff and rosary of black wooden beads, de Redon howled like a wild beast, and spun round and round, shouted something I could not understand, and dashed on— I at his heels, in the middle of the yelling and excited Arabs. They had evidently come into the city from the outside, being differently dressed from the townsmen, darker and hardier-looking toughs.

Some had long guns and some carried perfectly good rifles.

The street down which we ran, debouched into the big market-square, the Square of the Minaret, and this great place was packed almost solid with people, all moving in the direction of the Residency. Certainly " the heathen raged furiously together," and when we got fairly into the middle of them, I began to feel that it was as safe a place as any, so far as risk of discovery went, and I yelled and waved my sword with the best.

De Redon wriggled, thrust, and fought his way through the crowd aggressively, and with the air of an important person who has very urgent business in hand. In an exceedingly violent and truculent assembly of fanatical ruffians, he seemed the most violent, truculent and fanatical of the lot. I followed him as best I could, and endeavoured to behave as he did.

Suddenly the shouting crowd gave back, just as crowds do when shepherded by mounted police, and, in a few moments, de Redon and I found ourselves in the foremost ranks, and then in front, and ahead of the mob. Turning to face the swaying crowd, de Redon twirled his staff above his head and bawled in Arabic at the top of his voice :

"Back ! Back ! . . . Run ! Run ! . . . The Roumi dogs . . . the *Franzawi* are coming . . ." and pointed to where from a side-street, a detachment of Zouaves came charging at the double—stoned and shot-at from the roofs, and followed by a howling mob, only kept at bay by the rear-guard-action tactics of a Sergeant, who, every now and then, halted the end squad of the little column, turned them about, fired a volley, and rushed back to the main body, who slowed up during the operation.

Occasionally a soldier fell and was instantly the centre of a surging mob that slashed and tore and clubbed him almost out of semblance to the human form.

As the little column, evidently fighting its way to the Residency, debouched into the square, the officer in command, a young Lieutenant, charging at their head, threw up his sword-hand and shouted :

"*Halte ! . . . Cessez le feu ! . . . Formez le carré !*"

And, in an instant, the company was a square, bristling with bayonets, steady as a rock, front ranks kneeling, rear ranks standing close behind them, awaiting the next order as if at drill.

"Run ! Run ! My brothers !" yelled de Redon, in

the comparative quiet that followed this manœuvre, a slight lull before the storm.

"Run! Run! . . . The *Franzawi*! . . . We shall be slain!" and he dashed at the wavering crowd that hung uncertain whether to charge in holy triumph or flee in holy terror.

Following his voice came that of the French officer, full, clear and strong.

"*Attention! Pour les feux de salve! . . . En joue! . . .*"

"Quick! Quick! . . . Run! Run . . ." yelled de Redon.

A huge man, wearing the green turban of a *haji*, and bearing aloft a green banner, thrust through the crowd, sprang forward, sent de Redon sprawling and yelled:

"*Allah! Allah! Allah Akbar! . . . Fissa! Fissa!* . . . Follow me and die for the Faith. . . ."

The crowd howled in response and moved forward.

De Redon, apparently representing a different brand of holiness, and full of the *odium theologicum*, returned the violent assault of the *haji*. He returned it with his club. The *haji* dropped, and the subsequent proceedings interested him no more.

The crowd rushed forward.

"*Feu!*" shouted the Zouave officer, and either instinctively or because de Redon did so, I flung myself to the ground.

Crash! . . . rang out the volley of the Zouaves.

"*En joue! Feu!*" cried the officer.

Crash! came the second volley from all sides of the now surrounded square of troops.

The crowd about me scattered like leaves before the wind, and de Redon and I were two of dozens of motionless figures upon the ground.

"*Garde à vous!*" cried the officer. . . . "*Par files de quatre! . . . Pas gymnastique! . . . En avant! . . .*"

Before he could give the order, "*Marche!*" a great voice boomed forth from above our heads, as though from Heaven.

On a little balcony at the top of a needle-like minaret, appeared the *muezzin*, and, on a clarion note, fairly trumpeted forth the words:

"*Kill! Kill! . . . In the name of Allah! . . . Gazi! Gazi! . . . There is no god but God and Mahomet is His Prophet! . . . Slay! Slay! . . . Charge together, in the Name of Allah! . . . Burn! . . . Destroy! . . . Kill! Kill! . . .*"

The mob rallied and from every street, alley, courtyard and doorway poured forth again in hundreds.

"*Charge!*" boomed forth again the great voice of the mullah.

Bang! went a rifle and, as I glanced from the figure of the Iman toward the sound, I saw the Sergeant lower his rifle.

"*Marche!*" continued the officer, even as the body of the *muezzin* struck the parapet of his eyrie, reeled over it and crashed into the courtyard below.

A terrific yell went up from the vast crowd, and many rushed to the spot, while others turned to pursue the Zouaves, now retreating at the double.

In front of the following crowd, a recumbent figure sprang to its feet, and with extended hand and every appearance of tremendous excitement, pointed away to the opposite corner of the square.

"Beware! Beware!" he shouted. "A trap! A trap! . . . Danger! . . . Big guns! Cannon! *Boom! Boom!* . . . Run! Run! . . ."

Bewildered and excited eyes turned in the direction to which de Redon pointed.

"Follow me!" he shouted, and ran toward the nearest street.

I sprang up and dashed after him, waving my sword and yelling, "*La illah ill allah ill Allah!*"

It seemed to me as good a noise as any, and quite fashionable at the moment—in fact, literally *le dernier cri*.

As always happens when a mob is given a lead, a large number followed, and, though de Redon's heroic effort

did not prevent pursuit of the soldiers, it delayed it, as
our section of the crowd streamed across the front of those
who were dashing forward to avenge the death of the holy
man who, with his last breath, had incited them to rapine
and slaughter.

Keeping as near de Redon as I could, I galloped along
behind him, waving my sword and emitting appropriate
noises.

Into a side alley dashed de Redon still yelling :

"Big   guns !   Cannon !   Machine-guns ! . . .   The
French army ! The French army ! . . . Fly ! Fly !"
and in a minute it was filled from end to end with the surging rushing river of our followers, each man running because
everybody else did.

Out into another street we turned, and into yet another
and another, and along them kept the uneven tenor of
our way, until before us appeared a city gate, leading out
into the desert.

Toward this we streamed, some of us yelling, "_Kill !_"
others, "_Fly !_" . . . others, "_Franzawi ! Franzawi !_"
. . . some in search of secular salvation, others the salvation of their souls and life-everlasting, through the slaughter
of the Infidel.

Through the gate thundered the yelling mob and, as
the inevitable moment approached when those who run
begin to ask, "What precisely _are_ we running for ? " de
Redon began to slacken his pace, drop back into the crowd,
and to edge toward the side.

Snatching at my wrist as he did so, he turned about,
dropped into a walk, and, a moment later, limped lamely
and blindly into a yard-wide opening between two high
native houses.

Excited and hurried out of my normal poise and dignified deportment of a perfect little gentleman, I was moved,
for no particular reason, to smite him with the flat of my
sword where the seat of his trousers should have been,
and to hound him along with such opprobrious epithets as
I had learned.

"Quicker! Quicker! Misbegotten son of a dog!" I howled; and belaboured the poor half-blind tottering creature in the best Oriental manner.

We rounded a corner, and de Redon laughing heartily, straightened up.

"Splendid!" he said. "But I'll borrow the sword and drive *you*, next time. . . . Splendid!" he gasped. . . .

"Now we'll cut in ahead of Bouchard and his Zouaves and try to get you into the Residency with them. . . . Come on. . . ." and he started running again.

We turned a corner and ran into a gang of looters.

Some were yelling, wrangling, squabbling, in front of a house, while others appeared to be literally turning the house inside out.

As a bed, fittings and occupant complete, came flying over a balcony, de Redon executed a number of those dance-steps which had already won my admiration, while defying emulation so far as I was concerned.

Scarcely slackening his pace, he spun round and round like a top, whooping fiendishly. This interested the looters not at all, and we passed on unmolested—my immediate wonder being whether the occupant of the deciduous bed were an invalid, and my immediate decision being that at any rate he soon would be. . . .

Turning again and dashing through a narrow stinking close, we heard a dreadful scream, that pierced the more distant din of the shouting and fighting.

In a dark and deeply-recessed porch, the back of which was an open door, a man stood with one foot on the breast of a child—a little girl, whose skinny arm he appeared to be turning and twisting from her body in his effort to secure the wide thick armlet of silver, which was apparently too small to pass the elbow.

I have to testify that de Redon was into that doorway before I was.

Turning with a fierce snarl the brute snatched a great knife from his sash, as de Redon, unable to swing his staff up, used it like a spear. The end of the staff went home with a pleasant thud, and drove the man sprawling back against the wall.

Raising the knife, he sprang at de Redon, seizing the staff in his left hand as he did so; and I simultaneously swiped the brute with my heavy sword.

It was the first time in my life that I had struck a man in anger, and I did it unskilfully . . . so unskilfully that, though he had every cause for complaint, he had no opportunity. The sword was so sharp and heavy, and wrath and indignation had so nerved my arm, that I had split his skull and killed him dead as a door-nail.

"*Mon Dieu!*" observed de Redon, as the man went down, taking the sword with him. "Don't you hit me with that sword any more."

Picking up the sobbing child, I lifted her inside the heavy door, and shut her in the house.

"Papa and the men-servants all gone to the fair, I suppose," observed de Redon, as we ran on down the alley. . . .

This same alley became a tunnel which led into a small square. As we came out into this, the noise became terrific, and, looking down a narrow bazaar which joined it to a main street, we saw that this latter was packed with a dense crowd of armed men all streaming along past the end of it.

"Bouchard will never do it," said de Redon, slowing up. "He should have stayed where he was posted. . . . Perhaps they burnt him out, though. . . .

"Look here," he continued, "if you turn to the right at the end of this bazaar, I expect you'll know where you are. It leads straight to the Residency. . . . Suppose you try to get in, and let Levasseur know what's happening. . . . Tell him Bouchard is fighting his way from the market-square to the Residency, and that I say he'll need help. Then Levasseur can use his own discretion as to whether to make a sortie. . . . I'll go along with the crowd and try the ' French-Army-with-cannon-behind-you ' game again. . . . Good luck, *mon ami*. . . . If anyone interferes with you, give him one like you gave our late friend in the doorway. . . . Good-bye. . . ."

And those were the last words spoken to me by Captain Raoul d'Auray de Redon of the French Secret Service.

"Good-bye, old chap, and good luck," I said, and, a minute later, we were into the crowd, de Redon attracting all the attention he could by whooping, twirling his staff, spinning round and round, and howling like the demented dervish he was impersonating.

I, on the contrary, hugging the wall, made my way along in the opposite direction as unobtrusively as possible, and attracted no attention. It struck me as I dodged, elbowed, pushed and evaded the impulsive pedestrian traffic, that, in a way, a fugitive is a good deal safer in time of tremendous public uproar and disturbance than during profound peace, inasmuch as everybody is far too excited to be observant.

Anyhow, not a soul molested me as I went along muttering, gesticulating and foaming at the mouth. It is a curious fact that I did not taste the fragment of soap which I had placed beneath my tongue.

§ 3

In a few minutes, the throng thinned and slackened and I found that this crowd had detached itself from the outskirts of the vaster one that surrounded the Residency.

Here I made quicker progress, and eventually came, at a run, into a dense mob that filled the street and faced in the direction in which I was going.

Backward and forward they moved, as the front ranks advanced and retired, and into these front ranks I could only make my way by clinging tight to posts, throwing myself down against walls, or diving into doorways, whenever the mob was driven back.

At last I was where I wanted to be, and looked upon a stirring scene of battle, murder and sudden death.

A regular siege of the Residency was in progress, a siege enlivened by constant assault.

From every window, balcony, roof-top, wall, minaret, tower, doorway and street corner, a steady fusillade concentrated upon the building, while, every now and then, a great company of wild death-seeking fanatics rushed at the low wall that surrounded its compound, only to break and wither beneath the blast of the steady rifle-fire of the defenders, and to find the death they sought.

Crisp and timely, crash upon crash, came the volleys from the treble tier of fire of the troopers at the wall, the windows and the roof. Wave after wave swept forward and broke upon that steady rock, throwing up a white spray, as survivors of the ordeal-by-fire sprang on the low wall, and the bayonets of the French soldiers.

And, the whole time, a ceaseless rain of bullets struck the house, so that it was in a nimbus of its own dust—a kind of halo of its own glory and suffering, as each bullet registered its impact with a puff of whitewash, dust and powdered brick. . . .

How to get in there ? . . .

From the surrounding wall, from every window and balcony, and from the parapet of the flat roof, the rifles of the defenders cracked unceasingly. It would be plain and simple suicide to advance openly, dressed as I was, and it would be suicide of a more unpleasant kind to strip off my Arab head-dress and *burnous*, and so proclaim myself a Christian.

Edging along the walls of houses, crawling on all fours, dashing from doorway to doorway and shelter to shelter, I gradually made my way from among those who played a comparatively safe and waiting rôle—onlookers who would turn to looting murderers as soon as the wall was cleared, and the doors beaten in—until I was among the fighting fanatics who made the frequent hand-to-hand attacks upon the low wall, the wall that must be captured before the house could be set on fire or taken by assault.

There was a hellish din from the hundreds of guns and rifles banging in all directions, and the continuous animal howling of the mob.

It would have been impossible in this inferno to hear what anybody said, and the wild rushes that broke upon the wall were the outcome of herd instinct and mob-intuition rather than of any definite organization, orders and leading.

Suddenly everybody would dash forward, the mouth of every street vomit hundreds and hundreds of men, and a great sword-waving mob would surge across the open, hack and hew and slash as it reached the wall, waver and fall back—and then turn and run for dear life to the lanes, alleys, buildings and compounds from which it came.

And, each time, the litter of dead and wounded increased and lay ever thicker along the wall. Soon the besiegers would be able to charge straight over the wall on a ramp of bodies. . . .

From where I crouched in a deep gutter, my head and shoulders behind a stone post or mounting-block, I could see two sides of the Residency, and did not doubt that it was under heavy fire on its two garden sides.

As I watched and cast about in my mind for a plan, the strange psychology of mobs decreed another sudden simultaneous assault, and I found myself running and yelling with the best—or the worst—in a desperate charge upon the desperately defended wall.

Let it not be supposed that I displayed heroism or strove to find a hero's grave. Far from it. I displayed such prudence as was possible, to avoid getting into the front rank of the rush, and rather strove to keep a hero's body between me and the rifles as we ran. And when at last I reluctantly found myself bounding over the prostrate forms of those behind whom I had hitherto been sheltered, I promptly joined them in their biting of the dust, until a living wall of humanity was once more between me and the wall of stone.

Leaping to my feet again, I made another rush at the spot where the fighting-line was thickest and cast myself at the feet of the brave.

Of the feet of the brave I soon had more than sufficient, for they were planted heavily on every portion of my person, as the un-led unorganized hordes again retreated.

Left high and dry by this ebbing tide of horny-hoofed humanity, I found myself within a few feet of the wall, and one of hundreds of motionless, or writhing and twitching bodies.

Of the defenders of the wall I could see nothing save their gleaming bayonet-tips, the occasional *képi* of someone who ran crouching along, and the heads of watchful sentries placed at intervals.

A moving cap halted, rose slowly upward and a man looked over the wall.

Now was my chance.

Raising myself on my hands, I shouted :

"*Hi ! Monsieur ! Je suis Americain ! . . . Je suis un ami ! . . . Aidez-moi ! . . . Je viens. . . .*"

And down I flopped with the utmost alacrity as the worthy man, with a swift neatness, theoretically quite admirable, drew and fired an automatic pistol.

Though he had drawn and fired practically in one movement, his aim was extraordinarily good, for the bullet hit the ground within an inch of my head.

I believe I gave an excellent rendering of the rôle of a dead Arab.

And I decided to play this easy part until there were again some braver men than I, between myself and that wall. Nor did I have long to wait.

With a howl that seemed to achieve the impossible by drowning all other sounds, the mob charged again, materializing with astonishing swiftness, and in astounding numbers.

A shout, a whistle, a sharp order . . . the wall was lined with heads and rifles . . . and I fairly burrowed into the filthy dust with my nose, as a volley crashed out . . . again . . . again . . . and I felt as though I should be blown away upon the blast. . . .

With my hands protecting my head, I endured the rush and trample for a few seconds ; and then, with a bound and the record sprint of my life, I flung myself at the base of the wall, as a rifle seemed to blow my head off, and a bayonet tore my filthy *kafieh* just beside my neck.

As I fell and snuggled into the friendly base of that lovely wall, I thought I was blind and deaf and probably dumb, or " alternatively," as the lawyers say, quite completely dead.

Quickly, however, I decided that none of these things was so, as I could see filthy feet and brawny brown legs scuffling around me, and hear the sounds of combat, and shout a curse when a charging, bounding *ghazi* landed fairly on my stomach, and, for a few minutes, that seemed like a few hours, I was kicked, trampled, trodden and struck until I was almost driven to spring up and take my chance at the wall . . .

And suddenly I was free, and the feet that had trampled me, were either once more in headlong flight, or else stilled in death.

Free also I was to make all the row I wished, in French, and to tear off my Arab head-dress and reveal myself to whomsoever would lend me his ears. . . .

But I remembered the shoot-first-and-ask-afterward gentleman with the automatic, and restrained my inclination to poke my head over the wall.

Something had to go over the wall, however, so I lifted up my voice and started, more or less tunefully, to bawl in French, a version of a song which I had very often heard on the lips of Colonel Levasseur, and the tune of which I had often heard soldiers singing and whistling on the march. In point of fact, Major de Beaujolais had picked it out on the piano and sung it at Mary's request after dinner only last night—the Marching-Song of the Legion . . .

"Tiens voilà du boudin ! voilà du boudin ! voilà du boudin !
    Pour les Alsaciens, les Suisses et les Lorraines;
    Pour les Belges il n'y en a point,
    Pour les Belges il n'y en a point,
    Car ce sont des tireurs au flanc.
    Pour les Belges il n'y en a point,
    Pour les Belges il n'y en a point,
    Car ce sont des tireurs au flanc.

I sang, or rather shouted, and I was heard.

A head suddenly appeared over the wall. . . . Hell! It was my friend of the automatic, and most markedly I did not move.

"*Tiens!*" I cried. "*Voyez!* and also *Regardez!* and *Ecoutez!* and all that, *et ne tirez pas.* Don't shoot the singer, he's doing his best, and have you seen the pen of my aunt, *parceque je suis Americain et Anglais, et Français, et bon garçon et votre ami. Oui! Oui! Je vous aime, Monsieur le Sergent. Comment allez-vous ce matin, et Madame votre femme et tous les petits sergents?* . . . 'Kiss me Hardy,' said Nelson, and 'War is Hell' replied Sherman."

The man's head and shoulders came up over the wall, and, placing both hands upon it, he leant right over and stared at me, his mouth open and his eyes starting from his head.

"*Que le diable emportez-vous?*" the Zouave growled. "Who the devil are you and what the hell are you doing there?"

And with a watchful eye upon his empty right hand, I raised myself from the ground, swiftly gabbling that I was a friend and guest of Colonel Levasseur, that I brought most urgent and important information, and that he must either call the Colonel instantly, or let me come over the wall.

The wary man's right hand disappeared from sight, and I flopped back into the dust as it returned holding that beastly automatic.

Damn the thick-headed fool! I had torn off my head-dress exposing my fair neck, ears and hair, and the mob would charge again at any minute.

"When I shout 'Come,' jump over the wall and throw yourself on the ground," bawled the quick-witted clever man whom I had so miscalled. "And lie down quick on this side, or I'll blow your head off," he concluded and disappeared.

"*Come!*" he shouted a second later, and I fairly threw myself over the wall and at the feet of the Sergeant, while he and several of his officious braves covered me with their rifles.

"Colonel Levasseur will be round here in a minute. You stay like that till he comes," said the Zouave Sergeant, and, as he turned away, bade two of his men to shoot me if I moved, or if they felt like it.

I proceeded to play at Living Statuary and tried not to twitch a muscle even when flies endeavoured to explore my brain by way of my eyes, ears and nose.

Among the men who crouched lining the wall were many others who lay at full length upon the ground, dead or too badly wounded to make further effort. The garrison had suffered heavily, both from rifle-fire and from the constant hand-to-hand *mêlées*, when the swords of the Arabs had met the bayonets of the soldiers.

As I watched, a military surgeon, followed by four hospital-orderlies, or stretcher-bearers, came round the corner of the house, and, in spite of the continual heavy fire, had the severely wounded carried away, and the dead laid in a row where they would not cause the feet of the fighting-men to stumble. The less-severely wounded were bandaged where they sat with their backs to the wall.

" What's this ? " asked the Surgeon-Major, whom I knew well, as he passed me. " An Arab prisoner ? What do you want *prisoners* for ? "

" True," I answered, to his great astonishment, " especially when they are not only civilians but neutrals."

" *Mon Dieu !* " ejaculated the Major. " But you look a pretty bloody neutral and a fairly war-like civilian . . ." and he bent over the still form of a Zouave. . . .

Colonel Levasseur came round the same corner, cool as on parade, followed by his *officier d'ordonnance*.

" 'Evening, Colonel," I called, rising to my feet. " Excuse a certain disorder of dress. . . ."

" Good God ! It *is* you, Vanbrugh ! " he said, seizing my hand and leading me into the house. " *Where's your sister ?* "

" De Beaujolais has taken her away with him," I replied,

" and Captain de Redon says they have got clear of the town. . . . And I am to tell you that a detachment of Zouaves, under Bouchard, is fighting its way here, and is held up in the Street of the Silversmiths . . . a huge mob between them and you. . . ."

" And you fought your way in here to bring them relief ? " cried the good Colonel, and for one dreadful moment I thought he was going to embrace and kiss me. " You shall get the Cross of the Legion of Honour for that, my brave friend. . . . You have offered your life for Frenchmen and for France. . . ."

"Fought nothing, Colonel," I assured him. . . . " Offered nothing. . . . I snooped around in a great funk, pinched these rags from dead men's backs, and crawled in here on my tummy. . . . But if you'll give me a rifle and a quiet corner, I can hit a running Arab at twenty yards, especially if he is running at *me*."

Levasseur smiled.

" Up on the roof then," he said, " and snipe their snipers. There are some swine with Lebel rifles on neighbouring high buildings, who are doing a lot of damage. . . . Take care of yourself. . . . Better put on a *képi* and tunic before you go up—you look like the President of all the Dervishes and you might get a bayonet in you before you could explain. . . . Excuse me, I must get Bouchard's lot in. . . . Down the Street of the Silversmiths, you said ? . . ."

Outside the room which the Surgeon-Major had turned into an operating theatre, there was a pile of blood-stained clothing and accoutrements. From among these I took a *képi*, regimental jacket, pouch-belt and rifle, and made my way up through the well-known interior—so familiar and yet so utterly different—to the roof, the parapet of which was lined with sharp-shooters who kept up a continual independent fire at surrounding minarets, watchtowers, and roofs of higher houses, which overlooked and commanded this one.

"Hi! Who are you?" cried a bearded officer crouching against the wall opposite the little stone porch, built over the top of the steps that led to the roof.

I knew him by sight but couldn't remember his name. "Colonel Levasseur's guest, Vanbrugh," I shouted. "He told me to come up here."

"Run across and lie down here," he called back, and I noticed that he drew his revolver as I did so.

"Excuse me," he said, "I didn't recognize you—I don't think that *Madame votre mère* would do so, either. . . . Now, if you can get the sportsman who is ensconced in the corner of that roof *there*, you'll have earned your corn for the day. . . . He's shot four of my men already, in spite of the bad light. . . ."

So, for a brief space, I was an unenlisted man, fighting for France and my own skin. It was extremely exciting and thrilling, and one was too busy to be nervous. Snap-shooting by flickering firelight, mingled with bright moon-light, is very interesting.

The sniper and I fought our little duel out. . . . I got quite fond of him. . . . R.I.P. . . . Perhaps my rifle was better than his, though I had no fault to find with the latter when it took my *képi* from my head, nor when it spoilt the perfectly good collar of my unbuttoned jacket. . . . The light was good enough for him, any-how. . . .

I was aware of the increasing sounds of approaching volley-firing. Evidently Bouchard's detachment were over-coming resistance and fighting their way in.

The officer in command of the roof was sending more and more men over to the side that commanded the square, so I went across to that side too, chiefly with the object of getting a good view of the show when the Zouaves burst into the open, and charged through.

Cautiously I peeped over the parapet.

Another assault was impending, and down the Street of the Silversmiths came the swiftest of those who were fleeing before the Zouaves.

At their head was a figure that I recognized—an almost naked scarecrow that spun round occasionally as he ran, and twirled a great staff above his head.

I rushed to my officer and indicated de Redon to him, and then with a brief " Excuse me," cast military propriety to the winds, dashed across to the stairs, and down them in search of Levasseur. . . . I could not run round to every officer, non-commissioned officer, and soldier in the building, and point out de Redon to him individually— but I had some sort of idea that Levasseur might sound the " Cease fire ! " while de Redon did his work and then rushed off elsewhere. . . .

I made a swift tour of the upper floor, of which each window and balcony was crowded with soldiers, behind whom lay the bodies of those who would fight no more.

I had expected to find the Colonel on the big wide verandah that ran the length of the front of the house, on either side of the vast roof of the colonnaded porch. This verandah had a low wall or parapet and, like the compound-wall below, was lined with soldiers.

Levasseur was not here, and, as I glanced below, I saw great masses of men gathering to surge across the square in a mighty overwhelming wave once more. I saw a mob come rushing down the Street of the Silversmiths, and de Redon—far ahead of them—bounding, leaping, twirling and yelling in front of the main attack opposite the front of the Residency.

" *Back ! Back !* " he howled. " *Beware ! Beware !* . . . *The big guns are coming.* . . . *Run !* . . . *Run !* . . . "

I also ran, down the stairs that led to the entrance-hall, and out into the compound, where the soldiers—whose fire-control was admirable—crouched along the wall like statues with levelled rifles, awaiting the volley-signal.

As I rushed past the bearers of a pitiful blinded Zouave, and down the steps under the porch, I saw Colonel Levasseur, standing between his second-in-command and his aide-de-camp, pointing with raised arm, and, as I saw him, I received a tremendous blow that knocked me down. I thought someone had hit me, looked round, and got to my feet, feeling very queer. . . .

What was it that I had been about to do ? . . . Something very urgent and important. . . . De Redon !

As I reeled forward, trying to shout, Levasseur's voice rang out with tremendous volume and authority. . . . He was still pointing. . . . He himself was ordering a volley ! . . . I staggered towards him mouthing silently. . . .

With a great crash, every rifle along that side of the compound was fired. . . . The earth rose up and hit me or else I fell to the ground. . . .

Another great shout from Levasseur. . . . Another volley. . . .

I tore myself from what seemed the powerful grip of Mother Earth, steadied myself, and saw de Redon doing exactly what I was doing, standing, swaying, tottering, his hands pressed to his breast. . . . Why was he imitating me ? . . . Why could I not shout to Levasseur ? . . .

De Redon fell heavily, head foremost. . . . So did I. . . . Why was I imitating him ? . . . A great faintness. . . . A grim fierce face before my closing eyes. . . . An Arab about to slay me ? . . . No, a feathered head-dress —a face more powerful than that of any Arab. . . . Thank you, Chief. . . . Dogged does it. . . . Grit . . . and grit . . . and iron guts. . . .

I was on my feet again ; breathing more easily too ; pulling myself together again ; coming round ; blood running down my chest and arm. . . .

I reached Levasseur's side somehow—and found I could not speak !

" *Vous êtes bien touché, mon pauvre ami !* " he said, in his great rough kindly voice.

I could not make a sound in answer, and he turned from me and bawled another order. The aide-de-camp shouted something about going inside and finding the doctor.

I tried to pull my jacket off and he gave me a hand, thinking I was trying to get at my wound.

Dropping my *képi* on the ground by the jacket, I made

for the wall, wearing only an Arab garment like a long shirt, and very baggy Arab trousers—both garments filthy and covered in blood, mine and that of their late owner.

I managed to get over the low wall without being grabbed by one of the defenders, and a stumbling, tottering run brought me to where de Redon lay in his blood.

Stooping to give him a hand, I found that it would only be a hand, for my right arm had ceased to function. It merely swung numb and useless, as I bent down.

De Redon did not move. I seized him and began to drag him in the direction of the wall. . . . His rotten rags tore away, and I fell. . . . The pain, for which I had been subconsciously waiting, began then, and I think it stimulated me.

I got up again and turned de Redon over. I wanted to get a grip on something he was wearing. Lift him I could not, with only one arm and scarcely the strength to keep myself erect. It seemed beastly to pull him by the arm or leg or hair. . . . He was most obviously dead. . . . Horribly riddled. . . .

None the less, I must get him. . . . I would *not* go back without him, and, with a word of apology I seized his wrist and began to drag. . . .

I was astonished to find myself alive.

Why was I not shot by one side—or both ?

I concluded that the very few on either side who had time to notice me, took me for a friend. The French soldiers were not firing independently but were awaiting the order for the next volley, and they had seen me run out from the compound. The Arabs saw a blood-stained Arab, escaping presumably from the French ; but they would begin to shoot at me as soon as they saw me dragging a body to the compound. . . . Or would they think me mad ? . . . Anyhow I was going on the return journey, making good time, and in another minute I should be at the wall. . . .

Was it *possible* that not three minutes ago I had been up on the roof exchanging pot-shots in a friendly and sporting spirit with a very competent sniper ? . . .

A few more yards and . . .

There was a sudden deafening crescendo of the infernal din, a hellish roar from ten thousand throats . . . a crashing volley . . . another . . . and I was hurled head-long, trampled flat, smashed and ground and crushed, a living agony—until a smashing blow upon the head was a crowning mercy that brought oblivion.

§ 4

I must have been unconscious for a very long time— or, what is more probable, I must have been unconscious and semi-conscious, off and on, for hours—as I have a recollection of terrible battle-dreams, of receiving further injuries, and of being partly buried beneath a heavy weight.

When I awoke, or regained full consciousness, the sun was setting and the battle was over. . . . Gradually I realized that I must have been where I was, for nearly a day. . . . Absolute silence reigned where the very spirit of devilish din had so long rioted. . . . I was lying where I had fallen. . . . The body of a big Arab lay across my legs. . . . The head of another was on my stomach, face downwards. . . . More were sprawled and huddled close against me. All very intimate and cosy together.

With great effort and greater pain, I slowly turned my head in the direction of the Residency, and beheld its charred and blackened ruins affronting the rising sun. The compound wall appeared to be hidden by the piles of dead.

I hoped that the garrison had died in the compound and not in the burning building. I thought of the wounded laid out in rows in the corridor outside the operating-room.

My next effort was in the direction of self-help, and was fruitless. What I earnestly desired to do was to remove the head of the dead Arab from the pit of my stomach, where it seemed to have the weight and size of a mile-stone.

I soon discovered that it would be all I could do to re-move a fly from the end of my nose, and that by the time I did it the fly would be gone. I don't suppose I could

K

have moved if those two bodies had not been lying upon me. I had lost a great deal of blood, from two bullet wounds in the neck and shoulder, and a bad sword-cut on the head. . . .

It is a truth as well as a truism that we don't know our blessings when we receive them. In fact it is impossible to tell a blessing from a curse. But for those wounds, I should have got back into the Residency and died with the rest. When that enthusiast with the sword did his good deed for the day, he saved my life (and a life worth a thousand of mine, as well) and I never even saw his bright countenance.

That night was just endurable, but to this hour I do not greatly care to dwell upon the day that followed. How much was delirium, nightmare-dream, subjective horror, and how much was real, I do not know. But there were unutterable agonies of thirst and terrible pain, and the unbearable burning of the sun upon one's exposed unmoving flesh; there were vultures, kites and pariah dogs; prowling ghouls who robbed the pitiful dead ; times when I gained full control of my faculties and lost them again in paroxysms of screaming terror, pain and fear—silent screams that did not issue from cracked black lips.

And always there were flies in thousands of millions.

At times I was mad and delirious; at times I must have been mercifully unconscious; and at times I was quite clear-headed, and perhaps those were the worst.

I distinctly remember concluding that my father was right and that I was wrong. There was a Great Good God of Love and Mercy who let us be born filled with Original Sin and who had created an Eternal Hell for all that sinned. I had sinned—and here I was, nailed down and being slowly roasted, in unspeakable pain, for ever and for ever. Yes, Father was right, and Noel and I had been wrong in agreeing that such would not be the nature of a God of Love, but rather of a Devil of Hate.

I believe that I slept when kind beneficent Night succeeded hellish torturing Day. At any rate, I was unconscious for most of the time, and remember nothing but occasional glimpses of the stars, and then, with shrinking abject terror, seeing the sun rise.

That was the last of conscious suffering, for I remember no more, and I afterwards learned that I had a very narrow escape of being buried alive when the French relief-force arrived and began clearing up the mess.

It was my white skin that saved me. The men of the burial-fatigue party who were removing my body with those of hundreds of others, noticed that I was some kind of a European, and drew the attention of their Sergeant to the fact. This man informed an officer, and the officer discovered that I was alive as well as white—in parts.

In the military hospital I was most kindly and competently nursed, and, when fit to be moved, I was transferred to Algiers that I might have the benefit of sea-breezes, ice, fresh fruit, better food, and the creature comforts unprocurable in the desert city of Zaguig.

And here I told my tale to the authorities, or rather to the very charming representative of the authorities who visited me in hospital.

Having given all the information that I could, concerning the fate of the garrison of Zaguig, I sought for news of de Beaujolais, but I forbore to mention that my sister was with him. . . . He had seemed so very averse from taking her, and had made the military impropriety of such a thing so clear, that I thought it best to say nothing on the subject—particularly when I found that they knew absolutely nothing as to his fate, and did not expect to do so for weeks or months. My informant professed absolute ignorance of de Beaujolais' destination even.

I decided that, whether the doctors released me from hospital or not, I would remain in Algiers until there was definite news of de Beaujolais. I would then fit out a caravan and go in search of him and of my sister. . . .

After a certain point, I did not progress very favourably. My wounds healed well, but I suffered most appalling headaches—whether from the sword-cut or from sunstroke did not seem clear. At times I thought a splinter of bone must be pressing on my brain, but the admirable surgeon assured me that the bone was not splintered at all, and that the headaches would grow less frequent and less painful.

They did neither, and I decided that I would go to London and see Sir Herbert Menken, then considered the greatest consulting-surgeon in the world.

And while I was slowly gathering energy and still putting off the evil day of travel, Mary arrived, well, smiling, radiantly happy, and engaged to marry Major de Beaujolais.

She had accompanied him to his destination and returned with him to Zaguig, fearing the worst so far as I was concerned. Here they had heard of my escape, and a black cloud had been lifted from Mary's mind—for the joy and happiness of her engagement to the man whom she had "loved at first sight" had been darkened and damaged by her fear—fear amounting almost to a certainty—of my death.

However, she had hoped against hope, and had moreover been conscious of an illogical but persistent belief that I was not dead.

She assured me that one corner of her mind had not been in the least surprised when they got the astounding news that I had survived and was, in fact, the sole survivor of the massacre. . . .

Mary and I took up our temporary abode at the Hotel Splendide at Mustapha Supérieur, and she nursed me while de Beaujolais reported himself and his doings to the military authorities, and obtained furlough for his marriage and honeymoon.

I went with them to Paris after the wedding, where de Beaujolais shopped assiduously with Mary and showed himself not only brave but *foulard*-y, and thence, alone and very lonely, ill and miserable, I went on to London in the desperate hope that Sir Herbert Menken could do something to relieve my almost unbearable headache, insomnia, neurasthenia and general feeling of hopeless illness.

I was quickly coming to the point where either something must be done to me, or I must do something to myself —something quite final, with a pistol.

CHAPTER VI

HOW shall hasty and impatient Man know his blessings from his curses, his good from his evil?

Good came upon me at this time in most terrible form, and in my ignorance I prayed to be delivered from my good, from the blessing that brought me my life's usefulness and joy. . . .

I arose on this particular morning, in London, feeling ill and apprehensive, afraid of I knew not what, but none the less afraid. I was in the grip of Hell's chief devil—Fear—the fear of something wholly unspecified.

Having dressed, with trembling fingers, I avoided the hotel dining-room and, as early as was reasonable, I set forth, bathed in perspiration, to keep my appointment with Sir Herbert Menken.

"Taxi, sir?" inquired the Jovian hall-porter, as I passed the counter behind which he lurked, all-seeing and omniscient—and it was borne in upon me that his query was absurd. *Of course* I could not enter a taxi! What a horrible idea! . . . I would as soon have cut my throat as get into a taxi—or any other vehicle.

"Good Heavens, no!" I replied shuddering, and passed out into the street, much perturbed at the man's horrible suggestion.

Dreading and hating the throng, the noise, the traffic, I made my way along the street, feeling as I had never felt before, and as I pray God I may never feel again.

I would have given anything to have been back in Zaguig with all its murderous dangers, provided I could have felt as I did there.

I was not in pain . . . I did not feel definitely ill in any

149

definite part of my body . . . I was not afraid of anything to which I could give a name . . . And yet I felt
terrible. Every nerve in my body shrieked to God for
mercy, and I knew that unless I did *something* (but what,
in the name of Pity ?) and did it quickly, I should go mad
or fling myself under a street-car or truck. . . .

I fought my way on. . . .

Merciful Christ have pity ! This was suffering such as
the Zaguigans could never have caused me with knives
or red-hot irons. . . . Where was I ? . . . *What* was
I ? . . .

Suddenly I knew what I was. . . .

Of course ! I was a shell-fish deprived of its shell, and
wholly at the mercy of its environing universe. Yes, I
was a creature of the crustacean kind, a sort of crab or
lobster, without its armour. Every wave of ether could
strike me a cruel blow ; the least thing touching me would
cause me agony unspeakable—even rays of light impinging
upon my exposed nerve-surfaces would be,—nay, *were*—
as barbed arrows, spears and javelins. . . .

If a passer-by brushed against me, I should shriek—a
flayed man rubbed with sand-paper. . . . Yes—I was a
naked crustacean, and I must find a hole into which to
creep. . . . A nice hole beneath a great rock ; a hole just
big enough to contain, without touching, me. . . . There
I should be saved from the eyes and hands, the mouths
and antennæ of the million-headed . . .

But I could see no hole into which to creep. . . .

I took a grip upon my courage, and passed on, in search
of one—a beautiful dark cave, just big enough . . .

I reached the end of the block and was about to step off
the side-walk when I realized my new danger. If I stepped
into the road, the flood of traffic that streamed along it
would bear me away irresistibly ; away, on and on, into
some wild and whirling Charybdis, wherein I should for
ever go round and round with accelerating velocity for all
eternity, never, never to find the beautiful dark cave that
was my great necessity. . . .

I had had a narrow escape from a terrible danger, and I drew back from the gutter, and crouched against some railings. These seemed friendly. At any rate, they did not hurry along, nor whirl round. I clung to them, conscious of the stares of the curious as they hurried past, immersed in their own affairs, but with a glance to spare for mine.

Two errand-boys passed, one in a many-buttoned uniform.

" Blimey ! 'E's 'ad a 'appy evenin' somewheres," observed one of them. " 'E sang *'Won't be 'ome till mornin'*—and 'e ain't."

" Yus," agreed the other, eyeing me with a large toleration, " some people 'as all the luck."

I tried to give them money, to get them to go away and cease to look at me, but my hand so shook that I could not get at my pocket.

I turned my face to the railings and, peering through them, saw that they guarded an " area " or small paved yard on to which looked the basement-windows of the house. And into this yard, some twenty feet below me, opened the door of a coal-cellar, or some such place—a dark, quiet, beautiful cave into which one could crawl and be safe from mocking eyes and jeering voices, from touching hands and feeling antennæ, from *everything* that could, by the slightest contact, agonize one's utterly exposed and unprotected surfaces.

If only I could get to that dark beautiful cave ! . . . But if I loosened my grip of the railings I might fall, or be carried along until I was thrust into the dark river of the roadway and whirled to destruction never-ending.

I moved along the railings, not releasing one hand-grip until I had secured the next, and the perspiration streamed down me as I concentrated every faculty upon this difficult progress to the gate that I could see at the head of a flight of stone steps, leading down to my cave of safety. . . .

And then a Voice smote me, and I looked over my shoulder, my heart in my mouth.

" What's the game, Sir ? " said the Voice.

It was a vast and splendid London policeman, one of those strong quiet men, wise, calm, unarmed, dressed in a long authority, the very embodiment of law, order and security, the wonder and admiration of Europe.

Terrible as it was to be addressed and scrutinized, I felt I could bear the agony of it, because these men are universal friends and helpers to all but evil-doers.

" I am an unshelled crustacean . . . I want to get down to that cave," I said, pointing.

" Crushed *what* ? . . . Want to get home, you mean, I think, Sir," was the reply. " Where's that ? "

" In America," I said.

" Longish way," observed the policeman. " Where did you sleep last night, if it isn't asking ? "

" At my hotel," I replied.

" Ah—that's better, Sir," said the good fellow. " Which one ? . . . We might get back there perhaps, eh ? "

" No, no—I couldn't . . . I simply could *not*," I assured him. " I would sooner die . . . I *should* die— a dreadful death. . . ."

" *Pass along, please !* " said the policeman suddenly and sharply, to the small crowd that had collected. " 'Ere, you—'*op* it—quick," he added to a blue-nosed loafer, who stood gazing bovine and unobedient. . . .

I can remember every word and incident of that truly terrible time, for myself stood apart and watched the suffering wretch that was me, and could give no help, could do nothing but look on—and suffer unutterably.

" Now then, Sir," said the policeman, " if you can't go 'ome, an' you won't go to your 'otel, where *can* you go ? . . . We all got to go somewheres, y' know. . . .

" You don't want to come along o' me, do yer ? " he added as I pondered his dark saying that we must all go somewhere, shook my head in despair, and clung to the railings.

" With *you* ? Where to ? " I asked, with a new hope.

" Station," he replied. " Sit down in a nice quiet

little—er—room—while we find out something about yer."

"I should love it," I told him. "Could you put me in a cell and lock the door?"

"You'd have to *do* somethink first," the kindly man assured me.

This seemed a splendid chance! Fancy being concealed in a beautiful dark cell until my shell grew again and there was something between my exposed nerves, my bare raw flesh, my ultimate innermost self, and the rough-shod rasping world!

"If I gave you a sovereign and thumped you on the chest, would you arrest me for assault and lock me up?" I asked. "Do—for Mercy's sake . . . I'll give you anything you like—all I have."

"*Come*, come now, sir," expostulated the officer, "you let me put you in a taxi, and you go back to your 'otel an' go to bed an' 'ave a good sleep. . . . If you don't feel better then, you tell 'em to send for a doctor. . . .

"You a teetotaller?" he added, as I stared hopelessly at his impassive face.

"Practically," I said. "Not in theory, you know, but . . ."

"Any'ow you ain't drunk *now*," he admitted, sniffing, and added briskly, "Come along, now, sir! This ain't no way for a gent to be'ave at ten o'clock of a Monday morning," and, turning to the lingering passers-by, suddenly boomed, "*Will* you passer*long*, please," in a manner that swiftly relieved me of the painful stare of many gazing eyes.

One man did not pass along, however, nor go by on the other side. . . . No Levite, he. . . .

He was a small neat man, very well dressed in a quiet way.

"You are like a moth," I said. "For God's sake spread your wings over me. . . . My shell has come off. . . ."

Of course he was like a moth. He had great black eyebrows and deep luminous eyes . . . sphinx-like, he was . . . the sphinx-moth. . . .

I had seen moths with just such eyebrows, and eyes shining in the lamp-light. . . .

" Ill ? " he asked, and took my wrist between finger and thumb. " What's your name and address ? "

" I don't know," I replied. " Do help me . . . I'm in Hell—body and soul . . . and I shall shriek in a minute. . . . For the love of God help me to find a cave or a hole . . ."

" Come along with me," he said promptly, " I've got a beauty. . . ."

He stared hard into my eyes, and in his I saw goodness and friendship, and I believed and trusted him implicitly. . . .

I had fallen into the hands of the greatest alienist and nerve-specialist in England. . . . Coincidence ? . . .

Tucking his arm through mine, he detached me from the railings, led me to the house, close by, in Harley Street, where he had his consulting-rooms, gave me a draught of the veritable Waters of Lethe, and put me to bed on a sofa in a back room.

Without troubling to discover whether I was a pauper, a criminal, an escaped lunatic, or a prince in disguise, he took me that night to his far-famed nursing-home in Kent.

And here, my salvation, in guise incredible, most wonderfully awaited me.

§ 2

At Shillingford House, a great old mansion of warm red Tudor brick, Dr. Hanley-Blythe kept me in bed for a week or so, visiting me upon alternate days and submitting me to an extraordinarily searching cross-examination, many of the questions of which, I was at first inclined to resent. I soon realized, however, that there was absolutely nothing in the specialist's mind but the promotion of my welfare, and I answered every question truthfully and to the best of my ability.

One day, after carefully and patiently extracting from me every detail of a ghastly dream that I had had the previous night—a dream in which I dreamt that I murdered my father—he asked :

"Did you love your father when you were a boy ? "

"Yes," I replied.

"Certain ? " he queried.

"Er—yes—I think so. . . ." I said.

"*I* don't. In fact I know you didn't," he countered.

I thought a while, and realized that the doctor was right. Of course I had never loved my father. I had respected, feared, obeyed and *hated* him. . . . He had been the Terror that walked by day and the Fear that stalked me by night. . . .

"Face the facts, my dear chap," said the doctor. "What is, *is*—and your salvation depends on freeing your mind from repressions, and making a new adjustment to life. . . . The truth will make you free—and whole. . . . Get it up, and get it out. . . ."

I pondered deeply and delved into the past.

"I am sorry to say that I have always hated my father," I confessed. "Feared and hated him terribly. . . ."

"Yes—and you made your God in your father's image," said the doctor. . . .

"I have ' feared God ' but not hated Him," I replied.

"Nonsense ! " exploded Dr. Hanley-Blythe. "Don't we hate *everything* and everyone that we fear ? . . . Fear is a curse, a disease, a deadly microbe . . . the seed of death and damnation. . . . Since we are speaking of God—get rid of that foul idea of ' fear God.' . . .

"*Love* God. . . . What decent God would rather be feared than loved ? . . . Let's have a God that is a *little* more divine than a damned savage Ju-Ju ! . . . That cursed injunction to *fear* God ! . . . Killed more souls and bodies than anything else. . . . Love God and fear *nothing* ! . . . Some sense in that. . . .

"Now look here—get your father in perspective. He's a poor human sinner like yourself and me. A man of like passions with us. . . . Probably always meant for the best—and did his best—by you. . . . Nothing to *fear*— a frail sinner like the rest of us. . . . No power over you now, anyhow. . . .

"When you go to sleep to-night, say out loud :

"'Poor old Dad! I feared and hated you—but now I do neither. . . . I never understood you—but I do now.' Then say, also out loud, 'God means Good, and Good means God. . . . God is Love and Love is God.' . . . See ?"

And another time.

"You are a bachelor ? . . . Well, you shouldn't be. . . . No healthy man has a right to be a bachelor at your age. . . . And you have always lived the celibate life in absolute chastity ? . . . Hm ! . . . We shall have to find you a wife, my boy ! . . . I prescribe sunshine and fresh air, occupation and plenty of it, a trip to see your father—whom you will smite on the back and address as 'Dear old Dad—you heavy-father old fraud'—*and a wife.* . . . Yes, a wife, *and*, in due course, about three sons and two daughters. . . .

"What do I think caused your breakdown ? . . . I don't 'think'—I *know*. . . . Your father, of whom you had too much, and your wife whom you never had at all. . . . Caused a neurosis, and when you got physically knocked out at Zaguig, it sprang up and choked you. . . . And now get up and dress and go out in the grounds and sit in the sun and realize what a harmless old chap your father is, and what a kind friendly fatherly jolly old God made the beautiful jolly old world that we muck-up so much. . . . And think over all the girls you know, and decide which one you will ask to marry you. . . . *Marriage will be your sure salvation.* . . . I prescribe it. . . ."

A couple of nurses—kind devoted souls—helped me into an invalid chair and wheeled me out into the grounds. They found me a beautiful hidden spot among great rhododendron bushes where I should be safely concealed, protected from the rear and on either hand, and have a glorious view of the rolling Kentish park-land before me. They assured me that the path by which we had come was very rarely used, and left me in my wheeled chair to wonder whether I should ever be a man again. . . .

. . . " Think over all the nice girls you know, and decide which one you will ask to marry you. . . . *Marriage will be your sure salvation.*"

There was only one woman in all the world, and she was already married. . . .

I hope no-one in this world suffers as I suffered in mind and body during those days.

§ 3

I believe that there really are people to whom " experiences " of the psychic and super-normal order are vouchsafed.

I have both read and heard of well-attested cases of dreams and appearances, inexplicable voices, and waking visions whereby information was imparted, or help sought.

Nothing of that sort has ever occurred to me.

I have not, on looking into my mirror at night, beheld the agonized and beseeching face of the woman who needed my help beyond all things, the woman whom I was to love and to marry.

I have not dreamed dreams and seen visions in which such a woman has implored my instant aid and told me exactly what to do, and how, and when and where to do it.

I have not heard a mysterious voice, clear and solemn as a bell, speak in my astounded ear and say, " Come. I need you. Hasten quickly to such-and-such a place and you will find. . . ."

I have seen no ghost nor apparition that has given me a message.

Nothing of the sort.

But the following fact is interesting.

I sat in my retreat, one day, thinking of Isobel, wondering where she was and what she was doing, whether she were happy every minute of the day, and whether it would be my fate ever to see her again. . . . Long, long thoughts between waking and sleeping. . . . And then with shaking hand and fumbling trembling fingers I opened a book that one of the nurses had left with me, " in case I felt like reading for a little while." . . .

And, opening at random in the middle of the book, I read :

" . . . his vision of her was to be his Faith and Hope and was to be all his future. She was to be his life and his life was to be hers. . . . For he was a Worshipper, a Worshipper of Beauty, as were they who lived ' or ever the knightly years had gone with the old world to the grave,'—they to whom the Face was not the face upon a coin, the pale and common drudge 'twixt man and man, but the face of a beautiful woman, the Supreme Reality, the Focus of Desire—that desire which is not of the body, not of the earth, not of the Self, but pure and noble Love—God's manifestation to the world that something of God is in man and something of man is in God. . . . This knight thus worshipped God through the woman, with a love that was spiritual of the spirit, with no taint of Self. . . . And his motto and desire was Service. . . . Her service without reward ; the service that is its own reward. . . . For he felt that there must come for the World's salvation from materialism and soul's death, a Renaissance, a Reformation —of Love. . . .

" Love that was once the road to all perfection ; man's cry to God, to Beauty, to the Beauty of God and the God of Beauty. . . . Love that once leapt free from flesh and cried aloud, not, ' Love me that I may be blessed and comforted and rendered happy,' but ' Let me serve thee with my love, that I may help and bless and comfort thee and render thee happy. . . .' Love that was Service, the highest service of God

through the service of His noblest expression—Woman. . . .
Love, that divine selfless thing, Man's great and true salva-
tion, the World's one need, the World's last hope. . . .

" *He would dedicate his life to the service of this woman,*
asking of her nothing more than that he might dedicate his
life to her service in the name of Selfless Love, the Love that
is its own reward, its exceeding rich reward. . . ."

and at the sound of a footstep, I here looked up—and
beheld Isobel.

§ 4

Isobel, actual and alive . . . looking older and looking
ill and pale and too ethereal, and lovelier if possible.

Our eyes met. . . . For a second we stared incredulous.

" *Isobel !* " I cried, still dreaming.

" The dear nice American boy ! " she whispered.

Tears came into her beautiful eyes, her sweet and lovely
face grew yet paler, and she swayed as though about to faint.

With a strength that I certainly had not possessed a
minute before, I sprang to my feet, caught her in my arms
and lifted her into the chair. Her need and weakness
gave me strength, and I was ashamed—ashamed that I
had sat trembling and shaking there—envying any healthy
hobo that tramped the road—longing for death and thinking
upon ways of finding it. . . .

Isobel ! . . . *Here !* . . .

She must be a patient of Dr. Hanley-Blythe . . . ill
. . . in great sorrow, judging by the look upon her lovely
face. . . .

I was shamefully conscious of noting that, by her dress,
she was not a widow. . . . And then I rose above my
lowest, and strove to put myself aside entirely. . . .
Isobel was here—and ill. . . . Surely I could serve her
in some way, if only by wheeling her about in a bath-chair
. . . reading to her. . . .

" I can't believe it. . . . I must be dreaming . . ."

she said as these thoughts flashed through my mind.

" Oh, dear American boy—will you help me. . . . I am in such trouble. . . ."

Help her ! Would I *help* her !

My illness fell from me, and I stood erect, and strong— I who had recently been assisted to crawl to that invalid's chair, a wretched trembling neurotic. . . .

" John . . . my husband. . . . They have taken him. . . . Oh ! . . ." Her eyes brimmed over and her trembling lips refused their service. . . . She covered her face and gave way to tears. . . .

Her husband ! . . .

I knelt beside the chair. . . . By the time my knee had touched the grass, I had crushed back the thoughts, "Her husband. . . . ' They ' have taken him. . . . Dead by now, probably. . . . ' *Think of all the girls you know.* . . . *Marriage will be your sure salvation .'* . . ."—and I was unselfish and pure in heart—purified by the clear flame that burnt within me, before this woman's altar that was my heart.

" Tell me," I said. . . . "And then believe ! Believe with all your soul that I can help you somehow. . . . Be sure of it. . . . *Know* it. . . . Why—surely I was created for that purpose. . . ."

I was a little unbalanced, a little beside myself, and more than a little inspired. . . .

And I inspired Isobel—with hope. . . . And with faith and with belief—belief in me, her servant.

Under the influence of my assurance and re-assurance, she told me her pitiful tale from beginning to end. . . .

I sat on the ground beside her chair, and she forgot herself and me as she poured out her woe and trouble— poured them out until she was empty of them, and their place was filled by the hope which I gave her, the faith that I had—for the time, even the *certainty* that I felt.

When she had finished, I took her little hand in both mine, and looked into her eyes.

" I *know* he is alive," I said. " I am as certain of it as I am that we are here together. He is alive and I will find him. I will not only find him but I will rescue him and bring him back. *Alive and well, I will bring him back to you. . . .*"

And at that moment I believed what I said. There is no such thing as " chance "; and God had not brought me to that place for nothing—nor to make a mock of us for His sport. . . .

What Isobel told me on that golden English summer afternoon—as I sat beside her chair, in a short-seen Seventh Heaven of bitter happiness and sad joy, listening to her voice with its soft accompaniment of the murmuring of innumerable bees in immemorial elms—is indelibly written on the tablets of my memory, and I can tell it exactly as she told it to me.

CHAPTER VII

" I SHALL tell you absolutely everything—right from the beginning," whispered Isobel. " That is the least I can do—after what you have just offered . . . and promised. . . . Everything, right from the beginning. . . . What it was that caused them to disappear . . . and caused their deaths. . . . Oh, those splendid boys. . . . And John, my own darling, John . . ." and she wept anew.

" John is alive," I said. " And he's coming back to you. . . . Believe me. . . . Trust in me. . . ."

" I do," she answered. " Oh, I do. . . . You have given me new life. . . . I always felt that you could and would do anything that you promised. . . . I have always liked you so much. . . . Otis. . . .

" I'll tell you *everything*. . . . You would hardly believe it. . . . You remember Claudia, of course ? . . . The loveliest girl. . . ."

" Yes," I said. " ' Queen Claudia of the Band.' . . . Michael loved her very much, I think. . . ."

" Michael worshipped her," agreed Isobel. " He would have died for her. . . . He did die for her—in a way. . . . Poor wonderful noble Beau. . . . It nearly broke John's heart. He came back so different . . . poor John. Michael and Digby both. . . . Yes, John returned different in every way, except in his love for me. . . . Oh, John ! . . ."

" Michael and Digby *dead* ? " I exclaimed. " *Beau Geste* dead ? . . ." This was horrible. What had happened?

" Yes, and Claudia is dead too," replied Isobel. " She was Lady Frunkse. I expect you read that she married

162

Sir Otto Frunkse, 'the richest man in England.' . . . A motor-smash. . . . You must have seen it in the papers ? . . . She lived—or rather died—for three days. . . . Poor Claudia—she was blinded and terribly disfigured by broken glass, and her back was broken. . . . Her husband went out of his mind for some time. He loved her passionately—and he had bought her . . . and he was driving the car . . . and was not quite sober. . . .

"She asked for me on the last day. I was in the room at the time. . . . She knew she was dying. . . . Her mind was absolutely clear, and she did not want to die until she had made a confession. . . . She asked me to tell everybody— after her death. You are the only person I have told. . . . I want you to know everything that concerns John. . . . It was very dreadful. . . . Only her mouth was exposed. . . . In that vast golden room and colossal Chinese bed, poor lovely Claudia was merely a mouth. I knelt beside her and held her poor groping hand and she whispered on and on . . . and on. . . .

"I'll try to tell you.

"'Is that you, Isobel?' she said. 'There is no-one else here, is there ? . . . Listen. . . . Tell this to my Mother— Aunt Patricia is my Mother—and to John and Otto and George Lawrence, everybody—after I am dead. . . . I cannot tell my Mother myself . . . Digby knows, now . . . And poor little Augustus . . . My Father knows too. I think he knew at the time. The mad know things that the sane do not. . . . Poor darling "Chaplain,"—we all loved him, didn't we, Isobel ?

"'Didn't you love Beau too, Isobel ? Really love him, I mean. . . . I worshipped the ground he trod on. . . . But I was only a girl—and bad. . . . I was bad. . . . Rotten. . . . I loved money and myself. Yes, myself and money, more than I loved Beau or anything else . . . anyone else. . . .

"'And Otto had caught me. . . . Trapped me nicely. . . . It served me right. . . . How I loathed him, and feared him too—and I actually believed he would let me be disgraced—let me go to prison—if I did not either pay him *or marry him ! . . . It was more than two thousand pounds. . . . It seemed like all the money in the world to me, a girl of eighteen. . . .*

" ' *And if I married him I should be saved—and I should be the richest woman in England. . . . I thought it was a choice between that and prison. . . . Otto made me think it. I couldn't doubt it after he had sent his tame solicitor to see me. . . . The awful publicity and disgrace and shame. . . .*

" ' *But Michael saved me—for a time. . . . He saved me from everything and everyone—except from myself. . . . He couldn't save me from myself. . . . And when he was gone, and Otto was tempting me and pestering me again, I gave way and married him—or his money. . . .*

" ' *Isobel, it was I who stole the " Blue Water "—the mad fool and vile thief that I was. . . . I thought I could sell it and pay what I owed Otto—and a dozen others—dressmakers and people ; shops in London. I must have been mad—mad— with fear and worry. . . .*

" ' *Michael knew—before the lights came on again. . . .* ' "

Isobel broke off here and wiped tears from her cheeks.

" I must tell you about that, Otis," she said. " You heard about the great sapphire, ' Blue Water,' when you were at Brandon Regis, I expect ? It was kept in a casket in a safe that stood in the Priests' Hole—and the Priests' Hole is really undiscoverable. Its secret is never known to more than three people, though scores of people are taken to see the chamber. It is said that nobody has ever discovered the trick of it, in four hundred years.

" Aunt Patricia used to show the ' Blue Water ' to favoured visitors, and sometimes she would have it out and let us handle it and gloat over it. It lived on a white velvet cushion under a thick glass dome in the steel casket.

" One night—it was not long before I last saw you— we were sitting in the drawing-room, after dinner, and Claudia asked Aunt Patricia if we might have it down and look at it again. We hadn't seen it for ages. The Chaplain

—who was one of the three who knew the secret of the Priests' Hole—went and got it, and we all handled it and loved it. Then the Chaplain put it back on its cushion and put the glass cover over it—and suddenly the electric light failed, as it often used to do, in those days.

"When the lights came on again—the 'Blue Water' had disappeared. . . . Everyone denied having touched it—and next day, Beau ran away from home. . . . Then Digby disappeared. . . . Then John—and I was the most miserable girl in England. He told me, quite unnecessarily, that he had not stolen the wretched thing, and of course we also knew that neither Beau nor Digby was capable of theft.

"They joined the French Foreign Legion . . . and . . . and . . . Michael was killed . . . and Digby was killed . . . but John came back safe and sound—but *oh*, so changed . . . and now . . . *they have got him again*," and the poor girl broke down and wept unrestrainedly.

"I'll bring him back," I said, keeping a powerful grip upon myself, lest I put my arms about her, in my yearning ache to comfort her. "I *know* I shall find him and bring him back. . . ."

"Why—so do I," she smiled. "I believe it. . . . I feel it's *true*. . . . God bless you. . . . I . . . I can't . . . I. . . ."

My eyes tingled.

"I'll finish telling you about Claudia," she said. . . . "Poor Claudia went on :

"'Yes, *Michael knew*. . . . *He came to my bedroom that night*. . . . *I was in bed, wide awake, and in a dreadful state of mind*. . . . *I felt awful*. . . . *Filthy from head to foot*. . . . *I was a thief, and I had robbed my Aunt, my greatest benefactress*. . . . *I did not then know that she was my Mother—she only told me when the Chaplain died and she was broken-hearted and distraught*. . . .

"'*Michael crept in like a ghost*.

"'"CLAUDIA," *he whispered*, "GIVE ME THE 'BLUE WATER.' I AM GOING TO PUT IT BACK. THE KEY IS IN

THE BRASS BOX ABOVE THE FIREPLACE IN THE HALL AS
AUNT SAID."

"'*I pretended to be indignant—and talked like the hypo-
crite and liar that I am. I ordered him out of the room, and
said I'd ring the bell and scream if he did not go at once.*

"'"CLAUDIA," he said, "GIVE IT TO ME, DEAR. . . . IT
WAS ONLY A JOKE, OF COURSE. . . . LET ME PUT IT BACK,
CLAUDIA. . . . NO-ONE WILL DREAM THAT IT WAS YOU
WHO TOOK IT. . . ."

"'"*No-one but* you, *you horrible cad*," I said. "*How*
dare *you*. . . . *How* could *you*. . . ."

"'"DON'T, DEAR," he begged. . . . "DON'T. . . . I
KNOW! . . . YOU BRUSHED CLOSE TO ME AS YOU MOVED
TO THE TABLE AND AS YOU RETURNED TO WHERE YOU
WERE STANDING. . . . YOUR HAIR ALMOST TOUCHED MY
FACE. . . . DON'T I KNOW THE FRAGRANCE OF YOUR
HAIR, CLAUDIA? . . . COULD I BE MISTAKEN. . . .
SHOULDN'T I KNOW YOU IF I WERE BLIND AND DEAF—
AND YOU CAME WITHIN A MILE OF ME? . . . HAVE I
WORSHIPPED YOU ALL THESE YEARS, CLAUDIA, WITHOUT
BEING ABLE TO READ YOUR THOUGHTS? . . . I KNEW
IT WAS YOU, AND I WENT AND STOOD WITH MY HAND ON THE
GLASS SO THAT IT WOULD LOOK AS THOUGH I WAS IN THE
JOKE TOO, IF ISOBEL TURNED THE LIGHTS ON WHILE YOU
WERE PUTTING IT BACK. . . . GIVE IT TO ME QUICKLY,
DEAR—AND THE JOKE IS FINISHED. . . . OH, CLAUDIA
DARLING, I DO LOVE YOU SO—AND I HAD NOT MEANT TO
TELL YOU UNTIL YOU WERE OLDER. . . . GIVE IT ME,
DEAREST CLAUDIA. . . ."

"'*His voice came to me out of the darkness, like that—and
I was* racked, *Isobel*. . . . *I loved him, you see*. . . .
*And I loathed Otto, and I had to have two thousand pounds
or marry him—or go to prison—I verily believed.*

"'*And I stood out against Michael, and lied, and lied,
and lied, and pretended to be indignant—hurt—enraged—
wounded . . . and I called him horrible names, and all we
said was in dreadful tense whispers.*'

"'"CLAUDIA! CLAUDIA!" he said. "YOU CAN'T

POSSIBLY DO IT. . . . I KNOW IT'S ONLY A JOKE—BUT DON'T PLAY IT ANY FURTHER. . . . IF IT DOESN'T BRING HORRIBLE DISGRACE AND HURT UPON YOU, IT WILL BRING DISGRACE AND HURT UPON SOMEBODY ELSE—ISOBEL, DIGBY, JOHN, GUSSIE. . . . AND EVEN IF YOU WENT MAD AND DID SUCH A THING, YOU COULDN'T GET AWAY WITH IT. . . . NOBODY WOULD BUY IT FROM YOU. . . . GIVE IT ME, DEAR. IT IS SUCH A *DANGEROUS* PRACTICAL JOKE TO PLAY ON A PERSON LIKE AUNT PATRICIA. . . .''

" ' *And he begged and begged of me to give it to him—and the more certain he was that I had got it, the angrier I grew. . . . Isn't it incredible—and isn't it exactly what a guilty person does? . . .*

" ' *At last he said :*

" ' " LOOK HERE, THEN, CLAUDIA. I AM GOING AWAY TO MY ROOM FOR AN HOUR. . . . DURING THAT TIME THE ' BLUE WATER ' IS GOING TO FIND ITS WAY BACK. *SOME-ONE* IS GOING TO PUT IT IN THE DRAWING-ROOM BEFORE— SAY ONE O'CLOCK—AND AUNT WILL FIND IT IN THE MORN- ING. . . . AND NOBODY WILL EVER KNOW WHO PLAYED THE SILLY TRICK. . . . I SHALL GO DOWN MYSELF, LATER ON, AND SEE THAT IT IS THERE. . . . SPLENDID ! . . . GOOD-NIGHT, DARLING CLAUDIA . . .'' *and he faded away like a ghost.*

" ' *I lay awake and lived through the worst night of my life. . . . I could not go down and put it back—tacitly con- fessing to Michael that I was a thief. . . . I loved him so, and I valued his good opinion of me more than anything— except my beastly self. . . . If he had come back then, I should have given the horrible stone to him. . . . I should . . . And later I grew more and more angry with him for suspecting me—and I got up and locked my door and bolted it. At about four o'clock in the morning I weakened and grew afraid of what I had done. . . . I saw myself arrested by policemen. . . . Taken to prison . . . in the dock . . . tried and sentenced to penal servitude.*

" ' *I added cowardice to wickedness, and at last, overcome by fear, I jumped out of bed, took the " Blue Water " from the* toe of a riding-boot where I had hidden it, slipped on a dressing-gown and mules, and crept downstairs. Every board seemed to creak, and my heart was in my mouth. I dared not carry a candle nor switch on any lights.

"'Every stair and board, I trod on, creaked and groaned, and I felt that every soul in the house must know what I was doing. . . . And suddenly I knew I was being followed, and I think that perhaps that was the most dreadful moment of my life.

"'"AUNT PATRICIA," I thought, and I nearly shrieked. I felt that if she turned on the lights and caught me there, with the "Blue Water" in my hand, I should scream myself insane. . . . And then a cold hand touched me, and I did scream—or thought I did—before I realized it was the hand of a man in armour. . . .

"'And then my one need was to get rid of that awful jewel. I rushed to the fireplace and fumbled at the high mantel for the brass box in which Aunt Patricia had put the key. I found it, and hurried on, to the drawing-room door. The noise that I made in opening it sounded like thunder, but by that time, all that I cared about was to be rid of the sapphire, and back in my room before I was caught. It didn't matter to me who was suspected of having taken it. . . .

"'And as I reached the table on which the glass cover stood, someone entered the room.

"'Do you know, I believe my heart really stopped beating as I waited for Aunt Patricia to switch the lights on. . . .

"'And then a voice said, "OH, THANK GOD, DARLING. . . . I KNEW YOU WOULD. . . ."

"'It was Michael.

"'And in the sudden and utter revulsion of feeling, I could have cursed him. . . . I had been so absolutely certain that it was Aunt Patricia, that I was utterly enraged at the fright he had given me. . . .

"'And can you believe that I turned about and marched out of that room, to bed, without a word, still clutching the "Blue Water" in my hand? . . . Later he came and tapped softly

*and turned the handle. He stayed there for over an hour,
tapping gently with his finger-nails and turning the handle.
. . . And I lay there trying not to scream . . . trying to
get up and give him the sapphire . . . trying not to get up
and give him the sapphire. . . . And as the time wore on,
I got more and more frightened at what I had done. . . . In
the morning, I got up and went out into the rose-garden and
he came to me there.*

" " " LAST CHANCE, CLAUDIA DEAR," *he said.* " GIVE ME
THE 'BLUE WATER' NOW, AND THERE SHAN'T BE A BREATH
OF SUSPICION ON YOU. . . . IF YOU DON'T, IT IS
ABSOLUTELY *CERTAIN* THAT YOU'LL GET INTO THE
GHASTLIEST TROUBLE. AUNT IS BOUND TO GET TO THE
BOTTOM OF IT. . . . HOW COULD SHE IGNORE SUCH A
BUSINESS—EIGHT OF US THERE. . . ? AND SUSPICION
WILL BE ON POOR LITTLE GUS—AT FIRST. . . . YOU
CAN'T *POSSIBLY* SELL IT. . . . GIVE IT TO ME AND I'LL
GIVE YOU MY WORD NOBODY WILL EVER *DREAM* THAT
YOU. . . ."

" ' *I burst into tears. . . . I had had such an awful night,
and I was so filled with anger and fear and* hatred—*hatred
of Michael and Otto and of all the men in the world—that
I broke down. . . . I nearly gave it to him. . . . And
after breakfast I did give it to him, too late, and I told
him I loathed him utterly, and that I hoped that I should
never set eyes on him again ! . . . I never did, Isobel,
as you know. . . . And I have never had a happy hour
since. . . .' "*

Isobel paused and wiped tears from her eyes. I would
have left her but that I felt it was good for her to talk and
get it all out.

" Poor, poor Claudia," she went on. " She died that
night. Sir Otto Frunkse went insane for a time. I
thought Aunt Patricia would die too. Claudia was all she
had, after the Chaplain died and Michael was killed. . . .
She blamed herself for the boys' deaths. . . . And now,
John ! . . . Oh, John ! . . . John ! . . ."

"Why did she blame herself?" I asked. "Surely it was Claudia's—er—act, that led to Michael's and Digby's going away. . . ?"

"I will tell you everything, as I said," replied Isobel. "It's wonderful to have a Father Confessor and friend . . . and you are going to find John for me. . . . I *know* you are. . . . I feel as though I were coming out of a tomb. . . . You have lifted the cover a little already. . . . I shall tell you everything. . . .

"Michael knew that Aunt Patricia had sold the real 'Blue Water'—sold it to the descendant of the Rajah from whom it had been—acquired—by her husband's ancestor, in India. . . . She had a right to sell it, I believe, as her husband gave it to her as a wedding-present. . . . This man, Sir Hector Brandon, used to leave her for years at a time. He was a very bad man—a bad husband and a bad landlord. . . . I know that she put almost every penny of the money into the estate. . . . She had had a model of the 'Blue Water' made before she parted with the original. . . . Michael ran away with this model. He thought it would be a splendid way of covering up what Claudia had done, and of what Aunt Patricia had done, too —and Sir Hector was about to return to England. . . . Poor darling Michael—it was just what he *would* do! . . . It must have seemed such a simple solution, to him, and the end of terrible and dangerous trouble for the two women he loved. . . . It saved Claudia from shame and disgrace and from Aunt Patricia's anger, and it saved Aunt Patricia from her husband's. . . . Sir Hector Brandon would simply think that Michael had stolen the 'Blue Water,' and Aunt Patricia would think that he had stolen the dummy—in ignorance of its worthlessness."

§ 2

This Beau Geste! . . . It was an honour and a boast to have known him! . . . And those two women—that mother and her daughter! . . . My God! . . .

§ 3

"Uncle Hector never came home after all," continued Isobel. "Nor Beau either. . . . Nor Digby. . . . And now, *John*—my John! . . . Oh, Claudia, the trouble and misery and tragedy you caused that night! . . ."

"Tell me about John," I said.

That would do her more good than anything. . . . I had learnt from Dr. Hanley-Blythe, and from my own experience, what repression can do to one!

"When Michael ran away, taking the suspicion and the blame, and Digby followed him to share it, John felt that he must go too. You see the three boys had always done *everything* together, all their lives. And John felt that they were shielding him because nobody would dream of suspecting Claudia or me—and there was a reason why Gussie should not be suspected. As a matter of fact, I was in a position to prove his innocence—as well as my own—for I had hold of his arm the whole time that the room was in darkness. . . . So it was *John or Claudia*—and John went. . . . Then it *must* be one of the Geste boys. . . .

"John felt certain that Michael had gone to the French Foreign Legion because the very name of it had fascinated him, ever since a French officer had stayed at Brandon Abbas and told us about military life in Africa. . . . Why —you may have met him there! . . . De Beaujolais is his name. He was the son of an old school-friend of Aunt Patricia's and, at Eton, was the fag of George Lawrence, her second husband. . . ."

"No, I didn't see him at Brandon Abbas," I said. "But I saw him in Africa, in a place called Zaguig. . . . He saved my sister. . . . It's a queer little world. . . !"

"It *is* a queer world . . ." mused Isobel. "Think of that! . . . You know Major de Beaujolais! . . ."

"Related to him," I smiled. "My sister married him. . . . I mean he married my sister. . . ."

"*What* a coincidence!" said Isobel.

"Not it!" I ventured to contradict. "There are no

such things ! . . . It was no coincidence that Jasper
Jocelyn Jelkes ran away from Brandon Abbas and came
to my Grandmother's place . . . nor that a Colonel
Levasseur became enamoured of my sister and invited us
to Zaguig, with the result that I got all broken up . . . nor
that Dr. Hanley-Blythe chanced upon me when I was
just enjoying the nervous reaction from it ! . . . Go on
about John. . . ."

"He went to the French Foreign Legion, and there he
found Beau and Digby as he had felt certain he would.
. . . At the siege, by Arabs, of a fort at a place called
Zinderneuf, Beau was killed, and John stabbed the Commandant of the fort, in self-defence. . . . The man had
heard that Beau and Digby and John were jewel-thieves
and had a huge diamond ! . . . Digby wasn't at Zinderneuf. He came with the relief-party and was sent into the
empty fort. He saw Beau's body reverently laid out, beside
that of the Commandant—who had John's bayonet through
his heart. He went half mad and set the place on fire and
escaped to look for John, because John wasn't among the
dead. . . . He soon found him, because John had done
just the same thing—dropped from the wall furthest from
the entrance, and had run to the nearest sand-dunes. . . .
Then two friends of theirs, scouting or patrolling on camels,
found them, and the four of them got away together. . . .

"Then Digby was killed by a raiding party. . . ."

Her voice broke again and there was silence.

"Poor darling Digby. . . . He was such a kind, happy,
dear boy. . . . And after awful hardships and dangers,
just when escape seemed sure, the other three were stranded
in the desert without camels. . . . And they only had
about a quart of water. . . . And one of the two friends,
one they called ' Hank,' went off in the night . . . to give
John and the other man a chance . . . the water. . . .

"Then John and the other—' Buddy,' John called him
—got to a desert village and they stayed there a long time,
hoping to find the third man or to hear something of him.
. . . He had given his life for them. . . . And at last they

gave up hope, and found a caravan going south to Kano.
. . . There they got into touch with George Lawrence,
who was a Commissioner or something, in Nigeria. . . .

"And as soon as they were there, John's companion
turned round and went back to look for the lost man—
Hank. . . . They were a sort of David and Jonathan pair,
and the man said he was going to search until either he
found his friend or died. . . .

"John was too ill to go back with this man, Buddy.
. . . I have no doubt he would have done so, otherwise,
as soon as they had got camels and supplies. . . . Men
do such foolish things. . . . But John went down with
enteric, and nearly died. As soon as it was safe to move
him, George Lawrence brought him home. . . . Oh, I
nearly died of joy, although I cried and cried when I heard
about Michael and Digby. . . .

"And we were married. . . . And I was the happiest
woman in the whole world . . . for a time. I was *too*
happy, of course. . . . We aren't meant to be as happy
as I was, or we shouldn't want to go to Heaven. . . ."

"Oh, yes, we are," I interrupted, "and you are going to
be just as happy as that again. And it's *going to last*, this
time. . . ."

Isobel sighed and pressed my hand as she smiled gratefully at me.

"Yes—I was too happy," she resumed, "but it did not
last very long. . . . John did not recover properly. He
simply did not get fit again. . . . He had had a most
terrible time. . . . The deaths of Beau and Digby before
his eyes, and the awful hardships he had suffered, ending
up with this enteric or typhus, when he was so weak. . . .
George Lawrence said he looked like a dying skeleton when
he first saw him in Nigeria. . . . And even then of course,
he couldn't get proper nursing or invalid food. . . . It was
a marvel that he lived.

"Well—we hadn't been married long, before I saw there
was something very wrong with John. . . . He hardly
ate anything at all, and he scarcely slept. . . . I don't

think he ever got any sleep at all, at night. I used to hear him walking up and down, up and down, in the corridor. He would go out there so that he should not wake me, and then he would sit in his dressing-room and smoke for a while and read. He used to be able to doze a little in the afternoons, and I would make him sit in a long chair under the trees in the Bower—you know—where we used to play. . . . I couldn't get him to go to bed in the daytime, as he ought to have done.

" And if he fell asleep in the chair, he had horrible dreams and woke with a dreadful start, or else he would talk all the time. . . . That was how I found out what was really at the root of the trouble. He felt he had left his friend in the lurch—had deserted the man who would never have deserted him, abandoned the David who had gone back into the desert to look for his Jonathan instead of escaping when he had the chance. . . .

" I was so worried and frightened that I got Dr. Hanley-Blythe to come to Brandon Abbas. He wanted John to come here and be under observation, but John wouldn't hear of it. . . .

" Then one night, John was walking up and down in his dressing-room, and, as I was going to him, I heard him say, groaning, ' *I shall go mad if I don't go back!*' . . . I made up my mind immediately, and as I pushed the door wider open, I said :

" ' *John, darling, I know what is the matter with you,*' just as though I had had a sudden brain-wave. He stared at me. My heart seemed to turn right over—he looked so ill and so unlike himself, too—and I felt absolutely dreadful at the thought of what I was going to do. . . .

" ' *You must go back, darling,*' I said . . . ' *and find them. . . . I shall come with you—as far as Kano anyhow.*' . . . I meant to stay with him and never let him out of my sight, of course. . . . He stared and stared as though he could not believe his ears—and then his poor sad face lit up with joy, and I thought my heart would break.

" ' Isobel ! ' he said, and took me in his arms as though

he loved me more than ever, for what I had done. ' *You
see they may be alive . . . they may be slaves . . . they
may be in some ghastly native prison . . . they may be in
some place where they'll have to stay for the rest of their lives,
for want of camels. . . . Isobel—they offered their lives for
Digby and me when they helped us away from Zinderneuf.
. . . Hank gave his life for Buddy and me when he went off in
the night, and left us the drop of water. . . . Buddy saw me
safe to Kano before he went back to look for Hank. . . . And
I left them there, and am living in safety and luxury ! . . .
They may be alive. . . . There may be time to save them
even yet. . . . I can't sleep for thinking of them . . . in
Arab hands. . . .*'

" ' *We'll start as soon as you like, John,*' I said—and I
felt myself going dead, as it were—dead and cold at the very
heart of myself. . . .''

There was silence for a while, a silence broken only by a
little sob, and I looked away over the beautiful Kentish
scene. Should I let her go on ? Was it too painful to
be beneficial, or was it her salvation ? . . .

" You are distressing yourself," I said, moved almost
unbearably by her tears. . . . " Tell me the rest to-
morrow."

" Oh, no, no ! Let me tell you now. . . . If you
are not—tired. . . . Oh, if you knew the relief it is . . .
and the hope that you have given me . . . my friend-in-
need . . ." she answered at once.

" George Lawrence was wonderful," she went on, " and
Aunt Patricia did not raise a word of protest when he said
he would come with us. . . . Of course, his help would
be absolutely invaluable. He was in Nigeria for about
twenty years, himself, and could pull all sorts of strings,
give us the soundest advice and assist us in numberless
ways. . . . I think that Aunt Patricia realized it was a
life-and-death matter for John, especially after what Dr.

Hanley-Blythe had said to her. . . . What I did not then realize, was that George Lawrence's real object was to take charge of *me*, if anything happened to John when he went off into the real desert, right away from civilization and help. . . . He never expected that John would return alive, and he did not expect that John would ever get better if he did not go. . . .

" Do you know, John began to improve from that night —from the very moment that I had suggested his going back. . . . He went to bed and slept, and I heard him singing in his bath, the next morning ! . . . Several times during that day he actually whistled as he went about his preparations for the journey. He was a changed man, and I got some idea of what he had suffered by sitting idle while his friends whom he had ' deserted ' might be dying in the desert, or be living in captivity worse than death. . . .

" On the voyage from Liverpool to Lagos, he put on weight daily, and was almost himself again by the time we got there. . . . And then he revealed the plot hatched by George Lawrence !

" We were to go to friends of his, and I was to stay with them while John and he went on to Kano. After he had seen John off, with a proper caravan—to go to the village where he and his friend had lived while they had been searching for the third man—George was to return to me and take me home again ! . . . These two precious lunatics thought I was going to agree to *that*—and sit down quietly with George's friends for weeks and weeks, and then go quietly home without John.

" ' Oh, yes,' they said, ' George's friends are most delightful people ; have a charming house in quite the best part of Nigeria ; really very good climate at this time of year ; plenty going on, at the Club ; tennis, racing, polo, bridge and dancing ; I should have a lovely time. . . .'

" I didn't argue. I merely smiled and shook my head.

" When they realized, at last, that I was going with John, and that nothing on earth would stop my going with John, there was frightful consternation and alarm ! They even talked of abandoning the whole scheme and returning by the next boat. . . . I wouldn't hear of that, and they wouldn't hear of my attempting to make the caravan-journey into that part of the Sahara, one of the most water-less, hot and dangerous of deserts. . . . We compromised eventually. . . . I was to come with them to Kano, and John was to go on with the best guides, camels, camel-men, outfit and provisions that money could buy. He was to take special men, as messengers, too. He was to send a man back with a message, as soon as he reached the village, and send messages at regular intervals afterwards. . . . The men were to report to an English official at Kano, a Mr. Mordaunt—an old friend of George Lawrence, and he would cable news to us. . . . John promised that he would not go further north than Zanout, himself. . . . His idea was to promise a big reward to anybody who brought him genuine news, and he hoped to get into touch with one or two big men, Arab or Touareg chiefs, who are famous and influential in that part of the Sahara. . . . And to tell the great Bilma salt-caravan—thousands of people—about it. ...

"John thought that the 'desert telegraph'—that mysterious spreading of news which turns even the desert into a whspering-gallery—would soon make it known, far and wide, that a great sum was being offered by a rich European for news of two friends of his. . . . All sorts of *canards* would soon be flying about, and hundreds of false clues would be discovered. . . . And among tons and tons of chaff there might, one day, be found a grain of truth. . . .

"Poor John ! . . . Oh, my darling John ! . . . He was so hopeful. . . . He was so happy again, now that he was, at any rate, *trying* to do something for his friends—if only they were still alive. . . . There was hope that the second one was, and just a bare chance that the first one had been found and saved."

"You are tiring yourself," I said again, as Isobel fell silent.

" No, no ! Let me finish—unless you are tired yourself," she replied. " It does me good to tell you . . . and the sooner you know everything, the sooner you may be able to do something. . . ."

" John got to the place, where he had lived with his companion, in about three weeks, and sent back the first messenger. Nothing was known there, apparently, but he had hardly expected to get news so soon, and was still full of hope. Two more messages came, the second from Zanout, where he thought he had found a trace of the man he called ' Buddy.' . . . It seems the Touareg of those parts know the appearance and brand-marks of every camel, and the full history of every raid in which camels are stolen. John thought that Buddy and his caravan had been captured by Touareg or Tebu robbers, and the next thing was to find somebody who could give details as to the band and where they came from, and whether there had been any survivors of the caravan. . . .

" And then . . . And then . . . We got a cable from George Lawrence's Kano friend, *saying that John himself had been captured !* . . . Not by raiders. . . . He had been recognized by a French patrol and had been arrested. . . . Oh John, John, dear ! . . . I let you go back there —but you would have died if you had stayed here. . . ."

I could do nothing to comfort her—except reiterate my promise to find him and bring him back.

" George Lawrence was splendid again," she continued. " He took me back to Africa. . . . I would have gone alone if necessary. . . . Before going, he moved heaven and earth. . . . He went to the Foreign Office and the Colonial Office and to see several Members of Parliament and visited the offices of the London newspapers. Then he got into touch with his friend, Major de Beaujolais—who was at our wedding and knew all about John. . . . We went to Paris, and he saw various influential people there, and thence to Algiers to see the Commander-in-Chief. . . .

Everybody was most kind and sympathetic and helpless—
especially helpless in France and Africa. . . . '*Nothing
could be done. . . . The law must take its course. . . . We
civilian officials cannot interfere with the military authorities.
. . . We military officials cannot interfere with the civilian
authorities. . . . Fair trial, of course. . . . Court martial.
. . . Death penalty generally inflicted—very properly—in
cases of desertion in the face of the enemy. . . . Some very
peculiar features about this case moreover*' . . . and so-on.

"It was unspeakably dreadful to feel so powerless,
baffled and ineffectual. . . . I felt I must get as near as
I possibly could to the place—in Africa. . . . I must have
every scrap of news. . . . I lasted out—as far as Kano.

"Mr. Mordaunt was so kind and helpful. He had kept
the man who had brought the last information—a Touareg
camel-driver, hired in Kano. . . . This man had told the
whole story to George Lawrence, over and over again. . . .
They had found a soldier of the French camel-corps, who
had strayed or deserted from a patrol—apparently what
they call a *peloton méhariste*, out on a *tournée d'apprivoise-
ment* through the Touareg country. . . . John had be-
friended the man, of course—given him food, water and
a camel, and the man had gone straight off and brought
the patrol down on his benefactor. . . .

"From what this camel-man said, George Lawrence and
Mr. Mordaunt concluded that the soldier had recognized
John and had denounced him, for reward and promotion, or
else—having had enough of desertion in the desert—to
ingratiate himself with the leader of the patrol and palliate
his offence. . . .

"Anyhow, what was perfectly clear, was that John had
been captured and arrested in French Territory by the
'competent military authority'—as a deserter from the
Legion. . . .

"*Oh John, John, my darling! . . . Shall I ever see you
again! . . .*

"And when I had learned everything there was to learn
at Kano, I collapsed altogether, and only just didn't die.

. . . I think it was the belief that I might, somehow, be able to help John, that kept me alive. . . . It must have been a dreadful time for poor George Lawrence. . . . I remember very little about it, but I get fleeting glimpses now and again. . . .

"And here I am, Otis . . . and can do *nothing*. Everything possible has been done—and all we know, through the kindness of Major de Beaujolais, is that he is alive—or was—and is a convict in the Penal Battalions in Africa ! . . . Eight years ! . . . And then to return to the Legion to finish his five years there ! . . . *Eight years !* He couldn't survive eight months of that life. . . . And here am I—and I can do *nothing . . . nothing. . . .*"

"*I* can, though," I said, and arose to begin doing it.

§ 4

A week later, I was in Sidi bel Abbès—an earnest and indefatigable student of Arabic and of all matters pertaining to the French Foreign Legion and to the French Penal Battalions of convicts, as well—the "Zephyrs" or "Joyeux."

A fortnight later, I was an enlisted *légionnaire* of the French Foreign Legion, and, secretly, a candidate for membership of the Zephyrs.

It was my intention to see the inside of Biribi,[1] the famous or infamous convict depôt of the Penal Battalions, and only by way of the Legion could I do so. Thence, and only thence, could I possibly find John Geste, and until I found him, neither I nor anybody else could rescue him.

[1] Recently disestablished and abolished.

CHAPTER VIII

I HAVE very rarely found anything as good as I expected it to be, and almost never as bad. If the joys of anticipation are generally greater than those of experience, the terrors are almost always so, and the man who said, "We suffer far more from the calamities that never happen to us, than from those that do," talked sense.

I had expected life in the French Foreign Legion to be so rough, so hard, so wholly distasteful from every point of view, that I had anticipated something much worse than the reality.

It was hard, very hard; it was rough, wearisome, monotonous and wholly unpleasant; but it was bearable.

I don't think I could have faced the prospect of five years of it—unless, of course, it were for Isobel—but as things were, I contrived to carry on from day to day.

What made things worse for me than for some people, was the fact that I had no military leaning whatsoever, and that the soldier's trade is the very last one that I should voluntarily adopt.

Of course, if one's country is at war, and there is need of more men than the standing army provides, one is fully prepared to learn the soldiering trade, to the end that one may be as useful as possible as quickly as possible. But this was different, and to me, at any rate, the whole business seemed puerile, stupid, and an entirely unsuitable occupation for an intelligent man.

There was not one solitary aspect of life that was enjoyable, and I do not think that I was ever faintly interested in anything but the *salle d'honneur*.

This wonderful museum of military trophies and of concrete evidence of superhuman courage, devotion and endurance, did more than interest me. It thrilled me to the marrow of my bones, and I took every opportunity of gazing at the battle pictures, portraits of distinguished heroes, scenes from the Legion's stirring history—all of them, without exception, painted by legionaries who were survivors of the scenes depicted—or comrades of the men whose portraits adorned the walls.

Every captured standard, weapon, and other trophy, illustrated some astounding story, a story as true as Life and Death, and far, far stranger than any fiction that ever was conceived.

The single exhibit that thrilled me most was, I think, the hand of Captain Danjou in its glass case beneath the picture that told the story of the historic fight of sixty-five against two thousand two hundred better-provided troops ; a fight that lasted a whole day, and ended in the capture, by assault, of five wounded survivors—wounded to death, but fighting while strength remained to load a gun and pull a trigger.

What I suffered from, most of all, was a lack of companionship. There wasn't a comrade to whom I could talk English, and none to whom I cared to talk French, or what passed for French, in the Legion.

Stout fellows all, no doubt, and good soldiers, but there was not one with whom I had an idea in common, or who appeared to have a thought beyond wine, woman and song, unless it were food, money and the wickedness of non-commissioned officers.

One of my room-mates, a poor creature named Schnell, who appeared to me to be not only the butt and fool of the *escouade*, but also of Fate, attached himself to me and made himself extremely useful.

For some inexplicable reason, he developed a great admiration for me. He put himself under my protection, and in return for that, and some base coin of the realm, he begged to remain my obedient servant, and was permitted to do so.

I was to meet the good Schnell again—in different circumstances.

Things improved somewhat when, after some weeks, I completed my recruit's course, took my place in my Company and came under the more immediate notice of Sergeant Frederic.

§ 2

I did not look upon it as a piece of great good luck when I found that my Sergeant was an Englishman, and one of the best of good fellows. I regarded it rather as a Sign.

I never knew his real name, but he was a Public School man, had been through Sandhurst, and had served in a Dragoon regiment. How he had fallen from the Officers' Mess of a British Cavalry regiment to the ranks of the Legion, was a mystery, for he was one of those people in whom one cannot detect a weak spot, and with whom one cannot associate any form of vice or crime.

I often wondered.

It may have been debt, a love affair, or sheer boredom with peace-time soldiering, and I often hoped that he would one day be moved to tell me his story. Naturally I never asked him a question on the subject of his past. It can't be done in the Legion. . . . Not twice, anyhow.

Of course, a Sergeant cannot hob-nob with a *légionnaire*, walk out with him or drink with him, but Sergeant Frederic, as he called himself, gave me many a friendly word and kindly encouragement when we were alone ; and later, when we were away down in the desert, he would march beside me and talk, or come and chat in the darkness of bivouacs. On one occasion, when he and I were in the same mule-*peloton*, he and I were out on a patrol, or a *reconnaissance*, by ourselves, for a whole day, and he laid aside his rank and we talked freely, as equals, and man to man. It did us both good to talk English once again, and to converse with a man of our own level of education, social experience and breeding.

It made all the difference in the world, to me, that my Sergeant was a man of this type, and regarded me with the eye of friendship and favour. Moreover it was not unnoticed by the Corporals that I was a compatriot (as they supposed), and something of a protégé of the Sergeant.

Had I, at that time, proved a slack and inefficient soldier however, I am pretty sure there would have been a prompt end to the favour of Sergeant Frederic and his myrmidons.

Thanks to this position of affairs, I did not in the early days, have too bad a time in the Legion. It was hard, terribly hard, and I was only just equal to the life, physically speaking, when real marching began in earnest, and I took part in some of those performances that have earned the Legion the honourable title of " The Foot-Cavalry " in the XIXth (African) Army Corps.

At first I used to be obsessed with the awful fear that I should fail and fall out, and share the terrible fate of so many who have fallen by the wayside in Algeria and Morocco. But it is wonderful how the spirit rules the body, and for how long the latter will not give in, if the former does not. . . .

Time after time, in the early days, I was reduced to a queer condition wherein I was dead, not " from the neck, up," as we say, but from the neck, down. My head was alive, my eyes could see, my ears hear, but I had no body. My head floated along on a Pain. No, I had no body and I was not conscious of individual parts that had been causing me agony for hours—blistered feet, aching calves, burning thighs, cruelly lame back, cut shoulders. These were amalgamated into the one great amorphous and intangible Pain that floated along in the white-hot cloud of dust, and bore my bursting head upon it.

I used to think that I could be shot, when in that condition, without knowing it and without falling, provided that no vital part were hit, and that I should go on marching, marching, marching. . . .

For, once I had reached this condition, I was almost immune and immortal, indestructible and unstoppable—while the spirit held, high and unfaltering. But when the last " *Halte!* " was cried, and the voice of an officer rang out :

" *Campez*," and the Company Commanders bawled :

" *Formez les faisceaux*," and " *Sac à terre*," and the unfaltering spirit went off duty, its task accomplished, then the poor body had its way. . . . It trembled . . . it sagged . . . it collapsed . . . and it lay where it was, until kindly and more seasoned comrades dragged it aside and disposed its unconscious head in safety if not in comfort.

I fully and freely admit that this marching was the worst thing that I encountered in the Legion, thanks to my good luck in being in Sergeant Frederic's *peloton*. The next worst things were the lack of acceptable companionship and society, the deadly wearisome monotony, and the impossibility of natural self-expression for one's ego. I am no militarist, no " born soldier," and I wished at times that I had never been born at all.

It was on the occasion to which I have referred, the day when Sergeant Frederic and I were alone together, from before dawn to after midnight, that I asked him the question which probably surprised him more than any other that he had ever been asked. . . . We were riding at ease—so far as one can ride at ease on a mule. . . .

" How can a man who wishes to do so, make certain of getting sent to the Zephyrs ? " I inquired suddenly. " Just that and nothing worse—nor better . . . the happy medium between a death-sentence from a General Court-martial, and thirty days' solitary confinement from the Colonel." . . .

Sergeant Frederic laughed.

" The *happy* medium ! " he said. . . . " Well—they're called the ' *Joyeux* '! You're a queer chap, Hankinson.

. . . D'you mean you *want* to join the honourable *Compagnies de discipline?* Don't you get enough discipline here ? " and he laughed again. . . . " Well—I dunno— I suppose you'd find yourself in the Zephyrs all-right if if you gave me a smack in the eye, on parade, one morning. . . ."

That was a thing I most certainly should not do—and I little thought, at the time, that it would actually be through this most excellent chap that I should come to wear the military-convict uniform of the African Penal Battalions. . . .

" Better not risk it, though," he continued, smiling. " It is much more likely that you'd be shot, out of hand. . . . It is the law, even in peace time, that the death-penalty be awarded for the striking of any *supérieur*, no matter what the provocation—and no matter what the rank of the striker or the stricken. . . . And you know the awkward rule of the French Army, '*No man can appeal against a punishment until he has served the whole of it.*' "

" Yes. . . . Plenty of fellows do get sent from the Legion to the Zephyrs, though," I said. " What's the trouble usually ? . . ."

" You've got Zephyrs on the brain," was the reply. " Are you afraid you'll get sent there ? . . . Not the slightest fear of that, unless you wilfully get into serious trouble. . . . What do men get sent there for ? Oh, insubordination, desertion, damage to Government property, sedition—or just continued slackness and indiscipline. . . . The Colonel can give six months for that, and the General Court-martial can give you penal servitude, to any extent, for a serious ' crime ' or continued bad record. . . . Those who get themselves a term in the Zephyrs earn it all-right, and thoroughly deserve it, as a rule. . . . Almost always. . . . As far as I can remember the wording in Army Regulations, it is, ' *The Minister of War has full power to send to the Compagnies de Discipline any soldier who has committed one of several faults, the gravity of which makes any other mode of repression inadequate.* . . .'

I like that word ' repression ' ! . . . They *repress* them all-right, in the Penal Battalions ! . . . Of course, ' Minister of War,' in this case, means the General Court-martial that sits at Oran, and the General Court-martial knows that when the Colonel sends a man before it, something has got to be done with the sin-merchant.

" So they either shoot him, or plant him in the Zephyrs for a few years, and the Colonel is rid of him. . . .

" Naturally the Colonel doesn't want to lose any man who is a ha'porth of good—so you may take it a *légionnaire's* a pretty hard case and a Republic's Hard Bargain before he gets as far as the General Court-martial."

" Yes," I agreed. . . . " But one hears stories of innocent, harmless and well-meaning fellows who fall foul of a Corporal or a Sergeant, and are so constantly run in, by the non-com., that the Company Officer has to take notice of it, and begins doubling the dose that he finds put down in the *livre de punitions* against the man's name. . . . By the time the Captain has begun to give the maximum that his powers allow, the Colonel has got his eye on the poor devil, and starts doubling the Captain's dose, and, before long, the man has got the Colonel's maximum of solitary confinement and an ultimatum— reform, or six months deportation to the Zephyrs. . . . And he can't ' reform,' for the Sergeant won't let him— and it's the Sergeant's word against his. . . ."

" One *does* hear such stories . . ." said Sergeant Frederic, and changed the conversation.

§ 3

The days passed swiftly—swiftly as only days of continuous hard work can do, and I began to find myself becoming a routine-dulled *légionnaire*, with so much to do in the present that I could scarcely think of the future.

This would not do, and I must get action. I had not come to the Legion to settle down, serve my time, and take my discharge ! It appeared unlikely that there was anything more about John Geste, for me to learn, and it was high time that I decided on the course which I should pursue to achieve my safe transfer from the honourable ranks of the Foreign Legion to the dishonourable ranks of the working-gangs of the Zephyrs.

The great question was—should I embark on a course of slackness, insubordination, petty "crime" and general unsatisfactoriness, so that by the thorny path of more and more punishment, and increasingly long and heavy sentences of imprisonment, I should sound to their depths the Colonel's powers of "repression," until I touched the very bottom and was repressed from the regiment altogether for the space of six months—or should I conceive, and then commit, some crime for which no punishment was adequate, save such as could only be awarded by a General Court-martial—to wit, penal servitude or Death.

On the one hand, it would be a long and painful—a most distasteful and degrading—business, to play the bad soldier so sedulously that I went through the whole gamut of regimental punishment until the Colonel sent me to the Zephyrs for six months—a disgrace to my Corps, my country, and myself.

On the other hand, it would be unspeakably tragic, if, in attempting to qualify for penal servitude in the Zephyrs, I overdid it, and earned the death-penalty—thus failing in my task of finding John Geste; depriving Isobel of her last chance of happiness; ending in a felon's grave all the high hopes that I had held out to her; and breaking the fine promises that I had made.

In favour of the first course was its comparative safety.

Against it, was its protracted misery and moral abasement, and also the fact that the six months which the Colonel could and would give me, might prove all too short for my purpose—indeed would almost certainly prove too short. Twenty years would probably not be long enough.

In favour of the second course, was its comparative

decency and brevity. A serious military "crime," a Court-martial, a sentence.

Against it, was the possibility of the sentence being a death-sentence.

Which to choose? . . . I wondered whether, ever before, in the long and astounding history of the French Foreign Legion, a man had deliberately endeavoured to earn a sentence in the Penal Battalions, and had solemnly weighed the respective merits and conveniences of a Colonel's short-term sentence, and a Court-martial's penal servitude decree.

§ 4

I hate to look back upon the period of my life that now began. It was, in a way, almost a worse time than that which I spent in the actual Penal Battalion—as much worse as mental suffering is than physical suffering—for the misery of the constant punishment and imprisonment that I deliberately brought upon myself, was nothing in comparison with what I suffered in *earning* that punishment.

I loathed myself ; I loathed the thing that I had to make myself appear to be—insubordinate, dirty, untrustworthy, lazy, incompetent and wholly detestable to the normal military mind. What hurt me most, was Sergeant Frederic's disappointment in me, a hurt and bewildered disappointment that quickly turned to scorn and the bitterest contempt.

When I first began to lapse from grace—which was as soon as I had decided that I would lapse by slow degrees and a gradual slipping down Avernus, rather than by the commission of a General Court-martial crime—the good fellow did his best, by light punishment, by appeal to my better nature, and then by sharp punishment—to stay my downward course. He would send for me when I had completed eight days *salle de police* or some other punishment, and talk to me for my good.

"Look here, Hankinson," he would say, " what's the

game ? . . . You're in the Legion and you've got to stay in the Legion for five years, so why not make the best of it, and of yourself ? Why not go for promotion ? You could rise to Sergeant-Major and re-enlist for a commission. . . . And—other things apart—you might play the game, since you *have* come here ! . . . And I thought you were such a decent chap. . . .

" It's bad enough when some of these ignorant unintelligent clods are bad, dirty, and drunken soldiers. For a man like you, it isn't decent. . . . I can't make you out, Hankinson. . . . One of the weaklings with a screw loose somewhere, I suppose. . . . Come man, pull yourself together . . . for the credit of the Anglo-Saxon name, if for nothing else. . . . Dismiss ! . . ."

And I would salute, and go, without a word, but with a bursting heart.

Yes, what I was doing now *was*, undoubtedly, by far the hardest of the things I was privileged to do for Isobel.

§ 5

But, one day, a ray of light and warmth shone into the dark cheerlessness of my life at this period.

Sergeant Frederic had an idea.

He wasn't a brilliant man, but he was one of those sound solid, sensible Britishers who are richly endowed with that uncommon thing, common sense.

He sent for me, and said, as soon as we were alone, " I've come to the conclusion, Hankinson, that for some reason, best known to yourself, you are deliberately trying to get into the Zephyrs ! . . . If so, you're a damned fool—a mad fool. . . . But I can understand a mad fool, if there's a woman in it. . . .

" What I want to say is, I shall punish you exactly according to your deserts—without mercy. . . . But if you are trying to get into the Zephyrs, perhaps you'd better give me a smack in the eye, on parade, and get it over. . . ."

" And now get to Hell out of this," he concluded, with
an eloquent handshake.

. . . .

Fate was in a slightly ironical mood when all my painful
efforts to deserve and attain a Court-martial, were rendered
superfluous.

A sand-storm—aided by a brief failure of the com-
missariat, over-fatigue, and frayed nerves—provided me,
without effort on my part, with that for which I had
schemed and suffered for months.

The battalion formed part of a very large force engaged
on some extensive manœuvres, which were, I believe,
partly a training-exercise for field-officers, partly a demon-
stration for the benefit of certain tribes, and partly a
reconnaissance in force.

My Company was broken up into a chain of tiny outpost
groups, widely scattered in a line parallel to the course of
a dry river-bed which was believed by the more ignorant
legionaries to form a rough boundary between Algeria
and Morocco.

Small patrols kept up communication between the
river-bed frontier line and these groups, and one day I
found myself a member of such a patrol.

As it happened, the rest of the *escouade* consisted entirely
of Russians, with the exception of my friend Rien, a
Frenchman, and a couple of Spaniards and a Jew. All the
Russians were in a clique, except Badineff, who hated the
others.

This man, Badineff, a huge, powerful fellow, was a
gentleman, and was commonly supposed to have commanded a regiment of Cossacks. After his third bottle
of wine, he would talk of his " children," and say there
were no cavalry in the world to compare with them. . . .
" My regiment would ride round a whole brigade of Spahis,
while it galloped, and then ride through it and back." . . .
After his fourth bottle he would lapse into Russian, and
further revelations were lost to his interested audience.

Badineff had re-enlisted in the Legion twice, was now

serving his fifteenth year in the ranks, and must have been about sixty years of age.

He spoke perfect English, French and German, and had certainly seen a great deal of life—and of death too.

The other Russians were " intellectuals," political plotters and refugees—a loathsome gang, foul as hyenas and cowardly as village pariah-dogs.

Our patrol started from bivouac, after a sleepless night, long before the red dawn of a very terrible day—one of those days when a most terrific thunderstorm is always just about to break, and never does so.

By one of those unfortunate concatenations of untoward circumstance that render the operations of warfare an uncertain and much over-rated pastime, we had to start with almost nothing in our water-bottles, less in our haversacks, and least in our stomachs.

Sergeant Frederic, however, comforted us with the information that our march was to be but a short one—about ten *kilomètres*—and that the outpost to which we were going was actually holding a well, water-hole or oasis, and was properly provisioned.

All we had to do, was to step out smartly, arrive promptly, eat, drink and be merry, and then lie like warriors taking our rest with our martial cloaks around us.

It was Sergeant Frederic who lied.

The post was quite thirty kilometres away, and we had marched about twenty of them, through the most terrible heat I have ever known, when the sand-storm came on, and we were lost.

It began with a wind that seemed to have come straight from the opened mouth of Hell. It was so hot that it hurt, and one laid one's hand over one's face as though to save it from being burnt from the bones behind it. Dust clouds arose in such density as to obscure the mid-day sun. As the wind increased to hurricane force, the dust was mingled with sand and small stones that cut the flesh, and, before long, gloom became darkness.

We staggered on, Sergeant Frederic leading, and in every

mind was the thought, "How can he know where he is going? . . . We shall be lost in the desert and die of thirst."

Darkness by day is very different from the darkness of night, for at night a man can take a bearing from the stars and keep his direction.

It is difficult to give an adequate idea of the conditions that prevailed. We were deafened, blinded and suffocated.

To open one's mouth and gaspingly inhale sufficient air to rid oneself of the terrible feeling of imminent asphyxiation, was to fill one's lungs with sand; to open one's eyes to see where one was going, was to be blinded with sand; to stagger on, buffeted and bedevilled through that black night-by-day, choking and drowning in a raging ocean whose great breakers were waves of sand, was to be overwhelmed and utterly lost; to give up hope and effort and to lie prone, with face to earth, in the hope of escaping the worst of the torture, was to be buried alive.

Perhaps this was what Sergeant Frederic feared, for he kept us moving—in single file, each man holding to the end of the bayonet-scabbard of the man in front of him, and with strict orders to give the alarm if the man behind him lost touch.

Frederic put Badineff, Rien and myself last. . . .

How long we struggled on, bent double against the wind, I do not know, but I was very near the end of my tether, and feeling as though I were drowning in a boiling sea, when I was jerked to a standstill by the halting of the man in front of me.

A Russian *légionnaire*, one Smolensky, appeared to have gone mad, and with his clenched fists forced into his eyes, and face upraised as though to lift his mouth above the flying sand, screamed that he would go no further; that Frederic was a murderer maliciously leading us to our deaths, an incompetent fool who did not know in the least where he was going nor what he was doing, and a scoundrel who merited instant death. . . .

A man threw himself on the ground. . . . Another. . . . Another. . . .

N

As Rien, Badineff and I pushed forward, Sergeant Frederic loomed up through the murk of this fantastic Hell.

"What's this?" he yelled, leaning against the wind.

Another man threw himself on the ground, and the mad Russian began loading his rifle, shrieking curses at Frederic as he did so.

"Let's *die* like gentlemen, at least," cried Rien, as Badineff sprang on the madman, wrenched his rifle from him and knocked him down.

Another man, a friend of the madman, swung up his rifle to club Badineff, and I seized it as it came back over the man's shoulder.

Rien shouted something that was carried away by the wind, and I received a heavy blow on the head.

I saw Sergeant Frederic draw his automatic, as I stumbled and fell.

Like a prairie fire leaping from tuft to tuft, madness was spreading from man to man, and the unauthorized halt was becoming a free fight. The single-file column had become a crowd—a maddened crowd ripe for revolt and murder.

Sergeant Frederic acted with wisdom and his usual coolness. As I staggered to my feet he roared the blessed words:

"*Halte! Campez!*"

He was instantly obeyed, and everyone sank to the ground. Going from man to man he pushed, pulled, shouted, and exhorted, until he had got all but the weariest and most despairing, crouched on knees and elbows, soles of the feet to the wind, heads tucked in, chin upon chest, and the face in the little space protected by the body.

In this posture, such as the Arab assumes in the lee of his kneeling camel, when caught in a sandstorm, one might hope to breathe, and by frequent movement to avoid burial.

In a few minutes the patrol was almost obliterated and, to any eye that could have beheld it when that awful storm was at its height, it must have suggested an orderly arrangement of sand-covered boulders, rather than a company of men.

How long the sand-storm lasted I do not know, but it was only by dint of frequent change of position that we were not buried alive. Nor do I know how long it had been day when the sun's rays again penetrated the dusty gloom. Whether Sergeant Frederic really had the least idea as to where he was, or where he was going, I do not know, but he bravely strove to give the impression that all was well—that we were not lost, and that a brief march would bring us to water and to food. Encouraging, praising, shaming, exhorting, promising, he got the *escouade* on its feet and together, and after a brief brave speech, gave the order to march, and as some of us turned to step off, a Russian, Smernoff—a typical sample of " the brittle intellectuals who crack beneath the strain," a loathsome creature, mean as a jackal, and bloodthirsty as a wolf, suddenly yelled :

" *March ?* My God, yes, and where to ? . . . You have lost us ; you have killed us, you swine ! . . ."

And as Sergeant Frederic strode toward him, the beast threw up his rifle and shot him through the chest. Evidently he had slipped a cartridge in, during the storm.

Frederic fell, rolled over, gasping and coughing blood, drew his automatic, and, with what must have been a tremendous concentration of will-power, shot Smernoff just as Badineff swung up his rifle to club him.

" Hankinson," gasped Frederic as I sprang to his assistance. " Take command. . . . Shoot any man who disobeys you. . . . March straight into the wind—due south. . . ."

Hubbub arose behind me. A rifle was fired, and, looking round, I saw that Dalgaroff had fired at Badineff and apparently missed him, for Badineff sprang upon him and bore him to the ground, his hands at his throat.

In a moment the *escouade* was in two fighting factions, Smernoff's Russian gang against Badineff, Rien, myself, the Roumanian and the Spaniards. I rose to my feet, and, as I threw open the breech of my rifle, shouted words of command which I hoped might be automatically obeyed.

The result was a clicking of breech-bolts as rifles were loaded.

"Rally here, the loyal men," I shouted. "Come on, Badineff," and to my side sprang Rien, Jacob the Roumanian, Badineff and the two Spaniards, and stood shoulder to shoulder with me, between Frederic and the Smernoff faction.

"Now, you fools," I bawled. "Aren't we in danger enough? Follow me, and I will get you out of it. . . . I know the way."

There was a groan and a movement behind us.

"Stand aside," said the brave Frederic, who had struggled to a kneeling position, one hand pressed to his chest, the other holding his automatic steadily.

"Mirsky," he croaked, "return to your duty. Fall in here instantly."

Mirsky laughed, and Frederic shot him dead.

"Andrieff, return to your duty," continued Frederic. "Fall in here instantly."

Andrieff flung his rifle forward and they both fired. Frederic fell back. There was a thunder of hoofs, and a troop of Spahis came down upon us at the charge—their officer riding some fifty yards ahead.

"*Surrender!*" he roared, as he pulled his horse on to its haunches. "*Ground arms.*" . . . And as his troop came to a halt at the signal of his up-flung hand, he bade his Troop-Sergeant arrest the lot of us. Leaping from his horse he strode to where Frederic lay, bleeding to death, and knelt beside him.

"Tell me, *mon enfant*," he said, and put his ear to Frederic's feebly-moving lips.

"Mutiny," he whispered. "Not their fault. . . . *Cafard*. . . . No water. . . . Lost. . . ."

And with a last effort raised his hand, and, pointing to me, said:

"This man is . . ." And died.

"Ho, this man is the ring-leader, I suppose," snapped the officer, rising and glaring at me. "Tie his hands.

Tie the hands of the lot of them," and, drawing an officer's field pocket-book from beneath his Spahi cloak, he entered his observations—quite erroneous, as, at the Court-martial, they proved to be. Having noted that the dead sergeant had shot three of the mutineers in self-defence after being twice wounded by them, and that I was apparently the ring-leader, he made a list of the names and *matricule* numbers of the prisoners, snapped the elastic band upon his book, and returned it to his breast-pocket with a certain grim satisfaction. He then had the prisoners released and set them to work to dig two graves, one for the Sergeant and one for his murderers, while his troop off-saddled and took a mid-day rest. . . .

That evening, we found ourselves strictly guarded and segregated prisoners in the camp, and, after a brief field Court-martial next day, at which our Spahi officer testified that he had caught the lot of us murdering our Sergeant, we were despatched to Oran for the General Court-martial to decide our fate. Out of the mass of perjury, false witness, contradictory statements and simple truth—the latter told by Rien, Badineff, Jacob the Gypsy, and myself—emerged the fact that the *escouade* had murdered its Sergeant, losing three of its number in the process. . . . Further it was decided that if those three, as might be assumed, were the actual murderers, the remainder were certainly accessories, even if they did not include the actual slayers.

It was a near thing, and I believe that only one vote stood between the death-sentence, and that of eight years' penal servitude, *travaux forcés*, in the Disciplinary Battalions of France.

The President of the Oran General Court-martial was a Major de Beaujolais. . . .

CHAPTER IX

IT will perhaps be quite comprehensible that I do not care to dwell over-much upon the time I spent in the Penal Battalions of Madame la République.

I certainly am not going to complain of the treatment I received, inasmuch as I was there by my own desire, and had been at some considerable pains to arrive there.

Each country has its own penal system, and each country can criticize that of the other, if it has nothing better to do. Our own system is not without spot or blemish, and one has heard unpleasant things of the treatment of convict-workers in our coal-mines.

Charles Reade had considerable fault to find with the English convict system, and those exiled to penal servitude in Siberia have a poor opinion of Russian methods of punishment.

And I am the less disposed to assail the French convict-system because Biribi is now abolished (and also, perhaps, the Devil's Island, where Captain Dreyfus suffered, and the Guiana penal settlement), and the worst punishments that we endured were inflicted upon us illegally and in defiance of the law. These latter, generally the outcome of the vicious spite of some local petty tyrant, struck me as rather unnecessary, for the prescribed and lawful punishments were wholly adequate—apart from the fact that life itself was one long punishment.

For example, I personally needed nothing more in the way of correctional attentions than twenty-four hours of *la planche*. This ingenious device was, as its name implies, merely a plank. To the observer's eye, a simple plank, but to the sentenced man it was something more.

In the first place, the plank was some twelve feet above the ground. In the second place, it was neither sufficiently long, nor sufficiently wide, to enable a man to lie down upon it in anything but acute discomfort and danger of falling. He could merely sit upon it—and he could not do that for long, without changing his position in the hope of finding one less racking and tormenting. In the third place the heat and glare of that white-washed, white-hot prison-yard was a cruel and dangerous torture in itself.

The punishment of *la planche* sounds mild and moderate. So did some of those of the Holy Inquisition of old—particularly the worst of all, that of water dripping on the head.

Let anyone who thinks it mild and moderate, try it for an hour. Let him not try it for twenty-four hours, however, lest he do not regain his sanity.

But could not one throw oneself off this hellish perch of the devil ? One could. One did. But not twice. He was ready, willing, nay positively anxious, to return to that now attractive plank, by the time he had discovered what happened to those who voluntarily or involuntarily quitted the post of dishonour.

Nor indeed was there any real necessity to exceed the simple and lawful punishment of deprivation of water ; of standing facing the sun in a white-washed corner from sunrise to sunset without food or drink ; or of being chained to a wall with the hands above the head.

In fact one would have thought that " hard labour "—harder perhaps than that known to any other convict in the world—by day, and lying chained to an iron bar and to one's neighbour on the stone floor of a shed, by night, might, with the absence of all that makes life supportable, and the presence of everything calculated to make life insupportable, have rendered even " lawful " punishment unnecessary.

But no. Punishment beyond punishment had to be inflicted, and then illegal and indefensible torture added.

Chief of these were the *silo* and the *crapaudine*, both once permitted by law, and both absolutely prohibited and " abolished " by General de Negrier. I saw both these tortures inflicted, and I suffered one of them myself. But I wish to repeat, and to make it clear, that this villainous brutality was wholly contrary to law and in flat defiance of most definite military regulations.

Also, I wish to repeat that, in any case, I am not complaining. What I got, I asked for.

Further, if the system was severe to the point of savage and brutal cruelty, it is to be remembered that the bulk of the convicts were desperate and dangerous criminals, many of them barely human in their horrible depravity, and far more dangerous to those in authority over them, than any cageful of lions, tigers and panthers to the wild-beast-tamer who ventures among them.

While there was a sprinkling of soldiers whose horrible " crimes " were those of dirty buttons, slackness, drunkenness, earning the enmity of an N.C.O., and being generally and congenitally non-military, there was also a certain number of ordinary criminals who had been, perhaps, more unfortunate than wicked. But there was, as I have said, undoubtedly a very large proportion of the worst and beastliest criminals in the world, prominent among whom was the typical Parisian *apache*, who has no faintest shadow of any solitary virtue, save occasionally the savage courage of the cornered rat.

As is natural and very right and proper, the officers and non-commissioned officers—and more particularly the latter—are chosen with an eye to their suitability for the work they have to do.

Stern disciplinarians are required and stern disciplinarians are selected. Not only did the success of the system depend upon the iron discipline of these men, fierce, unbending, remorseless—but their own lives as well. Many have been killed in the execution of their duty, either by the sudden action of a maddened and despairing individual, or as the result of a cunning plot, planned and executed with fiendish ingenuity and ferocity.

They carry loaded revolvers in unfastened holsters, and their hands are never far from them. In time, they come inevitably to regard the convicts not only as enemies of the State and of Society, but also as personal enemies, and behave toward them accordingly. This is more particularly true of the non-commissioned officers, and in the conditions prevalent in far-distant desert places, where the great French military roads are in course of construction by convict labour.

And to one of these road-making gangs it was my fate to be drafted—the fate " written on my forehead," as the Arabs say—to which I had been destined, as I believed, from the beginning of time, that I might fulfil myself.

The latest road—a Road of Destiny indeed for me— was to run from the city of Zaguig, of horrible memory, to a place called the Great Oasis, a spot now of the greatest strategic importance to France. On this road were working a large proportion of the military convicts.

So, once again, to Zaguig I came, and from Zaguig marched out along the uncompleted high-way that was miraculously to lead me to my goal.

§ 2

Of that spell of road-work I remember but little.

Each day was exactly like its terrible predecessor. Each night a blessed escape from Hell, if not to Heaven, at any rate to a Nirvana of nothingness.

Often I wondered how men of education and refinement, such as Badineff and Rien, delicately nurtured, were able to bear the horror that was life, inasmuch as it was all that I, with my great sustaining inspiration and need to live, could do, to force my body to obey my will and keep my will from willing death.

In point of fact, it was patent to me that Rien was failing

and that both the temper and the body of the giant Badineff were wearing thin.

And then a spell of bad weather, with terrific heat and sand-laden winds, that seemed to have been forced through gigantic furnaces, precipitated, as so often happens, one of those catastrophes of madness, mutiny, murder and heavy retaliatory and repressive punishment.

I am sorry to say that I was the innocent cause of this particular example of these tragedies that are all too common, and indeed inevitable, in such circumstances.

Small beginnings ! . . .

As is so often the case, the beginnings of this affair which was to cost the lives of so many men, were small enough, God knows.

A Sergeant, one of those " hard cases " that are naturally selected for their aggressive harshness, merciless severity, and all the qualities that go to make the ferocious disciplinarian and martinet, stood watching me as I swung my pick ; with blistered hands, aching arms, eyes blinded with sweat, a terrible pain at the back of my neck, and the feeling that if I bent my body once again, my back would surely break. . . .

As I painfully straightened myself, he stepped towards me, and, with his stick, struck my cap from my head. To be quite just, I think he was only making a sudden raid upon that place of concealment, in search of tobacco, food, paper, pencil, a piece of steel, or a sharp-edged stone.

However, the stick struck my head as well as my cap, and I was still sufficiently near, in memory, to civilization, to find his act discourteous. I must have given expression to this wrong mental attitude, and looked upon him with the eye of mild reproach.

Now, in the ranks of *les Joyeux*, looking can be an offence. A cat may look at a king, but a convict may not look at a corporal—save with the glance of the most respectful, humble and obedient reverence. Any other kind of look may be mutinous ; a mutinous look may precede a mutinous act ; and a mutinous act precedes death. The red blossoms of wrath must be nipped in the bud, and the Sergeant promptly nipped mine.

In a second I was sent sprawling with a blow that partly stunned and wholly confused me—and it was with a sense of confusion worse confounded that I saw Badineff raise his spade and fell the Sergeant from behind, while Rien snatched the automatic that the man was in the act of drawing.

Ludicrously enough, Rien shouted at the stunned Sergeant, "You insolent dog! How dare you strike a gentleman!" and was himself struck to the ground by a convict, a Spaniard named Ramon Gonzales, a poor mean soul who hoped to curry favour for his virtue, and gain remission for his sins.

At the same moment, a Corporal dashed into the mêlée, kicked me in the face, fired his automatic at Badineff, and was promptly felled by a man belonging to another *escouade* —and, even in that moment, I noticed the splendid straight left with which he took the Corporal on the point of the jaw, and the fact (which should have astounded me) that he ejaculated in excellent English, "Dam' swine!" as he did so.

As to exactly what happened then, I am not perfectly clear, save that there was a rush of guards and convicts, as Badineff picked up the automatic dropped by Rien, shot the Spaniard who had felled the latter, shot the Sergeant who rose to his feet and pluckily tackled him with his stick, and then shot a guard who charged him with fixed bayonet.

There was a terrific hubbub, some more indiscriminate shooting, and within a few minutes of my original impious glance at the Sergeant, a number of bodies was lying prone upon the sand, whistles were blowing, voices barking orders, convicts shouting insanely, and chaos reigning in the very home of the world's most rigid discipline.

But not for long.

As always, discipline prevailed, and within another minute or two, order was restored. All the bodies but two or three, promptly came to life and were found to be those of wise men who had flung themselves down until the shooting was over, with the double view of dissociating themselves from the evil doings of wicked men, and of having a little nap.

Apart, very much under arrest, stood the villains of the piece, myself, Badineff, Rien; the Roumanian gypsy known as Jacob the Jew; the Spaniard, Ramon Gonzales; the man with the useful left who had knocked the Corporal out, and three or four more.

Well! We'd done it now, all-right! And it was a drum-head Court-martial for ours that evening, and our backs to a wall and our faces to a firing-party at dawn next morning. Except that there wouldn't be any wall.

There would be a grave though, and we should dig it. We should also stand by it and topple neatly into it when the volley was fired. I hoped I should be dead before they shovelled the sand in.

I also thought of a wily convict who was said to have toppled before he was shot, and to have crawled out before he was buried, and I pondered the possibility of contriving these duplicities.

It did not come to this, however, and I am still in doubt on the subject.

Chained together, and surrounded by guards with loaded rifles and fixed bayonets, we were marched from the scene of our sins—a long and miserable march, to the temporary depôt of the slow-progressing, ever-moving Company.

This depôt proved to be a deserted Arab village, and for want of better or worse accommodation, we were hastily consigned to its large underground grain-pit, or *silo*.

Confinement in these *silos* had been expressly forbidden because men had gone mad in them, died in them, been forgotten in them, had murdered each other in them for the last drops of water. But many forbidden things are done in those distant places where subordinates rule, where public opinion is not, where the secrets of the prison-house remain secrets, where the grave is very silent, and where necessity not only knows no law, but is apt to be the mother of diabolical invention.

Into this grain-pit we were dropped, one by one ; those who preferred to do so, being allowed to climb down a rope by means of which a large pail of water and a sack of bread were lowered for our sustenance until such time as a field Court-martial could be assembled.

That might be upon the morrow, or, again, it might not.

I do not think that there was any intention of actually imprisoning us in this *silo* as a punishment—our offence was too desperate for that.

I think that the officer commanding the Company—if he knew anything about it at all—merely gave the order to put us there as the simplest and easiest means of keeping us secure for the brief space that remained to us—probably only a day, or, at most, a couple of days—before we were tried and shot for murderous revolt against authority.

What then happened, above ground, we did not know— and only two of us ever did know—but by piecing together information which, as I shall tell, I obtained later, I came to the conclusion that a whirlwind attack by Touareg or Bedouin tribesmen, upon the Company, drew every man from the depôt to the scene of the fight, where they shared the fate of escort and convicts alike, there being not a single survivor.

What happened below ground may be quickly told, for the worst hours of my life, hours which seemed certain to be my last, hours during which I was compelled to abandon hope of helping Isobel, ended in the greatest moment of my life, *the moment in which I found John Geste*, the moment in which I knew that I had, against all probability, succeeded.

During those dreadful days, we died, man by man, according to our kind ; some in fear, some in wrath ; some in despair, some in faith and hope ; and one by his own hand.

The two Anglo-Saxons survived, whether by tenacity,

strength, the will to live, or the Will of God; and on the fifth day there remained alive only myself and the bearded man who had struck and damned the Corporal—*and who was John Geste*.

And then I should never have known him, but that he used an expression that I heard nowhere else but at Brandon Abbas.

Stout fella!

I really cannot, even now, give the faintest idea of my feelings in that hour. As nothing I can say would be adequate, I will say nothing.

I had found John Geste!

Think of it. . . .

CHAPTER X

A LIVE we were, but only just alive. Thirst, starvation, suffocation, corpses, flies and other attendant horrors had almost done their work on men not over-nourished, nor in too good condition, at the start—and when we were discovered it was none too soon.

We actually owed our salvation, I believe, to the predatory, or at any rate, the acquisitive, instincts of an aged party who, knowing of the existence of the *silo*, came to see whether it contained anything worth acquiring.

It did. And he acquired us.

I was lying beside the inanimate body of John Geste, and doing my utmost to persuade him not to die, when the light from the small man-hole in the roof was obscured suddenly, and I knew that we were either remembered or discovered.

I called out in French, and then in Arabic, seeing what I thought to be the silhouette of the head of a native.

And, in the same tongue, a thin piping voice called in wonder upon Allah, and then in question, upon us. I hastily assured the owner of the silhouette and the voice, that he was indeed the favoured of Allah in that he had discovered us, powerful and wealthy *Roumis* who would, in return for help, reward him with riches beyond the dreams of avarice.

Apparently my feeble croakings reached not only the man but his intelligence, for the head was withdrawn from the top of the short shaft which connected the *silo* with the ground above, and, a few minutes later, a rope came dangling down into our dreadful prison.

I promptly decided that it would be better for me to attempt the ascent first, for if I could get up I could certainly get down again, and I wanted to see who and what was up above, before fastening the rope to John Geste.

I did not like the idea, for example, of his being hauled up to the roof and then dropped. I accordingly passed the rope round my body beneath my arms, tied it on my chest, and shouted to whomsoever was above, to pull.

For several minutes nothing happened—minutes that seemed like hours, and then suddenly with a swift but steady lift, I rose the fifteen or twenty feet to the opening.

I thrust, fending, with my hands and knees, and was ignominiously dragged out into the blessed light and sweet air of day, at the heels of a camel to whose saddle-tree the end of the rope—the identical rope with which we had been lowered—was fastened.

The man leading the camel halted. I untied the rope, and perceived myself to be in the company of three extremely decrepit-looking old men, and three remarkably fine riding-camels.

It was soon quite evident to me that the leader, at any rate, of this aged trio was anything but decrepit mentally, and he quickly grasped the idea that I was to be lowered again into the pit, that I might bring up another man who was alive but too weak to help himself.

Not only did he grasp my idea, but produced a better one of his own—and I had only just understood it and ejaculated, " God bless you, Grandpa," when my knees gave way, my head spun round, and with infinite regret and annoyance, I collapsed completely.

When I again opened my eyes upon the glorious and wonderful world from which I had been absent for five days in Hell, I was lying in the shade of a mud wall, and John Geste was lying beside me.

Grandpa warmly welcomed my return to consciousness,

and explained that he and his young brother had been down quick into the pit, while his youngest brother—a lad who looked about eighty to me—had operated the camel. Also that he had only brought up this one, albeit a doubtful case, as the others were all dead, very dead indeed.

I commended Grandpa most warmly, and promised to set him up for life, whether in a store, a saloon, or a houristocked Garden of Eden, and to see both his young brothers well launched in life.

Not only had the excellent old man had the sense to bring up our own pail, and fill it with water, but he had concocted a millet-porridge abomination, which, with some filthy and man-handled milk curd, formed the noblest and most welcome feast which had ever been set before me.

More, and what gave me infinite joy on John Geste's account, he had sent one of the boys for the milk.

While I was wondering where the dairy might be, Grandpa mentioned that there was a Bedouin encampment "just over there", and any amount of fresh camel's-milk was to be had for the asking, and still more for the giving of a cartridge or two.

When I began to question the ancient as to who he was and whence he came, the light of intelligence faded from his eye, all expression from the mask-like mass of wrinkles which was his face, and he announced he was a very poor man—a *miskeen* of the lowest type, and that I was his father and his mother.

What he did tell us, and what was of the very deepest interest, was that, five days ago, there had been a sudden Touareg raid upon the road-gangs, a brief fight and a relentless slaughter. Apparently this had taken place a few miles from the deserted village where we lay, and the Touareg *harka* had swept through it, slaying every living soul they encountered.

As Grandpapa pointed out, it was lucky for us that they had not chanced upon the *silo*. Modestly he contrasted our present fortunate position with the fate that might have been ours.

o

Excellent as were the ministrations, however, of these three wise men of Gotham, or elsewhere, I doubt whether either John Geste or I would have recovered in their hands. We might have done, for we were both pretty tough and imbued with the most intense yearning to live ; but John, I learned, had recently been most desperately ill, and needed something more than curds and soaked millet-seed. That he lived at all, was due, in the first place, to the fact that we had a plentiful supply of fresh camel's-milk, and, in the second place, that we were promptly captured by semi-nomadic Bedouin, and, in a sense, fattened for the killing.

§ 2

On the second day after our rescue from the *silo*, as John Geste and I lay in a deserted mud-hut, a tall Arab, followed by our deliverer—volubly explaining that he had just found us—stooped into the hut and favoured us with a long, hard, searching stare, slightly amused, slightly sardonic and wholly unfriendly.

And the Arab was Selim ben Yussuf, that handsome human hawk.

There was no mistaking the high-bridged aristocratic nose, the keen flashing eyes beneath the perfectly arched eyebrows, the thin cruel lips between the canonically clipped moustache and the small double tuft of beard.

In the extremely dirty, dishevelled, unshorn and emaciated creature before him, Selim utterly failed to recognize the " wealthy tourist " whom jealousy had nearly prompted him to stab in the garden of Abu Sheikh Ahmed at Bouzen.

What he did see in me and John Geste, was a pair of French convicts, delivered into his hand—an extremely welcome capture, valuable whether for purposes of ransom, hostage, torture, or mere humiliating slavery.

" *Salaam aleikoum, Sheikh,*" I croaked. " I claim your hospitality for myself and my comrade. . . . And listen. . . . He is a great man in his own country, and his father would pay a ransom of a thousand camels, for he is a very wealthy man and loves his son. . . ."

But ere I could embroider the theme further, Selim ben Yussuf laughed unpleasantly, and with a contemptuous :

" Filthy convict dogs ! " turned to our ancient rescuer and bade him deliver us alive at the *douar*, whence he had been obtaining the milk for us.

With profound obeisances and assurances of the promptest and most willing obedience, the ancient backed from the hut, vanished into thin air and was seen no more.

When, a little later, a band of ruffians came to fetch us, my strength and temper were both sorely tried. For when I tried to carry John Geste to the miserable baggage-camel provided for our transport, I was tripped up, kicked, struck, reviled and spat upon, by these well-armed braves ; bitter haters, every one, of the Infidel, the *Roumi*, the invader of the sacred soil of Islam.

Luckily we were not bound, and I was able to hold John more or less comfortably on the camel. What I feared was that his illness was typhoid fever, and that rough movement would cause perforation and death. Luckily again, it was only a short ride to the encampment of the semi-nomadic tribe of which Selim ben Yussuf's father was the ruling Sheikh.

From what I saw and heard of the old man, I got the impression that he was a gentleman—a real courteous, chivalrous, Arab gentleman of the old school, a desert knight of the type of which one often reads, and which one rarely meets.

Unfortunately, like so many Oriental fathers, he was so besottedly devoted to his son that he could see no wrong in him, and would deny him nothing. Further, although the aged Sheikh had by no means abdicated, the reins were slipping from his feeble hand, and were daily more firmly grasped in the strong clutch of his son.

Selim, though not yet ruler, was the power behind the

throne—but there was another and a stronger power behind him.

It was before these three, as they sat at the door of a big white and brown striped tent, that we were driven, I staggering along with the unconscious John—who otherwise would have been dragged along the ground by one foot—on our arrival at the *douar*. And, in a moment, it was manifest that the old Sheikh spoke the final word, that the young Sheikh's thought was expressed by that word, while the third person's brain inspired the thought.

And the third person was the Angel of Death.

There, between the father and son, evidently beloved of both, sat the indescribably beautiful half-caste of Bouzen, the daughter of the Ouled-Naïl dancing-girl and the Englishman who had loved her and left her.

She knew me instantly, even as our glances met, and I was apprised of the fact by her long cool stare, and mocking smile, though she spoke no word and gave no sign of recognition.

Remembering the effect produced upon Selim by her previous recognition of my personal attractions, I welcomed her present reticence.

And now what ? . . . Here was a bewildering and astonishing turn of affairs !

I had fallen into the hands of a bitter enemy of France, who was also a bitter and jealous enemy of myself. Behind him, and swaying him as a reed is swayed by the wind, was a girl notorious for her destructive evil-doing—a girl who loathed Christians in general, for her hated father's sake, and me in particular for my lack of response to her overtures at the house of Abu Sheikh Ahmed.

If she had been ready to kill me then, when I was a person of some importance, and actually in the company of the all-powerful Colonel Levasseur, what would she do to me now that I was completely in her power—helpless and harmless—a miserable piece of desert flotsam, an escaped convict, whose killing the authorities would be more disposed to approve than to punish !

I addressed myself to the old Sheikh, throwing myself upon his mercy and appealing to his chivalry and honour— in the name of Allah and the Koranic Law and his own desert custom—for at least the three days' hospitality due to the " guest of Allah," the traveller who is in need.

" Traveller ! " sneered Selim. " Convict, you mean. . . . A pariah dog that is condemned even by its fellow dogs. . . ."

Evidently the gentle Selim knew our brown canvas uniform for what it was.

But the old gentleman rebuked him.

" Peace, my son," he gently chided, " the prayers of the unfortunate are acceptable to Allah, the Merciful, the Compassionate, for they are His children. . . . And he who is merciful to the children of Allah is pleasing in the sight of Allah, before Whom all True Believers must one day stand. . . . Let these two men be guests of the tribe for three days, and let them want for nothing. . . . Thereafter let them go in peace, praising God. . . ."

" So be it, my father," smiled Selim. And so it would be, I decided—but I doubted that we should go far " in peace."

" And if they be the condemned prisoners of the *Roumis*," he continued, " are they not then the enemies of the *Roumis* ? And are not the enemies of the *Roumis* thy friends ? "

" No dog of an Infidel is my friend," growled Selim, eyeing us savagely, and I felt truly glad that the old Sheikh was still master in his own house.

For the next three days we were regarded as honoured guests, and had we been the Sheikh's own sons, we could not have been more kindly and generously treated.

Our food was of the best, we were given complete and clean outfits of Arab clothing, and we shared a tent plentifully provided with rugs and cushions. We were favoured with the services of the Sheikh's own *hakim*, a learned doctor who did us no harm—as I did not give him the opportunity—and who did us much good by decreeing that we be immersed in hot water and then be clipped and shorn by the Sheikh's own barber. It was fairly easy to get the good doctor to prescribe this and whatsoever else I wanted him to prescribe, by pretending to assume that he *would* prescribe it. And I had only to say :

" I am sure that my sick friend will benefit *enormously* by hot broth of goats' flesh, provided you will add to it your learned and pious incantations . . ." to procure abundance of both.

That three days of perfect rest, with unlimited fresh milk, broth, cheese, curds, *cous-cous*, bread, sweet-meats, butter, eggs, lemons, and occasional vegetables, did marvels for both of us, and led me to the blessed conclusion that John Geste was not, after all, suffering from malignant disease so much as from general debility and weakness.

I had only been just in time.

But—Merciful, Gracious, Benignant God—I *had* found him. . . . I *had* found him. . . . *I had found John Geste and I had saved Isobel.*

And I was curiously content and unafraid—strangely happy and unanxious, in spite of our position, our almost hopeless position between the upper French and the nether Arab mill-stones—for I knew, I *knew*, I had not been allowed to go so far that I might go no farther. . . . I had not found John Geste to lose him again—by the hand of man or the hand of Death.

Curiously enough, John Geste and I talked but little during this time.

For the first couple of days he was so weak that I discouraged conversation ; and when, by the third day, he had turned the corner, and, thanks to his splendid constitution and great natural strength of mind and body, he was making a swift recovery, conversation was difficult.

There was so much to say that we could not say it, and our talk consisted quite largely of those foolish but inevitable repetitions of expressions of incredulity and wonder.

I think it was some time before he really grasped what had happened, and realized who I was; and when he did, he could only lie and gaze at me in bewildered amazement.

And when I had slowly and carefully told him my story from the moment when I had met Isobel at Dr. Hanley-Blythe's nursing-home, to the moment when he felled the Corporal who kicked me in the face, he could only take my hand and endeavour to press it.

As became good Anglo-Saxons, we were ashamed to express our feelings, and were, for the most part, gruffly inarticulate where these were concerned.

Obviously John was worried at his inability to thank me, and, every now and then, he would break our understanding silence with a slow :

" Do you really mean that you actually enlisted in the Legion in order to get sent to the Zephyrs on the off-chance of finding *me* ? . . . What can one say ? . . . How can I begin to try to express . . . ?   Isobel shouldn't have let you do that. . . ."

" Isobel had no say in the matter," I replied. . . . " Entirely my own affair. . . .   Gave me something to do in life. . . ."

" It's incredible . . ." said John.

" Yes. . . .   A wonderful bit of luck. . . .   No, not luck. . . ."

" I mean it's incredible that there should be a man like you, who . . ."

" Well, you yourself came back to Africa to look for a friend," I reminded him.

" Yes . . . but he had a claim on me. . . .   I owed him my life. . . ."

" Well . . ."   I fumbled, " a claim. . . .   If you're going to speak of *claims* . . ." and I stopped.

" God !   How Isobel must have *loved* you—to let you come," I said.

And :

" God ! How you must *love* Isobel—to have come,"
said John Geste, and from the great hollow eyes the
very soul of this true brother of Beau Geste probed into
mine.

I looked away in pain and confusion.

His hot and shaking hand seized my wrist.

" Vanbrugh," he said, " you have done for Isobel what
few men have ever done for any woman in this world—will
you now do something for me ? "

" I will, John Geste," said I, and looked into his face.
" What is it ? "

" It is this. . . . Will you answer me a question with
the most absolute, perfect and complete truth—the truth,
the whole truth, and nothing but the truth—without one
faintest shadow of prevarication or limitation.".

" I will, John Geste," said I.

" Tell me then," he begged, " does Isobel love you ? "

Let those who can, be they psychologists, physiologists,
psychotherapists, physicians, lovers, or plain men and
women whose souls have plumbed the depths of emotion
—let them, I say, explain why, in that moment I was
stricken dumb.

I could not speak.

I could see the lovely face of a girl bending down to me
from the back of a horse . . . I could see the boy, who
but those few years ago was myself . . . I saw her smile
. . . I heard her voice . . . I felt again the marvellous
and mighty uprushing of my soul to the zenith of such joy
as is known to human kind, when the declaration of my
love had trembled on my lips—and now, *I could not speak*.
I was stricken dumb—dumb as I was stricken on that
morning of my highest hope and happiness, that morning
of my deepest despair and pain.

John coughed slightly.

I fought for words. . . . For a word. . . . I wrestled
as with Death itself for the power to shout, " *No! No!
No! A thousand times, no !* " And I was dumb—sitting

smitten, aghast, horrified, staring into the tortured eyes of poor John Geste.

His pale pinched face turned impossibly paler and yet more pinched, and from the white lips in that frozen mask came hollowly the words that seared me so.

"Then what I ask of you, Vanbrugh, is this. Get you back safely to England. For the love of God, take care of yourself and get back quickly. . . . And with this message. . . . That I died in Africa—for die I shall—and that the very last words I said were . . . that my one wish was that you and she would be happier together than ever man and woman had been before."

And then I found my voice, a poor and ineffectual thing, hampered by a great lump in my throat, and after a cracked and miserable laugh, I contrived to say :

"Why now . . . that's certainly the funniest thing you would hear in a lifetime. . . . Isobel love *me* ! . . . Why she loves any pair of your old boots that you left at home, better than she loves the whole of the human race, myself included . . ." and I contrived another laugh. "Why, my dear chap, Isobel would rather be on the ground floor of Hell with you, than on the roof-garden of the Seventh Heaven with the greatest and finest man that ever lived, much less with *me*. . . ."

His eyes still burned into mine.

"You're speaking the truth, Vanbrugh ? . . . Yes . . . you *are* speaking the truth. . . . Isobel could only love once. . . . How could I doubt her. . . ."

"You're a very sick man," said I.

"I must be," he said, and coughed slightly, again. "But oh, Vanbrugh, you . . . you . . . you . . . *stout fella* ! . . . hero. . . . What can I say to you but that I understand, Vanbrugh . . . I understand . . ." and being at the highest pitch of emotion, his English hatred of showing what he felt, came to his rescue, and with an embarrassed grin upon his ravaged face, he squeezed my arm.

"Stout fella ! You're a stouter man than I am, Gunga Din," he said, and fell back upon his mattress.

Yes, the Gestes could *accept* generously, as well as give generously—which is a thing not all generous people can do.

§ 3

During the three days' hospitality and grace, we had received no visits save those of the doctor, the barber, and the servants who waited on us with food, clothing and hot water ; and though I had no doubt that our tent was pretty strictly guarded, we had been treated as guests rather than prisoners, in accordance with the order given by the old Sheikh.

On the fourth evening there came a change.

Instead of servants bearing a brass tray laden with excellent food, Selim himself, followed by some half-dozen of his familiars—young, haughty, truculent Sons of the Prophet—swaggered into our guest-tent.

The change which came over his face as he did so, would have been ludicrous had it been less ominous.

Expecting to see two foul and filthy ruffians, shaggy, unshorn—garbed in the tattered remnants of brown canvas uniforms, he beheld two clean and shaven gentlemen of leisure, clad much as he was himself.

And then he recognized me.

" *Allah Kerim !* " he ejaculated. " Our blue-eyed tourist of Bouzen ! The contemptuous, haughty *Nazarani* dog, who had not the good breeding to accept the kiss with which the Angel of Death would have honoured him ! . . . She shall be the Angel of Death for you indeed, this time. . . . A kiss ? . . . You shall kiss a glowing coal. . . . An embrace ? . . . You shall embrace a burning brazier. . . . Perhaps that will put some warmth into your cold heart, you dog. . . . And who is this other escaped convict, masquerading in that dress like a jackal in a lion's skin ? . . . Have you slept warm, you *Roumi* curs ? . . . You shall sleep warm to-night—on a bed of red-hot stones. . . ."

And he gave an order that I could not hear, to one of his followers. John Geste yawned.

"Chatty lad," he said. "What's biting him?"

"He doesn't like you much and he doesn't like me a little," I replied, "and I am a bit worried. I don't know exactly how far what he says goes, in this outfit. . . . He's the lad I was telling you about—the lover of the lady who was sitting in papa's pocket."

"And the lady?" asked John Geste. "I dimly remember that there was one."

I stole a glance at Selim. His back was turned—he had gone to the door of the tent and was looking out, seemingly in reflection.

"I am not sure that she isn't the *deus ex machina*—or shall we say the little 'dear' *ex machina*," I replied.

"Or *cherchez la femme*, since we're talking learnéd," smiled John. "You think she may be our fate, eh? Beware of a dark woman, what? . . . You know her?"

"I have met her twice, and I am not looking forward to the third time," I replied.

"What sort of a person is she?"

"Well, the gentleman at the front door has been calling us dogs quite freely—shall we say something of a lady-dog?"

"What poor old Digby used to call a bitchelor," grinned John. "Poor dear old Dig . . . God! I wish he and Beau were with us now. . . ."

"Amen," said I, and was moved to add, "I'll bet they're watching, mighty interested," and, at that moment, Selim's order bore fruit in the shape of some husky negroes.

"Get up, you dogs," he snarled.

"Why certainly, most noble and courteous Arab," said John Geste, as he rose painfully to his feet. "I have eaten of your salt, and I thank you."

"You have eaten of my father's salt and you may thank him—that three days have been added to your miserable life," was the uncompromising reply.

" The arm of the French is very long, Selim ben Yussuf,"
I said.

" Yes, convict," he replied, " it will reach you, I think,
or rather your body. . . . The terms of the reward are
' dead or alive ' I believe."

" Selim ben Yussuf ! " mused John, aloud. " Son of a
famed and noble Sheikh, and seller of dead men's flesh !
. . . Does he eat it too ? " he added, turning to me.

" Why no," I said. " He's far too good a merchant . . .
he can get money for it. . . . He sells those who eat his
salt too. . . ."

It was a dangerous line, but it *was* a line—on Selim's
pride and self-respect. Torture me he might, but I did
not think he would sell me alive or dead, much less John
Geste, against whom he had no grudge save that of his
nationality and religion.

My last remark had certainly got him on the raw, for
he strode up to me, his hand upon the big curved knife
stuck in the front of his sash.

" Lying Christian dog, you have *not* eaten of my salt,"
he shouted. " It was my father's. . . . ' Three days,'
he said . . . and he is no longer in the camp."

" A great gentleman," I observed. " The old order
changes . . ." and I shrugged my shoulders.

I had an idea that the old Sheikh had not gone very
far, nor for very long—or our shrift would have been
shorter.

" Throw the dogs out," he snarled, turning to his slaves,
and we were unceremoniously hustled from the tent, and
with sundry kicks, blows and prods with spear-butt and
matrack-sticks, we were personally conducted to some
low mean goat-skin tents, situated at a distance from the
main camp and much too near an enclosure obviously
tenanted by goats.

Into one of the tents we were thrown, and for the
moment, left—but around a camp-fire that burned in
front of it, certain unmusical loud fellows of the baser
sort rendered night hideous and escape impossible.

A glance round the filthy and dilapidated tent showed it to be entirely unfurnished, nor was anything added unto us save a huge and disgusting negro, who entered and made himself one with us, who were evidently his sacred charge.

John Geste, courteous ever, gave him welcome.

" Take a chair, Archibald, and make yourself at home," said he. " Take three, if you can. . . ."

Archibald, or rather Koko, as we later discovered his name to be, made no reply.

He merely sat him down and stared unwinkingly and unwaveringly.

If he had been told to watch us, he certainly did it. And after his eyes had bored into us like gimlets for a few hours, we were constrained, with many apologies, to turn our backs on him.

For more hours we sat and talked of plans of escape, and could only conclude that, in our weak state, our one hope was the good-will of the old Sheikh.

Nor was this hope a strong one, for however kindly the old man might treat us while we were in his power, it was too much to hope that he would do anything but hand us back, safe and sound, to the French authorities.

Any Bedouin tribe grazing its flocks in the neighbourhood of the Zaguig–Great Oasis Road, would act wisely in giving every possible proof of its innocence, virtue and correct attitude towards the French, in view of the recent attack upon the road-gangs.

CHAPTER XI

THAT night I was taken horribly ill; so ill that, after thinking it must be cholera, thought departed altogether, and I knew nothing more for several days.

When I did return to a realization of my surroundings, I found that I was back in the guest-tent, and that I was alone.

Where was John Geste?

My last memory was of his helping me in that foul goat-skin hole, while that beastly nigger, callous as an animal, sat and stared.

A horrible panic fear gripped my heart, and feebly I called John's name. And even as my heart almost stopped, I was reassured by the thought, the conviction, the certainty, that this wonderful thing, this finding of John Geste, against all probability, was no chance, no piece of luck—much less a colossal mockery. We are *not* the sport of mocking Fates.

But I called his name again, with what little strength I had.

Quite possibly the old Sheikh had returned, and, finding that we had been evilly entreated, had had us brought back, not only to the guest-tent, but had given us a tent each. The better sort of Arab is capable of much fineness in the matter of hospitality—a hospitality enjoined by his religion and by countless centuries of desert custom, the outcome of desert need.

At my second feeble call, a man stepped into the tent, in the shade of which he had probably been sleeping. He was one of the servants who had previously waited on us in this same tent.

"Where is my brother?" said I.

" Gone, *Sidi*," replied the man, and promptly departed, returning in a few minutes, accompanied by the *hakim*.

From this gentleman's delight in finding me conscious, I gathered that he had been strictly charged to effect my recovery, the credit for which he promptly awarded himself. To this he was very welcome, as was, to me, the broth which he prescribed—together with pills, potions and Koranic extracts. These last he painfully wrote on scraps of rag wherewith he enriched the mutton broth.

The pills I pushed into the sand beneath my rug. With the potions I watered their burial-place. The rags, in my gratitude and generosity, I bestowed upon the deserving waiter, by way of a tip. For the broth I found a good home, and felt the better for it.

But when, after thanking and congratulating the eminent physician I asked :

" And where is my brother, *Sidi Hakim* ? " I got the same unsatisfactory reply.

" *Gone !* " and a gesture of the thin hands and delicate fingers, to indicate a complete evanishment as of smoke into thin air.

In spite of my continued reassurement of myself, I was anxious, worried, frightened, and filled with a horrible and apprehensive sense of impotence.

However, there was nothing to be done, save to recover strength as quickly as might be possible.

" Now let me think—clearly and calmly," said I—and promptly fell asleep.

When I awoke, the Angel of Death was sitting beside me, chin on hand, and regarding me with a look which was anything but inimical.

Staring, startled from my sleep, I read her thoughts.

I am quite certain that at that moment, all that was European in her was uppermost. She was her father's daughter, civilized, white, kind.

She smiled, and while the smile was on her face she was

utterly and truly beautiful, more beautiful than any woman I have ever seen, save one.

Extending a gentle—and very beautifully manicured—hand, she wiped my brow with a small and scented handkerchief, product of Paris.

" Ze poor boy," she said softly. " But he has been so ver' ver' ill," and kissed me in the manner and the spirit in which a mother kisses a sick child.

"Thank you—er—Mam'zelle," I said. " Where is my friend ? "

" *Gone*," she replied.

For the third time I had received that sinister reply to my question.

" Gone—*pouff !* Like zat," she continued, and this time the gesture was that of one who blows away a feather.

" I play a trick on Selim, wiz him. . . . Zat Selim think himself too clever. . . . *Oui . . . Sacré Dieu. . . .*"

" What trick ? Tell me quickly. . . . Where is he ? " I begged

" Zat Selim ? " she asked.

" No, no, no ! My friend, my brother ! Quick ! Where is he ? "

She laughed mischievously, obviously quite pleased with herself.

" *Oh, la, la !* He does not matter. . . . He serve his purpose. . . . He serve my purpose too. . . . Oh ! zat great fool, Selim ! . . . But now you go sleep again. . . ."

" Yes, yes, but tell me first, where is my friend ? What have you done with him ? " I begged.

" What is he to you ? " she asked, and her pleased smile faded a trifle.

" My friend ! My brother ! " I replied.

Her expression changed. A look of doubt succeeded the smile.

" Oh, well ! . . ." she shrugged, as she rose to her feet, " . . . he is only a man ! . . . But *I* am a *woman* ! . . ."

And her smile, as she left the tent, was not in the least motherly.

§ 2

My state of mind may be imagined.

Against all probability, against possibility almost, I had found John Geste, had thanked God for that miracle —and John Geste had vanished. . . . The cup dashed from my lips. The fruit of my sufferings and labour— dust and ashes.

I groaned in spirit, and I was near despair. But, if I can be understood, I lost hope without losing faith—and did the one thing I could do. I strove to regain my physical strength, while I walked delicately in the path of friendship with the Angel.

That evening she visited me again, all smiles and honey, honey that grew a little over-sweet and cloying.

I learned that Selim ben Yussuf was away, with most of the fighting-men of the tribe, and that the old Sheikh was at Zaguig, presumably by pressing request of the Authorities, who would probably be making life a little difficult for every tribal leader within a hundred miles.

On this and other topics of local interest, she chatted freely, and seemed quite willing to tell me truthfully every- thing but the one fact I wanted to know.

The moment I spoke of John Geste she became evasive, laughed mischievously, and as I pressed for an answer, seemed first embarrassed and then impatient and annoyed.

After she left the tent, I thought I would see what happened if I attempted to leave it too.

Koko happened.

He made it quite clear to me, though without violence or even truculence of manner, that the guest-tent was my home and that from home I should not stray. As I returned and dejectedly dropped upon my mattress, the *hakim* entered and I had a bright idea.

I asked him whether he had any personal interest in my recovery.

He replied that my life was dearer to him than that of

his oldest son. I said that that was very nice, but ventured to point out that one would scarcely have thought it, when I lay practically dying, down by the goat-farm.

Ah, that was quite a different matter. Selim ben Yussuf had left no doubt, in reasonable minds, that the news of my early demise would be received with equanimity. Hence something in my *cous-cous*, which had nearly done the trick.

But the news of my approaching demise had not been received by the Sitt Jebrail, the Angel of Death, with any equanimity at all.

On the contrary.

She had left no possibility of doubt in any reasonable mind that my death would only precede that of the good *hakim* by a very few minutes—and hence the fact that my life was dearer to him than that of his oldest son, and that I, being possessed of the feelings of a gentleman would undoubtedly consider the feelings of another gentleman, and live for all I was worth.

This was most excellent, and I returned to my original point.

" So you *do* want me to live, *Sidi Hakim* ? "

" I desire nothing more fervently, *Sidi Roumi*."

" Well, I can and shall live, on one condition, and on one only. . . . That I am at once told what has become of my brother, and that I am thereafter at once restored to his society. . . . Get that right plumb in the centre of your intelligent and most noble mind, *Sidi Hakim*."

The good doctor's face fell.

" *Allahu Akbar !* " he murmured in astonishment. " I have heard of these things. . . . People pining for each other. . . . Men for women. . . . Women for men. . . . Even the lower animals. . . . But a man for a man ! . . . Is it possible ? . . ."

" It is here under your nose, *Sidi Hakim*," I said earnestly. " I'm going to die right here, to your great inconvenience, I fear. . . . Where is my brother ? "

" He is gone, *Sidi* . . . but do not grieve. . . . He is

alive and well—in the best of health, and full of happiness.
. . . And he is being *well* looked after . . . Oh yes. . . .
On my head and my life. . . . And on my son's head
and on my son's life. . . . I swear he is being most care-
fully looked after. . . . Yes. . . . By the Ninety and Nine
Names of Allah. . . . By the Beard of the Prophet. . . ."

I shut my eyes and fetched a fearful groan.

" Tell me everything quickly, for I am on the point of
Death," I whispered as deathfully as I could contrive.

" *Sidi ! Sidi !* " he wailed, " I dare not say a word. . . .
She would have my feet set in the fire. . . ."

" All-right. . . . Good-bye," I replied, and, like King
Hezekiah, I turned my face unto the wall, continuing this
death-bedlamite comedy, in the hope of getting some scrap
of information from this gibbering pantaloon.

" *Stop ! Stop ! Sidi,*" squeaked my medical attendant.
' Will you swear not to betray me to her, if I tell you what
I know . . . I know nothing really."

" I will not betray you, *Sidi Hakim,*" I said.   " And I will
not die if you tell me the truth."

" Your brother has gone back to—er—his—er—friends,"
announced the *hakim,* diffidently.

His information certainly brought me back to life, all-
right. I shot up in bed and seized him, almost by the beard.

" Do you mean to say that the *French* have got him
again ? " I shouted.

" Yes . . . Yes . . ." admitted the *hakim.* " He is
perfectly safe now. . . ."

I fell back upon my pillows feeling like dying in good
earnest. " He was perfectly safe now ! . . ."

*John Geste was back in the hands of the French and all my
work was to do again. . . .*

CHAPTER XII

I DON'T think I gave way to despair. Although my heart sank into the very depths, there was, as it were, a life-line to the surface—a line of faith and hope. I had found John Geste once. . . . What man has done once, man can do again. Evidently this girl knew something, and apparently had some hand in whatever had happened ; and almost certainly Selim ben Yussuf had played a part. I imagined myself with my hands at Selim's throat, squeezing and squeezing until either the eyes came out of his head, or the truth out of his mouth.

What had the girl said ?

" I played a trick on Selim with him "—and I half-wished it was recognized good form, and quite permissible if not praiseworthy, to serve her as, in imagination, I had just served Selim.

What I must find out was whether the *hakim* had spoken the truth—which was quite problematical—and, if so, whether John had been taken to Bouzen, Zaguig, or one of the construction-camps on the Road. Of course it was quite possible that he was even now within a few yards of me—either above ground or below it.

What in the name of God could be the trick that she had played on Selim ben Yussuf *with John*.

Followed by a fine-looking Arab, whom later I knew to be Abd'allah ibn Moussa, she again entered the tent.

" Tie his feet firmly, but without hurting him, and his hands in such a way that he is not uncomfortable," she ordered. "He will get strong very quickly now, and I don't want him to run away."

"Will you kindly tell me what has become of my brother, Mademoiselle?" I asked politely. "There can be no harm in my knowing, can there, especially now that you have tied me up so securely?"

"*Eh bien*, how he chatter about zis friend of his! I tell you he has *gone*—gone where you nevaire see him any more. . . . But you see *me*, isn't it? . . . Don't I look nicer than that friend of yours, *hein*?"

"You'd look a lot nicer than you do, if you told me everything, Mademoiselle," I replied. "You are a European—you are a woman—we are Europeans—we have done you no harm. Why behave like one of these uncivilized Arabs?"

"*Ah, oui*, zat's so," agreed the Death Angel. "You are both Europeans. I wish all Europeans have only one heart, and I can stab it. I wish all Europeans have only one throat, and I can cut it."

She looked like a tiger-cat, and while I watched, her face changed utterly, and, with a sweet and gentle smile, she dropped to her knees and leant over me.

"All Europeans except you, I mean, Blue-Eyes. You are nice and good and *gentil*. *You* would nevaire *desert anybody*, isn't it? *Nevaire would you do that*, I know in my heart." And she kissed me on the lips.

"You kiss me," she said. "You kiss me quick, and say you nevaire run away, and I untie your hands and feet, and take your *parole*, isn't it? Kiss me, *kiss me*, I tell you."

I closed my eyes, set my lips firmly—and received a stinging blow on the face.

§ 2

What shall I say about this astounding woman, known as "The Angel" among the Arabs, and as "The Angel of Death" to those Europeans who had the privilege of her acquaintance.

She was the most extraordinary and remarkable human being whom I have ever met, yet at the same time there was really no reason that she should astonish and astound, for she was the perfectly logical outcome of her heredity and her environment.

What should the daughter of a hundred generations of savage courtesans—unscrupulous, avaricious and unbridled —sometimes be, but an evil unscrupulous savage? What should the daughter of a blue-eyed Nordic sometimes be, but balanced, self-respecting and amenable to ideas of civilization.

We are assured that in every Jekyll there is some Hyde, and in every Hyde there is some Jekyll; and the best and the worst of us are well aware that the materials of which our characters are woven are not of even quality. But with this "Angel," it was not only a case of a mixed nature reflecting mixed descent, but a case of a complete and undisputed occupation of her body at different times, by two utterly distinct and different personalities.

For part of the time—for the greater part of the time— she was just herself, the Anglo-African, the half-caste, with all the expected attributes of the mulatto. But for the rest, she was either "The Death-Angel," the savage, the African, the lawless and evil native courtesan; or else Mlle. Blanchfleur, the European, the normal white woman, calculable, and, within her sphere, conventional. . . .

Be that as it may, she most certainly astonished and astounded me—this most pathetic, most terrible, nightmare woman. . . . Nightmare indeed—for, thinking of her frequently, as I do—I often dream of her, and though these dreams are not nightmares in the sense that dreams about my father are, their warp is horror and their woof is pity; and the dream is sad, melancholy and depressing beyond belief.

If I could but put the Angel from my mind! . . .

I cannot and I never shall. . . . I think of her, to this day, as frequently as I think of Isobel herself, and infinitely more unhappily. (That is a foolish thing to say, for there

is nothing whatsoever of unhappiness in my thoughts of
Isobel.   What did Isobel ever bring to any living soul but
happiness ?)

Some of the truth of what I have said of the Angel of
Death can be grasped by realizing that her actions ranged
from the decreeing and superintending of torture, to the
performance of acts of trusting and noble generosity ; from
venal bestiality, to a high idealism ; from a bitter savage
vengefulness, to a noble and generous forgiveness.

In short from the worst of her Arab mother to the best
of her Christian father.

§ 3

Whenever Koko, the negroid slave, whose precious
charge I was, took his yellow-whited eyes from me, yawned,
scratched himself, and stared vacantly out into the wonderful desert night, I gnawed at the palm-fibre cords which
bound my wrists.   Should I succeed in freeing my hands,
it was my unamiable intention to free my feet, and then
to do my utmost to incapacitate this gentleman.

He had a long sharp knife, and a heavy stick, short and
thick.   I had a hard and useful fist.   With one of these
three weapons something might be done.   I did not at all
like the knife idea.   My own fancy ran in the direction
of a swift and knock-out presentation of the fist, followed
by a more leisured confirmatory application of the heavy
stick.   This seemed to me a reasonable compromise between
the slaughter of a citizen, who after all was but doing his
duty, and my continuation in a position of extreme peril.

" *Eh bien !   On dîne donc, n'est-ce pas ?* " murmured a
silky voice, as I sat with down-bent head, my teeth fixed
in the unpleasant-tasting hairy cord.

" 'Ow you like it, *hein ?* . . .   Eat a bit more then,
M'sieur Blue-eyes.   P'raps that the las' food you get,
what ? "

" *Bon soir, Mademoiselle,*" I replied, with an attempt

at a debonair smile and an air of gay bonhomie that I was very far from feeling. " Won't you join me ? . . . Have a bite . . ." and I raised my bound wrists toward her.

" Ah, so you say, is it, Blue-eye . . . Yellow-hair. . . . Laughing face . . ." replied the Angel, and kneeling beside me, seized my wrists and deliberately bit my hand with the ferocity and strength of a wild beast.

" Laike what you call savage dog, *hein* ? " she said, thrusting her face against mine.

" Or a dog of a savage," I observed.

" *Sacré Dieu !* How I *hate* you . . . *hate* you . . . *hate* you ! " she cursed, and, even as I was thinking, " Better than loving me, anyhow," she seized my head and crushed her lips violently against mine. . . .

" *Baisez-moi !* . . . *Baisez-moi !* . . . *Baisez-moi !* . . ." she cried.

" Soh ! You will not kees me, noh ? . . . Naow, leetle Blue-eyes, you kees me, or see what come," and she took me by the throat.

I was revived from the faintness of strangulation by the pain of her setting her sharp teeth in my lip.

. . . Darkness, and a roaring in my ears. . . .

. . . A voice speaking from very far away. . . . Had I been clubbed on the head. . . . What was that ? . . . Oh yes, the gentle Angel.

" Oah, yon *won't* kees me, *hein* ? You won't lov' me, *hein* ? You won't 'ave me any price, noa ? S'pose I say you never kees any other girl, *hein* ? " she panted. " S'pose I cut your lips off, yes ? " and she seized my ears and shook my head violently to and fro. . . .

Most painful, undignified and humiliating.

" Uh ! You say nothing on that, is it ? You don't grin some more, *hein* ? . . . What s'pose I say you never *look* any other girl ? . . . What s'pose I have those blue eyes for myself. . . . 'Ave them out your silly 'ead, yes ? . . ." and as she spoke, she thrust her thumbs violently and most painfully beneath my eyes. I suffered most horribly in the next few minutes, but I can truthfully say that the idea of surrender to this tempestuous petticoat absolutely never entered my head. I don't know why, but the idea simply never occurred to me. Nor do I think that the reason for this lay in any Joseph-like virtue inherent in my character, nor in any definite feeling that when I did fall from grace, it would not be with the Angel of Death as a companion.

I think my resistance was simply and solely due to the fact that I am one of those stubborn creatures whom you can lead on a hair, but cannot drag with a cable. Also I have Red Indian blood, and my " No " means " *No*."

Every fibre of my being rebelled against this coercion, and the Angel was beating her head not only upon mine but against a stone wall—compounded of the dogged, unyielding rock of Anglo-Saxon stubbornness, and the cement of Red Indian stoicism, tenacious and prideful.

Not unto me, but unto mine ancestors the credit, if I bore well the sufferings and the temptation—the temptation to escape torture—that were put upon me. . . .

But always I had to remember that a dead, maimed, or blinded Otis Vanbrugh would be of but little service to John Geste . . . to Isobel. . . .

Springing to her feet, the Angel of Death (by means of a violent kick upon his latter end, tactfully turned towards us) attracted the attention of our chaperon, who squatted in the doorway of the tent, pondering perchance, Infinity, Life and the Vast Forever—or indeed, his latter end.

With a nasty oath and a stream of guttural orders, in Arabic, she drove him from the tent.

During his absence, the Angel gave me what she termed my last chance, and made it clear to me, beyond the peradventure of a doubt, the terms upon which I might retain my right to life, liberty and the pursuit of happiness.

By the time I had made it equally clear to the Angel

that, since I was not a person to be led along the primrose paths of pleasant dalliance, still less was I one to be scourged adown their alluring ways, the good Koko had returned and entered with seven devils worse than himself.

By the Angel's clear and explicit direction, I was roughly jerked to my feet, dragged from the tent, and thrown down at the root of the nearest tree.

With promptitude and dispatch, a young palm was cut through, some six feet from the ground.

Impalement! Surely not? It could not be possible that this girl, who had European blood in her veins, who had consorted with Europeans, who knew something of Christian teaching, and who was, after all, a woman—was going to have me stripped and stuck upon the sharpened end of this tapering stump, to die miserably . . . to die a lingering death of unspeakable agony, while a crowd watched, jeered and gloated.

A woman! . . . But Hell hath no fury like a woman scorned. . . . If Hell had a fury such as this Angel at that moment, the Devil himself must have felt unsafe. . . .

No, they were not sharpening the top of the stump.

I was again jerked to my feet, held in position and tightly bound to it.

It was to be a stake and not a spear.

Surely she was not going to have me burnt alive. . . . Burnt before her eyes. . . .

A woman! . . . But a woman scorned. . . .

What should I do as the flames mounted, and death was imminent. . . . Plead to the woman? . . . Agree? . . .

Dead, I could not serve Isobel. . . . A hard choice. . . .

No. I saw no preparation for a fire.

Their immediate task completed, the black soldiers stood about—incurious, stupid, animal. The Angel gave them a curt order and they went, with scarce a further glance at me—and I and that she-devil were alone.

§ 4

" Now, my friend," she said when we were alone, " we just see 'ow long you defy ze Angel of Death ! . . . *Sans doute* you t'ink yourself ver' fine man and bear pain like Aissa dervish, *hein* ? But I tell you somesing. . . . Don't you leave it too late, so that when you say ' *All-right, Mademoiselle; I finish—I give in—I do what you laike,*' you are not already too spoilt, see ? . . . No good saying zat after you gone blind for always, or after your tongue cut out for always, or you are too burnt ever to walk about any more, see ? "

I saw.

" Tell me, Blue-Eyes," this well-named young woman continued, " you rather be deaf and dumb both, or blind only—if I be kind and give you choice ? . . . Perhaps you anger me, and you get all three ! . . . Perhaps I get ver' angry and you 'ave no 'ands and no feets. . . . *Oh, la, la,* zis poor lil' Blue-Eyes ! . . . He ver' proud man until one day he got no eyes, no tongue, no ears, no hands, no feets. . . . Oh, ver' proud man—ver' 'andsome man—till someone cut off his lips and his nose and his eye-lids—not so pretty then. . . . What you t'ink ? "

I remembered John Geste's cold iron courage, and yawned. The Death Angel was certainly taken aback.

It then occurred to me to use my lips, while I had them, to whistle a little air. And the first that came to my mind was the one I had sung, or howled, to the Zouave Sergeant as I lay under the wall in Zaguig.

" *Mon Dieu,*" whispered the girl. " Is it you are ze bravest man ever I have met—*or is it perhaps you t'ink I am making ze bluff and will not torture you ?* "

A little bit of both, I thought. I am playing at being a brave man—and surely no human girl could cut a man's eyes out, stab his ear-drums, hammer a wedge into his mouth and cut his tongue out. . . . Not even an " Angel of Death." . . .

" Because if it is *zat*, I soon show you," continued this she-devil. And drawing her knife she ripped my *jubba* and *kaftan* downward from the throat, exposing my chest.

" Kees me," she said softly, rising on her toes, and placing her lips on mine.

" *No ?* " . . .

And on the right side of my chest she made a horizontal gash.

I started and quivered with the sudden pain, and was thankful that she had not, as I had expected, driven the knife into my throat or heart.

She stepped back a pace.

" 'Ow you like *zat*—for start ? " she asked, and, again placing her lips on mine, whispered " Kees me."

" *No ?* "

And again she slashed my breast with a horizontal gash an inch below the other.

" *Now* kees me," she said, and put her lips to mine.

" *No ?* "

And with a sloping cut she joined the ends of the two gashes with a third.

" See ? " she asked. " Ze letter Z ! . . . I write my name on you—ZAZA. . . . Always you remember Zaza then. . . . For ze little time you live, I mean. . . . Twelve cuts, it is. I do it ver' neatly now."

Evidently a case of practice making perfect, I thought.

" You kees me now, *hein* ? "

I tried to think coolly. If I let this fiend kill, or utterly incapacitate, me, there was the end of my search for John Geste—the end of my service to Isobel. I must give way, for their sakes. But, I told myself, were John Geste safe in England, this young woman should not defeat me. Pride is a poor thing to be proud of, and so is stubbornness, but I freely confess to being proud of both.

Well, the dozen cuts would not put me out of action, so she could carry on. . . . But if it really came to blinding, she would win—and, as she felt my unresponsive lips, she changed from cold anger to red-hot rage—which was probably my salvation.

"*Kees me ! Kees me ! Kees me !*" she screamed, hammering my face and body with her clenched fists.

"You *won't, hein* ? . . . Then I'll waste no more time ! . . . Now you kees me and say you love me—or you die . . . and you die *slow*—and blind," and she pressed the point of her knife sharply in under my right eye.

I saw the grim face of the Sioux Chief, my ancestor, but even to be worthy of him, I must not hold out longer. She was going to blind me—and no blind man could help John and Isobel.

I gave in.

"*Zaza*," I began—and the word was drowned in a scream, as the girl flung down the knife, threw her arms about my neck, and kissed me passionately and repeatedly.

"Oh, forgive, forgive !" she cried. "I was mad. . . . A devil comes into me and I must be cruel—cruellest to what I love best. Forgive me, dear Blue-Eyes, and see—promise me you will come back to me, and I will let you go after your friend—I will do anything for you if you will promise to come back to me. . . . I cannot live any more without you. . . . Look—I will do *anys*ing—*everys*ing if you promise to come back," and, with a slight return of her former manner :

"And I swear to God, on this piece of the True Cross" —and she touched her book-shaped locket—"and to Allah, by this Hair of the Beard of the Prophet, and by my mother's soul, that, if you do not promise, I will stab you to the heart, and then stab myself to the heart also, and we will die together here."

"I promise," I said, only too thankfully—"that I will come back to you as soon as I have seen my friend leave Africa in safety—if you will tell me the truth and give me every help you can."

"Yes, and suppose zat is not in many years—in ten years and twenty years, when I am ugly old woman ?

"I give you one year," she added. "You come back

to me in one year, or directly you save your friend," and picking up her knife she placed its point above my heart, and I knew with perfect certainty that, if I refused, I should die.

" I will return to you in a year," I said, " or before, if I have found my friend within that time, provided you tell me the truth, and help me in every way."

" And you will marry me ? " she asked.

" Of course," I replied.

" And you will take me from this vile country where I am a wicked woman, and neither Arab nor European ? "

" I will," I said, " but get this clear—the sooner my friend is found and saved, and sent out of Africa, the sooner will you get what you want. . . . Now tell me. . . . What was this trick you played on Selim ben Yussuf ? "

As she cut at the cords that bound me, she told me how Selim ben Yussuf, in jealous rage, had decided to torture me to death, as soon as his father went safely away to Zaguig.

At that moment, a French patrol, a *peloton méhariste*, had ridden into the camp, and Zaza had pointed out to Selim ben Yussuf that a far finer vengeance than mere death by torture, would be to hand me back to the ghastly slavery from which I had escaped ! . . . Moreover, he would be killing two birds with one stone, for, by giving up an escaped convict, he would be doing a good deal to sweeten the somewhat unsavoury reputation that he bore with the French.

Selim ben Yussuf had agreed that the idea was a splendid one, and had given orders for the *Roumi* prisoner, in the white burnous, to be brought and handed over to the *goumiers* of the patrol.

Anticipating this, she had instructed Abd'allah ibn Moussa to take away John's blue burnous and give him my white one. . . .

So the *hakim* had told the truth ! . . .

After chafing my limbs, and lavishing upon me the

loving tender care and kindnesses of a mother or a wife, Zaza helped me back to my tent—did everything for my comfort, and suggested that, since our bargain was made, I should now relax my foolish and insulting behaviour, and show myself as fond and loving toward her as she was more than willing to be toward me.

The position was a delicate one.

The last thing in the world, that I wanted to do, was to offend her, to bring back her spirit of savagery, to make her anything but my most earnest helper. And the last thing but one, that I wanted to do, was to make love to her.

"Zaza," I said. "Listen. We've made a bargain. Are you going to keep your side of it ? "

"Most pairfectly," she replied, " but, oh, most truly."

"And so am I," I said. "When I come back I will be your husband. I will be kind, and gentle, and everything you want me to be to you, but now it is business, work, planning and thinking—not love-making. Do you understand ? "

"I onderstand," said Zaza. "You *will* come back to me. Yes, yes, I trust you. . . . I *know* you will come back—my dear. . . . *You* would never desert a woman. . . ."

CHAPTER XIII

I SUPPOSE that it is a perfectly vain imagining when I wonder whether the Angel's last fiendish outbreak —that so nearly cost me my sight, if not my life—*was* her last. It would give me very great peace of mind to think that the mood that followed, the mood of remorse and utter repentance, could be thenceforth her normal condition, and that her vehemently expressed hatred of savagery, violence and vice, would last.

Vain imaginings and foolish hopes, I fear. For a temperament is a temperament and she was as much the daughter of her Arab mother as she was of her Christian father.

But the girl that sat the night through, beside my couch, was lovable, gentle, a civilized white woman and rather the ministering angel, "when pain and anguish wring the brow," than the sinister Death Angel of so short a time before. She was, moreover, pathetic and pitiful, and it touched my heart to hear her aspirations to that way of life, way of thought, and way of conduct, that befitted the daughter of her father.

"We will never come near this accursed country ever again, my dear one, when you are my 'usban'. . . . We will go to Paris, and Wien, and Londres, an' I will be so good an' r-r-respectable. . . . An' everyone will call me Madame and Missis, an' not silly evil names like Angel of Death. . . . An' we will have a fine 'ouse an' everysing *comme il faut*. . . . An' all my clo'es shall be make in Paris. . . . An' we will go to the Opera. . . . An' we will ride in ze Bois. . . . An' I will not be Moslem at all, but all Christian. . . . An' scorn all zem *demi-mondaine* like 'ell. . . .

"You *will* come back to me. . . . You will start to come back to me ze day your frien' go on board his ship ? . . . Or else you give up ze search for 'im, an' start back to me, one year from zis day, *hein* ? . . . You *promise* ? . . .

"Yes . . . Yes . . . I know you speak truth. . . . I know men. . . . I know ze true voice an' ze false voice. . . . Ze true eyes from ze false eyes. . . . From us of ze Ouled-Naïl no man can hide behind his face. . . . No, no. . . . I am *not* of ze Ouled-Naïl. . . . *À bas les Ouled-Naïls*. . . . I am English. . . . I am daughter of Omar ze Englishman. . . . Yes . . . Yes . . . I know you speak truth. . . . Your blue eyes are true eyes. . . . Your kind voice is true voice. . . . I *know* you will come back to me. . . .

"Look, dear one, . . . will you not swear it for me on Bible and Koran both ? Swear it before your God and my Allah. . . . Will you not swear it on zis leetle gold book I wear roun' my neck. . . . Nevaire I take it off . . . it is a great talisman an' great amulet. . . . One side is my Father and a piece of True Cross. . . . That is God side. . . . On other side is my Mother an' one hair of ze Beard of ze Prophet. . . . Zat is Allah side . . . Ze Sultan himself gave it to her mother. . . . No harm can come to me while I have such a thing as zis, can it ? . . . I would put it roun' your neck, dear one, an' give it to you, but I dare not let it go from me. . . . All would be good for you, an' that I would laike. . . . But it might not be bringing you back to me. . . . If I keep it, all will be good for *me*, an' then it will be bringing *you* back to me. . . . But when you come back to me, you shall have it an' wear it always, night an' day, an' then no harm can ever come to you. . . . I will show you ze pictures of my Father an' my Mother to-morrow. . . .

"Always I am afraid to open it at night-time, lest I lose ze piece of ze True Cross which is only a tiny splinter ;

Q

or ze hair of ze Beard of ze Prophet. . . . Zat would be too ter-r-rible. . . . I should die. . . .

"Oh, it will be bringing *you* safe back to me. . . . Yes . . . Even though I wear it you will be safe, because unless it kept you safe and brought you back to me, it would not be bringing good to me, an' making me happy, isn't it ? . . . Yes . . . it will keep you safe for me. . . . An' your truth, honour and goodness will make you come. . . .

"Oh ! an' I know. . . . Such fun. . . . Old Haroun el Rafiq shall do a sand-reading and tell us. . . . Now I have nevaire spoke your name an' you have nevaire seen him, so he cannot know. . . . We shall see. . . ."

Calling to Koko, she bade him fetch Haroun el Rafiq, and, half an hour or so later, a strange hairless creature of indeterminate age and with the deadest features and the livest eyes I have ever beheld, followed Koko into the tent, salaamed humbly to the Angel, fixed his burning eyes on mine, and squatted cross-legged on the ground. From a small sack he tipped out a pile of sand before him, smoothed it flat with the palm of his hand, made a geometrical pattern upon the surface with white pebbles, and studied his handiwork with rapt attention.

After a minute or so of this contemplation, he wiped out the pattern, smiled as to himself and at his own thoughts, shook his head, rose to his feet and made to leave the tent.

"Stop ! Stop !" cried the Angel. "You've told us nothing. . . ."

"What does the Sitt desire to know ? " inquired the soothsayer.

"First of all, whether this Sidi will return ? "

"Return where ? " asked the man. "To this place ? "

"Will return to me, I mean," said the girl frankly.

"He will," promptly replied the man, and the enigmatic smile again disturbed the frozen calm of his dead features. "I saw him riding at the head of a goodly company. . . . Riding from the north, straight to you. . . . I saw the *kafilah* arrive amid scenes of joy and welcome. . . . I saw him stride to your tent and I saw you rush forth and embrace him as a lover. . . . I saw you feasting with him, alone, in a bridal tent. . . ."

The Angel sat with parted lips and shining eyes.

"Did you see more ? . . . More . . ." she urged.

"No," answered the man, and I knew he was lying. "It is enough. . . ."

"Yes, it is enough," murmured the Angel.

"More than enough," I thought.

The sand-diviner's prophecy elated my companion as unreasonably as it depressed me.

"Yes . . . You will come back. . . . *C'est vrai.* . . . I feel it *here* . . ." she said, laying her hand upon her heart.

"Yes, I shall come back, as I have promised," I said, "if I live. . . . But the more immediate question is when shall I *start* ? "

"Oh, my dear one . . . my dear one . . . my love. . . . *Must* you leave me at all ? . . . Why must you go ? . . . He is only a convict . . . a *scélerat.* . . . A what-you-call dam' rascal. . . ."

"He is an innocent man, and the finest man that ever lived," I remarked, "and he is my friend. I only came to this country to find him. . . . And through you I lost him. . . . The sooner I go to look for him, the sooner I shall be able to return to you."

"Oh, my dear one, my dear one, if I had only known ! . . . What a *fool.* . . . What a *devil*, I was. . . . Oh, cannot I come wiz you ? . . . Yes, *why* cannot I come wiz you ? . . . It is not zat I do not trust you, but I cannot bear zat you should leave me. . . ."

"You cannot come with me," I said. "In the first place, Selim ben Yussuf would be on our track with half the tribe, the moment he returned to find you gone. . . . In the second place, you cannot live like a hunted wild beast, as I may have to do. Besides, I may give myself up to the French again, if I can get news of him in no other way."

And I pondered the fact that there would be no record

nor witness of the mutiny that had led to our incarceration in the *silo*, if, as our deliverer had told us, the whole unit had been surrounded and wiped out, to a man. John Geste and I, if I returned, would merely be two of the convicts who had somehow escaped the massacre.

"No, I cannot come wiz you," sighed the Angel. "I should be 'indrance an' not ze 'elp, an', as you say, Selim ben Yussuf would capture us and keel you. . . . But I can help you. . . . Yes, I can send you off wiz ze best of everysing. . . . You shall have my own camels an' men—when you mus' go. . . ."

"You cannot go until you are stronger," she added.

"I must go before Selim ben Yussuf returns," I reminded her.

"Yes . . ." she agreed. "But you need not go far until you are strong. You could go a day's ride and camp. . . . An' I will tell Selim zat you, zat is to say *your frien'*, as he thinks, died. . . . The *hakim* will swear it. . . . He fears me greatly. . . ."

"He certainly does," I agreed.

"Yes . . . I have one or two spells . . ." she smiled. "Spells an' magics zat you buy in ze chemist's shop in Algiers. . . . An' potions. . . . Ah, *oui*! . . . potions. . . . One drop of which makes ze hard stone or ze steel, bubble an' smoke. . . . An' I will send Abd'allah ibn Moussa wiz you. . . . My own faithful servant. . . . He is faithful as ze horse of ze Arab, an' ze dog of ze Englishman. . . . He is as brave as ze lion, an' as true as Life an' Death. . . .

"He was ze devoted servant an' frien' of my Mother, an' he nurse me when I am a baby. . . . An' now he lof me laike he lof my Mother. . . . If I say to 'im, '*Go you, Abd'allah ibn Moussa, wiz zis man. He is my lover . . . die for him, or die wiz him,*' he will not come back wizzout you, an' I will feel comfor'ble in my 'eart. . . . Nevaire, nevaire will he leave you. . . ."

I felt that such fidelity might prove embarrassing.

"He'll be a useful guide, anyhow," I agreed. "But

I'll send him back as soon as I am well on my way, and feeling fairly strong."

" I shall tell him not to leave you," said the girl.

" Well, I may have to leave *him*," I replied. . . . " But anyhow, the sooner you give him instructions to get your camels and people together, the better."

I knew something of Arab dilatoriness and the utter meaninglessness of time, in the desert.

Without further remark, she rose to her feet, drew her veil about her face, and left the tent.

I followed her to the entrance, with some vague idea of escape from the terrible silken meshes of the dreadful web that this jewelled spider was spinning about me.

" Salaam, *Sidi*," grinned the unutterable Koko.

" Hell ! " I replied, and again flung myself down upon my cushions.

§ 2

A few minutes later, the Angel returned, followed by an Arab, whose fine and noble face was that of a man of middle age, great intelligence, philosophic calm, high courage, and great determination and tenacity.

I speak without exaggeration. The man's face was noble and he proved to be a noble man, if fidelity, endurance, unswerving loyalty and courage, connote nobility.

" Zis is Abd'allah ibn Moussa," said the Angel, and the man salaamed respectfully. " Zis is a *Roumi* lord," she continued, turning to Abd'allah.

" Also he is my Lord and my Master, and your Lord and your Master. . . . He is my lover and he will raise me up to be his wife. . . . Go with him, Abd'allah. . . . Follow where he leads. . . . Sleep where he sleeps. . . . Live where he lives. . . . And die where he dies. . . . But he will not die, Abd'allah . . . for you will guard his life with yours, and you will bring him back to me. . . ."

" On my head and on my life be it," replied the man.

" Go and make ready," said his mistress, and he went away.

There was a commotion of hails, shouting, and men running—alarums and excursions without, in fact.

Abd'allah ibn Moussa turned back into the tent.

" A *kafilah* comes," he said, and went about his business.

The Angel's eyes met mine and her face paled.

"Zat Selim!" she said, as with a bitter laugh, I ejaculated:

" Selim ben Yussuf ! "

" I will keel heem, zat so-clever Selim," whispered the Angel, and the European side of her character seemed to fade somewhat.

" I must hide you. . . . I must hide you. . . . He must not see your face. . . . See ! You must go back to the goat-herds' tents as soon as it is safe. . . . I will keep Selim in his tents. . . . I will send Abd'allah to take you back. . . . I will tell zis Selim zat ze frien' of ze blue-eye Nazarani is dead, an' Abd'allah shall disguise you. . . . Yes, like a poor blind *miskeen*. . . ."

Well, things seemed to be going wrong indeed.

What would I not have given for a few hours of normal health and strength.

I must leave it to the wit and the wiles of the Angel to keep me hidden until I could get away.

The estimable Koko stooped into the tent, very full of himself.

" His Highness, the Sidi Emir, the Sidi Sheikh el Hamel el Kebir, Shadow of the Prophet, and Commander of the Faithful, has arrived with his great Wazir, noble sheikhs, captains, and many soldiers," he announced pompously.

" He calls for the high Sheikh Yussuf ben Amir, and for Selim ben Yussuf his son, and for the Sheikh's captains and *ekhwan* of the tribe."

The Angel's face relaxed and she heaved a sigh of relief.

" Ze good God be praised ! It is not zat Selim ! "

" But who is it ? " I asked.

"*Oh, la, la !* He is ze gr-r-reat big man ! He is ze chief of ze chiefs. . . . He mak' treaty wiz ze French. . . . He is ver' civilized an' important ! He marry English girl—laike me. . . . He is frien' to French an'

treats well all *Roumis*. . . . Oh, he is *ver'* big man. . . .
An' often, before, I have want to see him. . . . But now
I have you, dear one, I care not at all. . . ."

A pity !

And now, what ? How was this going to affect me and
my fortunes ?

If this Emir were a staunch ally of the French and
" kind to all *Roumis*," presumably he would be kind to
me—until he handed me back to his allies.

How long would he stay here ? What exactly was the
extent of his power over this tribe ?

Would the *hakim*, or one of the servants, attempt to
curry favour with him by informing him that there was a
captive *Roumi* in the camp—or would they fear the Angel
more than they feared him ?

An idea occurred to me.

If this Emir were truly great, as the Angel implied, might he
not be touched by a truthful " David and Jonathan " story ?

Suppose I told him everything, threw myself upon his
mercy, and begged him to help us. . . . Might he not
accede, and, moreover, be a very tower of strength, if his
heart were touched and his imagination fired ? I would
speak of John Geste figuratively as my brother, and quote
the Arab proverb :

" The love of a man for a woman, waxes and wanes as doth the moon:
But the love of brother for brother is constant as the stars,
And endureth like the word of the Prophet."

And if I failed, and if he were inimical, or merely disposed
to do his duty to his allies, the French, should I be in any
worse position ?

If he handed me over to the nearest " competent military
authority," I should be promptly sent to Zaguig, and
thence to the nearest road-gang, where, in all probability,
John Geste had already been sent.

That would be something, but now that I knew of his
whereabouts, I could probably help him better from
without than from within.

It was almost impossible—it was certainly too much to hope—that another such series of events as had set us free together, could ever happen again, even if he and I were in the same *escouade*.

What to do ?

As these thoughts passed through my mind, I watched the face of the Angel, who also was pondering deeply, pinching her lower lip the while. . . .

" I sink I will go an' see zis Emir," she said at last. " Perhaps I will make him do somesing, *hein* ? "

Doubtless she had excellent reason for putting faith in her powers of persuasion where Arabs were concerned. It was wholly hateful, but I brought myself to say :

" You know best. . . . If this Emir can and will help us. . . ."

" *Enfin :* If he get your brother for you, *he get you for me*, isn't it ? . . . *Oui !* . . . I mus' quickly see zis Emir. . . . He will camp close by. . . . I will send Abd'allah to say zat I will pay heem a leetle visit. . . . I sink he has heard of me. . . . Oh, yes. . . . Zen he will make feast, an' I will see which way ze cat jump. . . . If he get *ver'* friendly, I will tell heem he must help you and your brother. . . . Ze good God grant zat zat Selim does not return before I get you away. . . . Ah, but if I mak' *great* frien's wiz ze Emir, I could mak' him keep Selim in his camp as hostage for ze good be'aviour of zis tribe. . . . I will *tell* him sings about zat Selim. . . .

" Now do not let anybody see your face until I come back, dear one. . . . And you go to sleep and get strong while I am gone. . . . I will send some more of ze beef-tea of muttons. . . ."

§ 3

And sleep I did, long and heavily, possibly by reason of some unusual ingredient in the beef-tea of mutton.

When I awoke, it was as a giant refreshed, and I was filled with an unwonted sensation of hope and confidence.

My first visitor was the *hakim*, followed by a servant bearing hot stew in a jar, and most welcome coffee in a brass bowl.

So much better was I feeling, that I wondered whether my excellent medical attendant, having poisoned me at Selim's request, had administered an antidote when ordered by the Angel to save my life if he wished to save his own.

In point of fact, the creature did not strike me as being of sufficient intelligence and medical knowledge to deal with a cut finger or a blistered heel, but undoubtedly some of these rascally quacks are familiar with poisons unknown to the European pharmacopœia.

Anyhow, I felt unexpectedly stronger and fitter and, having finished the stew and enjoyed the coffee, I demanded more.

Having fed, washed and been shaved, I peeped from the door of the tent to see what was doing in the great world.

The first object that met my interested gaze was the indefatigable Koko, leaning against the stump of a tree, just in front of the entrance to my tent, and gazing at it— gazing and gazing.

I wondered whether the creature ever shut his eyes at all. Certainly the Angel knew the secret of inspiring obedience and fidelity in her servants.

About a quarter of a mile away, a couple of remarkably fine tents, marquees almost—before which flags and pennons fluttered from the hafts of spears stuck in the ground—marked the temporary residence of the Emir.

Near to these big tents was the extremely orderly and well-aligned camp of his followers or body-guard, a camp much more like that of European troops than of a band of Arab irregulars. . . .

Once more I wondered what had taken place in those pavilions—whether the Angel had visited the Emir, and if so, with what success her power of intrigue, allurement and diplomacy had been brought to bear upon the incalculable mentality and character of this powerful lord of the desert.

I was soon to know.

A little later, she entered my tent, threw back her *haik*, and seated herself upon the cushions.

Obviously she had succeeded beyond her wildest hopes. Seizing my hands in hers she laughed gleefully.

" Oh, my dearest dear one. . . . It goes well. . . . I am so happy. . . . Ze Emir is *gentilhomme*. . . . Oh, he is gr-r-reat man . . . civilized and good and kind. . . . And oh, zat Wazir of his. . . . *Oh, la, la !* Oh, he is one naughty little man. . . . Oh, *mais c'est un grand amoureux*, zat one. . . . He mak' lof to me . . . oh, laike 'ell. But listen. . . . What you sink ? Zis Emir, he know all about everysing. . . . He know there is a *razzia* on the French. . . . He know zat some of you are hiding down in a pit, an' all die excep' two. . . . "

" But how on earth does he know that ? " I exclaimed.

" Oh, I don' know. . . . He know everysing zat happen in ze desert. . . . Everysing. . . . They say ze vultures tell him. . . . He know two of you are in zis camp. . . . So when I find zat he know everysing, I tell him ze truth. . . . Oh, he was ver' angry wiz zat Selim. . . . I tell him old papa Yussuf ben Amir go to Zaguig before ze French come to *him*. . . . An' I tell him Selim give back one prisoner to ze French patrol. . . . An' now he want to see you. . . . Do not be afraid. . . . It is good zat you go to his camp, then Selim cannot do anysing at all. . . . An' ze Emir promise me he will not give you up to ze French. . . . Now I tell papa Yussuf ben Amir, an' zat Selim, an' everybody, zat you are *died*. . - . "

CHAPTER XIV

ACCOMPANIED by Abd'allah ibn Moussa, Koko, the *hakim*, and the Angel's servants who had waited upon me, and knew me to be a *Roumi*, I set forth, my *haik* well across my face, to visit the Emir el Hamel el Kebir, Chief of the Confederation of Bedouin tribes that inhabited the desert country which extended from Zaguig to the Senussi sphere of influence, and had its capital or centre in the Great Oasis.

His name, titles and position I had learned, as far as possible, from the Angel; from Abd'allah ibn Moussa, who appeared to have for him an admiration almost amounting to veneration; and from the *hakim*, the tribal gossip, scandal-monger, and news-agent.

Seated on a rug-strewn carpet in front of the largest tent, were two richly dressed Arabs. They were alone, but within hail was a small group of sheikhs, *ekhwan*, and leaders of the soldiery.

Sentries, fine up-standing Soudanese, stood at their posts, or walked their beat in a smart and soldier-like manner.

I got an impression of discipline and efficiency not usually to be found about an Arab encampment.

From the little group of officers and officials, a broad squat figure detached itself and came to meet us—a deformed but very sturdy dwarf, whom I knew later as Marbruk ben Hassan, the Lame. He saluted me politely while my following salaamed profoundly.

" His High Excellency the Sidi Emir bids you welcome

and gives you leave to approach," he said, and bidding the others remain where they were, he led me to the carpet, whereon sat the man who so mysteriously "knew all things" that happened in the desert.

With a wave of his hand, the big man dismissed the dwarf, and beckoned me to draw near.

The huge Emir, and his small companion, presumably the "naughty Wazir," eyed me with a long and searching stare.

I decided to stand upon what dignity I had, to hold my peace, and let the Emir speak first.

He did.

"Mawnin', Oats," he said casually. "How's things? . . . Meet my friend El Wazir el Habibka, known to the police and other friends, as Buddy. . . ."

What was this? . . . Sun, fever, lunacy, hallucination? . . . Most annoying, anyhow. . . . How could one carry on, if one's senses played one such tricks as this? . . . One expects to be able to believe one's own eyes and ears. And yet here were my eyes apparently beholding the face of my brother Noel—bronzed, lined, wrinkled and bearded—and my ears apparently hearing his voice. His absolutely unaltered voice. With regard to the face I might have been deceived; as to the voice, never—much less the two in conjunction. Besides, the man had called me "Oats," Noel's own special nickname for me since earliest childhood.

"Pleased to meet any friend of Hank's," said the smaller man, his grey eyes smiling from an unsmiling face.

"He's my young brother," said the Emir.

"Oh?" observed the other slowly. "Still—that ain't his fault, is it, Hank Sheikh? Why couldn't you say nothing, an' give the man a fair chance?

"Don't you brood on it, friend," he added, waving his hand, "and anyway I don't believe it."

Fever, sun, hallucination? Only in dreams and in the delirium of fever do typical Arab potentates talk colloquial English. These men *were* most obvious Arabs; Arab to the last item of dress and accoutrement ; Arab of Arabs in every detail of appearance and deportment.

But could my eyes be normal while my ears deluded me ? No. This *was* real enough. This *was* my brother. This man with him *was* talking English.

"*Noel !* " I said, beginning to recover and accept and believe.

Noel winked heavily, and laughed derisively in a manner most familiar. This was real enough anyhow.

"*Noel !* " I said again—helpless but beginning to be hopeful.

"*Know-all !* " ejaculated the little man. " It's what he thinks he is, anyhow. . . . But that ain't his name. . . . B'jiminy-gees, yes it is, though." . . .

And turning to Noel he said :

" You *said* your name was Know-all Hankinson Vanbrugh . . . after Miss Mary come to the Oasis. . . . Gee ! I believe you had an accident and spoke the truth, Hank Sheikh. . . . Ain't it some world we live in ! . . ."

"*Noel !* " I said again for the third time. "*Hell !* Am I mad, or drunk, or dreaming or what ? "

" Say, sport, if you're drunk, tell us where you got it, quick," interrupted the little man urgently.

"*Oats !* " mocked my brother, my obvious, undeniable indubitable brother, Noel.

" Say, did Mary send you ? . . . I've been wearing mourning for you, Son. . . . Mary said you were all shot up, in Zaguig. . . . In a regular bad way about you she was—only she was in a worse way about her Beau. . . ."

" Sure—Beau Jolly," put in the incredible nightmare Wazir. " Ol' friend o' mine, only he don't know it. . . ."

" Mary been *here* ? . . . Excuse me if I sit down. . . . Will it be in order ? . . ."

" No, most certainly not," said my brother. " Common people like you don't sit down in the presence of royalty . . . don't you know *that* much ? . . . We'll go into the parlour. . . ."

And the two rose and led the way into the tent, the Wazir dropping the felt curtain behind us as we entered.

And then my brother fell upon me, and there was no illusion about the thump and hand-grip with which the proceedings opened.

And Buddy was real. Quite as real as anybody I have ever met, by the time he finished welcoming me as the accepted and undeniable brother of " Hank Sheikh."

And at the tenth or perhaps twentieth attempt, sane and coherent conversation took the place of ejaculation, marvellings, and the callings upon various deities to bear witness that this was indeed a staggerer.

" I am still dreaming, or wandering in my mind, Noel," I found myself saying. " But *did* you say that Mary had been here ? "

" Not right here, but down this way. . . . In our home town. . . ."

It was his turn to marvel.

" And she never said a word ! . . . Gee ! And they say women can't keep a secret. . . ."

" It was to *you* then, that de Beaujolais was coming on his secret mission from Zaguig. . . . And of course brought Mary with him . . ." I said.

" It certainly was, Boy. . . . But he didn't know it then. . . . And he don't know it now. . . . And as far as you was concerned you wasn't going to know it either, it seems. . . . Gee ! What do you know about that, Son ? . . . Good for lil' Mary ! . . ."

" She always loved you very dearly, Noel," I said.

My brother smiled.

" Yes, sure," he mused. " And now she loves de Beaujolais a whole heap more very dearly. . . . It's for him, and from him, she's keeping the State Secret."

" What ? . . . Doesn't de Beaujolais know who you are ? "

" Not a know to him," replied my brother. " He thinks

I am the Emir el Hamel el Kebir, Shadow of the Prophet,
Commander of the Faithful, Protector of the Poor . . .
Mahdi, Shereef and Khalifa . . . Overlord, Ruler, Spiritual
Head and War-Lord of the great Bedouin Confederation
of the North South Western Sahara . . . Friend and
ally of France. . . . So I am too. . . . Three loud
cheers."

"Don't foam at the ears, Son," observed the Wazir
gravely. "Mustn't let no loud cheers in the hearing of
the Injuns."

And then I sprang from my cushions and certainly there
could have been no sign of weakness about that uprising
. . . and probably my hair stood as erect as I did.

"*Hank!*" I shouted, pointing in Noel's face.

"*Buddy!*" I yelped, pointing in the face of the little
man. They regarded me tolerantly.

"*Hank and Buddy!*" I cried. "*The men that John
Geste came back to look for!* . . . Hank went off and left
them the water. . . . Buddy stayed by sick John Geste
and took him to Kano. . . . Buddy went back to look
for Hank. . . . John Geste came back to look for
Buddy. . . ."

"*What?*" the two shouted as one man.

"*Yes!*" I shouted in reply. "And *I* came out to
look for John Geste and *I found him!* . . . And Selim
ben Yussuf has just sold him back to the French, thinking
it was I. . . ."

Both were staring.

"*Hell!*" growled my brother. "I'll take that Selim
ben Yussuf on the ball of my thumb and smear him on a
wall . . . the damned dog's-dinner!"

And:

"I'll so take him to pieces that no-one won't ever be
able to put him together again," promised the little man.
"I'll sure disestablish him."

"God!" breathed my brother, "*John Geste?*"

"Say!" whispered Buddy. "John Geste come back
to find *me*? . . .

"What! Didn't his gel marry him then? . . ." he added.

"She did," I replied. "He went home nearly dead, and they were married—and he could hardly eat, sleep or breathe for thinking of you two in the hands of the Arabs. . . . When he did get a sleep he'd start yelling, '*Hank gave his life for me,*' or, '*Buddy went back and I slunk home,*' until his wife said what he'd been praying God for her to say, and told him to come back and look for you. . . ."

"She must be a fine woman," said Noel.

"She's the finest and noblest woman in the world— the truest, the sweetest and the loveliest. . . ." I said.

Noel gave me a long and searching look.

"Gee! I wisht I were an orayter!" said Buddy. "Sure ain't it the biggest tale you ever heard tell! . . . And ain't he the White Man? . . . My God, he's like his brothers! . . . Come back to look for *me*! . . ."

And we three sat and stared at each other in silence, each thinking his own thoughts, realizing fresh aspects of this astounding business and trying to grasp the stunning fact that, approaching from opposite directions, and in ignorance of each other's movements, we had met at the heart and centre of this wonderful maze of circumstance.

"And how in the name of the Almighty Marvellous, did *you* come to know John Geste?" asked Noel suddenly.

"I knew all three of them," I said, " . . . when they were kids. . . . Their home is at a place called Brandon Abbas, a regular castle . . . only a mile or two from Granny's place at Brandon Regis. . . ."

"If anyone rises to remark that it is a small world we live in, I'll hand him one," observed Buddy. "Gee! Ain't it some world!"

We pondered the smallness of the world and the marvels packed into its limited space.

There literally was so much to be said that there was nothing to say.

" And why on earth did those three boys from the Stately Homes of England come to the Legion ? " asked Noel. " The three of them combined couldn't put up half a dirty trick, if they gave their whole time to it."

" Beau Geste ran away and enlisted to shield a girl—she's dead now—and the other two followed him to share the blame."

" Something about a dam' great di'mond, weren't it ? " said Buddy.

" Something of the sort," I agreed.

" And how did you come to know that ? " continued Noel.

" I met his wife in a Nursing-Home after I had been shot up, in Zaguig," I said. " She was a kid at Brandon Abbas too."

" And she told you that John Geste had come back to look for *us*, she not knowing we were *your* Brother and Co. ? " said Noel.

" He come back to look fer *me*, I tell you," put in Buddy. " He didn't give a curse for you, Hank Sheikh."

" And you offered to come and look for him ? " continued Noel, contemplating me thoughtfully. " And you joined the Legion to get sent to the Zephyrs on the chance of getting in touch with him. . . . ?

" Good Scout. . . ." he murmured, and sat pondering, stroking and fingering his beard in true Arab fashion.

" Well, Son, the good God Almighty meant you to find John Geste," he observed at length. " Fancy your getting sent to the same Battalion, and then being stuck down in the same *silo* together, and then the Touareg swiping every living Frenchman between there and Zaguig."

" Yes," I agreed. " . . . And this is what I want to know. . . . How in the name of the Almighty Marvellous once again, do *you* come to know all about *that* ? Who told *you* that there were two French convicts in Sheikh Yussuf ben Amir's hands, and that they were saved from a *silo* after a massacre ? "

R

"Who saved you, Son?" smiled Noel.

"Three aged scarecrows—village beggars, loafers. . . . United ages about three centuries . . ." I said.

"Meet Yacoub-who-goes-without-water and his two young brothers. . . ."

"Alf and Ed," murmured Buddy.

" . . . the Chiefs of my Desert Intelligence Department. You were hardly above ground before I knew that there had been a raid on the road-gangs, and you were hardly in the power of Selim ben Yussuf, before I knew that a couple of French prisoners had been found down a *silo*. I learnt that much while I was on the way here. . . . I'm Keeper of the Peace in these parts. . . ."

"And the pieces . . ." murmured the Wazir.

" . . . And I rushed my Camel Corps straight for here when Yacoub sent me word that the Touareg had got busy in my country. . . . I surely will learn Mr. Selim ben Yussuf a lesson he'll remember, and let him know who's Emir of this Confederation—when there are any deals to be done with the French. . . . It was his business to treat you properly and to notify me that he'd got you. . . .

"Yes, damn him," he went on. "It would have been you he'd have handed over, but for that Death Angel girl. . . . And as it is, it's *John Geste*. . . ."

"And now we got to go get John Geste. . . ." put in Buddy. "And that's a game what'll want some playing. . . . Blast Selim ben Yussuf. . . . I'll hang him on his own innards. . . .

"One thing," he added, "I kissed his gel for him, an' that surely doth get the Arab goat *sur*-prising. . . ."

Silence.

"Bud," said my brother to the Wazir, "we've built up a big business here. . . . We've put the Injuns wise to a lot of things. . . . We've made the old man's seat safe for the boy. . . . We've taught 'em how to handle the Touareg, and we've got 'em in right with the French. . . .

It's a fine, sound, going concern, with me President, you Vice-President, and the Board of Directors hand-picked, and a million francs invested under the old apple tree. . . . We're made for life. . . . We pay our own salaries and we fix our own pensions . . . also age of retirement. . . ."

" Sure, Hank Sheikh," said his Wazir. " We sure are the deserving rich. . . ."

" . . . On velvet," continued my brother. " Just made good and got all the lovely things that was coming to us. . . . Why, we're Near-Emperors. . . . Sure-enough Presidents of a Republic, anyhow. . . . And now here this John Geste comes along, gets into the Zephyrs, Our Own Representative gets him out, and he gets in again. . . . Are we to lose everything to save him again ? . . . *Let's leave him where he is*. . . ."

" Let's don't, Hank Sheikh," replied the Wazir.

" Are we to undo our life's work ? "

" Sure," said the Wazir promptly.

" Are we to lose everything we've worked and toiled and suffered and risked our lives for ? "

" Every last thing," agreed the Wazir.

" Are we to break our Treaty with the French ? . . . Break our word to the Tribes ? . . . Break the hearts of the men who love and trust us ? . . ."

" Break everything," assented the Wazir.

" Are we to start life afresh at our age ? . . . Take the road again ? . . ."

" Sure. . . . Take the road and everything else we can get. . . . What's bitin' you, you ol' fool ? "

" You mean you'll throw away *everything*—chuck up the grandest golden success two hungry hoboes ever made. . . . Go back from wealthy prince to tramping beggar ? " . . .

" Ain't our friend in trouble, Hank ? " replied Buddy. " What you talkin' about ? "

" Shake, Son," said my brother. And the two men shook hands.

"Some folk'd say our duty to the French and these Arabs came first," said Noel.

"Let 'em say," answered Buddy.

"Some folk'd say a man ought not to go back on his word," continued Noel.

"*Word!*" spat Buddy. "Ain't our friend in trouble? What's the word you've spoke, against the word you *haven't* spoke? . . . That you stand by your pard through thick and thin. . . . You remember what you said to me, Hank Sheikh? . . . '*It's all accordin'* to what they call your "*Bo Ideel.*"'"

"Goo' Boy," observed my brother, taking the small man by the scruff of the neck and shaking him affectionately. "When your friend's in need, he's your friend indeed."

"Sure thing, Hank Sheikh. . . . For a minute I wondered if you'd gone batty in the belfry or woozy in the works."

"I was only trying you out, Son. . . . I apologize. . . ."

"So you oughter, Hank Sheikh," snorted Buddy.

"Don't think I doubted you, Son, but I thought I'd remind you that it's a hard row to hoe, and ruin at the end of it."

"Harder for you, Old Hoss," grinned Buddy. "You got a wife, an' I ain't. . . . Me! . . . I got more sense. . . ."

"Married, Noel? . . . My congratulations. . . . An Arab lady?" I said. "Why, no, of course, I remember . . . the Death Angel said you'd married an English girl like herself. . . ."

"An English girl—very unlike herself," replied Noel, and eyed me queerly.

"I shall look forward to meeting her and paying my respects as a brother-in-law," I said, wondering what sort of extraordinary person my brother could have picked up in this part of the world.

"You have met her, Oats," replied Noel, and I stared astounded, beginning to wonder again whether this were not, after all, an extraordinary dream.

No, it was not a dream. It was more like a good dream wasted.

"Met her ? " I said. "Where ? "

"She was a Miss Maud Atkinson," said my brother with excellent nonchalance, and both he and Buddy watched me expectant, and, I thought, a little on the defensive.

I don't think my jaw dropped, nor my face expressed anything other than what I wished them to see.

"Congratulations again, Noel," I cried. "When I congratulated you before, it was the usual form of words. . . . I can now congratulate you on having married one of the bravest and best little women that ever lived. She went *literally* through fire to help a friend—in a burning house in England. . . . She's pure gold."

"Thank you, Oats," said my brother, extending his hand.

"Nearly married her meself," observed Buddy glumly. "He butted in, the day before. . . . Stuck his great hoof in our love affair before I . . ."

Spreading a useful hand across his Wazir's face, the Emir thrust his Minister out of the conversation.

"And Mary never told you *that* . . ." continued Noel.

"No. . . . She just mentioned that Maudie was married," said I. "Doesn't she rather complicate the situation ? "

"Like Hell she does," pondered Noel. "She'd be the first to chase me off to get John Geste. . . . She'd never forgive us if she knew we'd left a friend in trouble. . . ."

"Where is she now ? " I asked.

"At my headquarters at the Great Oasis," replied my brother. "In the charge of my Council and a great old bird who is Regent of my chief tribe. . . . At least they think she is in their charge. . . . As a matter of fact she is the best man of the lot."

"Did she marry you as an Arab ? " I asked.

"She married me as a Lovely Sheikh, out of a book," was the reply. "Going to marry me again as a common man, out of a job, when we go home. . . . I'm still a bit of a mystery to her. . . . Girls like mysteries. . . . She always wanted a Sheikh and now she's got one. . . . And she's a *houri*. . . ."

" Wicked shame," muttered the Wazir. " Married the gel under false pretences. . . . Tole her he'd bought a book an' learned English so as he could talk to her— the rambunctious ole goat. . . . Spoilt the one and only love affair of my life. . . ."

" Never mind, Son," soothed the Emir. " You started another last night."

" I certainly did," agreed Buddy with prideful mien. " I'll tell the world she fell for me, right there. . . . And she cert'nly is the Tough Baby. . . . I'm going over to call on her, bye-and-bye."

" You certainly made an impression on her," I said. " She spoke of you when she returned from the visit."

" And that brings us to the point," said Noel. " She tells me that Selim ben Yussuf handed a convict over to a *peloton méhariste* some days ago ; and that means that he was taken straight to Zaguig, examined on the subject of the Arab raid, and sent back to a road-gang. . . . Now by the mercy of God, old Yacoub-who-goes-without-water knows his face—and I back him to pick him out from ten thousand. . . . I'll have him and his gang off within the hour, and as soon as John Geste is working on the road again, I shall know it. . . ."

" What will Yacoub do ? " I asked.

" Everybody," grunted the Wazir.

" Beg mostly," replied my brother. " Loaf about . . . cadge . . . steal rusty cans and run for his life . . . look silly . . . do a bit of water-carrying . . . pick up a job . . . hold a horse . . . lead a camel. . . . They're the three finest old actors that never went on the stage. . . . Believe me, Henry Irving never had anything on Yacoub-who-goes-without-water. . . ."

" And when he locates him ? " I asked.

" Them *un*corrigible Touaregs again . . ." suggested

the Wazir. " There'll be another raid and John Geste
will be took captive by them. . . . Even the Zephyrs
will pity the pore feller. . . ."

" That's the scheme," said Noel. " It'll want some
planning. . . . I don't want to hurt anybody, and I
don't want to get my people shot up, either ; but John
Geste's coming right out of that road-gang. . . ."

" I get the idea," I mused. " In the meantime what
becomes of me ? "

" You're dead and buried, Son. . . . Your ghost turns
Injun and stays with us, keeping its face hidden. . . .
We'll brown it up a bit. . . ."

" But there are half a dozen people who know I'm alive,"
I said. " The lot out there who brought me over. . . ."

" That's Miss Death Angel's trouble. . . ." replied my
brother. " They're her people. . . . It's up to her to
see they don't squeal about her little games, to Selim ben
Yussuf, or anybody else. . . .

" I don't think they'll talk much, when I've had a word
with them," he added, and the Wazir chuckled grimly.

" I'm dead of course, as far as the French are concerned,"
I remarked.

" You perished in the massacre, Son. . . . Poor old
John will be in a bad way," he continued. " He can't
very well tell the French you're alive and ought to be
rescued from the wild Bedouin, and he can't very well leave
you to be tortured by Selim ben Yussuf, as he thinks. . . ."

" I suppose Selim ben Yussuf couldn't do any good, if
you were to put the screw on him ? " I asked.

" No," replied my brother. " *He* can't do anything.
. . . Once he's handed an escaped prisoner back, there's
an end of it. . . . I myself couldn't do a thing, although
I'm Emir of the Confederated tribes of the Great Oasis,
and ally of France.

" . . . No, Selim can only tell me all about the patrol
and then take what's coming to him. . . . The fool ! . . .
The damned impudent presumptuous *fool* ! . . . Why, I
could prevent him succeeding his father as Sheikh of his

Tribe. . . . If I were staying on, that is . . ." and he smiled wryly. " I'll get him, as it is . . . if he comes back in time. . . ."

" He's bound to come back soon, I should think," said I. " The girl expected him to roll up at any minute. In fact, when we heard the commotion of your arrival, we thought he had come. . . ."

" What's the position there exactly . . . d'you know ? " asked Noel.

" Yes," I replied. " I do. . . . It's the hell of a position. . . . Selim is madly infatuated with the girl, which you can quite understand. . . . And the girl is apparently madly infatuated with me . . . which you probably cannot understand. . . .

" I met them both in Bouzen a long time ago, and the trouble began as far back as that. . . . Selim was after her then, and wanted to stab me because she singled me out at a dancing-show. . . .

" I gather that, being heartily tired of Town, she came for ' a day in the country ' . . . Giving Selim a trial trip before marrying him, perhaps. . . . Just as likely to become his step-mama I should say. . . ."

" And then you came on the scene and the scene was changed. . . ." suggested my brother. " Friend Selim did himself some good when he brought you home, didn't he ? "

" Yes. . . . And me too . . ." I sighed. " I paid her rather a high price for my freedom to go off again in search of John Geste. . . . Noel, old chap, *couldn't* you have come a day sooner ? . . ."

" No, Son . . . nor an hour. . . . Why ? "

" Because I made a fair and square bargain with the Death Angel that I'd come back to her as soon as I had seen John Geste out of the country, or else at the end of a year. . . ."

" Come back to her ? . . . What for ? . . ." asked my brother.

" To marry her," I said.

My brother stared incredulous, and then laughed harshly.

"Marry her ? . . . Well, that's an engagement that'll be broken off," smiled he.

"Not by me, Noel," I told him. "It's a 'gentleman's agreement.' . . . I gave her my word and my hand on it. . . . She has done her part and I'll have to do mine. Just as soon as we've got John Geste out of the country. . ."

"You'll come too, Son—if you have to come in a sack," affirmed my brother.

"Noel," I said, "listen. . . . Before you came, this girl made a bargain with me. On her side she was to help me get John Geste out of the country. . . . In return for that help, I gave her my solemn promise that I would come back. And I shall do so. . . ."

"I get you, Son," he answered thoughtfully.

Silence fell, and we sat, each thinking his own thoughts —if gazing in wonderment upon incredible but undeniable facts, can be called thought.

The Wazir was the first to break the silence, and the trend of his cogitations was apparent.

"Do I understand that you are reg'larly engaged to this young woman then ? " he asked purposefully.

"Yes," I said.

"You *would* be . . ." he observed glumly, and in reply to the inquiry of my raised eyebrow, added :

"I was going to propose to her meself, to-day. . . ."

"Then I sincerely hope you'll do it, and be entirely successful," I replied.

"Well, you cut in first, Bo. . . . We'll leave it at that. . . . I ain't bad at heart. . . ."

"No. It's your head that's bad," observed my brother. "Brains went bad long ago. . . . Now stop jabbering and put Marbruk ben Hassan wise. . . . I want Yacoub here quicker than Marbruk can get him. . . ."

The Wazir left the tent.

"Who *is* he, Noel ? " I asked.

"The biggest little man that ever lived. . . . And my

friend," replied my brother. "I took up with him when I ran away from home, and we've been together ever since. . . . He's the bravest man I ever saw and there never lived a stauncher. . . . He's true, Son. . . . And when you want him, he's *there*. . . ."

"What's that language he talks?" I asked.

"Well, he was born in the Bowery, New York, and that's his mother tongue. . . . And he got his schooling in South State Street and Cottage Grove Avenue, Chicago, and the slums thereabout, and he talks the dialect. . . . He graduated on the water-front at San Francisco, and learnt some good language there. . . . He was a bar-keep in Seattle, and went to the gold-diggings. . . . He was a cow-puncher in Texas and Arizona, and he's used the roads of the U.S.A. a lot—and the railways more so, but I don't think he ever bought a ticket. . . ."

"And why do you talk like him when you are talking to him?" I inquired.

"Because I've got good manners," replied Noel. "And what's good enough for Bud is good enough for me. . . .

"Now you stay where you are for a bit, Son," he continued. "I'm going to hold a *mejliss* and get busy. . . ."

A few minutes later, the Emir and his Wazir were seated on the carpet and cushions of State outside the big tent in which I was concealed.

The Oriental Potentate was seated in judgment; if not "in the city gate" as of old, then in the door of his tent and shadow of the palm, as in days far older.

The dwarf, Marbruk ben Hassan, brought to the judgment-seat the party who had escorted me.

"And so there were two *Roumi* prisoners . . ." said the deep voice of the Emir, " . . . and one of them was given up to the French, and the other died. . . . Is it not so? . . ."

"It is so; O, Emir," said the voice of the good *hakim*.

"It is so indeed; O, Emir," said Abd'allah ibn Moussa.

And the voices of the servants chorused the refrain.

" And his body was buried in the sand," continued the Emir. " You were all present I think ? "

" All ; O, Emir . . ." was the unanimous reply.

" There could be no mistake about it ? " suggested the Emir. " I should be sorry for one who made a mistake about it. . . . Sorry for him, and his son, his son's son, and his wives and his children, his camels, his goats, and all that he had."

All appeared perfectly certain that there could be no mistake on the subject.

" Was it a deep grave or a shallow grave, in which you buried this unfortunate prisoner ? " pursued the Emir.

And it was the voice of Abd'allah that answered promptly :

" Oh, a very shallow grave ; O, Emir. . . . It might be found that jackals had removed the body . . . should any search be now made for it. . . ."

And the voice of the *hakim* chimed in with :

" And it was a much-trodden spot, O, Emir, near the camel-enclosure. . . . A very difficult spot to find . . . even had the jackals not rifled the grave. . . ."

" It is well," concluded the Emir. " Go in peace, making no mistake . . . for my arm is long—long as the Tail of the Horse of the Prophet."

CHAPTER XV

I SPENT the following days in a curious condition of mind, and much comfort of body. I had complete and much-needed rest, and freedom from all personal anxiety and fear; and my hope concerning John Geste was rising high. . . . I had had him in my hands and I should have him again. . . .

This brother of mine was a strong man—a strong man armed—influential and powerful, unless he came into deliberate conflict with the French, whose friend and ally he was.

With him I was absolutely safe, and, though idly quiescent myself, I felt that everything possible was being done to further my affairs—which were now equally those of my brother and his friend.

I could lie upon my cushions, resting and relaxed, yet happy in the knowledge that more was being done to further John Geste's rescue than at any time since Isobel had told me of his capture.

I could not talk with these two without becoming imbued with a feeling of completest confidence. They were so sure that their Desert Intelligence—which had never yet failed them—would speedily discover John's whereabouts, and that their brave and faithful fighting-men would effect his rescue.

Naturally I had my moments of fear, gloom, anxiety and doubt, but I had my hours of hope and joy, and certitude that all would be well, and that I should live to see John Geste step upon the deck of a British or American ship.

And at that point I always awakened myself from my day-dream and refused to envisage the future.

Life—with the Angel of Death as my wife!

Well, I must make the best of it, and the best of her. There is good in everyone, and, probably, in her way—and given a fair chance—she was quite as " good " as I was. . . . And in any case I should be a happy man, if only I succeeded in saving John. . . .

I grew very near to my brother again, during this brief period of waiting, this tiny oasis in the desert of strenuous life, and got to know him very well.

The more I learned, the more was I filled with admiration at his astounding feat—his rising by sheer unaided ability, from being a practically dead man, possessed of the remains of one ragged garment and nothing else, to his present position—as a man of wealth, power and importance.

His was indeed a wonderful story, and in my private mind I ranked him with such men as that Burton who became an Arab and made the pilgrimage to Mecca, earning the title of *Haji*, a Mussulman of Mussulmans.

Little wonder that Major de Beaujolais, with all his Secret Service training, had found no grounds for suspicion, since the Arabs themselves believed him to be an Arab.

His years of wandering in the desert with John and Digby Geste must have been a hard apprenticeship, but the only possible one for such success as this.

And the same applied to my brother's *fidus Achates*, Buddy.

Neither of them was a man of book-education, but both were men of brains, ability, determination and character.

Noel was his father's son there, but oh, how different a man—with his wise broad tolerance.

When I endeavoured to discover Noel's mental attitude to our Father, I was somewhat baffled, but came to the conclusion that if he did not still actually hate him, he thought of him with some bitterness, and promised himself the pleasure of, some day, returning home, and " having it out " with him, " mastering him " as he expressed it. . . .

Not in a spirit of bitterness and revenge, or with the least idea of humiliating him, but rather as a sop to his own self-respect and to meet him on an equality, on his own level, and as man to man ; and particularly, I think, Noel wished to demonstrate to him that a son of Homer H. Vanbrugh could, unaided, amount to something, without dwelling for ever in Homer H. Vanbrugh's pocket, or in the shadow of his crushing and overwhelming bulk.

Not only did my affection for my brother increase, as we talked together, but my respect also. And I envied him. . . . He was the Happy Warrior. He had deliberately chosen the way of life that suited him, and for which he was suited, rejecting the job of rich man's son, offered him by circumstance, and going out into the high-ways and by-ways of the world, the open roads that called to him.

He had climbed a steep and rugged path, and he had enjoyed the effort and the danger. He had made contact with realities, looked life in the face, and acknowledged the great God of Things As They Are.

And of all the interesting things about him, what interested me most was the fact that, having literally and actually been crowned with success, he was, without an instant's hesitation, prepared to cast that crown away at a word—a word of a friend in danger.

A crown was not his *beau idéal*.

A man who thought like Don Quixote though he chose to talk like Sancho Panza.

And, too, the more I saw of his friend, the more I liked and respected him, for my brother's standards and values were his in equal measure.

To what extent this was due to the uninfluenced nature of the man, and how much to the fact that my brother was his untarnishable hero, and impeccable model, I do not know—and if the latter, the more credit to him that such a man could be his ideal.

Yes—I liked Buddy. And I wrote him down a bold, unconquerable spirit, sterling and faithful and fine.

" Lie low, Son," whispered my brother, entering my comfortable tent wherein I lay restfully at peace—in the peace of the great desert.

" French patrol coming. . . . You're all right behind that face-stain—your own father wouldn't know you. . . . No need to chuck your weight about though. . . . If you like to put an eye to one crack and an ear to another, you may have some fun. . . ."

It wasn't exactly fun, but it was very interesting, to hear the officers of the Patrol talking with the Emir el Hamel el Kebir and the Sheikh el Habibka el Wazir, over their three rounds of ceremonial and complimentary mint tea.

Marvellous was the impassive Arab dignity with which the Emir, his Wazir, Sheikhs and chief men met and greeted the French *sous-officier* and his European subordinates, and with which they conducted them to the rug-and-cushion-strewn carpet before the Emir's tent.

When all customary and proper formalities had been observed, the French *sous-officier* got down to business.

It appeared that the French authorities at Zaguig appreciated the Emir's prompt action in hurrying to the scene of the massacre, and hoped that, by now, he had some information on the subject of the raiders. . . .

Of course the Touareg at once came under suspicion . . . but it was easy to cry, " *Touareg* "—and there were certain features of the raid that might or might not indicate Touareg. . . . The said features might have been covered by the Touareg face-veil, so to speak. . . .

But, and here was a point to consider, might not those veils have been borrowed, and might they not have veiled features that were not those of Touareg faces at all ?

There were reasons for thinking so, and if the slaughter had been Touareg handiwork, why was the life of at least one of the road-gang spared ? . . . And how had this man come to be in the hands of Selim ben Yussuf ?

The convict himself would say nothing . . . absolutely nothing . . . though he had undoubtedly received every encouragement to speak. (My fists clenched as I listened and thought of poor John. . . . I cursed the Angel of Death.) . . . Of course he may have been knocked on the head and really remember nothing, as he said. . . . But *how* did Selim ben Yussuf get him ? . . .

And what exactly was Selim ben Yussuf doing within a few miles of where the massacre took place ?

Old Sheikh Yussuf ben Amir, his father, was all-right, no doubt, but Selim ben Yussuf was quite another coconut. . . .

His record was a bad one, or rather it was a record of strong continual suspicions. . . . It was firmly believed that he had been prominent in the Zaguig massacre, though as there was no survivor of that, except an American tourist, no evidence could be got against him. (Here I was indeed interested.) . . . Still, Major de Beaujolais had reported that he had seen Selim in Zaguig just before the massacre—and pray where was the gentleman at this very minute ? . . .

The Emir stroked and fingered his beard, gravely nodding as the Frenchman talked. . . . And the Emir's Wazir stroked and fingered his beard, gravely and wisely nodding as his master did so.

It appeared that the Emir had himself entertained suspicions concerning Selim ben Yussuf, and had his eye upon him . . . and in fact, the sole reason why he remained encamped at this spot, with his Camel-Corps, was to see whether Selim returned to the Tribe and, meanwhile, to make wide inquiry as to his whereabouts and movements.

And had the Emir heard the rumour which *l'Adjudant* Lebaudy had picked up somewhere . . . that Selim ben Yussuf had had *two* French prisoners ?

Here the Emir stroked his beard very thoughtfully.

" If he has another prisoner, he has taken him with him," he said. " There is absolutely no question whatever of there being another French prisoner in their camp over there. . . ."

" That's certain, is it ? " asked the officer.

" As absolutely certain as that Mahommed is the Prophet of Allah. . . . Have a tent-to-tent visitation if you like, but 'twill be but a waste of time . . ." said the Emir.

" It would be like the young fox," he added, thoughtfully frowning, " if he *did* have two, to give one up in token of good faith, and to keep the other as a hostage— or to torture, if he hates the *Roumi* as some say. . . ."

" H'm. . . . Give up one to show his love, and keep one upon whom to show his hate, eh ? " said the Frenchman.

The Emir then inquired as to this curious rumour, and learned that an Arab *méhariste* with *l'Adjudant* Lebaudy's patrol had been told by a boy, a goat-herd, of whom he bought some dates, that there had been two *Roumi* prisoners, but one was said to have died. . . .

Probably nothing in it—except that one of the Secret Service spies had also brought in a story, admittedly somewhat fantastic, about a *Roumi* prisoner having been tortured to death by a woman. . . .

The Emir did not appear to be impressed.

" It'll be ten by the New Moon . . ." he smiled. " However, our young friend, Selim, shall enlighten us. . . . Oh, yes . . . Selim shall talk. . . ."

" Selim shall squeal, eh ? " smiled the French officer grimly.

The Emir looked up.

" What does old Sheikh Yussuf ben Amir say ? " he asked.

" He says he knows absolutely nothing about either Selim's movements or about Selim's prisoner or prisoners, and I think he is speaking the truth. . . ."

And the Emir bade the officer rest assured that he, El Hamel el Kebir, would know the truth, the whole truth, and nothing but the truth, as to there having been one or two French prisoners in the hands of Selim ben Yussuf, and as to the precise manner in which that suspect had acquired them.

S

One more thing—and the officer picked up his riding-switch and *képi*—orders were coming, for Sheikh Yussuf ben Amir's tribe, to migrate at once to the Oasis of Sidi Usman, near Bouzen, there to concentrate and remain until further notice.

Would the Emir facilitate their departure and keep a patrol in the neighbourhood, so long as it seemed likely that Selim ben Yussuf, and the fighting-men with him, might return to where he had left the tribe encamped. . . .

§ 3

And, next day, as we three sat in dignified isolation apart from all men, a servant came running, spoke to the Soudanese sentry—whose business it was to see that none unauthorized approached within hearing—and drew near.

" Yacoub-who-goes-without-water sends a messenger ; O, Emir," the man said, making obeisance.

" Bring him instantly, el R'Orab," ordered the Emir, and, a minute or two later, an aged and filthy beggar approached, a man so old and decrepit that the flesh of his bent and trembling legs seemed covered in dry grey scales rather than brown human skin. His face expressed nothing but senile imbecility and, as his shrivelled lips opened, exposing the toothless gums and a tongue like that of a parrot, one expected to hear nothing but the shrill piping voice of a pitiable dotard, well advanced in second childhood.

Supporting his emaciated frame with the help of a staff, he salaamed profoundly, glanced at me inquiringly, and, on receiving the Emir's kind permission to speak freely, changed astonishingly.

Certainly he was still a dirty old man, but one whose face now expressed shrewdness, alertness, and ripe wisdom. A hopeless, helpless, doddering old pantaloon turned, before my eyes, into an extremely knowing, spry and competent old gentleman.

" May the Sidi Emir live for ever ! " quoth he, " and

dwell in the protection of Allah and the care of His Prophet.
. . . Humblest greetings from his meanest slave, Yacoub-
who-goes-without-water, and this message. . . .

"'Know, O, Emir, that the *Roumi* prisoner sold by
Sheikh Selim ben Yussuf to the *Franzawi* was taken to
the city of Zaguig and there cast into prison. . . . At the
gate of the prison have I sat, a blind and naked beggar,
asking "Alms for the love of Allah! Alms for the love of
Allah, the Merciful, the Compassionate. . . ." I have not
left this place by day nor by night, and all who have entered
in unto it, and all who have come out of it, have I seen. . . .
Yea, every one. . . . And behold, three times has the
Roumi prisoner been taken by soldiers from this old
prison to the new barracks. . . . And three times has
he been brought back. . . . Each time did I follow afar
off, and what happened when he was taken to the barracks
of the *Franzawi* soldiers, I do not know, save that high
officers assembled and questioned him . . . for I climbed
on the back of a passing camel and saw through the iron
bars of the "hole through which one looks out. [1]" . . .

"'. . . And the fourth time he was taken from the
prison, he marched with others like him, and with soldiers
about them, down the Road that the *Franzawi* build from
Zaguig to the Great Oasis. . . . And each night they
halted for a night in an armed camp. . . . And now he,
and those others with him, have come to the place of the
deserted village, and they carry on the work of those that
are dead. . . . With my own eyes I am watching this
man and with my brother's voice am I speaking these
words. . . . And may the peace of Allah abide with the
Sidi Emir, and encompass him about. . . .'

"And that is the message of my brother, Yacoub-who-
goes-without-water, O Lord. . . .'"

And:

"It is well," replied the Emir. "Go and eat."

And as the intelligent old gentleman lapsed back into
the idiot centenarian and tottered out of earshot:

[1] Window.

"Good God above us!" said Noel. "*John Geste!* John Geste, himself, is not ten miles away from where we're sitting now, Otis!"

And I could answer nothing.

§ 4

We instantly became a Council of War.

My brother is a man of prompt action, but he is not of those who act first and think afterwards. I imagine his marvellous success among the Arabs was as much due to his wisdom in the Council-tent as to skill and courage on the battle-field.

In the strange rôle that my brother played at this period of his life, tactics and strategy counted for more than swashbuckling. It interested me greatly to see how he considered the views and opinions of Buddy and myself, and then of his most trusted Arab lieutenants, weighed them carefully, discussed them, and then produced his own, and his reasons for holding them.

Inasmuch as I had worked in the road-gang and knew, to the last detail, the method and routine of the daily and nightly procedure, my advice was asked, my suggestions invited, and I was flatteringly bidden to say precisely what I would do if I were the executive in charge of the work of rescue.

To me, it at once appeared that there were two methods open to us—that of force, and that of guile, and I promptly propounded this platitude.

"Take the force-idea first, Son," said Noel, "bearing in mind it's not to be a raid like this last one. I'll have John Geste if I kill every Arab and Frenchman in Africa, but I intend to get him without killing anybody."

"That rather cramps one's style for force, doesn't it?" I said. "Limits one's scope of action, a little. . . . What would happen if we swooped down upon the working-party in overwhelming strength, but unarmed. . . . Simply kidnapped John by main force. . . . We three seize him, while a hundred good men and true scatter everybody, all ends up, and we ride for it ? "

" What would happen, Son ? . . . We should leave about thirty dead . . . probably including John Geste and certainly ourselves. . . . As I say, I don't want anybody killed, especially my own men. . . ."

" What about a hand-picked party, to surround the spot in the dark, and shoot straight and fast—but high. . . . While they're carefully hitting nobody, we three, armed, say, with ' a foot of lead-pipe ' each, dash in and get John. . . ."

" Dash in and don't get John," said my brother. " We get about seven bullets each, instead. . . ."

" Well . . . what about this idea ? . . . Let your man, Yacoub, get a word of warning to John to be *ready* at sunset to-morrow . . . expecting something to happen. . . . Then let Selim ben Yussuf's tribe start their trek in the afternoon, and pass along the road just before the gang is due to stop work. . . . All your men might join in the procession, camels and all complete, and the more dust they raise the better. . . . We three, and a few chosen lads who can be trusted, can be in a bunch, and one of us carry a spare *haik* and *burnous*. . . . As we pass and jostle along the road, Yacoub gets beside John and says ' Now ! ' to him, and I shout ' Come on, John.' . . . He just steps into the midst of the crowd and we throw the spare *burnous* round him to hide his uniform, and he pulls it over his face. . . . Let Buddy be leading a spare camel, and we three push forward as quickly as we can, to the head of the column, and then ride for it. . . ."

My brother smiled.

" Bright idea, Oats," he said kindly. " But it would be ' Keep off the grass ' as soon as the mob tried to use the Road. . . . ' *At the stiffs in front, at five hundred metres, seven rounds rapid fire.*' . . . No, Son . . . especially after the recent raid, no clouds of dust are coming near any Zephyr party. Neither along the Road nor across it. . . ."

"Well, let's try guile," I said. "What about old Yacoub slipping John a file and hanging around until John makes a quiet get-away. . . . We're waiting near, with fast camels, and old Yacoub brings him to us. . . ."

"Waiting how long, Son? We might grow grey, or strike roots into the earth before John got his chance. . . . There won't be much slackness for a long time to come. . . . Suppose he's caught using the file? . . . Suppose he is shot, getting away? . . . You know about how many single-handed escape-attempts succeed. . . ."

"What about this? . . ." I tried again.

"Supposing you, in your own proper person, as the Emir el Hamel el Kebir, in your whitest robes, heavy corded silk head-dress and scarlet and gold camel-hair ropes round your head, visited that particular section of the Road—with your Wazir, and high Sheikhs, chief executioner, cup-bearer, baker, butler, soothsayer, and holy panjandrum and all—and had an afternoon tea-party with the nice friendly White Men. . . . And while all goes merrier than a marriage-bell, there is a sudden raid by a few score of your best, unarmed . . . and, as they appear, some of us seize the rifles of our friends, and the rest of us seize the friends themselves. . . . While we hang on to them—grapple them to our hearts with hoops of steel, so to speak—the new-comers guided by Yacoub, simply cut out John from the herd and make their get-away. . . ."

"Leaving us in the soup, like . . ." murmured Buddy.

"Well . . . we'd have the rifles, and they'd simply have to 'hands up' while we backed away to our camels and cleared off. . . ."

"Gee! Hasn't he got a mind, Hank Sheikh," admired Buddy. "He sure is your brother. . . . Sim'lar kind o' train-hold-up nature. . . ."

"It's a scheme," mused Noel. "It's an idea, Bud. . . ."

"Or there's that *silo*," I suggested. "Suppose Yacoub provisioned it, and we three made a regular Red Indian swift-and-silent sort of raid, dressed in brown paint and coco-nut-oil. . . . We might get him and rush to that *silo* and lie low there . . ."

" 'Down among the dead men,' " murmured Buddy.

" . . . until the first wild hurroosh is over. . . . That wouldn't lead a pursuit back to your own camp, either. . . . Sneak away from the *silo* the following night to where Yacoub has the camels. . . ."

Noel shook his head.

"Too risky, Son," he mused. "That *silo* may have been discovered and be in use again. . . . And if it hasn't, it sure is an unhealthy spot. . . . What's your idea, Bud ? " he continued, turning to his friend.

"Well, Hank Sheikh, I'd like a good up-and-down dawg-fight—a free-for-all, knock-down-an'-drag-out, go-as-you-please, bite-kick-or-gouge turn-up—an' run that boy, John Geste, outa gaol. . . . Life's gettin' a dam' sight too peaceful. . . . An' you're gettin' fat. . . .

"But since you've got so partic'lar an' no poor fightin'-man's to get hurt, what about dopin' the guard ? . . . Have a party. . . . Have a supper-party an' hand out the free drinks generous an' hearty *an'* doped. . . . You don't taste *hashish* in coffee, an' if we couldn't do anything else, we could work off three rounds of sweet coffee an' three rounds of mint-tea on 'em . . . not to mention something funny in the *cous-cous*. . . . Nothin' serious. . . . In the mawnin' twenty-five headaches *come*, an' one prisoner *gone*. . . . Hardly worth noticin'. . . ."

"Gee ! Hasn't he got a mind, Oats ? " admired the Emir. "Filled with treacly treachery, putrid poison, and mouldy mellow-drama. . . . But it cert'nly is an idea. . . ."

He turned to Buddy.

"Don't I seem to remember we already had one misfortunate igsperience with poison, Son ? "

"Misfortunate Hell ! " snorted Buddy. "It clinched the deal anyhow. . . . That's all the thanks *I* get. . . . That, and a broken heart. . . ." he added.

"It's an idea, Son. . . . It cert'nly is an idea. . . ."

admitted Noel. "The fierce and treacherous Sheikh stuff, eh? Invite 'em to a hash party an' poison 'em . . ."

"Look here, Noel," I broke in, "excuse the question. . . . But where do you draw the line? . . . You want no bloodshed, and I can quite understand that, and I entirely agree. . . . But about the treachery part of it, since the word's been used. . . . If I know you, old chap, and I think I do, you'll hate that more than a fair and square fight—openly showing your hand as having suddenly become an enemy of the French. . . ."

"I needn't appear in the fair-and-square fight, Son," replied my brother.

"I could very easily turn a picked lot of my braves into Touareg, and let there be another raid. . . . When the Guard was disposed of, Yacoub could identify John Geste, and they could bring him along . . . bring the whole lot along, if Yacoub got knocked out. . . . I should never be suspected. . . . It isn't that. . . . I simply don't want any killing, and I'll try everything else first.

". . . As to the treachery, that's the only alternative to fighting and that's why I'm considering it. . . ."

"Suppose the French ever find you out?" I asked.

"They're going to find me out, Son. . . . Out of the country . . ." was the reply. "It's like this, Boy. . . . John Geste came back to save us. . . . I'm going to save John Geste. . . . I'm going to do it without hurting a man, if I can, and that means I've got to play false since I won't play rough. . . . Well . . . I've taken their money and I've given them good value and a fair deal. . . .

"Now here endeth the good value and the fair deal— so I take no more money. . . . I throw in my hand. . . . I'm a Bad Man all-right, Oats, but I've never double-crossed and I won't start now. . . . The day I break my side of the contract, the contract's broken, and I won't benefit by it any more. . . . I've kept the Treaty that I made with my young brother-in-law, good and proper, but it's got to lapse directly I start monkeying-about with

" None are to die, Yussuf Latif . . . neither in fight nor in willing surrender of their lives . . ." said the Emir.

" Speak again; O, Yussuf Latif. . . ."

" What of this then, Lord ? When our peaceful and humble disposition has disarmed suspicion, and we have gradually been permitted to mingle with the soldiers of the escort, every one of these shall be allotted to two of our strong men. . . . Of every two men, one shall have two stout thin cords about his waist, or otherwise hidden. . . .

" At the given signal, every soldier shall be seized by the two appointed to him, and the moment that one has snatched his rifle, the other shall seize him round the arms and body. . . . The rifle-snatcher shall then bind the man's feet together and his arms to his sides. . . . The two shall then carry the man to an appointed place, where all the soldiers shall be laid together unhurt. . . . Except one. . . .

" This one shall be laid a mile away—his feet most strongly bound and one arm bound to his body tightly. . . . It shall be shown to him that there is a knife stuck in the sand, afar off. . . .

" When we have departed—taking with us the man whom you desire—this bound soldier will roll and wriggle toward the knife, and by the time he gets it and contrives to free himself and his comrades, we shall be very far away, and, making a détour, return hither. . . ."

" Leaving a track for all men to see ? " asked the Emir.

The Arab smiled at the joke.

" Nay, Lord," he said, " the détour would take us up the stony Wadi el Tarish where a million camels would leave no trace. . . ."

" Do you like this plan ; O, Yussuf ? " inquired the Emir.

" Each man thinks his own fleas are gazelles," quoted Yussuf Latif ibn Fetata.

" And what do you think the prisoners will do, when the guards are bound and you are gone ? " asked the Emir.

The Arab smiled and put his hand to his throat.

" They must be bound too," he said.

The Emir stroked his beard thoughtfully and pondered awhile.

" You have spoken well; O, Marbruk ben Hassan and Yussuf ibn Fetata. . . . I will reveal my mind later. . . . Meantime, each of you select two score of the best. . . . Yes, yes, I know that all are best—but select the coolest and steadiest. . . . Men who do not fire at shadows nor foam at the mouth as they fight. . . ."

The two withdrew, salaaming profoundly.

" A fine combination, those two," said Noel. " Cautious age and daring youth. . . . And both stauncher than steel and braver than lions. . . ."

" I surely am sorry for that Yussuf Latif boy," observed Buddy. " What's wrong with him is a broken heart. . . . I know the symptoms—none better. . . ."

" That's so, Bud," agreed Noel, and added :

" The wonder to me is that you ain't egsperienced the symptoms of a broken neck—or a stretched one anyhow. . . ."

The smile of the Wazir combined pity, superiority and contempt in exactly equal proportions.

" The point is, have you got a plan . . . chatterbox ? " he said.

" I have," said the Emir, and he detailed it to us.

" It ain't perfect," he mused, " but it's the best we can do. . . . It's funny without being vulgar. . . . It oughta succeed. . . . An' there won't be any killing. . . .

" The young woman would help us, all-right, Otis ? " he asked, turning to me.

" She certainly would," I assured him. " Only too glad to bring me a day's march nearer home. . . . Or right home in a day's march. . . ."

" That's the scheme, then," concluded Noel. " . . . And we'll bring it off to-morrow night. . . . I'll hate doing it—but I'd hate any other plan worse. . . . And the job's got to be done. . . ."

CHAPTER XVI

IN all the changing scenes of life, one of the several that
are indelibly printed on my mind, and which I shall
never forget, is that of the feast and entertainment, given
by the Emir el Hamel el Kebir, to the men of the advance-
party of those who were the pioneers on the Road that was
eventually to link the Great Oasis with Zaguig, the uttermost outpost of the African Empire of France.

Having a deep personal interest in this Road, the Emir
el Hamel el Kebir had, with a considerable bodyguard,
come from where he was encamped, to see with his own
eyes something of the great Road's swift progress and to
greet the fore-runners of its makers.

The feast was, of course, an Arab one.

Surrounded by cushion-strewn rugs, on a large palm-
leaf mat, slaves placed a shallow metal dish so vast as to
suggest a bath. In this, on a deep bed of rice, lay a mass
of lumps of meat, the flesh of kids, lambs, and I feared, of
a sucking camel-calf. A sea of rich thick gravy lapped
upon the shores of surrounding rice, with wavelets of
molten butter and oily yellow fat.

In the centre of the bath was a noble mound of heads
crowned with livers, intact and entire. Among the mass of
chops, cutlets, joints, scrags, legs, shoulders, saddles, and
nameless lumps of meat, were portions of the animals not
usually seen on Western dishes. These, however, could
be avoided by the prejudiced.

I noticed that the genuine Arabs present, were not prejudiced. Around this dish we knelt, each upon one knee,

his right arm bared to the elbow, and, with the aid of our good right hands, we filled our busy mouths, and ate . . . and ate . . . and ate . . .

And ate.

There were present, the Emir el Hamel el Kebir; his Minister el Habibka el Wazir; a gloomy taciturn Sheikh, dark of face and blue-black of hair and well-clipped beard, a man supposed to be under a curse and also suffering from the effects of a highly unwholesome love-potion administered to him by a jealous wife—a potion from which he would probably never recover, as the Emir, indicating my morose and surly self, explained to the French *Adjudant*; also Marbruk ben Hassan; Yussuf Latif ibn Fetata; and some half a dozen leading Sheikhs of the tribe to which the Emir belonged; and four or five Frenchmen.

From time to time, the Emir would fish out a succulent morsel and thrust it into the mouth of the guest of honour on his right, *l'Adjudant* Lebaudy, a man who interested me much. I had put him down as very true to type, a soldier and nothing more, but a fine soldier, rugged as a rock, hard as iron, and true as steel—a man of simple mind and single purpose, untroubled by thoughts of why and wherefore, of right and wrong, finding duty sufficient and the order of a superior more important than the order of the Universe. . . .

And by no means stupid—in fact watchful, wary, and fore-sighted, as we were to discover.

We ate in stark silence—as far as speech is concerned that is—lest light converse offend our host with indication that we were finding but light fare and entertainment. . . . When we had finished, and not a stomach could hold another grain of rice, we rose, indicated our profound satisfaction by profound hiccoughs, went to the door of the tent, wiped our greasy hands upon its flap, and then held them forth while servants poured streams of water upon them from long-necked vessels.

Meanwhile, other servants removed the depleted hip-bath, and so re-arranged rugs and cushions that, when two of the wall-curtains were rolled up to the tent roof, each man of the company reclined with his back to a tent-wall and his face to the star-lit night without.

The great guest-tent, in which we sat, was illumined by a hanging lamp within, and the flames of a great fire maintained at sufficient distance to cause no discomfort. A few yards from us, between the tent and the fire, servants laid palm-leaf mats, upon which they placed a rug.

Coffee was brought, glasses and clay cups upon a huge brass tray, and, to do them signal honour, the Emir himself, with his own hand, took glasses of coffee to his European guests.

But *l'Adjudant* Lebaudy excused himself, and I caught Buddy's eye as the *Adjudant's* deep voice, in very fair Arabic, rumbled words to the effect that so enlightened and understanding a man as the Emir would not wish him to drink coffee—which disagreed with him—merely for politeness' sake. . . .

The Emir was obviously greatly concerned and somewhat hurt. . . . Never in his two score years of desert experience had he met a man who did not enjoy coffee, or with whom coffee disagreed. . . . *Coffee !* . . . One of the choicest of gifts that the Mercy and Munificence of Allah had placed at the disposal of man. . . .

Perhaps the *Sidi Adjudant* could not approve such poor stuff as the Emir had to offer ? . . .

Not at all, not at all, explained the Frenchman. Doubtless there was none better than that of the Emir in all Algeria, nay in all the Sahara from Kufara to Timbuctu. . . . No, it was merely an affair of the digestion and strict injunction of the *Medécin-Majeur* against the drinking of coffee. . . .

The Emir expressed deep sympathy and great regret—the latter undeniably genuine.

However . . . the failure of hospitality could be rectified when the tea was brought. . . . That should be made entirely to the taste of the principal guest. . . . Either with or without *zatar*, which gives tea a scent and flavour so beautiful (to those who like it); thick with sugar . . . the first cup rich with amber; the second with lemon; and the third with mint. . . .

But, lo and behold!—an astounding thing—a shocking thing for any host to learn, the guest of the evening could not take *tea* either. . . . Tea had the same distressing effect upon his internal economy. . . .

This time the Emir was indeed concerned. . . . Scarcely could he believe his ears. . . . *Not take tea?* Tea of ceremony! . . . *Tea*, without which no host could honour a guest; no guest refuse without gravest discourtesy, nay, intentional insult! . . .

The Emir smiled tolerantly. His guest was of course jesting, as would be seen when the tea was brought. . . .

Meanwhile, at least five men in the tent could scarcely repress the sighs of relief they felt at the sight of the other Frenchmen who sipped and sipped, gave up their empty cups and twice accepted fresh ones. . . . Had they also refused, our plot had been frustrated.

The senior officer's refusal had filled those five with the fear that his continence had been pre-determined and enjoined upon the others. I decided that the incident was merely the outcome of his acquired or inborn mistrust of taking from an Arab host, food or drink so highly flavoured that the taste of a deleterious " foreign body " would be concealed. Also that he had no actual suspicions and had suggested none to his colleagues. . . .

Turkish cigarettes followed coffee. Turkish cigarettes, we learned, were also unacceptable to the digestion of *l'Adjudant* Lebaudy! . . .

In a quiet gentle voice, the Emir inquired whether a cigarette lighted and partly smoked by himself would be likely to disagree with the digestion of *l'Adjudant* Lebaudy.

" *Touché!* " smiled Lebaudy to himself, and hastened to assure the Emir that if there were a cigarette in this world that he could smoke and enjoy, it would be such a one—but alas, tobacco was not for him. . . .

Tea followed the cigarettes and, at last, the Emir was

brought to understand that the guest of the evening actually *was* refusing ceremonial tea !

He swallowed the insult in a way which showed that he could not be insulted. Mannerless conduct hurt none but the person guilty of it. Gross discourtesy merely labels such a one as grossly discourteous. . . .

It was well acted, and the other Frenchmen hastened to show the excellence of their manners, and drained their cups—special white-ware cups for the European guests only—at each of the three ceremonial drinkings.

As the third was ended and the cups collected, strains of lively music burst from the adjoining tent, and out on to the carpet floated a cloaked, mysterious form. Her cloak being thrown aside, the lovely and enchanting figure of the Angel of Death was revealed, and *l'Adjudant* Lebaudy had evidently at length discovered a kind of hospitality prohibited neither by his doctor nor by his digestion.

That is the picture I shall never forget—the Death Angel dancing beneath the desert sky by the light of a great fire, to the insistent sensuous music, the soothing-maddening-monotonous strains of the tom-tom, the *raita*, the *derboukha* and the flute.

At a respectful distance, in staring silence, sat the soldiers of the Emir's Bodyguard, rapt, enthralled, stirred, excited.

Apart from them, French soldiers off duty—all indeed who were not actually on guard or sentry—also sat and stared, entranced, enchanted.

Only those who have not seen a woman of their own sort and kind, for years, can measure the meaning and appeal to these men of, not merely a woman, but a singularly lovely and bewitching woman, trained and experienced in every art of fascination and allure.

And undeniably the Angel moved more like a winged being from another sphere, than like a creature of flesh and blood.

As the music abruptly ceased, and her dance finished, there was a space of utter silence, followed by wild and

T

tumultuous applause, as the Angel retired to her tent, wherein waited her negro women.

Before this tent sat Abd'allah ibn Moussa, guarding his mistress during her visit to the Emir's camp, but in a position from which he could watch me the while.

I fear that the next item on the programme, the singing of frank love-songs by an Arab youth with a beautiful voice and a remarkable repertoire, fell a little flat.

At its conclusion, the Emir gave orders for fresh coffee to be brought to us, and that yet more refreshment be served to the watching soldiers who had already been regaled with *cous-cous*, mutton-stew, sweetmeats and coffee.

Thereafter the Angel danced again, and her reappearance galvanized into fresh life and renewed interest, the now somewhat somnolent Europeans among the audience.

Again her performance was rapturously hailed and wildly applauded.

During the succeeding turn—some exceedingly clever juggling and conjuring—it was evident to a watchful eye that several of the French soldiers had lain back where they sat, as though overcome by sleep. . . .

For the third time the Angel emerged from her tent and danced, but, on this occasion, introduced a variation. From her dancing-carpet she moved across to that around which we sat cross-legged upon our cushions.

In this confined space she floated, whirling upon tip-toe.

Lebaudy's eyes shone and his lips parted. The Frenchman who sat on the Emir's other side, stared with a glazed and drunken gaze, though drunken he was not. His colleague, next but one upon his left, was frankly asleep. I watched the other *sous-officier*, and saw that he was struggling to keep awake—happy, drowsy, but desiring to see some more of this vision of loveliness before he went to sleep.

Next but one to him, the remaining *sous-officier* was making an effort to keep awake, while his head nodded abruptly at intervals, as his eyes closed and he relaxed for a second or two.

I admired the foresight of the Emir, who had so arranged his guests that they sat in a straight line to right and left of him, with Lebaudy between himself and the Wazir. Only by craning rudely forward, could Lebaudy see what was happening to his subordinates, who, so far, had not given way to snores as well as slumber. Furthermore, by no amount of craning, could he see the spot where his soldiers sat feasting eyes, ears, and stomachs.

Before *l'Adjudant* Lebaudy, the Angel paused, smiled seductively, and hovered, dancing divinely with her arms and body, while remaining stationary on the tiny spot covered by the tips of her bare toes. Anon she turned her back and bent right over until her face looked up into his. . . . French *sous-officiers* do not carry gold coins and place them upon the foreheads of appellant dancing-girls—but kisses are another matter, and, taking her face between his strong short-fingered square-nailed hands, he kissed her ardently, and again, with right good will.

With a ringing laugh, the Angel of Death swung her lithe body erect, and began to do her utmost to fulfil her name.

Before Lebaudy she danced, and with eyes for no-one else—not even for the great Emir ; and we sat and watched a wonderful exhibition of purposeful seduction—seduction, fascination and captivation.

And, as was her wont, the Angel succeeded in her task. None watching the face of *l'Adjudant* Lebaudy could think of the simile of the fascination of the rabbit by the deadly serpent, but at least one watcher of this sinister drama thought of Samson and Delilah.

Before my eyes, this brave strong man weakened and deteriorated ; ceased to be watchful, wary and alert ; forgot his duty and his whereabouts—forgot everything but the woman before him, and succumbed.

Only two of the musicians had accompanied her to our tent, one with a two-ended little drum which he played with palm and finger-tips, the other with the *raita*, and between them and the girl was complete understanding.

I have heard the world's greatest musicians interpret the music of the world's greatest Masters, and I have been greatly moved. But never in my life has European music, rendered on European instruments, *affected* me, as did that Arab music, played upon the *raita* and the drum.

Well do the Bedouin call the *raita*, the Voice of the Devil, and I was but an onlooker, while Lebaudy was an actor in this drama of two.

I do not know for how long the girl postured, danced, beguiled, knelt beseechingly before him, sprang away ere his hands clasped her, teased, maddened, promised—all in gesture and dumb-show; but suddenly, after a quick look at four sleeping Frenchmen, she glanced at the Emir, flashing a message, ' I have done my best and can do no more,' and floated backward from us, turned, and disappeared into her tent.

As her intention of departing became obvious, Lebaudy, still but semi-conscious of his surroundings, involuntarily it seemed, rose on one knee as if to follow, remembered where he was, and sank back, " sighing like a furnace."

But only for a moment.

Distracted as was his mind from affairs mundane, he seemed suddenly to realize that he had seen something— and heard nothing.

He had seen a colleague most unbelievably asleep, and he had heard no applause.

Something was wrong. . . .

His trained military instinct of the approach of danger was awakened and, shaking off the last vestiges of the spell, he arose briskly to his feet, with a peremptory,

" Come along ! Time we turned in ! "—and realized that his four colleagues were all most soundly sleeping.

" *What's this ?* " he shouted, half alarmed, half incredulous, and, striding across his left-hand neighbour, he nudged the nearest sleeper with his foot.

To speak more exactly, he fetched him a remarkably sound kick.

" Get up, you swine," he growled in French.

Receiving no response, he knelt swiftly, seized the man's collar, shook him so violently that his head rolled to and fro—and realized the state of affairs.

In that instant all alarm and bewilderment left him. He became as cold and hard as ice, and won my warm admiration.

Without haste or agitation, he coolly raised an eye-lid of the sleeping man, and gave a brief hard bark of disgust.

"*Drugged!* . . ." he growled in French, and glanced at the other sleepers, the only men now not upon their feet.

The raised tent-walls were lowered from without, and the *Adjudant* Lebaudy stood in a closed tent, and a circle of armed Arabs.

His hand went swiftly to a pocket, and ere he withdrew it with another short snort of disgust, I heard a voice whisper beside me. And the whisper was :

"It hath went before, Bo!"

As a guest, the *Adjudant* had worn no weapons, but he had certainly carried one, and the Wazir, his attentive host, had picked his pocket.

He was a brave man, this Lebaudy.

"Well, noble and honourable host," he said, with a bitter smile, and, with a swift change from sarcasm, added,

"What's the game, you dog ? You treacherous slinking jackal. . . . What now ? . . . Do you hope for the pleasure of hearing me bawl for help—to my poisoned men ? . . . What's the game, I say ? . . . ."

"One that I play with the utmost distaste, with the deepest regret, and with the profoundest apologies," replied the Emir. . . . "A game, I may add, in which you have made the wrong move . . . from my point of view, that is. . . ."

"Huh ! . . . I was to be poisoned too, *hein* ? . . . But I am too old a fox to be tricked by a mangy jackal. . . ."

"No, no, *Sidi Adjudant*. . . . Not poisoned ! . . . No-one has been poisoned. . . . You were to have been our honoured guest—for the night—like these other gentlemen who sleep where they dine. . . ."

" And while I slept ? " snapped Lebaudy. " All our throats cut ? Rifles and property stolen ? . . . More ' *Touareg* ' work, *hein* ? . . ."

" No, no, again, *Sidi Adjudant*," the Emir declared " Not a throat. . . . Not a rifle. . . . Not a *mitka* worth of property. . . . It was something wholly worthless that I propose to take—a convict. . . ."

" Indeed ! . . . You interest me . . ." sneered Lebaudy. " And might one venture to inquire which convict you kindly propose to liberate, and why ? . . . He must have some very wealthy friends. . . .

" And the sentries . . . and the guard . . . ? " he continued. " To be stabbed in the back . . . treacherously rushed at dawn ? . . ."

" Not a stab . . . Not a shot . . ." the Emir assured him. . . . " One or two of my Chiefs who speak French —sufficient for the purpose—were going to borrow, with many apologies, uniforms from a sleeping Sergeant and Corporal. . . . Half a dozen others, again with many apologies, uniforms from your excellent soldiers, now sleeping so soundly, as you rightly assume. . . . Everything would have been returned safe and sound and, in the morning, my dear *Adjudant*, we should all have awakened together, merry and bright, in the very places where we laid us down to sleep. . . . And by-and-bye you would have discovered that a prisoner was missing—and none so surprised as your simple Arab hosts, on learning the fact ! . . . *Voilà tout*. . . ."

As the Emir spoke, the *Adjudant* nodded his head from time to time, a thin and tight-lipped smile distorting his face.

" And now ? " he asked briefly.

" Ah . . . *now* . . . my dear *Adjudant* . . ." silkily replied the Emir, " . . . things are different. . . . You have been so wise . . . so cautious . . . so careful of your digestion . . . that you have changed my plans. . . . The ' game,' as you call it, will be a different one, and you will play the leading part in it. . . ."

"Again you interest me," sneered Lebaudy. "I might almost say you surprise me. . . . *I* shall play a leading part, *hein* ? And pray what might that be ? . . ."

"Listen, my dear *Adjudant*, and listen carefully—lest France have cause to mourn your loss. . . . You will lead a small party of *my* people—dressed in the uniforms of *yours*. . . . You will—er—' make the rounds,' do you call it ?—reassuring each of your sentries with the counter-sign and the sight of your countenance, to which you will raise a hand-lamp.

"You will then proceed to the tents of the convicts, and will release the one indicated by the man who will go with you in the uniform of a Corporal, and who will hold a knife within an inch of your back the whole time. . . . That convict you will bring here. . . . I and my followers will at once depart with him . . . and we shall do ourselves the honour of inviting you to accompany us. . . ."

"And if I refuse ? "

"You will accompany us all the same, my dear *Adjudant*. . . ."

"I mean if I refuse to have anything whatsoever to do with your infernal rascality ? . . . To Hell with your sacred ' games.' . . . Are you a mad dog as well as a treacherous one ? . . ."

"At least I am not mad, *mon Adjudant*," replied the Emir.

"But *you* are . . . if you refuse. . . . On the one hand, merely a convict the less—and *you* know how easily *they* can die, be shovelled into the sand, and struck off your roll. . . . On the other hand, the loss to France of a brave, resourceful, and, I am sure, valued officer. . . ."

"Murder, *hein* ? " remarked Lebaudy.

"And worse I fear," confessed the Emir sadly.

"Torture ? "

"Alas ! " admitted the Emir.

"And what becomes of *you*, my friend ? " sneered Lebaudy. "Are you not forgetting such trifles as the

French Republic, the French army. . . . How long will *you* live, you treacherous rat, after this ? . . ."

" Mourn not for me, *Sidi Adjudant*," besought the Emir. " One thing at a time, and first things first. . . . Listen again, I beg—it is for the last time. . . . One of your prisoners is going to be liberated *now*, by me. . . . It will be done more quickly and more easily with your help and presence, but done it *will* be. . . . Give us that help, and I give you my word, a word I have never broken, that you shall be set free—unhurt. . . . And not only unhurt, my friend, but rewarded. . . . As you remarked, the convict has wealthy friends—and I am one of them. . . . What do you say to fifty thousand francs ? . . . A fortune. . . . Would you care to leave the desert, to retire to your home in France ? . . . Beautiful France. . . . And sit beneath the shadow of your own vine and your own fig-tree, a wealthy man. . . . And no harm done, mark you. . . . No betrayal. . . . No treachery. . . . No selling of the secrets of France. . . . Just an act of mercy to an innocent man. . . . What do you say, *Sidi Adjudant* ? . . . What do you say to fifty thousand francs ? . . ."

Profoundest silence in the tent.

Not one of the watchful circle of armed men made sound or movement. All seemed even to hold their breath as they awaited the Frenchman's answer.

" I say *nothing* to them," he shouted. " I spit on them. . . . And on you. . . . Now, you dog—lay a hand on me as I go to leave this tent, and you have assaulted a soldier of France—obstructed him in the execution of his duty. . . . Already you have bribed and threatened him. . . . *You*, calling yourself an ally of the Republic. . . . *You*, who have made a Treaty with France. . . . *You*, who have taken French gold and would use it to bribe a servant of France . . . and if I live, I will command the firing-party that shall shoot you like the dog you are. . . ."

" And if you die ? . . ." asked the Emir.

" Then with a French rope will you be hanged by another servant of France. . . ."

And upon my soul, I almost whooped " Hear, hear ! "

The man was fine, as he stood there surrounded by his enemies, stood firm—wealth on the one hand, and torture on the other.

I felt sorry for Noel, for I knew how he must loathe the part he had to play, and I could not but admire the way in which he played it.

" Believe me, *Sidi Adjudant*, nothing but the sternest necessity could drive me to do this—to offer a bribe of gold or a threat of torture and death, to a soldier of France. . . ."

" Not to mention a guest, I suppose," observed the *Adjudant*. " . . . An invited guest. . . . The world-famous Arab hospitality ! . . ."

" Indeed if anything could further blacken my face and make more evil and distasteful my deed, it would be that fact . . ." admitted the Emir with sincerity. " By the Beard of the Prophet, and the Ninety and Nine Sacred Names of Allah, I loathe what I have to do. . . . Come, come ! . . . It is but a little thing I ask. . . . Just the life of one of those wretched prisoners. . . . And let me whisper to you, a Frenchman, a man of sensibility. . . . *There is a lady in the case . . . a beautiful woman . . . a sweet and lovely lady whose heart is breaking. . . .*"

I thought for a moment that Lebaudy wavered then—but he yawned, tapped his mouth once or twice with his open hand, and with a formal :

" It grows late. . . . I thank you for your hospitality, Emir. . . . You must excuse me . . ." he turned to go.

Noel, Buddy and I seized him—and I for one, hated the job—and the others drew their knives.

" Ah ! . . ." said Lebaudy.

And :

" Forgive me," said the Emir, and took him in a huge embrace as Marbruk ben Hassan, swiftly stooping, bound the Frenchman's feet together.

"*Sidi Adjudant,*" said the Emir, "I detest doing this . . . more than I can say. . . . Is there any hope for a *parole* ? . . . Give me your word to make no effort to escape, and I will not have you bound. . . . Nor shall you be gagged . . . Nor blindfolded when we shoot you. . . .

"Help us to treat you well. . . . To torture you, to make you aid me, would sadden me for a year. . . . To kill you, to shut your mouth, would sadden me for a lifetime. . . ."

Noel released his grip

The Frenchman drew back his clenched fist to strike, and his arms were instantly seized by Buddy, and pinioned behind him. "Carry him to the small tent," said the Emir, and the order was quickly obeyed.

Lebaudy made no resistance, but, the moment he was outside the large pavilion, he gave vent to the most tremendous shout I have ever heard from human lungs. . . .

"*À moi !* . . . *À moi !* . . ." he bawled.

And the sound of his voice was enough to awaken the dead.

Marbruk ben Hassan and Yussuf Latif simultaneously drew their knives, and put the points of them to the Frenchman's throat and heart respectively.

"Another sound and you die," growled the Wazir.

"*Garde* . . ." roared Lebaudy instantly. And the hand of the Emir was clapped over his mouth.

"Into the tent with him, quick," he said. "The sentries may have heard him. . . ."

And in a moment, the brave Lebaudy was hustled into the tent.

"The uniforms ! . . . Marbruk, Yussuf, and the rest of you . . . Quick. . . ." And all left the tent save my brother, Buddy and myself.

"Now then," he continued, addressing the *Adjudant*, and his voice and manner changed. "You saw that fire out there. . . . Suppose you were bound to a pole and fed into it, feet first ? . . ."

" Then I should hardly be able to make the rounds with you, if I wanted to. . . . Even your intelligence might follow that. . . ." was the reply.

" Of course. . . . How foolish of me. . . . Thank you . . ." replied the Emir. " We shall need your feet, as you say. . . . But we could lead a *blind* man, of course. . . . Or another idea. . . . We have ten minutes to spare while my men are dressing in the uniforms of yours. . . . Suppose we take off a finger a minute until you change your mind ? . . ."

" A bright idea ! . . . Guards and sentries are quite accustomed to seeing their commanding officer approach with both hands streaming blood ! . . ." sneered Lebaudy.

" Well then, suppose we agree that you are incorruptible and immovable ! Also that as you insist on spoiling our plans and thwarting our modest desire to take but one convict, we are going to give ourselves the satisfaction and compensation of torturing you to death as painfully as we know how. . . ."

" That is as you please," replied Lebaudy, " but I shall only get for a few minutes what you will get for all Eternity, you foul dog."

" No, no, *Sidi Adjudant* ! The removal of an Infidel is an act of merit on the part of a True Believer. . . ."

It occurred to me to feel glad that Lebaudy, whom my brother, of course, had no intention of injuring, much less of killing, had no suspicion that the Emir was other than he seemed. It would be a terrible blow to Mary should her husband's great drama be discovered to be farce.

" We shall know more about that later," growled the Frenchman. " What is not in doubt, is the question of your fate when my countrymen catch you. . . ."

" We shall know more about that later," smiled the Emir. " Meantime your fate takes precedence, *Sidi Adjudant*—and I will be generous. . . . For, in spite of your recalcitrance, and the trouble and annoyance you have given me, I will let you choose. . . . Shall it be the

fire, feet first . . . Impalement on the sharpened trunk
of a young palm . . . Or pegged out for the
vultures ? . . ."

The *Adjudant* shrugged his shoulders.

" It's a matter of complete indifference to me," he
yawned.

And before my brother could reply, Yussuf pulled aside
the curtain at the entrance to the tent.

" One came running," he said quickly, " a soldier. . . .
He heard the cry of this officer. . . . We have bound
him. . . . He is unhurt."

" He may have saved your life," remarked the Emir,
turning to the *Adjudant*. " Perhaps he will help us in the
little play-acting and give us the countersign, in return
for his life."

" If he is one of my *légionnaires*, you will get nothing
out of him," was the reply.

" Well, hope for the best, *Sidi Adjudant*. . . . If the
man is amenable, I will not torture you. . . . Perhaps
even I will not kill you. . . ."

The Emir then bade Yussuf bring four men and order
them, on peril of their lives, to guard the French officer and
see that none held communication with him.

He then led the way to my tent, where Marbruk ben
Hassan awaited us with a bundle of French *képis*, coats,
trousers, leggings, boots, side-arms and equipment.

In a surprisingly few minutes I was a French Sergeant,
dark and bearded, it is true—but then the night was dark,
and many of the soldiers were bearded—inspecting a guard
consisting of a Corporal and eight men.

" Now then," said Noel, ". . . the captive. No need
for him to see me, but he's got to see this guard. . . .
You'll talk French to him, of course, Otis. . . . Also let
him see, from not too near, the dead bodies of his slumber-
ing comrades and of the *sous-officiers* in the pavilion. . . .
Tell him his top-sergeant is elsewhere, tortured to death.
. . . That was his dying yell he heard. . . . If he's only
too glad to get his own back on the *Adjudant*, by helping,

all's well. . . . If he's staunch, try fright, bribery and corruption."

"Suppose he double-crosses . . . gives us the wrong countersign, and lets a yell when we get into the convict camp. . . ." said Buddy.

"Well, we've got to take a chance," replied Noel. "It's up to you to be right in judging your man. . . . He may jump at the chance of gaining a few hundred francs and his liberty, especially if Lebaudy is as popular as he used to be. . . ."

"*Used to be?*" I said.

"Yes. . . . Used to be . . . when Buddy and I were in his *peloton*. . . ."

"He surely was some nigger-driver," confirmed Buddy.

"*What?* . . . When? . . ." I said. "What *are* you talking about?"

"When we were in the Legion, Son. . . . You've heard the great tale of the Relief of Zinderneuf, where Beau Geste was killed, and we started out with John Geste and his other brother, and tramped the desert for two years. . . . Well, old Lebaudy was Sergeant of our *peloton*, under our smart-Alec brother-in-law. . . . Lord, yes. . . . Lebaudy is a great old friend of ours!"

"Only he's another that don't know it . . ." said Buddy, and added:

"It surely hath been a pleasure to twist his tail this night. . . . He's give us many a unhappy night, an' I allow we've give *him* one, now. . . ."

I said nothing but thought much.

In the best Legion manner, I stepped back, rasped a "*Garde à vous! Par files de quatre. En avant! . . . Marche!*" and the drilled men of the body-guard, to whom none of this was new except their unaccustomed uniforms, moved smartly beneath the ferocious eye of the Corporal-Wazir.

We had not marched more than a few yards before I cried:

"*Halte!*"

I had had an idea, and turned back to the Emir's tent. Noel was reclining on his rugs, looking thoughtful and somewhat dejected.

" Son," he said, " I don't like it. . . . I can't sit here in safety and let you go into that camp. . . . If they pinch you, you'll never be seen again. . . . Nor Bud either. . . . The Legion wants him—just like the Zephyrs want you. . . ."

" I'm going anyhow, Noel," I said, " whether you go or not. . . . It's my privilege and my right. . . . I found him, old chap, and I'm going to save him. . . . It's you who are saving him really, but I mean—I must be there—and take the lead too. . . ."

" True, Son . . . but I don't like it. . . . For two pins I'd come along, as one of your men. . . . But I mustn't be caught and be found to be an American from the Legion —for Mary's sake. . . . And for the sake of my Arabs too. . . . I hate letting Bud go without me. . . . But I can't let you go alone with the men, and Bud insists because John came back to look for *him*! . . ."

" What did you return for ? " he added.

" Why—I had an idea . . ."

" *No!* " said my brother, in feigned surprise.

" Yes, I've been thinking."

" You aren't here to think, Son. . . . You're here to obey orders, you know. . . . You go and collect the ideas of that man they've caught. . . ."

" What occurred to me," I continued unmoved, " . . . was this . . . I'm every inch a French Sergeant. . . . Suppose we put this disguised squad on their camels, and we make a little détour. . . . Then I ride in here again, at their head, and with some more of your body-guard behind us as *goumiers*. We ride in where this prisoner is, and he would at once see, with his own eyes, that we are a perfectly good French *peloton méhariste*. He'll shout for help, and you'll look guilty and confused. . . . I'll be haughty and truculent, and moreover I'll refuse to camp with you. . . . I'll have the man set free, and tell him to lead us into the convict camp. I'll take command, in the inexplicable absence of Lebaudy and the *sous-officiers*, voice my suspicions that something is wrong, visit the sentries and tell them to be watchful. . . . Count the convicts—and bring one away with me to this camp. . . . With a good nerve and a little luck, that ought to work perfectly. . . ."

Noel smote his thigh.

" Oats," he declared, " you've said something. . . . Go and fetch Buddy. . . ."

I bade my squad—or *troupe*—" Stand easy ! " and, in Arabic, told the Wazir that the Emir would fain have speech with him.

In the tent I repeated and elaborated my plan. It appealed to Buddy at once, and he preferred it to the other scheme on account of the human factor.

That was uncertain in both, but less so, perhaps, in my scheme. A bribed and intimidated man might well double-cross us—fearing the French authority more than us, and doubting whether he would ever get his thirty pieces of silver. He would probably agree to all that we suggested and then betray us—instead of his own people —as soon as we were well into their camp, and he in safety.

In a very few minutes my proposal was carried unanimously, the more readily in that none of us was at all enamoured of the debauching of a simple soldier from his duty, if it could be avoided.

" It looks water-tight to me," decided Noel. " So far, the prisoner has neither heard nor seen anything suspicious in this camp. All he knows is that they thought they heard Lebaudy shout. . . . The Corporal of the Guard, or someone, sent him down to see if anything was wanted, and he was seized and held as he came running into this camp. . . ."

" Quite right too," observed Corporal Buddy, with some indignation. ". . . Rushing into a respectable camp like this in the middle of the night. . . . Barging about like a steer at a rodeo. . . . *Course* he were arrested. . . ."

"Send a man for Marbruk ben Hassan," said Noel.

Buddy stepped out of the tent and, a few minutes later, Marbruk entered with him.

On being questioned by the Emir, it turned out that, as we hoped and supposed, the prisoner had been seized by the guard at the very entrance to the camp, had been put in the guard-tent, and could know absolutely nothing of what had occurred.

All seemed propitious for the success of my plan, and Marbruk was sent back with certain instructions to the guard—one of which was, to place the prisoner where he could see anyone who went by.

Marbruk was then to get my uniformed squad of hard-bitten dependable ruffians mounted, and to have them, with a dozen others in Arab dress, awaiting me at the opposite side of the camp.

Men and camels were of course drilled and experienced members of the Emir's body-guard, picked from his famous Camel-Corps.

"Good-bye, Son, and may God help you," said Noel, as I left the tent. "Keep cool, and act up to me and Bud, and we'll have John Geste here in an hour. . . . Now, don't forget. . . . You're an indignant and suspicious French Sergeant. . . . And you don't hold with Arabs as such. . . . You don't use language *too* frequent and free, to me, because I'm a Big Noise, and the French Government's very fond of me. . . . Still, you don't like having French soldiers arrested by Arabs, and you want to know all about it. . . . Play up, Son. . . . We'll get away with it. . . ."

His farewell to Buddy was less impressive, for, as that Corporal-Wazir turned on his heel without a word, the Emir's sandalled foot shot up and encountered ill-fitting French trousers.

Yussuf Latif ibn Fetata, in French uniform, stood at the head of my kneeling camel, his foot upon its doubled fore-leg to prevent its rising to its feet. He saluted as I approached and handed me the rein-cord.

I mounted, the camel rose, and I rode away from the camp, followed by my mixed *peloton méhariste*.

The night was dark and very still, and, at that hour—about three o'clock in the morning—*I* would willingly have been dark and very still, upon the comfortable rug and cushions of my tent. . . .

A quarter of an hour later, I approached the tents of the quarter-guard, and, as we drew near, the Soudanese sentry challenged and brought his rifle from the slope to the ready. I replied with a loud hail and the announcement that we were friends, come in peace.

The sentry turned and shouted, and from the guard-tent a powerful, mis-shapen dwarf came hurrying with a well-tended slush-lamp in his hand.

The guard turned out in fine style.

"*Franzawi!*" cried the dwarf, in great surprise. "Come in peace. . . . By Allah, is it well?"

"A *peloton méhariste Français!*" I cried. "What camp is this?"

"The camp of His Highness the Emir, Sidi el Hamel el Kebir, Leader of the Confederation of the Tribes of the Great Oasis. . . ."

"Sir!" cried an indignant voice in French from the guard-tent. "I have been arrested by these Arabs. . . . Been taken prisoner, I have! . . ."

And a man in uniform struggled from the tent, closely followed by two Soudanese.

"Here! What's this?" I shouted, my voice hard with wrathful surprise. "A French soldier in uniform? By whose order was he arrested? Where's he from? . . . Send my compliments to the Emir. . . .

"Come here, you," I called to the man. "Tell me about it. . . . I'll look into this. . . ."

And with gentle taps of my camel-stick upon its neck, I brought my camel to its knees.

The light from the slush-lamp fell upon my face and upon that of the French prisoner.

"*Hankinson !*" he cried, using the name which had been mine in the Legion.

"*Sergeant* Hankinson, please ! " I replied instantly, with stern reproof in my voice. "Have you gone blind, *Légionnaire* Schnell ? . . ." And I brought into prominence the gold stripe on my cuff.

Yes. . . . I had been quick ! . . . For once I had risen to the occasion with absolute promptitude and *aplomb*. And, by so doing, I had turned a ghastly contretemps into what might prove a piece of amazing good luck.

It was the miserable Schnell, the butt and buffoon of my barrack-room in the Legion, and, in another second, I should learn whether he had heard that I had been courtmartialled and sent to the Zephyrs. It was extremely improbable, as he had gone from Sidi-bel-Abbès to Senegal when I had gone to the Moroccan border.

"I—I—I beg your pardon, *Monsieur le Sergent*," gasped Schnell, saluting repeatedly. "I knew your voice and I recognized your face, and I called your name without stopping to look. . . . I am very sorry, *mon Sergent*."

All was well. The miserable Schnell had heard nothing.

"That's enough ! Don't chatter like a demented parrot. . . . Tell me how you come to be here. . . . And where the end of the Road is. . . . That is what I was looking for. . . ."

"Oh, close here, *mon Sergent*," replied Schnell, standing stiffly to attention. "It's like this, sir. . . . The convict camp is just back there and this Arab—he's a big Chief, a 'friendly'—he gave a *fête*, a feast, and dancing-girls and all that, and invited the Commandant and *messieurs les sous-officiers*, and all men who were off duty. . . . I was on guard, and me and Schantz and Slinsky and Poggi were sitting outside the guard-tent, when suddenly Corporal Blanchard said, 'Silence, you ! . . . Hark ! '

"And we listened, but we heard nothing, and the

Corporal said he thought he had heard the voice of *Monsieur l'Adjudant* Lebaudy. They say he has the biggest voice in the French Army. . . ."

" Oh, for God's sake," I growled, " cut it short. . . . And tell me what you are doing here. . . . You mean you assaulted some harmless Arab I suppose. . . . Or was it one of their women ? "

" Oh, sir ! No, no, no ! " protested poor Schnell. " Corporal Blanchard said he thought he must be mistaken, but said I'd better come across and see whether everything was all-right. . . . And they arrested me. . . ."

" I suppose you came rushing into the camp like a Touareg . . . like a whole Touareg raid, a host in yourself . . ." I sneered.

" The Corporal said ' Run across,' sir, and I came *au pas gymnastique* and . . ."

" Silence ! " I roared. " Don't you back-answer me, you jibbering jackass. . . . How long have you been here ? "

" About half an hour, sir," admitted Schnell.

" Well, I'll have you put somewhere else, for about half a month," I bullied. " You blundering half-witted . . . half-baked . . . half-bred . . . half-addled . . . half-man you. . . ."

I was, I fear, beginning thoroughly to enjoy myself. Probably I was uplifted by excitement, hope, fear and tautened nerves. I then turned upon the dwarf.

" And you ? " I stormed in Arabic. " How dare you arrest a French soldier on his way to speak with his commanding officer ? "

The dwarf spread deprecating hands and shrugged tremendous shoulders.

" By Allah ! A mistake . . . an accident. . . . Such fools as these Soudanese are. . . . But the *Roumi* soldier came running, and was violent. . . . His Highness the Emir will be distressed beyond words. . . . But the man was *very* violent. Some say he slew two with his bayonet . . . others say three. . . ."

"What!" I cried, "absurd! . . . Was the man
drunk then ? "

"Well, *Sidi*, *this* one was not very drunk," replied the
dwarf.

"What do you mean ? " I cried. "Let your speech
be plain. . . . 'This one was not very drunk.' . . .
Who *was* very drunk then ? . . ."

A quiet and orderly body of men, several carrying
lamps, approached.

The dwarf was flustered.

"Our Lord, the Emir himself," he whispered.

And at the head of a body of Sheikhs, officers, officials,
soldiers, and slaves, appeared the Emir el Hamel el Kebir.

"Please Allah! Well ? . . . Come in peace! . . .
The Peace of Allah be upon you! "

I saluted the Emir, military fashion.

"Health and the Peace of Allah upon you, O Emir ! . . .
Le Sergent Hankinson, peloton méhariste, numero douze,
for Number One Construction Camp. . . . I saw your
fire and came to ask. . . . In your camp I find a French
soldier arrested and detained. . . . I have to request
that you hand him over to me at once, with explana-
tion. . . ."

"What is this, Marbruk ben Hassan ? " inquired the
Emir of the dwarf. His voice was harsh.

Marbruk, with low salaam, hastily repeated what he
had said to me.

It appeared that the man had been very violent . . .
some said five had been killed . . . or gravely injured.
. . . The dwarf feared that the man had been under the
influence of the strong *sharab* of the *Roumis*. . . . Fighting
drunk, in fact. . . .

Indignantly Schnell denied that he had so much as seen
liquor, for years.

"But how *could* he be drunk ? " I interposed angrily.
"Where would he get it ? Do the wells then contain
sharab in this part of the desert ? "

The Emir smiled and stroked his beard.

"Nay, I never thought so," replied the Emir. "Until this day I had not thought it. . . . Strange indeed are the ways of the *Roumis*—but let us thank Allah for the diversity of His creatures. . . . Verily wine is a mocker . . . and well is it prohibited unto us. . . ."

"What is behind your speech, O Emir ? " I asked. "Give me not twisted words from a crooked tongue, I beseech you. Let our speech be short and plain."

"Will the Commandant come with me a moment ? " asked the Emir with quiet dignity. "And if perhaps he would bring this soldier who has seen no *sharab*. . . ."

"Corporal ! " I shouted over my shoulder. "Let the men dismount and take an ' easy.' Each man to stand to his camel with rifle unslung."

And Corporal Buddy's salute and reply were the authentic thing. It would have taken a quicker brain than Schnell's to have found anything wrong with me and my *peloton*.

As I moved off with the Emir, followed by Schnell, the former remarked confidentially, but with care that Schnell should hear him :

"I did not wish to say too much in front of your men, Commandant. . . . And also I thought you would believe your own eyes more quickly than my voice. . . ."

Bidding his followers to halt and to await him where they stood, the Emir led me and Schnell to a tent.

"I regret this most deeply," he said, " . . . and I would fain have concealed it. . . . I gave a poor feast in my humble camp and invited all who cared to come. . . . It is not for me to make comment. . . . But my men are accused of arresting one who knows nothing of any drunkenness, any imbibing of *sharab* . . ." and he pulled aside the curtain of the tent.

By the light of the lamp in the tent, we beheld the distressing spectacle of three uniformed non-commissioned officers, deep sunk in drunken slumber.

I shrugged my shoulders and clucked my tongue in disgust.

"Tch! Tch! Tch!... And what of their men?" I asked, shamefaced and angry.

It was the turn of the Emir to shrug his shoulders.

I stirred one of the sleepers sharply with my foot, and shook the other by the shoulder (but not too violently).

"And the *Adjudant* Lebaudy?" I asked.

"Do not ask me, *Monsieur le Sergent*," said the Emir pityingly.

"Where is he?... I will see him.... I must satisfy myself...." I said sharply.

"*Légionnaire* Schnell," I added. "Remain in here until I return.... Leave this tent at your peril."

The Emir led me away.

CHAPTER XVII

I RETURNED and entered the tent, grave-faced, sad, indignant, but with the look, in my eye, of a good Sergeant who sees promotion in the near distance.

"Schnell," I said, " listen, and be careful. . . . A still tongue runs in a wise head. . . . Get you back at once to camp, and report to Corporal Blanchard that all's well here . . . *all's well*, d'you understand ? . . . *Monsieur l'Adjudant* Lebaudy did not call for you. . . . He and the Sergeants are remaining longer. . . . *Remaining longer*, d'you understand ? . . . Be very careful what you say. . . . I should be sorry for you if it were found that false reports—detrimental to *l'Adjudant* Lebaudy and your superior officers—were traced to you. . . ."

The good Schnell apparently understood very clearly.

"Very good. . . . Get along back then and . . . oh . . . report that a *peloton méhariste*—Sergeant, Corporal, eight soldiers and ten *goumiers*—is arriving at once. Tell Corporal Blanchard to warn the sentries. . . . I may as well have the countersign too. . . . What is it, '*Maroc*' still ? . . ."

"No, sir, '*Boulanger*,' " replied simple Simon Schnell.

"Well, be off then . . . and don't run like a mad bull into your own camp. . . . Get a bullet in your belly one of these days. . . ."

Schnell saluted and departed with speed, filled with the best intentions.

"Now for it ! " I said, as we hurried forth to rejoin my circus of camels and performing Arabs.

"Great stuff! Son, you're The Goods!" whispered Noel, as he gripped my arm. . . .

I gave the order to mount, and, a minute later, I led the *peloton*, in column of files, at a swinging trot toward the convict camp.

Anxiously as I was awaiting it, the sentry's loud:

"*Halte!* . . . *Qui va là?*" brought my heart into my mouth.

I switched my mind from thoughts of John and Isobel —and became a French Sergeant again.

I answered, and gave the countersign in correct style— the style with which I was only too familiar—halted my *peloton*, and went forward.

"That you, Schantz?" I snapped.

"No, Sergeant," replied the man. "I am Broselli. . . ."

"Has Schnell just come into camp?" I asked.

"A few minutes ago, Sergeant," was the reply.

"Ah!" I said mysteriously, called my *peloton* to attention, and led them to the camp.

"*Halte!*" I cried at the top of my voice. "Dismount! . . . Stand easy!"

The guard turned out, the Corporal came hurrying, followed by a man bearing a lamp.

He saluted me smartly.

"Urgent and in haste," I said. "Take me to *l'Adjudant* Lebaudy, at once."

"He's over at the big Emir's camp, Sergeant," replied the Corporal. "A *fête* . . . a big show. . . . Everybody's there. . . ."

"So I gathered," I said grimly. "A little awkward if there was another raid, *hein*? However, that's the *Adjudant's* affair. . . . You in command here?"

"Yes, Sergeant. . . . I am senior Corporal," replied the man.

"Well, you'll do," I said. "They want that man back, in Zaguig. . . . The convict who says he was the only item not on the last Touareg butcher's-bill. . . .

They seem to think, now, it wasn't a Touareg show at all. . . ."

"What! The convicts themselves?"

"No, fat-head. . . . They wouldn't all have killed themselves, would they?" . . . and I leant over and lowered my voice confidentially. "*Selim ben Yussuf!* . . . And his tribe one of the Allied Confederation and all! . . . Yes, that's the latest idea. . . . It was he handed the man back, y'know. . . . And there's about a dozen not accounted for. . . . Smart bit of bluff, what!"

"He hasn't a cold in the eyes, that one," opined the Corporal.

"No," I said. "Come on . . . I can't stop chattering here all night. . . . You know the man, I suppose?"

"Well . . . not to say *know* him, Sergeant. . . . I daresay I can . . ."

"All-right," I answered. "I know his ugly mug well enough. . . . I had charge of him at the Zaguig Court-martial. . . . We shall be old friends by the time they *do* make him squeal. . . ."

I turned to Buddy.

"Corporal," I snapped. "We shall be off again in a few minutes. . . . Where's that spare camel? You'll be in charge of it. . . . Tie the man's hands behind him, and the end of the cord to your wrist. . . . The men will mount again in five minutes. . . .

"Come on, Corporal Blanchard," I added. "That damned Court-martial sits to-morrow."

And, preceded by the man with the hand-lamp, we marched off, my heart beating like a trip-hammer.

Apparently this worthy soul was more observant than his Corporal, for if he did not know the desperado by sight or by number, he knew which tent he was in.

With a murmured, "*Tente numero B7*," he led us straight to one of the tents.

"The bird's in here, Corporal," he said, as the sentry came to attention.

"Fetch him out then," said Corporal Blanchard.

" And be quick about it," I snapped.

There were rustlings and growlings within, the kind of sound of movement one might hear on stirring up a cageful of straw-couched feral beasts, at night.

Two minutes later, the man with the lamp reappeared with the sentry—and *John Geste . . . John Geste!* . . . ill, and broken and worn, but still firm of lip and grim of jaw.

It was an anxious second. . . .

Just kicked from slumber and flung out into the night, face to face with me, would he cry my name aloud in his incredulous surprise ? . . . If he did, I would take the same line that I had taken with Schnell, but with greater sternness.

I might have known ! . . . I need not have feared. . . . *" Bon chat chasse de race."* . . . Blood tells. . . .

John gave me a quick look, and then stood with the surly hang-dog convict slouch, his eyes on the ground.

" Here, you, put that lamp to his ugly mug. . . . I don't want to take the wrong man," I snarled, giving him what cue I could, and putting my hand beneath his chin, I rudely jerked his head up.

" That's the swine," I said. " Take him along and sling him on the spare camel."

And we marched off.

Buddy's reception of the prisoner was not calculated to raise suspicion in the slow mind of Corporal Blanchard.

With a business-like contemptuous roughness, he pinioned the prisoner. And with a brief :

" *Voilà !* Undo that if you can ! " he pointed with a jerk of his thumb to the spare camel, now attached to his own.

" Get on, and enjoy your last ride in this world," he growled, " and if you so much as *look* crooked, I'll drag you behind it. . . ."

" Well, good-night, Corporal," I said to the excellent Blanchard, and mounted my camel, every second expecting that the man's detestable voice, with a tinge of respectful surprise, would utter the words for which I had been waiting from the first.

"*What about the warrant, Sergeant? You haven't handed it over.*" Had he demanded it, as, of course, he should have done, it had been my intention to say :

"Ah, yes! Of course!"—to feel for it in my inner pocket, and—slowly, reluctantly, with growing horror, consternation, and alarm—to come to the conclusion that I had actually left it at Zaguig! I imagined Blanchard hastening to reassure his superior officer, and disclaim the slightest desire to embarrass him. . . . The warrant could be sent out with the next ration-party. . . .

In that case I would nod my agreement and offer to scribble him a receipt for the goods, as his authority meanwhile.

As I gave the order to march, another idea occurred to me, should he yet remember and yell for the warrant. I would say stuffily :

"Warrant! *You?* . . . How long have *you* been *l'Adjudant* Lebaudy? I think I'll hand it to him, thank you . . ." (very sarcastically).

But the fool never thought of it at all, God bless him! "*Walk . . . march . . .*" I intoned.

The camels shuffled forward, the sentry saluted, and . . . *John Geste was free.*

§ 2

During the short ride between the two camps, I kept silence and stared straight ahead into the night.

I could not have spoken without disgracing myself. A choking held my throat, a smarting blinded my eyes, an acute pain stabbed my heart, and I trembled from head to foot.

Nor did I hear a word pass between Buddy and John Geste, close behind me.

I think that both, like me, had hearts too full for speech, and that John was being wary—riding, as it seemed to him, among French soldiers.

By our own guard-tent, I halted and dismissed the *peloton*, the admirable small-part characters of my caste, who hastened away to return their " properties " to their rightful owners. It would not be seemly that any good French soldier should awake to find his trousers missing.

One on each side of John, we marched to the Emir's tent, entered it, closed the opening and stood together—an Emir, a French Sergeant, a French Corporal and a convict !

Three Americans and an Englishman !

Shall I attempt to describe that meeting ? . . . Tell of how John cleared his throat with a slight cough and remarked :

" Thanks awfully, you fellows. . . . These cords are very tight. . . . Anybody got a drink on him ? . . ." —and collapsed in a dead faint.

. . . Of how we worked over him and brought him round, Buddy weeping freely and swearing fiercely . . . my brother, in grim silence, save when he blew his nose violently . . . I swallowing, and swallowing, and swallowing, while words of fire capered about my aching brain.

" *John Geste is free . . . John Geste is saved . . . Isobel . . . Isobel . . . Isobel . . .* "

Of how, in silence, John Geste put his left hand on my shoulder and with his right gripped mine with what strength he had left to him. . . .

Of how he did the same with Hank, saying nothing. . . .

Of how he did the same with Buddy, saying nothing. . . .

Of how we four men, stirred to our deepest depths, as perhaps never before in our lives, tried to behave as reticent white men should, with decent repression of emotion . . . though Buddy was once or twice shaken from head to foot by a spasm—followed by a torrent of shocking profanity . . . though Hank was constrained to blow his nose with a violence that shook the camp and caused Buddy to request him not to wake the Seven Blasted Sleepers . . . though John Geste, from time to time,

"Marbruk ben Hassan," said he. "I need not give thee detailed instructions. A line of men behind a ridge across the Zaguig Road. . . . Camels twenty yards to the rear. . . . Orders to section leaders for ten rounds of rapid fire when Yacoub's rifle goes off, or your whistle blows. . . . Pickets far out, all round the camp. . . . Send out Yussuf Latif with a swift patrol, with Yacoub's messenger as guide. . . . Not a shot to be fired on peril of their lives. . . . We want to be 'surprised'—at fifty yards. . . ."

Marbruk ben Hassan, the happy light of battle on his soldierly face, departed, and the Emir turned back into the tent.

"Here's a pretty kettle of fish!" said he. "Bud, set R'Orab and all the servants to chucking water on that fire, and then on the drunks. . . . See there isn't a light in the camp. . . . You try and fetch the Sergeants round. . . . You come with me, Oats. . . . John, you lie low. . . . Go to bed, in fact, on those cushions. . . ."

John shook his head.

"Can't you find me a rifle?" he asked.

"On to that bed with you, Boy. . . . I do most solemnly swear that I'll bind you hand and foot, if there's another word out of you . . ." and he strode from the tent.

As we hurried to the small one in which Lebaudy must have been having one of the worst hours of his life, Noel remarked:

"If I see Selim ben Yussuf over the sights of my rifle, doing the early bird, this morning, it'll be more worms than early bird for his. . . ."

The four men in charge of Lebaudy were ordered to report to Marbruk ben Hassan immediately.

"*Sidi Commandant*," said the Emir, "no man can withstand his fate. . . . To some, good fortune; to some, bad. . . . What is written is written. . . . Your camp will be attacked at dawn. . . ."

"By *your* orders, you treacherous devil, of course. . . . I quite expected it," was the reply. "Huh! The faith of

the Arab! . . . The noble untamed unsullied Son of
the Desert, whose word is better than his bond! . . .
you pariah cur! . . . Now we know who made the *last*
raid! . . ."

"I think we do, *Sidi Commandant*—one Selim ben
Yussuf. . . . It is he who will attack now. . . ."

"By *your* orders," sneered the *Adjutant*. "Do you
take me for a fool—an Afflicted-of-Allah? . . . By your
orders, of course. . . . I, in your power, bound hand and
foot. . . . Three-quarters of my men decoyed here and
poisoned . . . and my camp 'will be attacked at dawn.'
. . . I've no doubt it will, you devil, you treacherous
hound . . . you lousy, begging, lying oasis-thief. . . .
Attacked at dawn, *hein*? . . . In other words, when
you've cut the throats of everyone of us here, you and your
foul gang of murderous ruffians will visit my camp with
knives and pistols in your sleeves, and make a massacre
—to avoid a fight! . . . That'll be your 'attack.' . . .
My soldiers shot in the back . . . stabbed in the back . . .
butchered. . . . More 'Touareg' work, *hein*? . . . Dead
men tell no tales, *hein*? . . . And all that you may earn
some gold for rescuing some rich criminal. . . .

"But you hear my last words, and remember them.
. . . The arm of France is long. . . . You'll hang. . . .
You'll hang—at the end of a rope, in Zaguig gaol. . . ."

"Are those the *Sidi Commandant's* last words? . . .
Because, if so, I would fain lift up my own poor voice and
utter one or two . . ." replied the Emir.

"Listen. . . . I have received information from my
spies, that Selim ben Yussuf will attack your camp at
dawn. . . . A sudden swift raid from the Zaguig side.
. . . His object revenge—he does not greatly love the
French, as you know—loot, rifles and sport. . . .

"As you have shown me, that would wipe out this
night's work, for me, nicely. . . . I have but to saddle-
up and go, with all my men—and the convict whom I
wanted—and all record of my (shall I say?) impropriety of
conduct, will vanish, even as will the aforesaid convict. . . ."

"*Lies!* . . . *Lies!* . . ." roared Lebaudy. "*Lies.*
. . . You father of treachery and son of filth. . . .
Words. . . ."

"Words *and* deeds, *Sidi Commandant* . . ." interrupted
the Emir. "Time flies . . ." and he drew a great knife
which, with its gold-inlaid hilt, worn upright in the middle
of his sash, marked his rank.

"*Deeds!*" sneered the undaunted Lebaudy. "Worthy
deeds! . . . Cut my throat, you Arab hero . . ." and
throwing back his head, he closed his eyes.

My brother cut the cord that bound Lebaudy's feet,
and set him free. Lebaudy stared incredulous.

"*Now* what's the game?" he growled.

"The game, *Sidi Commandant*, is this. . . . You jump
on to a swift camel and ride with us—you to your camp to
make those dispositions which will mark you as a second
Napoleon—I to my men who are by now ambushed across
the line of the Road from Zaguig to your camp, awaiting
the attack which will come within the hour. . . .

"Meantime the very utmost will be done to revive your
sleeping men, and to send them over, on camels, to your
camp. . . ."

"Are you speaking the truth?" incredulously asked the
astonished Lebaudy.

"Ride with me straight to where my men are protecting
your camp," said the Emir.

"I will," replied the Frenchman grimly. "I shall be
able to make my dispositions better when I have seen
yours," he continued. "Not that I believe a word of it.
. . . But I am in your power for the moment, and must
play your game, I suppose. . . ."

"It would be wiser, *Sidi Commandant*," said my brother,
helping the *Adjudant* to his feet.

"I will put my few men in, to stiffen your line . . . if
there *is* a line," growled the latter.

"It will need no stiffening, *Sidi Adjudant*," smiled the
Emir. "Might I respectfully suggest they be used as a
mobile reserve under your command . . . reconnaissance

. . . pickets . . . scouts . . . or even to cut off such retreat as will be left to friend Selim ben Yussuf. . . ."

" Seeing's believing . . ." growled the *Adjudant*. " I'll make my own arrangements, thank you. . . . And defend my own camp. . . ."

" Not with three men and a boy," smiled the Emir. " I'm going to fight Selim ben Yussuf when he attacks your camp, and you can help me as you like."

" Come on then," snapped the *Adjudant*, half-convinced. " If you are speaking the truth, they may come at any minute now. . . ."

" Arrangements have been made for their reception," said the Emir, and led the way to where the camels awaited us.

As we passed, I thrust my head into the Emir's tent, where John lay at rest upon the rugs.

He was awake.

" Look here, John—orders are that you don't leave this tent till we come back. . . . That'll be all-right, won't it ? . . . Then I can push off with Noel and help save the French camp. . . . He's hopping mad that that young swine, Selim, should have gone on the war-path like this. . . . And on the one and only night when the French can't look after themselves—thanks to Noel himself ! "

" Why, no, Vanbrugh, I'm not going to sit here, if Hank and Buddy are going out scrapping . . . I'm coming too. . . .

" Didn't I come out to Africa *to save those two* ? " he laughed, " and now I've *saved them*, do you expect me to let them out of my sight—scrapping around in the dark and all ? "

I grinned at this John Geste.

" Well, and didn't *I* come out to Africa to save *you* ? " I asked. " And now I've saved you, do you expect me to let you out of my sight—scrapping around in the dark and all ? "

" Better go together then," was the reply.

" Not a bit of it. . . . I must go and back my brother

up, and you must have the decency to remember that it's
cost us all no end of time and trouble to put you where
you are—and you've got to stay put."

"Oh, well, of course," replied John Geste, "if you put
it like that. . . . All I can say is—what I said before . . ."
and here he laughed out-right, "we'll go together. . . ."

And we went together—a pair of perfectly good Arabs
following their Emir.

§ 4

A short ride brought us to where we were challenged
by one of Marbruk ben Hassan's vedettes, and, a few
minutes later, we were being led by Marbruk himself,
along the line of his ambush-defence.

If Yacoub's information were correct, and Selim and his
raiders were going to attack in this direction, it would
probably be Selim's last exploit, and the end of his career
of treachery to the French.

The wily and experienced Marbruk had proceeded
sufficiently far from the camp to be at a spot where the
raiders would still be riding in a crowd. A little nearer
to the camp, and they would have spread out into a line
—a line that would have outflanked Marbruk's, and soon
become a circle completely enveloping the camp.

Already a scout, mounted on a fine Arab horse, had
ridden in with information which entirely corroborated
that of Yacoub—a *harka* some two to three hundred strong,
had ridden toward the line of the Zaguig–Great Oasis
Road, and, turning half-right, had swung on to it.

Having seen this, the scout had galloped back at once.

Adjudant Lebaudy grunted, and, with a guide, rode
hard for his camp.

A quarter of an hour later, as I sat beside John, behind
the ridge—possibly the most triumphantly happy person
in the world—and wished the wretched Selim would
hurry up, for I was very cold,—a rifle cracked.

I scrambled to the top of the ridge and looked over.

"Hullo!" said John. "What do you put that at—five hundred yards?"

"Or nearer," I said. "Now Noel will let them know that they don't surprise the camp, whatever else they do. . . . Nasty four-o'clock-in-the-morning shock for Selim. . . ."

A whistle blew near-by. A few minutes later a couple of short blasts were blown, and a crashing volley was fired from a distant section of the ridge.

Almost simultaneously, other volleys followed from other sections, and then the ceaseless banging of rapid independent fire from a hundred rifles.

A pandemonium of noise broke out from what had been the silent mysterious space in front of us . . . a noise to which wounded men and camels contributed, as well as every subordinate leader who had anything to shout—their cries varying in portent from charge to flight. Some I believe did one, and some the other, for I certainly saw vague blotches of white receding, while vague forms loomed up quite near.

A whistle blew loudly, a long strong blast, and all firing ceased. It blew again twice, and volley upon volley banged clean and crisp. The fire-control was astonishingly good.

The whistle blew again. From our front a few rifles cracked irregularly, and what other sounds could be heard indicated the retreat of our assailants.

"Got a bellyful, as well as a nasty shock!" observed John, as he jerked the empty shell out of his rifle.

"Hullo! There's a side-show," he added, as brisk firing broke out on our left-rear.

Evidently Noel had issued orders, for a section of men, running down the slope, mounted their camels and rode off, followed by myself and John.

Flashes were coming from distant sand-dunes on our left-front. The camel-section was halted in line, the men dismounted, and, a couple of minutes later, were enfilading the crest of the occupied sand-dune.

Undrilled, undisciplined and without any but mob-tactics, this body of raiders, who may have been an independent private effort, or a feint by Selim ben Yussuf, retired in a body to another sand-dune, offering an admirable target in the growing light, as they did so.

Commanded by Lebaudy in person, a small French party pursued in skirmishing order—there was always a number dashing forward and there was always a number firing—and drove them across our front.

As they retreated toward the main body, and in fact, finally fled in that direction, our line swung half-right, prolonging Lebaudy's line until both prolonged that of the Emir, and the whole advanced in skirmishing order from both flanks.

The Emir's aim and object was not, of course, slaughter, nor even the most severe and crushing defeat that could be inflicted upon Selim ben Yussuf. What he wanted to do was to defeat this attack, and in such a way that there would be no fear of its repetition until the French were in a position to deal with it themselves. Selim ben Yussuf's plan had most signally failed, thanks to the presence of the Emir's forces; the raiders were on the run, and the Emir's Camel Corps would keep them on the run. By the time the latter called a halt and returned to their camp, Lebaudy's force would be in a position—and a condition—to deal with any subsequent trouble.

As our line skirmished forward, a long low hill that lay at right-angles to the battle line, cut off Lebaudy's flank from our view. This long low hill, or high ridge, was about a mile in length and a half-section of our men advanced along it's narrow top. Suddenly one of these went running back to where his camel knelt, while another signalled " Enemy in sight," in spite of the fact that there was a retreating enemy in sight of all of us, in one direction or another. The signaller's meaning was made clear, however, when the messenger arrived at a lumbering gallop, and told his tale. Riding to where the Emir sat on his gigantic white camel, on top of a sand-dune, he told how there had been a sudden lightning raid, a veritable hawk-swoop, on the left flank of the line. A band of picked fighting-men mounted on the finest camels, and led by Selim ben Yussuf himself, had made a détour, and had approached unseen, by riding up a deep *wadi* and between high sand-dunes. They had approached sufficiently near the French flank to launch a charge and drive it home with terrific impact, before the flank-section could be swung back into line to meet them. The enemy, using shock-tactics, had broken and scattered Lebaudy's men, and, by the time Marbruk ben Hassan had got the flank-section of the Camel Corps in position to protect his flank and prevent the line from being rolled up, the raiders had wheeled about and fled.

" Fled ? " said the Emir. " Then why all this chatter ? "

" Yes, fled," said the messenger, and added deprecatingly and as though he were to blame—for every Oriental loathes to be the bearer of bad tidings—" They have taken the French officer with them."

Selim ben Yussuf had captured Lebaudy ! The Emir raised himself in the saddle and looked behind him.

" Horse," he shouted in a voice that would have done credit to Lebaudy himself, and waved a beckoning arm. Within a minute, his standard-bearer was beside him, and sprang from the back of the magnificent stallion that was the Emir's favourite.

" Oats," he said to me, as he sprang into the saddle, " find Buddy quick, and tell him I am chasing Selim, who's got Lebaudy. Tell him to follow with Yussuf Latif's section. He'll get his direction from the men on that ridge," and he bade the messenger ride back to the hill-top and watch. As he finished speaking, the Emir dashed off like a racing Centaur.

While I watched him go, I was struck by the disquieting thought that, riding at that pace in pursuit of camels, he would very soon overtake them. A camel will always beat a horse in the long-run, but not in the short. The speed is with the horse and endurance with the camel.

To me it appeared inevitable that my brother would over-take Selim ben Yussuf and his cut-throats, long before he had the support of the section that was to follow him. . . .

I quickly found Buddy, in command of the right flank of our line, and following on his camel, with critical eye, the orderly and regular advance of his dismounted skirmishers. I shouted the news to him and, as he shook his camel into movement and wheeled off, he shouted:

"S'pose the old fool thinks he is going to hunt 'em about with a stick! . . . Chase after him, Son. . . . I'll be along in two minutes. . . . Wish we'd got some more horses. . . ."

CHAPTER XVIII

A S I turned to go, I discovered that John had disappeared, and guessed that he was already trailing Noel. Urging my camel to its top speed—an undeniable canter—I took the straightest line for what I supposed to be the scene of the coming conflict. This took me across the ridge from which the messenger had come. From this eminence I could see, in the clear morning light, the fleeing band of camel-riders, a galloping horseman quickly overtaking them, and a solitary rider urging his camel in pursuit—Selim ben Yussuf and his raiders, my brother, and John Geste.

Careering in break-neck fashion down the slope of the ridge, I saw much of what then happened, and learned the remainder later from John and my brother.

§ 2

At the head of the fleeing raiders, rode Selim ben Yussuf on his famous horse. Its speed was restrained to that of the camels. By him, on a giant camel, also famous in that part of the desert, rode his cousin, one Haroun el Ghulam Mahommed, behind whom the unfortunate *Adjudant* Lebaudy hung across the camel like a sack of potatoes, his arms bound to his sides and his feet tied together—a most undignified, painful, and dangerous situation. In a close group round this camel, rode the remaining dozen or so of Selim's selected ruffians, some of whom found time in the lightness of their hearts and the heaviness of their hatred, to award the unfortunate *Adjudant* a resounding blow with a *mish'ab* camel-stick, or a violent prod with the butt end of a spear. Suddenly, one of the raiders, hearing the drumming of a horse's hoofs behind him, looked over his shoulder and then shouted to his leader.

Selim ben Yussuf looked round, saw, and understood. Wheeling out from his position in front of the camels, he shouted "*Ride on*," and, lowering his spear-point, charged head-long at the Emir.

Had the latter also carried a lance, the beholders would have seen a tournament like that of the knights of old— a combat belonging rather to the days of Saladin and Richard Cœur de Lion, the days of chivalry, when foemen met in single combat, man to man, horse to horse, and spear-point to spear-point. The Emir, however, carried only the Arab sword which he always wore, and an automatic pistol in a holster attached to the sword-belt which he wore round the sash beneath his *burnous*. . . .

Almost in the moment of impact, the Emir, a most perfect and powerful horseman, checked his horse, pulled it back on to its haunches and wheeled it from the line of attack—so deftly, so exactly, and so absolutely at the right second, that not only did the lance-point merely tear his wind-blown *burnous*, but the furious charge of his assailant missed him completely.

He drew his sword, but not his automatic, and spurred his horse at Selim as the latter was wheeling about, to return to the attack. It was too late for the Arab to attempt to charge, for the horse and man were upon him, and he could only lower his spear-point, that his charging opponent might impale himself upon it. The Emir's sword flashed down with tremendous force, and the deflected lance—either cut through or broken—was dashed from Selim's hand. Again checking and swerving his horse, the Emir wheeled away and gave Selim ben Yussuf time to draw his sword. Had he unslung the rifle from his back, the Emir would have shot him.

Selim spurred his horse and, rising in his stirrups, delivered a downward cut at the Emir's head. The Emir parried, feinted like lightning, and, in his turn, aimed a downward stroke at the head of Selim. Selim parried, but a downward blow from the mighty arm of the huge Emir, delivered with all his strength as he stood in his stirrups, was a different thing from a stroke delivered by the slight but wiry Arab.

It was parried correctly enough, but Selim's sword was struck from his hand as though by a thunderbolt, and the Emir's weapon smote him a heavy glancing blow that caused him to reel in the saddle. Instantly the Emir, dropping his sword, grappled the Arab in his great hands, dragged him from his saddle, dropped him to the ground and fell heavily upon him. For the moment, Selim ben Yussuf was out of action and had ceased to interest himself in the phenomena of this world.

Rising, the Emir took the stunned man's rifle, slung it over his own back, and then took the reins of both horses. Mounting his own, and seeing John Geste and myself approaching, he again galloped off in pursuit of the retreating raiders. It was not long before his race-horse of a charger again brought him near to the band of camel-riders. There was now no horseman to meet him on equal terms and charge him, lance in hand. As he drew near, two or three of those whose slower camels kept them in the rear, turned in their saddles and opened fire. But it takes a somewhat better marksman than the average Arab raider, to hit a man on a galloping horse, when shooting from the back of a trotting or cantering camel; nor did the plan of halting and dismounting appeal to any of these stragglers, in view of the fact that he would almost inevitably be cut down or shot, in the act of doing so.

With a wild whoop, and raised automatic, into and through the fleeing band, the Emir dashed. Men shouted, swung long lances round, un-slung long guns, drew swords, fired rifles, wheeled outward from the pursuing Vengeance —did anything but halt.

" *Ride on* " was their last order, and their very present inclination. At anyone who shot, cut or thrust at him, the Emir fired, and, in a tenth part of the time that it takes to tell, he was beside the leading camel—that of Haroun el Ghulam Mahommed. With a curse, the raider thrust his rifle sideways and downward and, without troubling to bring it to his shoulder, fired. Although the muzzle was not a yard from the Emir's body, the bullet missed him, thanks to the movements of both horse and camel. But an automatic pistol is different, and the robber Haroun el Ghumal Mahommed died, as he would have wished to die, weapon in hand and facing his man. With him died his camel which the Emir instantly, though reluctantly, shot through the head—and the band swept on, leaving behind it, its fallen leader, its best camel, and its prisoner, *l'Adjudant* Lebaudy.

The half-hearted attempt at a rally and a stand was quickly abandoned as the orderly line of the section of the Emir's famous Camel Corps, riding at top speed, came into sight.

§ 3

L'Adjudant Lebaudy interested me greatly that night, when he returned the Emir's hospitality.

He was not a man of breeding, culture and refinement, but he was a man of courage and tenacity ; he was not what is called a gentleman, but he was a strong man. He may have been a petty tyrant, but he was not always and wholly petty. He somewhat pointedly assured the Emir that the latter could drink his coffee without fear, and that he could please himself as to whether he slept where he dined. He was grimly jocular, and his jokes were not always in the best taste, but when we rose to depart, he shook hands with the Emir, stood to attention, honoured him with a military salute, and said :

"You are a brave man, Sidi Emir. You should have the Medaille Militaire for what you did this morning. Instead, you have my complete forgetting of all that

happened before dawn to-day. . . . And if there should
be a prisoner missing, I shall notify the authorities that
it is extraordinary that only one has been killed. Good-
bye, Emir el Hamel el Kebir."

Yes, an interesting man, our friend *l'Adjudant* Lebaudy,
and true to type, save that he was perhaps a little bigger
than most of his kind, and capable of a certain generosity
and magnanimity.

My story grows long—and it might be very, very long
indeed.

We set out, next day, for the Great Oasis. Here I did
what I had hardly expected ever to do—embraced and
warmly kissed my sister's maid, Maud Atkinson—now
my sister-in-law and something of a desert princess.

I should love to have time and space to detail our con-
versations and to describe our Maudie in her new rôle. She
obviously worshipped Noel, and confided to me that,
much as she loved Sheikhs, she was, on the whole, glad that
her Sheikh-like lord had proved (by slow degrees) to be a
white man. Repeatedly she assured me that he was a
" one," and when, at length, the dear girl realized that I
was Noel's own brother, and her own brother-in-law, she
could only ejaculate a hundred times,

" Fancy that now ! . . . Whoever would have thought
it ! . . . I can't hardly believe it ! "

.   .   .   .

I will not describe the solemn *mejliss* in which Noel took
leave of the assembled Sheikhs of his own and other tribes,
after telling them that he was going on a long journey to
visit his allies the *Franzawi*, nor of the really heartrending
and pathetic farewells between him and the men with,
and for, whom he had striven and worked and schemed
and fought.

But, at length, a large well-equipped and well-armed
caravan set out from the Great Oasis, and with it went
Marbruk ben Hassan and Yussuf Latif ibn Fetata in com-

mand of the fighting men of the escort; and, in time, by slow stages and by devious ways, the caravan arrived and encamped not far from a town into whose fine harbour came the ships of many nations—as they had done since the days of the Phœnician tramp and the Roman trireme.

On to a ship flying the French flag, my companions dared not go; and decided to voyage forth beneath either the American or the British flag, according to which entered the harbour first, for the sooner they were away the better.

To the delight of Noel and Buddy, it was an American ship that came—a huge vessel carrying a few hundred tourists and returning to New York from Japan, visiting the ports of the Southern Mediterranean, as she had visited those of the Northern shore, on her outward voyage. A cable to Isobel ensured that she would be awaiting John on the landing-stage at New York.

§ 4

I feel that I have not told all that I should have done, about John Geste. . . .

This dear wonderful John Geste. . . . This true brother of Beau Geste and of Digby Geste. . . . This man who could not settle down in happiness even with Isobel,—the wonderful and glorious woman who had given my life a purpose, my mind a lifelong dream, my soul a *beau idéal*— could not live even in that Paradise that her presence made for those she loved, while his friends were stranded where he had " deserted " them. . . . The man who loved Isobel so deeply and truly and nobly, as he most surely did—to *leave* her, after he had incredibly won back to her—to leave her, with little probability that he would see her face again! This is the greater love.

Poor John Geste. . . .

I was almost amused—grimly, sadly amused, when he again tried to thank me and to say good-bye, on that last night.

His repressed emotions, his repressed British soul, almost escaped. His British public-school reserve almost melted.

. . .

He, Noel, Buddy and I, had eaten our last supper together, and in silence smoked the last pipe of peace. As the time drew near for us to seek our sleeping-rugs, John Geste rose to his feet, stretched himself and yawned most unconcernedly, and strode from the tent.

As he did so, he glanced at me, and with a jerk of his head, bade me accompany him. I rose and followed him as he strode out towards the cliff. Suddenly he wheeled about.

"Vanbrugh," he said, as he held out his hand. "I want to say . . ." and his sudden spate of words ended in the little nervous cough that, in him, indicated strong feeling.

"What I want to try to tell you . . ." he began again, and got no further.

I would not help him. He was suffering an agony of emotional discomfort, and was utterly inarticulate. But I, too, was suffering an agony of pain, misery and grief.

He was going back to Isobel; and I—to the Angel of Death. . . .

I had grown to love him as much, I believe, as one man can love another. I had saved him. By God's grace and mercy and help, I had saved him, and kept my word to Isobel. . . . Yes, I loved him, but I would not help him.

And more than anything I wanted to see whether he would be able to "let himself go."

For myself, I somehow felt that had our positions been reversed, and had he been sending me back to Isobel, I should have embraced him. I should not have been able to refrain from hugging him. . . .

Not so John Geste.

"What I mean, Vanbrugh," he tried again, "is that. . . .

"Well. . . . You understand, don't you. . . . You know what I mean. . . ."

And I heard my knuckles crack, as his grip tightened, and he said it all in four words.

"My   God ! . . ." he ejaculated. . . .   Er. . . . Oh ! . . .

"*Stout fella !* "

§ 5

For the sake of his followers, Noel decreed that the three were to remain Arabs until the ship sailed. Those of the passengers, if any, who saw three Arab Sheikhs and a heavily-veiled Arab woman arrive, must have been more than a little astonished to behold them, next day, in the ready-made reach-me-down garments of " civilization," previously purchased in the town.

To this day I hate to think of that parting.

In one way, it was wonderful as being the consummation of a life's work, or rather of the work for which I had been born ; in another way it was terrible, tragic, unbearable.

I admit I was tempted—horribly tempted—and I thought it was fine of the other three to say nothing whatever to shake my resolution. They knew that I had given my word, and they would not ask me to break it, and when the Devil whispered in my ear, " A dancing girl—a half-caste, half-savage thing from the bazaars of Bouzen. . . . She doesn't expect it of you " . . . I clung grimly to my poor honesty, and replied, " It's not a question of what she is, but of what *I* am ;—and I *do* expect it of me." But it was a hard struggle. Nor was my misery lightened by the sights and sounds around me, as the ship steamed out of the harbour.

On a cliff, a mile or two from the town, my brother's followers abandoned themselves to such transports of grief as I have never witnessed before nor since.

With Oriental lack of restraint, they wept—literally rent their clothing, and exhibited every symptom of unappeasable misery and heart-breaking grief. Brief—perhaps as brief as violent—but starkly genuine and very terrible.

It was long enough in the case of a man called el R'Orab, my brother's body-servant, and caused his death. From the moment that he took leave of his master, he neither ate nor drank nor spoke a word. He went about his duties until he collapsed from weakness, and in his weakness he died, refusing even water. Pitiful and absurd as such conduct may seem to the European, it was highly approved by the Arabs, not one of whom dreamed for a moment of urging the man to eat or drink.

Just before he died, he painfully raised himself from his prayer-rug and, seizing the hand of Yussuf Latif ibn Fetata, who, with the help of Marbruk ben Hassan and myself, was nursing him, said:

" We shall never look upon his face again."

Apparently this statement—regarded as inspired because spoken by a dying man—was the last straw upon the load of unhappiness borne by the fated Yussuf Latif.

That night, he left his sleeping-place beside Marbruk and myself, and was seen by a sentry to go forth and stand beneath the stars, his arms out-stretched towards the East. With a loud and anguished cry of " *Leila Nakhla !* . . . *Leila Nakhla !* . . ." he plunged his knife into his heart, and ended the tragic life that had now become insupportable. . . .

My own parting with Marbruk ben Hassan and the rest, near Bouzen, did nothing to cheer my depressed and miserable spirit, and it was in a most unenviable frame of mind that I rode away with Abd'allah ibn Moussa toward the camp of the old Sheikh Yussuf ben Amir at the Oasis of Sidi Usman.

Abd'allah ibn Moussa was to ride in and discover if the Death Angel was still under the old Sheikh's protection, or whether she had returned to The Street, in Bouzen.

We camped, that night, beneath some palms, a far-outlying picket of the great host of trees of the Sidi Usman Oasis, and after a meal of dates, unleavened bread, and curded cheese as hard as stone, Abd'allah ibn Moussa rode off, bearing the message that I had seen my friend set

sail, and that I was here to fulfil my promise ; also that
Selim ben Yussuf was a prisoner in the hands of the
French at Zaguig.

At the close of one of the most miserable days that I
have ever spent—somehow uncheered even by the realization that I had saved John Geste and sent him back to
Isobel—Abd'allah returned. The Death Angel was in
the tents of old Yussuf ben Amir. Apparently she went
almost mad with joy at the news of my return, and Selim's
capture. She was coming out on the morrow, with a small
caravan of her own, to where Abd'allah and I now were.
Her message to me was :

" Await me there. I send you my heart and my soul,
and my life. I have given Sheikh Yussuf ben Amir that
which has made him the happiest man in the Sahara, and
my slave for ever—that Hair of the Beard of the Prophet
that the Sultan brought from Mecca and gave to my
Mother. I have done this to show you that I have
given up Allah, and now belong to God altogether, and
am a perfect Christian because you, my husband, are
one."

It may be believed that I did not sleep that night.
Perhaps I sub-consciously feared somnambulism, and
that I should arise and ride for my life, even while I
slept.

§ 6

She arrived next day.

Certainly her own resources, and those of Sheikh Yussuf
ben Amir, had been strained to their uttermost, judging
by the pomp and state in which she travelled. Quite a
small village of tents sprang up, as I saw when, at the
invitation of her messenger, I rode over to the spot
where she had pitched her camp. That the Sand Diviner's
words might prove true in every detail, it had been her
whim that I should come riding into her camp, and that
she should run forth from her tent to welcome me.

In her present manifestation she was wonderful—gentle, sweet, submissive, and most obviously longing to be " good " —to play the rôle of civilized and Christian gentlewoman, and be wholly the white daughter of her white father.

It was piteous and pathetic.

Her plan was that we should go to Bouzen, where we should at once be married by a missionary, either Catholic or Protestant, or both if I liked. There she would get her jewels and instruct her Bank—as she was, I learned, quite wealthy. From Bouzen we were to go to Algiers and become European in every detail. From Algiers we were to take ship for Marseilles and become more fashionably European. From Marseilles we were to proceed to Paris and become the last word in European fashion.

We were then to live happy ever after, wheresoever I preferred, but the further we were from Africa, the happier she would be.

Poor little soul !

A great feast was provided in the evening, and when we could eat no more, we sat together upon the wonderful cushioned rugs with which her tent was beautifully provided. And when I, unintentionally, evinced my unconquerable weariness, she bade me retire to the tent which she had provided for me, and sleep my last sleep as a lone and unloved man. As I rose to go, she held forth her tiny hands, and, as I took them, drew me down beside her.

From her neck she took the curious book-like amulet which was her most cherished possession and, putting its thin gold chain over my head, bade me wear it next my heart, for ever. That it would shield me from every danger was her deep certainty and sure conviction.

" My darling husband," she whispered, " I feel in my soul—yes, from the very depths of my soul—that this will save you. . . ."

It did. . . .

With her impassioned kisses warm upon my lips, I retired to my tent and threw myself down upon its sumptuous bed of cushions. The previous night I had not slept at all, and life had been a burden and a misery since I had said " good-bye " to John two weeks ago—two weeks that seemed like years.

I was too tired to sleep. The hours dragged by with leaden feet. Tossing and turning, groaning and cursing, I longed for daylight—and longed that it might never come.

Sitting up, I fingered the locket-amulet, now denuded of its greatest and most sacred of all Arab charms the (doubtless genuine) Hair of the Beard of the Prophet, but still enriched by its (doubtless equally genuine) Christian relic, the splinter of the wood of the True Cross.

Better not to open it now, by candlelight—as she herself had once said, the tiny splinter of wood might fall out and be lost—a loss that I could bear, but one which would probably trouble her beyond measure. . . .

But open it I did. Why, when I had just definitely decided not to do so ? The psychologist can, of course, give the reason. I cannot. I know that my fingers opened the locket without any conscious instructions from my brain. I looked at the lovely face, beautifully painted on ivory— of " Zaza Blanchfleur," the Ouled-Naïl dancing girl, whom mighty Rulers had loved, and who had loved an ordinary Englishman, who had deserted her.

Almost in the same second I glanced at the other face, the face of that same man " Omar, the Englishman," the father of the Angel of Death.

I then closed the locket and sat awhile in thought. During that half-hour, my mind was as a leaf upon the sloping surface of a whirlpool ; as a straw in an eddy of wind ; nay, in a cave of all the winds, blowing in every direction at once.

Twice or thrice I rose to my feet, and then sank back upon my cushions.

Finally I rose, scribbled the Death Angel a message of four words, in French, on a scrap of paper, dressed myself fully, and crept forth like a thief in the night. This was not the camp of the Emir el Hamel el Kabir, or it would have been impossible for me to do what I then did. No wakeful sentries moved, watchful and alert upon their beat; none listened, stared, and challenged. Apparently not a soul was awake in the camp, except myself.

Creeping like a sneaking jackal to where the camels knelt, I thanked God that mine and Abd'allah ibn Moussa's were tethered in charge of our own camel-men, apart from the rest. With ungentle toe, I roused the man who had been in charge of my camel, ever since he became mine, and bade him saddle both it and Abd'allah ibn Moussa's beast. If I took this man with me, he could tell no tales in the morning.

A few minutes later, the camel-man and I were travelling at maximum speed in the direction of Bouzen.

CHAPTER XIX

ARRIVED at Bouzen, I gave the camel-man money and a letter for the Death Angel, and bade him await me for three days in the market-place, and, at the end of that time, to take the camels back to Abd'allah ibn Moussa and tell him that I had gone on a journey.

I went straight to the railway station and, squatting down, awaited the train for Algiers, as many other Arabs were doing. Arrived at Algiers, I walked warily, gradually accumulating a European outfit, and storing it in the second-rate, or perhaps twenty-second rate, hotel, in which I lived in the native quarter of the city.

It was a different Otis Vanbrugh, who now shuffled about Algiers in *burnous* and heel-less slippers, from that Otis Vanbrugh who, ages and æons agone, had descended from his Mustapha Supérieur hotel to escort his sister on her visits to the romantic Oriental bazaars.

In the crowd, hooded and bearded as I was, I was perfectly safe ; and in restful peace and safety, I abode until the day when, having paid my bill, I went back to my room, shaved my face completely, dressed myself in my European clothes, seized my suit-case and grip, and marched straight out of the house, picked up a ramshackle carriage and drove to the quay where the good ship *Hoboken* awaited me and divers other items.

By way of Oran, Marseilles, Gibraltar and Tangier, she ploughed her uneventful way to New York, and, as in a dream, rather stunned and stupid and mechanical, I stepped once more upon my native soil.

My desire was to get home at the earliest moment and

to hear, once and for all, that John had, at last, safe and sound, whole and hale and hearty, reached Isobel, and turned her life from a nightmare of suffering into a reality of happiness indescribable.

I endured the long, long train journey ; I endured the apparently longer journey by stage ; and the third and penultimate lap, by hired buggy, which brought me to where I was right welcome to a night's shelter and the loan of a good horse.

I started at dawn next morning, and a couple of hours' ride brought me on to my Father's land. By afternoon, I sighted the Ranch House, and, soon afterwards, drew rein by the great verandah on which the family spent the major part of what little time it lived indoors.

"Morning, Oats," drawled my brother, without rising from the rocking-chair in which he was seated.

"Hullo, Boy," spake the voice of Buddy, and, as my sun-dazzled eyes penetrated the shadow of the deep verandah, I saw that I had arrived in time to interrupt a family conclave.

There sat my Father, mighty, massive, domineering and terrible as of old, glaring at me with an expression which appeared to rebuke the presumption with which I dared present myself before him unheralded. Obviously he was in a towering rage.

Before him, miserable and shameful culprits, stood Buddy and my sister Janey, tightly clasping each the other's hand—Buddy white under the stress of some emotion, his eyes blazing, his mouth a lipless gash in his set face—Janey, of course, wilting and drooping, and dissolved in tears.

"*Otis*," cried Mary's voice, and she dashed forward from the side of a tall dark man arrayed in smart riding-kit—the wide-cut tight-kneed style of which our Western horsemen are supposed to despise—and, without quite believing my eyes, I saw that it was her husband Major de Beaujolais. . . . (But of course it had been Mary's intention to bring him, sooner or later, to see her home, and

something of the life that she had lived almost to the time
that she had met him.) Dismounting and dropping my
rein over the horse's head, I took Mary in my arms for a
brief sound hug, and then followed her up the steps into
the verandah.

"What's the row ? " I whispered before turning the
corner, to enter the grim presence of my irate parent.

"Janey wants to get engaged to Noel's friend Buddy,"
she whispered. "Says she'll die if she doesn't. Dad says
she'll die if she does—and without his blessing—die of
poverty, misery, shame, hunger, Father's curse, domestic
slavery in a log cabin, disgrace, remorse, housemaid's
knee. . . . Puritan Father . . . Scarlet Letter . . ."

"In fact, Dad says ' No '—and there's an end of it,
eh ? " I asked.

"Of course," replied Mary. "Naturally he'd say
' No,' and there'd naturally be an end of it ! . . . Who's
Janey—to dare to breathe, if Dad says she mustn't."

"And Buddy ? " I asked.

"He's torn between a longing to pull his gun on the
old man before doing a Young-Lochinvar-*into*-the-West
with Janey, and his fear that Janey will never speak to
him again if he dares be so impious and blasphemous as
to thwart our so-religious Dad."

"So she'll either die of thwarting Buddy by obeying
Dad, or else of thwarting Dad by obeying Buddy, eh ? "
I observed.

"That's the position," agreed Mary, "and before Dad's
much older, he's going to hear something."

"From whom ? " I asked.

" *Me*," said Mary, with jutting chin, " and Noel. . . .
Saintly old man ! . . . While boundlessly hospitable to
my husband, he is far from cordial, in fact barely courteous,
and alludes to him—not in his hearing of course—as ' that
Godless Frenchman,' or ' that foreign idolater.' He gets
more holy-righteous, every day ! . . . But come on, or
he'll think we're conspiring, if you don't come and prostrate yourself before him."

I greeted my Father with a respectful warmth and cordiality that I did not feel, and received a grunt and a contemptuous stare in reply. The old man certainly was in a rage, and in one of his most violently autocratic and overbearing moods.

I kissed Janey, and also gave Maudie a warm fraternal embrace, wrung Noel's hand and that of Buddy, greeted de Beaujolais diffidently—and selfishly obtruded my own affairs immediately. The other matter could wait and I could settle it.

" John safe ? " I asked.

" Oh, sure," was the reply.

" And with his wife ? " I asked.

" Right there," was the reply from Noel.

" England, I suppose ? "

" They wasn't, an hour ago," drawled Noel.

" Where are they ? " I said, mastering a desire to hit him.

" Now be reasonable, Son. How should I know where they are ? " replied Noel. " They went riding together about an hour ago, and at the present moment they may be here or there, or somewhere else. . . . She met us at New York," he continued, " and as there wasn't a suitable ship for a week, and John was ill, we just naturally brought them along here."

" Then I may see them at any moment ? " I gasped.

" You certainly may, Son, at any moment or any other moment."

I sat down heavily on the nearest chair, for all my strength had suddenly gone, and my knees were trembling. *I might see Isobel at any moment !* . . . And John Geste ! . . . Should I mount my horse again, and ride . . . and ride . . . and ride . . . ?

I could not ride away from myself, if I rode away from her.

No, I would see Isobel, *once* again. . . .

What was that booming, in my ears ? Of course, the voice of my Father.

" And that's that," he was roaring, " and let me hear
not another word about it, Janey. . . . And as for *you*,
my friend, you can get out of this just as quick as the
quickest horse will take you—and don't you come on to
this ranch again until you are quite tired of life. Get me ?
Good afternoon." Buddy licked his lips, and stood firm.

" Now, Dad," said Noel, laying his hand on my Father's
arm. " Remember Janey's a grown-up woman, and
Buddy's my best friend, and I say. . . ."

" I'll tell you when I want your say," shouted my Father,
" and Janey can sling off with him, and with my curse too,
if she likes, and they'd better go while the going's good, and
not come back either."

A wail and a fresh shower of tears from Janey, and an
oath from Buddy.

" Coming, Janey ? " he asked, as he turned to go.

Janey literally threw herself on her knees before her
father. Noel rose from his chair, and Mary put her arm
round Janey.

" *Go*, my dear," she said. " *Go*, you little fool, and be
happy. . . . I'd be ashamed ! . . . Don't you call your
soul your own ? "

But Janey had no soul to call her own. It was her
father's, stamped and sealed. It was not filial love that
was working, nor wholly filial fear, but rather the unbreak-
able habit of a lifetime, the inhibitions of a father-
complex.

I conquered my selfishness and, for the moment, thrust
self aside.

" Will everybody please go away—for exactly ten
minutes," I said, and became indeed the cynosure of
neighbouring eyes.

" Come on," I urged Buddy. " Get out, and take Janey
with you—and come back in ten minutes. Off you go,
Mary ! Go on, Noel," and something in my voice and
manner prevailed, and I was left alone with my Father, to
face him and out-face him for the first time in my life. He
gave a bitter ugly laugh.

" Are you graciously pleased to allow me to remain ? "
he sneered, " or do I also leave my house, to oblige
you ? "

From sarcasm he leapt to violent rage.

" Why, you insolent half-baked young hound," he roared,
springing to his feet, and, meanwhile, I had produced and
opened the Death Angel's locket.

As he advanced upon me, with blazing eyes and clenched
fist, I held it toward him, and his eyes fell upon the two
portraits. . . . It was dreadful.

I thought, for one awful moment, that I had killed my
Father.

He staggered back, smote his face with his clenched
fist, and dropped into a chair, white, shaking, and stricken.

I felt dreadful, guilty, impious. . . .

" *Oh, God! . . . Where is she ?* " he gasped, fearing,
I suppose, that she was near.

" Dead," I replied.

He drew a deeper breath.

" *How did you get it ?* " he asked, white-faced and
frightened.

" From your *daughter*," I answered, " . . . from my
sister." . . .

" *My God . . . Where is she ?* " he asked again, and I
pitied him even more than I hated myself.

" In Bouzen," I said. " Where you bought the Arab
stallion . . . and—other things. . . ."

" *Does she know ?* " he groaned.

" No," I replied.

" *To how many have you shown that ?* " he asked, and
it seemed as though his whole life hung upon my answer.

" To no-one—yet," I replied, and added, as I pocketed
the locket :

" By the way, Father, this chap Buddy is one of the
very best, a real White Man. . . . He'd make a wonderful
overseer for this ranch, and a wonderful husband for Janey.
. . . And I might add that Major de Beaujolais is a most
distinguished officer, whose visit to us is a great honour :

and further, that Noel's wife, Maudie, is one of the best
and bravest little women that ever lived. . . . You see,
Father ? . . ."

A long silence. . . .

" I see, Son," replied my Father, at last, " and you can
give me that locket."

" Why, no, I can't do that, my dear Father," I replied.
. . . " When Janey's married, and Mary and de Beaujolais have gone, and Noel and Maudie have settled down
here happily, and Buddy has an overseer's job, I must
take it back to its owner. . . ."

" *Be careful of it*, meanwhile, Boy," said my Father.

" *Very* careful, Father," I replied, and shouted to the
others to return.

They found Father wonderfully changed, and all went
merry as a wedding-bell.

§ 2

John and Isobel returned by moonlight.

John clasped my hand, held it, stared me in the eyes—
his fine level steady gaze—gave his little cough of deepest
feeling and embarrassment, and went into the house without
a word. Our silence was very eloquent.

I sat down on the verandah steps, and Isobel, who had
stopped to give sugar to her horse, came toward me.

She did not know me until I removed my hat, and the
moonlight fell full upon my face.

Like John, she said nothing, but, putting up her little
hands, drew my head down and kissed me on the lips.
She threw her arms tightly about my neck and kissed me
again. The embraces and kisses were just those of the
child Isobel who had walked and talked and played with
me in our Dream Garden—as sweet and dear and beautiful
and innocent as those. Her little hands then stroked my

hair, and again we kissed, and then, still without a word, Isobel turned and ran into the house.

That is the moment in which I should have died.

Instead, I took a horse and rode away.

I rode further and harder than I had ever done in all my life, but I was not cruel to my horse. Who, that had been kissed by Isobel, should be cruel, or ever mean or base or bad?

Am I happy?

Dear God! Who that has been kissed by Isobel is not happy?

EPILOGUE

" *H*E shall know a joy beyond all mortal joy, and stand, silent and rapt, beside the Gate. . . . There is but one Way to that Gate. . . . It is not Love Aflame with all Desire—but Love At Peace. . . ."

THE SONG OF THE LEGION

March Theme of the Paramount Picture
BEAU GESTE

Music by
Frank Tours, James Bradford and Hans Spialek
Lyrics by Edward Lockton

By kind permission of
The Sam Fox Publishing Co. (London) Ltd.

THE SONG OF THE LEGION

1. The fier - y sun comes
2. The sun is sink - ing

up ___ to make the day, Hark to the
low ___ the stars burn bright, Death stalks a -

-broad "Up and a - way," The
Far thro' the night, ___ Our

blaz - ing des - ert gleams ___ A track - less sea ___ But
fate with Al - lah rests ___ So what care we ___

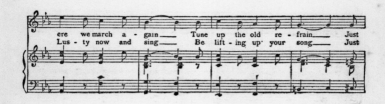

ere we march a - gain ___ Tune up the old re - frain ___ Just
Lus - ty now and sing ___ Be lift - ing up your song ___ Just

gath - er round and sing with me:— Here's to
gath - er round and sing with me:— Here's to

REFRAIN

you, you blighter and me, ___ Here's to an - y old wine we can find, Here's to

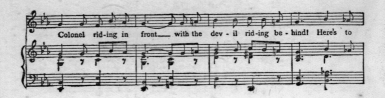

Colonel rid-ing in front___ with the dev-il rid-ing be-hind! Here's to

sweet hearts mer-ry and· fair.___ Raise your glass-es brim-ming and free, Here's to

roll-ing roll-ing a-long Here's to you, you bligh-ter and me!___

me!___

Made and Printed in Great Britain by Butler & Tanner Ltd., Frome and London